Blood & Water

Blood & Water

A Pacific Northwest Mystery

Lori Fairweather

WILLIAM MORROW AND COMPANY, INC. NEW YORK

Library of Congress Cataloging-in-Publication Data
has been applied for.

ISBN 0-688-16118-9

Printed in the United States of America

First Edition

2   3   4   5   6   7   8   9   10

BOOK DESIGN BY DESIGN 2000

www.williammorrow.com

For my mother,
Jeanne Fairweather Halverson,
in loving memory

Acknowledgments

Many thanks to the following people for encouragement, criticism, inspiration, and friendship: Kathy Halverson Testa, Shelley Singer, Jim Frey, Janet LaPierre, Charles Hine, Lori Greenberg, Kate Limanek, Kip Sheeline, Mary Ann Byrnes, Jennifer Robinson, and Zach Schisgal.

And, especially, thanks to my husband, Dan Schryer, for his unfailing love, support, and faith in me. Without him this book would never have been started, much less finished.

Blood & Water

1

I didn't hate my sister. At times I may not have liked her very much, but I swear I didn't hate her—notwithstanding any comments to the contrary I may have made along the way. How she felt about me was her business.

Sid and I were twins. Sidney Charlotte LaSalle and Frances Ann LaSalle, born six minutes apart on October 8, 1966. We were nearly identical in appearance, nearly opposite in everything else.

My last argument with Sid was on a miserable rainy night in November, the kind of night when the Pacific winds wreak havoc on power lines and weak-rooted trees, when the rain comes at you from all directions, when most folks stay safely indoors hoping their windows will hold. It was a night I'd like to add to my long list of painful old memories now forgotten, but one I fear will haunt me for a long time to come.

Sid had asked me to meet her at eight o'clock at the Seahorse Pub, a local beer joint on the coast highway three miles from our childhood home. It had been her idea to go out. We could have pulled a couple Michelobs from the refrigerator and talked across the kitchen table, but Sid never was much of a homebody—and neither of us was the type to let a rainstorm stand in her way.

I stumbled into the pub right on time, soaked and muddy from my dash across the unpaved parking lot. Sid had gotten there early and was lounging at the bar, propped up on her elbows, puffing on a skinny brown cigarette and blowing smoke rings at the bartender through her smudged red lips. Under a baggy denim jacket she wore a lacy black camisole cut well below the protruding ridge of her collarbone and an ankle-length skirt of crinkly tie-dyed cotton that fell open to reveal a seductive slice of thigh when she crossed her legs. A pair of scuffed black clogs lay empty on the floor beneath her bar stool. Classic Sid. She looked great. Certainly Woody Hanks, the bartender, thought so. He was leaning toward her across the bar, practically drooling, while she came on to him in her sultry, sullen way.

I glanced down at my own outfit—faded Levi's, white cotton blouse, tan wool blazer. Stylish enough, but not likely to attract any drooling admirers, not like Sid. We could trade clothes and I'd still feel the same.

I slid onto the stool beside her and said hello, vowing to ignore her cigarette. Woody wrenched his gaze from her chest long enough to acknowledge me with a cold nod and a frown—a less than rousing welcome, perhaps, but more than I had gotten from my sister. She peered down the throat of her long-neck Budweiser as if she were searching for a genie in the half-empty bottle, already too far gone to bother with me. Lost in space. She reeked of nicotine and musk perfume.

"Hello," I said again, this time louder. "Been waiting long?" By now I wasn't expecting a response.

She took a long drag on her cigarette and let the smoke slide slowly out her nostrils. Then she turned to me and proved, once again, I didn't know her as well as I thought. She gave me a wide grin and said, "Hi-ya, Fran. How-you-doin?"

Sid was an unpredictable drunk, sometimes morose, sometimes silly, often a bit of both. That night she seemed to be in fine spirits, although not entirely coherent. She tossed her cigarette in the general direction of an ashtray and tipped her stool toward me so she could plant a sloppy kiss on my lips. In the process she slipped off her seat and wound up sprawled across my lap, which struck her as tremendously funny.

I laughed along with her as I maneuvered her back to vertical. "I'm fine, Sid. How are you?"

"Hangin."

She gripped the bar with both hands to keep from toppling over backward, managing after a wobbly moment to stabilize herself enough to pick up her cigarette, which was smoldering on the bar beside her beer. She flipped back her curly brown mane with a jaunty snap of her head and sat up straighter, pursing her lips to hold back a wave of giggles. "There," she said with an air of accomplishment. "Where were we? Oh yeah. Good to see you, Fran."

Across the bar Woody Hanks tugged on his stubbly gray beard and gaped at us through wire-rimmed granny glasses. He wore a Grateful Dead T-shirt, filthy blue jeans slung low beneath his paunch, and a moldy-looking leather vest with a roach clip sticking out of the pocket. He slid a mustard-stained menu in my direction and retreated to the far end of the bar, where he busied himself polishing beer mugs, stealing glances at Sid, and chatting with a drunken workman in a hard hat.

I pushed a clump of wet bangs out of my eyes and scanned the menu. "It's a monsoon out there," I said. "I heard on the radio this is the rainiest fall Black Bay has had in fifty years."

Sid emitted one last perfectly round ring of smoke and watched it float away. "Monsoon is right. Fucking hurricane." She stubbed out her cigarette and traced her fingertips across the surface of the bar until they reached her half-eaten cheeseburger, from which she began to extract ketchup-soaked rings of raw onion. "Jesus, Woody. I told him no onions," she said as she piled them one by one onto the green tin ashtray beside her plate. "Looks like a bunch of bloody worms."

I glanced at her growing mound of ash-coated red onions and shoved my menu aside. I waved to get Woody's attention and ordered a Diet Coke, figuring I would fix myself something to eat later, at home.

She slid her Budweiser toward me. "Have a beer, Fran. My treat."

I took a sip and handed it back to her. The beer was lukewarm, but its sour bite was appealing.

"Two Buds," she said to Woody. Then she swayed back at me and whispered, "I gotta pee."

I watched her weave her way across the room, wishing we had picked somewhere else to meet. A place called the Seahorse Pub should be a haven on a stormy November night, warm and cozy with worn oak booths, scuffed wood floors, and a fireplace in the corner, the kind of place that served fish and chips and crusty brown bread with goat cheese. Unfortunately, the Seahorse is nothing like that. It has a linoleum floor, Formica-top tables, and the worst greasy burgers in town. There's a pinball machine in the corner where the fireplace should be.

When Woody delivered our beers I sent him back for two glasses of ice water. Sid slithered onto her bar stool a minute later, under marginally better control than before. She pushed aside the water and went for her beer. "Cheers, Fran. Here's to my doctor, who'd have a fit if he could see me now." She clinked my bottle and took a long thirsty drink from her own.

We made small talk for the next half hour, very small talk, the kind of inane conversation only possible when one person is slobbering drunk and the other is stone-cold sober. Sid rattled on about nothing in particular in her charming, if somewhat frenetic, stream-of-consciousness style, and I nodded periodically and laughed when I suspected she was making a joke. I knew if I hung in there long enough she would eventually get to the point, which I feared might have to do with money.

Sid had been after me for a loan for much of the past year, having latched onto the ridiculous notion that my husband, Peter, and I were flush with cash. Several months ago she had asked me for fifty thousand dollars. Fifty thousand. We could barely spare five hundred, especially after the three grand I had leaked out to her behind Peter's back over the past year and a half. She hadn't broached the topic since she arrived in Black Bay for our mother's funeral ten days ago, but I had been bracing myself. When she asked me to meet her at the Seahorse Pub and didn't say why, I automatically assumed she was planning to hit me up. I wasn't naive enough to think she simply wanted to spend time with me, although I guess in the back of my mind that's what I was hoping.

That night Sid seemed more interested in telling jokes than in talking about money, and even though she was too drunk to get the punch lines straight, she was still pretty funny. When she had not so much as alluded to the desperate state of her finances a full hour into our visit, I allowed myself to wonder, somewhat sheepishly, if perhaps there was no ulterior motive behind her invitation.

That triggered it. I've heard it said that twins can communicate on an extrasensory wavelength, but I'd never seen evidence of any such phenomenon between Sid and me until that moment. Not ten seconds after I let down my guard, she said, "So, Fran . . . I need to, um, talk to you about something. . . ." Her voice was suddenly serious, her words not so slurred as before. This was not the opening line of another joke.

I let out a chestful of air. Here we go, I thought. "Yes? What is it?" *Please don't ask for money. I'll help you any way I can, just not that.*

She picked up her beer and began peeling off its red-white-and-blue label. She opened her mouth, closed it again, and cleared her throat, but she didn't say what was on her mind. Just like the other times she had come to me for money. Why was she doing this again? She knew damn well Peter and I had nothing to spare.

Apparently she couldn't bring herself to say the words, so I saved her the trouble. With a quavering voice, I said, "Never mind, Sid. I know what you want to talk about. I'm sorry, but the answer is still no." She started to interrupt, but I held up my hand. "You know I'm broke. It's been a long year for Peter and me. We just don't have it. I'm sorry. Really."

She took a swig of beer and slammed the bottle down on the bar, but I saw that her hand was trembling. "Fuck you."

"Please, Sid, I understand you need—"

"No you don't understand. You haven't got a goddamn clue."

I reached for her arm, but she jerked away and spun around so her back was to me, leaving me to watch in silence as she fumbled for her cigarettes, lit one, and inhaled deeply.

"You're selfish," she said between puffs, and then more quietly, "fucking selfish bitch."

I filled my mouth with Budweiser and forced it down, my earlier hopefulness drowning quickly in the pool of sour beer sloshing around in my empty stomach. Why did I always think things could be better between Sid and me?

When Sid and I were kids, we'd had a different kind of relationship. We were never particularly compatible—Sid had always been a rebel and I was a loner—but our differences hadn't mattered so much back then. We'd had something in common too—a stubborn, wild streak. More important, we had been friends. Like sisters should be.

I glanced over at her. She was contemplating the green tin ashtray and mumbling that something or other was "life or death" and that I was "self-centered and uncaring." I didn't attempt to decipher her garbled complaint. I caught enough of it to know I was better off tuning it out.

When Woody brought another round of beers I drank mine down halfway in one long chug and focused on the fancy liquor bottles lined up along the back wall of the bar. Above the bottles was a dreamy poster of a man and a woman reclining on a white sand beach under a red and green umbrella, gazing out to sea. It was an advertisement for Myers's rum. The man wore a white shirt and sailor's cap, the woman a strapless red sundress. They were holding coconuts with straws sticking out of them. The poster reminded me of a game Sid and I used to play when we were kids, watching reruns of *Gilligan's Island* on television and afterward acting out imaginary episodes in the woods behind our house. Sid always got to be Ginger. I was Gilligan. The glamour girl and the goofball. I smiled at the memory, but my eyes burned with bottled-up tears. Funny, to look at us now. Sid was anything but glamorous, and I had grown up serious instead of goofy. And we were no longer friends.

I finished my beer and ordered another, my fourth. And then another. Why I went off like that, I have no idea. I just lost control. At some point I decided I'd had enough Budweiser, so I followed Sid's lead and switched to rum and Coke. I guess she'd noticed the poster too.

Tossing them back on an empty stomach, I quickly became as drunk as Sid, but unlike my sister I'm never a happy drunk. With a few drinks to lubricate my tongue, I let her have it.

Sid had stayed in Los Angeles the past year and a half while I looked after our dying mother five hundred miles up the coast in Black Bay. I dropped out of law school in San Francisco and moved back to our childhood home, working part-time as a paralegal for a two-man law firm headed up by an old family friend. Ten months into my stay, Peter gave up his marketing job at a Bay Area software company and moved north to lend his support through the worst of it. Sid, on the other hand, ignored the situation entirely. As Mom's condition deteriorated, she grew scarcer than ever. She hadn't bothered to come home the previous Christmas or for Mom's sixtieth birthday in August, said she couldn't afford the airfare to San Francisco and couldn't take the days off work to make the ten-hour drive. At the time it hadn't mattered much to me. With the cancer closing in, Mom wasn't strong enough to appreciate visitors, even family, and I certainly was better off without having my sister around to bicker with. But now, with Mom gone and Sid in town for the funeral, I could no longer see why she should get off so easily. For not the first time since Mom's death, I told her so.

She let me vent for several minutes before she cut me off. "Can it, Fran. I'm not interested." She stubbed out one cigarette and went for another. "The trouble with you is you're so goddamn high and mighty. Struttin' around the house like goddamn King Tut. I don't know how Peter stands it."

"My relationship with my husband is none of your business," I said.

"See? There you go. *My, my, my.* Trouble with you is you're selfish. Admit it."

For ten long days I had listened to my sister tell me what was wrong with me. She had been staying in the guest room above the garage since she arrived in Black Bay the morning of the funeral. Our father had built the room when we were little to use as an office for his insurance business. After Dad walked out on us when Sid and I were ten, Mom converted it into a bedroom so we could take in a boarder. It had its own bathroom and a separate phone line, so Sid was able to keep her distance from Peter and me while she was in town.

Her stay had been tolerable at first, thanks to the detached guest room, but the situation went downhill fast when she didn't return to Los Angeles within a few days after the funeral. She told us she was scared to go home because she had been having trouble with her boyfriend. They had been arguing, she said, although I suspected worse, judging from the bruises on her arms when she first arrived. I tried to get her to confide in me, but she made it clear she wasn't inclined to discuss the matter, and in the end I didn't push it. Knowing my sister, I suspected the boyfriend might have a few bruises of his own.

I had done my best to get along with Sid during her stay. Once or twice I made an effort to reminisce about our fun times together as kids, but she didn't seem interested, so for the most part I just left her alone. That seemed to be how she wanted it, and in my grief I guess that's how I wanted it too.

Our argument that night at the Seahorse Pub, or what I remember of it, escalated rapidly, first into a shouting match and then worse. I think Sid was the one who started the shoving. As best I recall, she blew one too many mouthfuls of smoke in my face, so I reached out to swipe the cigarette from between her lips. She misinterpreted my clumsy grab and counterattacked with a body blow that sent me tumbling off my bar stool hard onto the unforgiving linoleum floor.

I let out a cry of pain as I struggled to my feet, and then, to make matters worse, I stumbled backward and staggered into a pool table halfway across the room where two tough truck-driver types were in the midst of a serious game. I fell down again when I hit the table and somehow slid beneath it. When I stood up I whacked my head on the underside of the table and nearly went down once more. Before I had fully regained my balance, the larger of the two pool players, a black-bearded Goliath, came at me. He was brandishing his pool cue like a javelin and screaming obscenities, but I didn't hang around to hear what he had to say. I scrambled back across the room toward Sid, tripping over a bar stool she had overturned in her hasty retreat. She made it to the door and managed to get it open before I caught up with her. I grabbed the sleeve of her jacket and stumbled out after her into the muddy parking lot.

It was still raining, not as hard as before, but I was conscious of the cold drops pelting my face and spiking my eyes, and of the wind whipping the tops of the redwoods. I jerked hard on Sid's sleeve and heard the denim tear. She careened toward me with both fists flying.

I don't remember much about what happened after that, except I felt sick to my stomach and dizzy, as if I was getting the spins. My head was pounding so hard I wondered if I had given myself a concussion when I rammed it into the bottom of the pool table. My view of Sid went in and out of focus but grew progressively blurry. At one point I dove directly at her but missed entirely and slammed headlong into the side of my Jeep Cherokee.

Increasingly, I sensed I was losing the battle. I threw punches ever faster and ever more desperately, but few connected. My last clear thought was a terrifying conviction that I was fighting for my life. It was accompanied by a surge of panic-driven adrenaline—an uncontainable, unexplainable survival instinct that propelled me back at my sister with newfound fervor. Then it all gave way to blackness and silence.

2

My first sensation as I struggled toward consciousness was a ringing in my ears. That and a strange smell, something sour, like spoiled milk.

It was hailing. I could hear the frozen pellets bouncing off the roof and rolling onto the balcony outside my bedroom window. I was buried under three layers of wool blankets, flat on my stomach, spread-eagled like a Gumby doll.

The ringing stopped for a moment, but then it resumed. The doorbell, I realized, relieved the sound wasn't coming from inside my throbbing head. I didn't move. I wasn't sure I could. If Peter was home, he would get the door. If not, whoever was ringing could come back later.

The bell rang again, this time longer, the plea of an impatient caller who knew we were home and wasn't giving up. In slow motion I rolled to the edge of the bed and kicked off the covers. I instantly regretted it. A whiff and a glance jolted my senses like a dose of smelling salts. I still wore the blue jeans and white cotton blouse I'd had on the night before, and the sour milk smell was coming from my blouse. It wasn't sour milk. It was vomit.

Disgusted, I pulled up the covers and closed my eyes. By now Peter had gotten the door and was talking with our visitor in low tones. I recognized a familiar male voice but couldn't place it, so I tuned out the sound and retreated to a queasy semiconsciousness, hoping I would wake to find my adventure the night before had been just a bad dream. But I didn't and it wasn't.

The events of the previous evening came back to me gradually and in disjointed snippets, like pieces of a jigsaw puzzle scattered on a tabletop. I could patch together the first part fairly well. Sid and I met at the Seahorse Pub. We drank, we argued, we fought. Afterward I had somehow gotten myself home, although that part was obliterated in a haze of rum and beer. I hoped Sid had been as lucky. The two-lane highway between the pub and our house was narrow and slippery, and Sid was a reckless driver, even sober.

"Frannie?" Peter's voice pulled me from my foggy thoughts. It took me a moment to realize he was calling to me from the stairs.

"Yes?"

"You awake?"

"Not really."

"Could you come down here?" He sounded nervous.

I struggled to sit up and slid gingerly to my feet. The blood rushing from my head threatened to make me sick all over again. I stripped off my smelly clothes and dropped them in a heap at the foot of the bed beside my blazer and mud-caked shoes. Either I had managed to get them off by myself the night before or Peter had lent a hand at six o'clock that morning when he got home from work.

I pulled on a tattered terry cloth robe and shuffled downstairs, sliding my hand along the banister to keep my balance. When I rounded the corner into the foyer, I was surprised to find that our visitor was Andy Saybrook, a former classmate of mine and now a local cop. Andy's mammoth frame filled the doorway. He looked like a big red-haired ox next to Peter. He wore his police uniform and held his cap in his hands.

"Hello, Andy," I said as I approached, uncertain whether to give him a hug or stick out my hand. The look on his face stopped me before I could decide. It hit me he wasn't here for a social call. I glanced at Peter's grim expression and turned back to Andy. "What is it?"

Andy seemed more interested in inspecting the plastic rain cover on his cap than in talking to me. Without looking up, he cleared his throat and said, "It's your sister."

At the sound of his voice, my knees buckled and I collapsed against the wall. Peter managed to catch my elbow to save me from going down. The foyer and everything in it seemed suddenly flat and off-kilter, like a snapshot taken through a tilted camera. I stared up at Andy, towering above me, but it was Sid that I saw, not Andy. Her wild brown curls and violet blue eyes, so like my own, her taunting half-smile and strong square jaw. Her face was as clear to me as it had been the night before, as clear as if I were looking in a mirror. I could picture her lean, leggy body—thinner than mine and wiry, like an adolescent boy—only now it was crushed and bloody, being pulled from her VW bug. The deathtrap, Peter called it. It didn't even have seat belts.

"Car accident?" I asked.

Andy kept his eyes glued to his cap, which he was twisting in his big freckled paws. "Sort of," he murmured.

I leaned toward him, but still he wouldn't look at me. How could Sid have *sort of* been in a car accident? Either she was or she wasn't. Yes or no. "What happened, Andy? Is she—" I hesitated, unable to say what I was thinking. "Is she okay?" I finally asked, although I already knew the answer. They didn't send out a police officer to notify the family in person if the victim was okay.

Andy took his time responding. When he did, his voice was low and scratchy. "We got a call early this morning. Her car was found at Pirate Point . . . at the bottom of the cliffs."

"Are you saying she's . . . ?"

He sucked in his breath and let it out slowly, tainting the air with the smell of coffee and onions. "We don't know for sure yet. We haven't recovered the body. But her car fell fifty feet and landed nose down on the rocks. It's a total wreck." He paused to let the news sink in. "We think she was either thrown out on impact or pulled out afterward by the current. Trouble is, with the tides being what they are down there and with the swells from this lousy storm, we'll have a tough time getting a boat in close enough to look for her. Odds are we won't find her, unless she's lodged in the rocks."

I flinched at the image of Sid's body, bloody and battered, trapped at the base of the cliffs and pummeled by the force of the waves against the ragged boulders. I started to shake.

"Come on, Frannie. Let's sit down." Peter's voice was hollow, but calm. He wrapped his arm around my shoulders and guided me toward the couch.

Andy followed us to the living room, but he stopped at the French doors, as if he didn't want to intrude on our private misery. Maybe he just didn't want to track mud onto the rug. He was mumbling something about how sorry he was, but I wasn't listening. Reality had begun to take hold.

Pirate Point is four miles north of Black Bay, along the coast highway.

It's on the way to the Seahorse Pub, another mile up the road, situated on a notoriously rough section of the northern Sonoma County coastline. It got its name from local lore about a pirate ship that had gone down there sometime back in the late 1700s, sucked into the cove by the treacherous currents and smashed to bits against the rocks. Ten outlaws were sent to a watery grave the night their ship went down at Pirate Point. According to the legend, they're still buried there, two centuries later, under the waves at the bottom of the sheer cliff wall. It's said if you sit quietly at the top of the cliff and listen carefully, you can hear the echoes of their cries in the sounds of the sea. I knew it was true. I had heard them myself.

In fact, I knew Pirate Point intimately, having lived within hiking distance of the spot for most of my life. It is a menacing, godforsaken place, even on a sunny day. There are no trees on the point, and no wildflowers grow there in the springtime. Only rock. Massive black rock, beaten for centuries by the constant crashing of the waves, the brutal rains of winter, and the relentless coastal winds. I used to go there when I was a kid to sit on the boulders atop the craggy bluffs, watching and listening. Sometimes I would stay for hours at a time, bundled in a heavy woolen blanket I would sneak from the back of my father's car, hypnotized by the rhythm of the surf. I still went there occasionally, but less frequently than before. Pirate Point didn't soothe me anymore, not since my return home a year and a half ago, three months after the body of a young Black Bay woman had been found there, at the base of the cliffs. She had been raped and beaten and stabbed to death.

The sound of Andy's hoarse stammer brought me back into the room. He still stood at the French doors and was still inspecting his cap. "I— I need to get back to help with the search. Unless there's anything I can do for you folks, I'll be going now. I'll let you know when we get more information. God, I'm just so sorry—'' His voice faltered, and he hurried toward the door.

Peter rose to let him out. I got up too. "Wait, Andy. I have a question.''

He stopped and looked directly at me for the first time. His eyes were wide and unfocused. For an experienced officer, he wasn't handling this very well.

"The cliffs at Pirate Point are a good fifty yards off the road,'' I said. He nodded.

"This wasn't an accident, was it?''

"I don't think so, Fran.''

Then he turned and was gone.

3

Peter and I watched through the screen door as Andy hurried up the walk to his black and white Blazer. He had parked near the end of the driveway, not far from my Jeep, which was angled haphazardly onto the edge of the front lawn. It was raining hard now, but Andy had no umbrella, and it hadn't occurred to me to offer him one of ours. He had put his cap back on and was bent forward to keep the rain out of his face.

We stood at the door for several minutes, staring out at the bend in the highway where Andy's Blazer had disappeared into the fog. Neither of us made any effort to speak. I hadn't the strength to try, and I imagine Peter had simply no clue what to say.

In my mind's eye I could picture exactly where Sid's little convertible had been found, smashed on a jagged outcropping, half under water, half above, at the bottom of a fifty-foot rock wall. Pirate Point was one of the area's most photographed landmarks, by tourists for its legendary past and rugged beauty, and more recently, by gawking scandal-seekers caught up in the grisly glamour of what had happened there twenty-one months ago.

The murdered woman, April Kaminsky, had lived in Black Bay all her life and had gone to school with Sid and me. As young girls the three of us had been close, members of the local rat pack, and Sid had remained friendly with April in high school and after. I had drifted apart as an adolescent and had fallen completely out of touch when I left for college. Still, April's brutal slaying came as a serious shock to me, and I had done my best to avoid the local buzz still raging when I moved back to Black Bay twelve weeks after it happened.

The incident had occurred on the night of February 14, Valentine's Day. April's body, raped and sexually mutilated, was found the following afternoon inside her wrecked car at the bottom of the cliffs. Nearly two years had passed since then, but the police were still no closer to catching the killer than they had been on the cold clear winter day they hauled her body out of the Pacific. Further from it, I figured, since evidence and memories fade quickly.

When I finally turned to Peter, he was biting his lip and blinking back tears. I forced a numb smile to show I was okay and then walked past him, toward the stairs.

"I need a shower," I said.

He let me go and didn't follow, no doubt relieved I hadn't gotten hysterical, as I had when my mother passed away. He needn't have worried. I was coping, I suppose, but my emotional fuel gauge was still in the red zone. I simply had nothing left for Sid.

I headed for the bathroom and turned the shower on hot. The water nearly scalded me when I stepped in, but I stood there without turning the heat down, leaning against the cool tile wall, watching my paper-white skin turn pink, and thinking of my sister.

From the day we were born thirty-two years ago, Sidney Charlotte LaSalle had been, at best, an enigma; at worst, a pain in the ass. She had been a mischievous child, a wild teenager, and a defiant young woman. I had always admired her spunk, but in truth it was more than spunk, and I was one of the few who found it admirable. One time when we were in junior high Sid attempted, halfheartedly, to kill herself by slitting her wrists. I don't remember why. Maybe there was no reason; maybe it was all a big joke to her. She succeeded in ruining the cream-colored rug in her bedroom and in causing our mother to nearly have a nervous break-down, but not much else. I wondered if she had tried again last night and this time had done the job right.

I must have stood in the shower for nearly a half hour because when I came back to reality the water was turning chilly. I washed up quickly, toweled off, and pulled on a sweat suit. I tied my wet mass of curls into a ponytail and gently ran my fingertips over the surface of my head in search of a bump or tender spot from my collision with the bottom of the pool table the night before. Finding nothing, I brushed my teeth, forced down two aspirin, and went to gather my soggy, vomit-stained clothes, taking care not to inhale too deeply the sweet-sour smell of thrown-up beer and rum and Coke. I figured I would rinse out the jeans and blouse before tossing them in with the other laundry. The blazer would have to go to the dry cleaner. I picked it up with two fingers, wondering where to keep it until I could make the trip into town.

It was then that I noticed the red-brown blotches on the tan wool. I looked closer and picked at one of the spots with my fingernail. At first glance I thought it was mud, but on further inspection it didn't look like mud at all, not the kind of mud we have around Black Bay. Our mud is a rich, fertile black-brown. This was a reddish color. Like blood. There were large splotches of it all over the front and sleeves of my blazer and more on my blouse and jeans.

I staggered back to the bed and took a hasty inventory of my body and surroundings. I had a pair of purple welts on my left forearm and what felt like bruised ribs, but I hadn't noticed any cuts when I was in the shower, and there were no bloodstains on the sheets or my pillow. Had I given Sid a bloody nose the night before? It wouldn't have been the first time.

I gazed at the mound of clothes and tried to summon the energy to pick them up, but my hands lay limp in my lap and I didn't move off the bed. I thought back to the night before, to the Seahorse Pub, to the fight, to what might have happened afterward. Nothing came to me. One minute Sid and I were going at it in the parking lot; the next minute I was waking to the sound of Andy Saybrook ringing our doorbell. Everything in between was gone.

With shaky hands, I scooped up the clothes and headed back into the bathroom, where I turned on the water and dug out a bottle of Woolite from beneath the sink. Starting with my blouse, I wetted a stained spot, soaked it with Woolite, and rubbed it hard between my fingers. After a full minute of scrubbing I rinsed the spot in cold water, and holding my breath, I checked it. The fresh blood was gone but a dark shadow of the stain remained. I tried again with hot water. It worked no better. Frustrated, I tossed the blouse on the floor and went for my blazer. The tag inside the collar said DRY CLEAN ONLY, but I sloshed on the Woolite and went to work. When I rinsed away the soap, the stain was still there, as I was by now expecting. My blouse and blazer were ruined. I didn't need to try the jeans to know that they were too.

Feeling suddenly feverish, I splashed cold water on my face and tugged at the neck of my sweatshirt, wondering if Peter had cranked up the furnace. I half expected him to walk in on me to see what was taking so long. What would he say when he saw my clothes? What could he say? How could I possibly explain this? *I punched out Sid last night, Peter, must have given her a bloody nose. But somehow I managed to black it all out, so I really don't know what the hell happened....* Except that Sid had ended up dead and I woke up safe and sound with a pile of bloody clothes at the foot of my bed. It didn't sound so good.

I pushed myself back from the counter slowly, but with renewed determination. Peter mustn't find out about my bloodstained clothes. There was no good reason for anyone to find out, especially Peter. I had been leaning on him hard the last several months, taking advantage of his strong spirit and steady good nature, but my husband was human after all, and lately he had been snapping at me when I provoked him or picked a fight with Sid. The past year hadn't been easy for him either. I tended to forget that.

I pulled out a plastic garbage bag from the supply under the sink, filled it with my soiled clothes, and fastened it shut with a wire tab. Gripping the bag in one hand and the banister in the other, I crept downstairs and slipped out to the garage, where I pushed the bag to the bottom of one of two large plastic garbage cans. The clothes would be on their way to the town dump later that afternoon, and no one would ever know.

I could see Peter through the French doors that led from the foyer into the living room. He was on the couch, practicing his guitar, thin shoulders bent forward so he could read the sheet music spread across the coffee table. He looked up and smiled when I walked in, but the concern showed in his tired green eyes. Old eyes, I thought, too old for someone who hadn't yet seen his thirty-fifth birthday.

I eased myself onto the couch beside him and fixed my gaze on the green-and-blue plaid of the flannel workshirt he wore untucked over his Levi's. Eight months in Black Bay and my husband looked like a country boy born and bred, thanks in no small part to his shoulder-length sandy hair and the scruffy goatee he'd been so assiduously cultivating despite my pleas that he shave the stupid thing off. Ironically, he looked just like the guys Sid used to date when we were in high school—wannabe rebels, middle-class kids trying a little too hard to look tough. Sid had noticed too; I could tell by the catch in her eye when she first saw him the day she arrived for Mom's funeral.

He gave me another smile, weaker than the first, and set his guitar aside, but he didn't speak. Neither did I. We sat side by side in gloomy silence, staring out at the rain through the big picture window that overlooked the meadow between Mom's house—now our house—and the rocky Pacific coastline. The fog had cast a shadowy gray film over most everything beyond the scraggly rosebushes that dotted the small yard immediately in front of the house. I could just barely make out the silhouettes of the cypress trees that grew along the cliffs some seventy yards in the distance. Their tops were bent over like hunchbacked old ladies, tired and arthritic and battered by the wind.

I watched a raindrop trickle down the glass and flow into a puddle on the windowsill. A tear followed it down my cheek and dropped onto the front of my sweatshirt, but I didn't notice I was crying until I felt Peter's fingertips gently wiping away the wetness.

"Oh, Frannie," he said quietly. "How could this happen?" He sounded close to tears himself, although I suspected his distress was caused less by what had happened to Sid than by the inevitable delay it would cause in our plans to leave town. Peter had insisted on joining me in Black Bay the previous March during one of Mom's bad spells, rather blithely trading a high-powered software marketing position in San Francisco for a minimum-wage clerk's job in a twenty-four-hour backwoods convenience store. He perhaps had not adequately prepared himself for the magnitude of his sacrifice. Certainly neither of us had dreamed my mother would hang on as long as she did.

I closed my eyes and shook my head. "I don't know how it could happen, Peter. I just don't know. Sid was drunk when we left the Seahorse, but she seemed fine."

"Fine?" He pulled his hand away. His voice was sharper now. "How could you tell, Frannie? Were you fine too?"

I struggled not to snap at him and wound up saying nothing.

"You shouldn't have driven home drunk."

"I know that." I deserved this, but that didn't make it any easier to take.

"You shouldn't have let Sid drive either."

"For Chrissakes, Peter, it's not my fault. Sid wouldn't have listened to me. She could take care of herself."

He let out a long, slow sigh. "Under the circumstances, my dear, I'd say you're wrong about that."

"Come on, Peter. For all we know, Sid drove her own damn car off the cliff. If it hadn't been last night, she would have found another opportunity. I'm just grateful she waited until after Mom was gone."

His mouth dropped open. "My God, Frannie. You think Sid committed suicide?"

"She might have." I felt my theory crumbling under the weight of his incredulity. "Remember the money she wanted to borrow? She must have been in trouble. When she couldn't come up with the cash . . . well, maybe she panicked."

"I don't think so. Your father bailed her out."

"My father? No way."

"He did. His bimbo girlfriend was ranting and raving about it at the funeral. I overheard them arguing. Sounded like your dad took the money Barb was planning to use to remodel their house and he gave it to Sid."

I thought back to the night before. Sid hadn't actually asked me for a loan. I hadn't let her get that far.

"I'm just telling you what I heard, Frannie. But either way, I can't believe your sister would kill herself over fifty thousand dollars. That's not the Sid LaSalle I know."

I bristled at his last comment. *The Sid LaSalle he knew.* Who was that, I wanted to ask. Certainly not my sister. He'd never known my sister, never shown any desire to. Even while Sid was staying with us, she and Peter had spent almost no time together. Peter worked most nights, and during the day Sid avoided both of us. As far as I knew, the only time Peter and Sid had ever been alone together for more than a few moments was over a year ago when he'd been in Orange County on business and had driven into Los Angeles, at my insistence, to take her to dinner. He said they had a fine time, but I noticed he never spoke of her again.

"So you think she was murdered?" I felt my stomach rising to my throat.

He nodded. Of course he thought that. I did too, deep down.

"Why, Peter? Who would kill Sid?" I squeezed my eyes shut until a vision of my bloodstained clothes forced them open. "She hadn't lived in Black Bay for years. Nobody around here even knew her anymore. Who'd have reason to kill her? Who?" I sounded like a tape recording with the speed and volume turned up.

He shrugged. "I don't know. Who would kill that Kaminsky woman?"

I pressed my fingers against my throbbing temples, unable to respond.

"There are lots of crazy people out there, Frannie." He gathered me into his embrace and made comforting sounds in my ear. "Maybe you're right. I hope to God you are. At least if it was suicide, we know there isn't some lunatic out there on the loose."

I laid my head on his shoulder and thought of April Kaminsky. There was a lunatic out there on the loose. The lunatic who killed April hadn't been caught, thanks to the ineptitude of Andy Saybrook and his fellow incompetents on the Black Bay police force. The Valentine's Day Killer, the locals called him. He was still at large, free to kill again if he got the urge.

After a moment I slid out of Peter's arms. "You'll be late for work if you don't get going." He had the two-to-ten shift at the MiniMart that day, and like it or not, we badly needed the extra income.

He placed his guitar in its case and moved it to the far side of the couch—off-limits to my clumsy fingers. "Will you be okay by your-self?"

I nodded.

"You sure?"

"I'm sure."

With weak knees, I followed him to the garage door, kissed him good-bye, and watched as he carried our garbage cans out to the end of the driveway where they would be emptied later that afternoon by North Coast Disposal. I sucked in my breath when he picked up the can that contained my bloodstained clothes. He had no reason to lift the lid, and he didn't, but I was tempted to run out to him, pull the plastic bag out of the can, and dump the clothes at his feet.

In the end, my shame outweighed my need to confide. I stood rooted at the door, watching in guilty silence as his beat-up Volvo sedan fish-tailed out of the driveway. I waited there a few minutes after he was gone, leaning against the door with my forehead resting on the cool damp windowpane. Then I marched down the hall to the coat closet, pulled on my boots and rain slicker, and headed out through the garage. I needed to see for myself.

4

I drove north on the coast highway, faster than I should have, given the dense fog and slick road conditions. My palms were sticky with sweat and my breath was short, but I leaned forward and gripped the steering wheel with both hands, accelerating through the curves. It was cold outside, no more than fifty degrees, and drizzling, but I rode with the windows wide open.

The police had strung yellow tape across the turnout for Pirate Point, so I parked illegally on the east side of the highway and ran across. On the other side I ducked under the tape and stopped for a moment to compose myself before I began to pick my way along the muddy driveway that led to the end of the point.

I could barely see five feet in front of me, the fog was so thick. The only sounds were the waterlogged earth sucking at my boots and, ahead of me, the distant rhythm of the waves crashing against the rocks at the base of the cliff. I glanced back toward my Jeep, for reassurance, I guess, that I had come here under my own power and could leave when I pleased. But the Jeep had already evaporated into the mist.

I had to concentrate to keep my balance in the disorienting grayness as I staggered toward the point. My throat had started to constrict when I stepped out of the Jeep, and by now I was gasping for air. I slogged on for a minute or two, then paused to get my bearings. The sound of the waves seemed to come from all around me now. I put a hand out to brace myself against the trunk of a redwood. My fingers dug into the moist porous bark until little crumbles of it were imbedded under my nails.

After forcing down several deep breaths, I continued in what I believed was the direction of the cliff. I wasn't sure anymore. The farther I went, the muddier my path became and the more difficult it was to maintain my footing. When I got to within what I estimated was no more than a dozen yards of the edge, three shadowy figures emerged. I could make out two cops in uniform and a man in a trench coat holding an umbrella. They were huddled together, seemingly deep in conversation, just off the driveway near the tip of the point. A couple more cops climbed on the boulders at the edge of the cliff.

As I approached the group of three, I recognized Andy Saybrook's hulking frame and his partner, Harlan Fry. I winced at the sight of Harlan, although since Andy was working on Sid's case, I should have known his longtime partner would be too. Harlan is several inches shorter than Andy, but a lot tougher and a hell of a lot less friendly, a pumped-up Napoleon with a thick neck and tattooed biceps that bulge from too many hours in the gym. His intense black-eyed stare would be mysterious, maybe even sexy, on someone less menacing, but on Harlan it's frightening.

The man in the trench coat was Dominick Carbone, Black Bay's chief of police. For Nick Carbone to endanger the sheen on his Gucci loafers by making an appearance at the scene of an investigation, in a fifty-degree drizzle no less, was truly a rare occurrence. I looked around for the television cameras, which would have explained it, but there were none.

Carbone and Andy had their backs to me, but Harlan saw me coming and called out. "Hey! What the fuck are you doing out here?"

I stopped and stared, shrinking an inch as the mud swallowed the heels of my boots.

Andy interceded before I could respond. He strode toward me with his arms stretched open wide to block my path. "Fran, this is a crime scene. Nobody's supposed to be here while we're collecting evidence. That's why we put up the tape." He refused to meet my eye.

I looked beyond him to Harlan and Carbone. Their faces were grim and unyielding, a unified front. Apparently they felt the same as Peter. They thought Sid had been murdered.

"Crime scene?"

"The tape says DO NOT CROSS. It's there for a reason." Andy's voice was cold and curt.

I scowled at him from under the green plastic brim of my hood, wondering what had become of his sympathy from earlier that day.

"Fran, you asked if it was an accident. I told you it wasn't. I thought you understood."

"Yes, you told me. I was thinking suicide, Andy. Not . . . this."

His cheeks had been rosy from the cold. Now they were on fire. "We don't know yet. We have to treat it as a possible homicide until we determine otherwise. I'm sorry I didn't warn you not to come out here. I didn't think it was necessary." He glanced over his shoulder at the other officers. "It would be best if you left."

I didn't budge. Despite his show of authority, I had trouble accepting Andy as a real policeman. He looked more like a hot dog vendor at a ballpark. I nodded toward the guys on the rocks. "What are they doing?"

"We're trying to get the car out. They're looking for a place to set up a tow."

From their movement on the rocks I could tell Sid's car was just where I had pictured it, immediately beneath the farthestmost edge of the point, precisely where the rocks at the bottom of the cliff were the most treacherous. "Who could have spotted her car down there, under the lip?"

Andy hesitated before responding. "Woody Hanks. He was walking his dog on the bluff by his house." He gestured to his left, in the general direction of an invisible point a quarter mile to the north. It projected farther into the bay than Pirate Point, affording in better weather an unobstructed view back to the spot where Sid's car must have been.

"And her body?"

"Haven't found it yet. We pulled out a black leather clog, but so far no body. The Coast Guard is sending a boat and some divers, but . . ." He shrugged and stared at his boots.

"But what?"

"If the current's got her, she may be gone for good." He said it as if he already knew the answer. Sid's body was not going to be recovered. We would never really know exactly how she died.

Before I could ask another question, Dominick Carbone stepped between Andy and me, knocking Andy in the face with the spiky edge of his umbrella. "Miss LaSalle, you'll have to leave immediately. We've got to conduct a proper investigation. I'm sure you can understand that."

"It's Mrs. Estes now, Mr. Carbone," I said. "I'm married."

He took a step closer and leaned toward me so we were eye to eye. The spicy smell of his aftershave nearly made me sneeze. "I'm delighted you have a husband, but frankly, I don't give a damn if you're Mrs. Bill Clinton. You've got to go."

Without giving him time to enforce his order, I sucked in a gulp of sea air and took off at a brisk clip for the edge of the cliff. I listened for footsteps in the muck behind me, half expecting to be tackled from behind, but they let me go. When I got within several feet of the lip, the road gave way to a sloping muddy outcropping that stretched out over the sheer rock wall. This was the route Sid's car would have taken, the only clear pathway to the edge, but it was too steep to walk without risking a tumble down the sharp grade and over the drop-off. Ominous though they looked, the boulders on either side of the gap were safer. One could climb on the rocks all the way to the end and get a clear view down to the bottom of the cliff.

I scrambled onto the slippery boulders and made my way toward the two cops setting up the tow. They were well disguised in rain gear and hoods, but I was pretty sure I had never seen either of them before. They seemed young and uncertain of what they were doing, which bolstered my resolve. I was within a couple feet of them before they noticed me.

"Hey, what are you doing out here?" asked the taller of the two. Up close he looked to be about six foot five. His partner was my size.

I nodded in the direction of Sid's car. "I'm her sister. Carbone said I could take a look."

The cop looked skeptical, but he reached out to give me a hand. "Better be careful. These rocks are blame slick."

I nodded and inched my way past him to a spot where I could catch a glimpse of Sid's car.

"We're real sorry about your sister," said his partner.

"Thanks." I was lying flat on my stomach now. My legs were stretched straight out behind me, my feet wedged in a crevasse between two boulders, my arms extended, hands pressing against the cold smooth surface. I craned my neck out over the edge and forced myself to look down. It was a long windy drop to the black swells at the bottom of the cliff, but even fifty feet up, the sound of the waves slamming against the rocks was deafening. I pressed my hands harder against the boulders to brace myself and fought off a wave of nauseating dizziness by focusing on the horizon. To my right, due north, was the vantage point from which Woody Hanks had spotted Sid's car. It was rugged and uninviting, like Pirate Point, but in a totally different way. Unlike Pirate Point, which was barren and rocky, the point to the north was overgrown with tall dense brush that blanketed the ground to the edge of cliffs.

When I looked back at the water beneath me, a bit of yellow wreckage caught my eye. The rear fender of Sid's Volkswagen was jutting out of the barnacled black rocks. When the waves weren't splashing over it, I could see much of the bright yellow back end of the vehicle. There was no sign of life. The car was totaled. Worse than totaled. It looked like a squashed beer can.

I lasted only a minute in my precarious perch before the police chief caught up with me. "Mrs. Estes, come back here. Now!"

His voice was barely audible over the crashing of the waves, and I considered pretending not to hear him, but he was closer than I thought. An instant after he yelled to me, he clamped onto my ankle. The shock of his grip nearly sent me shooting over the edge. I looked back to see him squatting beside me with one hand on my ankle and the other on the rocks to steady himself.

"Goddamnit. You get your ass off of these rocks. Now! Or I'll place you under arrest."

He had abandoned his umbrella and trench coat, sacrificing his gangster-striped suit and starched white shirt. His eyes threatened to burst from their sockets, and his immense body shook as if he were having some sort of epileptic attack. I didn't like the man, but I surely didn't want him to have a seizure while he was holding my ankle at the edge of a cliff, so I slid back along the rocky surface and pushed up to my feet. I stepped around him and scrambled from boulder to boulder along a familiar childhood climbing route until I was able to hop down onto the muddy drive. I landed face-to-face with the two young cops who had allowed me out there. They stared at me, paralyzed. Above us a white-breasted gull soared in a wide circle, confirmed its disinterest, and flew off.

I shot the two cops a miserable little smile that was more grimace than grin and averted my eyes while we waited for Carbone. It was then that I spotted a brown object about the size of my thumbnail lying in the mud just beyond my left toe. It was a button, a typical nondescript little button, made of marbleized brown plastic. From what I could make out, it appeared to be similar to the buttons on the tan blazer I had been wearing the night before, not as big as those on the front of the blazer, but approximately the same size as the six smaller ones at the ends of the sleeves.

My breath caught in my throat. The police would find the button. It was inconceivable that they wouldn't. And then what? What if they asked me if I recognized it? If I admitted that it looked like the buttons on my blazer, they would ask to see the blazer and I would have to tell them I had thrown it away that morning—and why.

Reflexively, I scooched my foot forward so my toe covered the button. The cops were watching Carbone crawl toward us across the boulders and were too concerned about him to pay attention to me, so I pressed the button firmly into the soft soil with the ball of my foot and rolled my boot from side to side to cover it with mud. When I pulled my foot back, it was buried safely out of sight.

A moment later Carbone stumbled down from the last boulder. He grabbed me roughly by the arm and dragged me back to Harlan and Andy. "You're lucky I don't throw your ass in jail," he said in a voice just this side of berserk.

I twisted out of his grip. "Go ahead. Throw me in jail. How will that play in the *Recorder,* Mr. Carbone? 'Police Chief Jails Bereaved Sister for Visiting Scene of Twin's Death.' You go right ahead. Arrest me."

That shut him up, so I continued. "You listen to me, Carbone. That's my sister's car down there, and if somebody put it there, I want to know who. You guys screwed up when April Kaminsky was dumped down there and now you're about to do the same thing all over again."

Carbone looked ready to blow. "You don't know what the hell you're talking about."

"No? I read the papers, Mr. Carbone. You ripped up April's car trying to drag it up the side of the cliff and you're fixing to do the same with Sid's."

Andy's stupidity got the best of him and he broke in. "Jesus, Fran. The vehicle's totaled anyway."

"The back fender's not totaled, Andy. If Sid was pushed over the edge by another car, there might be damage to the fender."

Andy started to make another smart remark, but Carbone cut him off. "Save it, Saybrook. Fry, make sure Cruise and Walters don't touch the car until I say so." He grabbed my arm again and turned me so I faced the highway, but his voice was softer now. "Now please leave, Mrs. Estes. Your concern is understandable, but I must insist that you stay out of the way. I personally assure you we will conduct a thorough investigation. Nothing will be overlooked."

Small comfort, I wanted to say but didn't. Instead I took my leave, confident I had made my point. They would be held accountable for this investigation, and Carbone knew it.

Andy escorted me back to the Jeep. He steered me along a path through the trees so I didn't walk on the road or across the turnout, where another officer was preparing to take imprints of the tire tracks. Neither of us said a word, although I was tempted to tell Andy what I thought of his attitude. He was my friend, or so I thought.

When we got to the highway, Andy stopped and waited while I ran across and climbed into the Jeep. My hands were shaking and I felt light-headed, but I managed to get the key into the ignition. I waved as I pulled onto the road. He didn't wave back.

A cop is a cop, I told myself. Even Andy.

5

The face staring back at me from the bathroom mirror was not a pretty sight. This is what a beer-and-rum-and-Coke-on-an-empty-stomach hangover looks like, I thought. Like Sid after a long night of partying—only ten times worse. My skin was devoid of color except for the purple-gray bags under my bloodshot eyes. My lips were dry and tinged with brown. The damp weather had frizzled my curly hair, most of which by now had escaped my ponytail and was hanging in my face. I looked as if I had stuck my finger in an electrical socket. I felt that way too. No wonder Andy had been afraid to look me in the eye.

Over the objections of my upset stomach, I forced down a full glass of water with two aspirin. Afterward, not knowing what to do next, I wandered down the hall to my mother's bedroom and stood at the doorway, looking in. The room had white wallpaper dotted with tiny pink roses, a matched set of delicate antique reproduction furniture, and lacy white curtains. Mom had redecorated two years after Dad left, as if to symbolize her final acceptance that he wasn't coming back. I had helped her put up the wallpaper and could still find each of the secret flaws in our handiwork, the handful of wrinkles where we had trouble smoothing out the air bubbles, the narrow strip behind the door where the roses were upside down. Last week Peter had cleared out most of the medical paraphernalia that had accumulated over the past year, but I hadn't ventured

into the room since the day Mom died. I sensed that now was not a good
time to try.

With a knot of grief and exhaustion swelling in my chest, I turned
away from the door and made my way down the hall to Sid's old room,
where I stretched out on my back atop her crimson-covered bed. The
room had been left just as it was when we were in high school, decorated
with punk rock posters and dozens of creepy black and red candles, with
not a trace of the adult my sister had become. As far as I knew, Sid had
not set foot in here during the past two weeks, preferring instead the
relative seclusion of the guest room above the garage, where she could
more easily avoid my sentimental attempts to connect. I stared up at the
glow-in-the-dark decals on the ceiling, feeling lonely and tired and sorry
for myself.

Eventually I would go back downstairs and put on my game face for
the hard days to come, but there was no need to hurry. Peter didn't get
off work until ten, so I had plenty of time to indulge my self-pity and
then pull myself together before he got home. I dragged a pillow over
my face and closed my eyes, imagining my mother was alive and healthy
and working outside in her garden, clipping roses to float in a glass bowl
on the kitchen table or collecting petals for potpourri. For a minute it
eased the terrible ache in my heart, but only for a minute. Then reality
intruded. I saw her fragile, cancer-ridden body, and I knew I better think
of something else.

I started a mental list of things I needed to take care of in connection
with Sid's death. First I would call the relatives. That wouldn't take long,
since there weren't many left, just Mom's sister Clara in Pennsylvania,
some cousins in Phoenix, and, of course, Dad. Like it or not, I would
have to call my father. I would rather let him find out some other way,
like maybe when he sent Sid's birthday card next October and it came
back stamped RETURN TO SENDER. He would call to get a forwarding
address and I'd say, "Sid? She's been dead almost a year. Guess I forgot
to mention it." I was sure my sister, wherever she was, would appreciate
the gesture.

The possibility of a memorial service occurred to me, but I couldn't
bear the thought of putting my grief for my sister on public display so
soon after going through it all for my mother. If Sid's body was found,
I would arrange for her to be buried next to Mom in a private ceremony.
Peter and I would attend, and maybe Sam Goldman and Millicent Trimble, my friends from work, and our neighbors, the Olsons. There was no
one else to invite.

*   *   *

I was disoriented at first when I heard the click of the front door. It was pitch black and cold in the room where I lay, and the soft beat of the rain came from an unfamiliar direction. When I recovered my bearings I realized I had fallen asleep in Sid's room. I could smell the candle wax. By the light of my Timex Indiglo, I saw that it was only seven-thirty, not the dead of night, as it seemed.

I was still groping for my senses when I heard voices downstairs and then footsteps softly treading up the carpeted stairs. I was instantly alert. Peter didn't get off work for another two and a half hours, so who was creeping up the steps? With Sid gone, there was no one else who belonged in our house. No one.

"Frannie?"

I let out a groan. It was Peter, home early.

"Frannie, where are you? There's someone here to see you."

"What can I get you? Coffee? Tea? Coke?"

My husband the stewardess had welcomed Andy Saybrook and Harlan Fry into our home with an irritating overabundance of hospitality. He was eager to hear the latest news about Sid and unaware of the shabby way they had treated me earlier that day out at Pirate Point. I followed them into the living room, but I was too tired, too hungry, and too annoyed to mimic Peter's enthusiasm. I took it as a good sign that neither of the officers took him up on his offer of refreshment. Maybe they would finish their business quickly and be on their way.

Peter and I sat together on the couch, facing Harlan, who had helped himself to my mother's antique platform rocker on the other side of the coffee table. Andy was the last to find a seat, so he was left with a strategically inferior overstuffed easy chair near the fireplace. In a better mood I would have brought in a chair from the dining room so he didn't have to sit in the corner, but I wasn't in a better mood, so I didn't bother. He balanced on the edge of his seat with his elbows on his knees in a futile attempt to keep the goose down cushions from sucking him farther away from center stage.

Harlan pulled a scrap of paper from his jacket pocket and pretended to read it, slowly and with great interest. I figured he knew very well how anxious we were and was torturing us intentionally, so I clamped my mouth shut and stared at the red scratches that marred the backs of his hands. Beside me, Peter fidgeted and cracked his knuckles, but he too waited for one of the cops to speak first.

Andy's furtive glance bounced from Harlan to Peter to me and back to Harlan, but he didn't hold anyone's eye for more than a second. Eventually he squirmed forward in his chair and said, "Sorry about the, um, misunderstanding this afternoon, Fran."

I ignored Peter's questioning eye and shrugged. Apology noted but not necessarily accepted.

Before Peter could ask what "misunderstanding" he was referring to, Andy said, "I hoped we'd have some news for you by now, but I'm afraid we haven't made much progress. With the strong current we haven't been able to find the body. It was pretty rough out there today."

I nodded. "You're certain she was in the car when it went over the edge?"

Harlan cleared his throat in a not-too-subtle signal that he would take over. "Miss LaSalle was wearing a tie-dyed skirt last night, wasn't she?"

"Yes."

"We found a piece of it in the latch for the convertible top of her car. The top was partially torn off when the vehicle hit the rocks. It appears that the current dragged your sister's body out through the opening and her skirt got caught in the latch."

My stomach lurched as I pictured Sid's body being sucked out of her car into the icy Pacific chop. Peter noticed and took hold of my clenched fist.

Harlan noticed too. He sat up straighter and pushed back his shoulders. "There was a strong ebb tide last night," he said. "And the undertow is fierce near Pirate Point. Our only realistic hope of recovering the body had been if it was stuck in the car or lodged in the rocks. Unfortunately, when the current pulled it out through the convertible top, the undertow got it."

I nodded at my knees, unable to look at him. Through some unfortunate quirk of his facial muscles, he was grinning at us.

"We'll keep up the search for another day or two, but there's no way we'll find her now," he said. "Not a chance in hell."

Peter spoke up before I could find my voice. "Okay, so Sid is dead, and if we understand you correctly, it could be that she was murdered. Assuming that's the case, we'd like to know what you're doing to find the killer."

"We're on top of it, Mr. Estes. You can be sure of that."

Peter nodded and waited for him to continue. "Care to elaborate, Lieutenant?"

"For one thing, we found multiple tire tracks on the road out to the cliff. We've taken imprints and are waiting for the results. That may tell us if there was a second vehicle involved."

"Any footprints?" I asked.

"None but Woody Hanks's from this morning, and of course *yours* from this afternoon. Any others have been washed out by all the rain." He emphasized the part about my footprints. He must have noticed Peter's confusion when Andy mentioned they had seen me that afternoon.

Peter's face revealed nothing, but by now he surely knew what I had done. He didn't take his eyes off Harlan. "Woody Hanks? That old derelict who tends bar at the Seahorse Pub? What was he doing out there?"

"He found the car. Took his dog for a walk early this morning on the bluff near his house, just north of Pirate Point. He noticed the rear end of Miss LaSalle's vehicle sticking out of the rocks so he went over to get a better look. Then he called us."

Peter frowned, but he seemed satisfied with the explanation. "What else have you got?"

Andy coughed and ran his hand across his wide freckled forehead, which had turned a blotchy pink and was glistening with perspiration. He'd been sitting so quietly in the corner I had almost forgotten he was in the room.

"We're not at liberty to disclose the details of the case, Mr. Estes," Harlan said. "I'm sure you can understand that."

"What about suicide?" I asked. "Have you considered that possibility?"

His surprised expression answered my question. "Do you think that's what happened?"

"I think it's possible."

"Have you found a note?"

"No."

"Had your sister spoken to you of an intention to kill herself?"

"Sort of. We got into an argument last night. I thought she wanted me to lend her money and I told her no, but now I'm thinking she may have wanted to tell me something else. She said it was a matter of life or death."

"Was it unusual for her to say something like that?"

"Not exactly unusual, but—"

"Did she seem upset? Was she crying?"

"My sister wasn't the crying type, Lieutenant. She—"

"What about before last night? Had she been behaving strangely? Unusually depressed or despondent? Withdrawn?" He pulled out a pen and pocket-size notebook and scribbled a quick note. "I realize Miss LaSalle had come to Black Bay to attend your mother's funeral. Obviously, we would expect a certain amount of grief, but did it seem to you she was inordinately distraught?"

I examined my bitten-to-the-quick fingernails. Despondent? Inordinately distraught? Hardly. Sid had shown her typical lack of compassion at the funeral and during the days that followed, including the previous night at the Seahorse Pub. She had been short-tempered and quarrelsome, but hardly distraught.

"I guess not," I said quietly.

Harlan smiled and rested his case.

So much for my theory. I thought again of April Kaminsky's brutal murder and swallowed hard through my pinched throat. I slid to the edge of the couch to convey my desire to end our visit. They had delivered their news. Sid had not committed suicide. She had been murdered.

Andy mopped his forehead and Harlan scrawled more notes, but neither made any move to leave. I knew I should be grateful for their diligence, but I wasn't. I just wanted to be rid of them, to be done with the whole horrible day.

"Fran, did your sister receive any threats while she was staying with you?" Andy asked. "Anonymous calls, maybe? Had she noticed anyone following her?"

The obvious connection to April Kaminsky. According to the newspapers, April had been getting anonymous phone calls shortly before she was killed and had told her parents she thought she was being followed.

"Fran?"

"Oh, sorry. Nothing that I know of."

"Did she have any enemies? Anyone who might have had it in for her?"

I stared into Harlan's hard dark eyes. They were the eyes of a thug. He had a recent wound over one of them, a raw purple track with stitches that stretched from the outside corner of his left eye to the middle of his thick black eyebrow. I was tempted to say yes, that Harlan Fry was Sid's enemy. Harlan knew it was true. Andy knew it too. Fifteen years ago Sid had implicated Harlan in a police brutality scandal, and it had nearly cost him his career. A high school Halloween party had gotten out of hand and someone called the cops. Before the night was over Harlan had savagely beaten and nearly killed a black student, one of Sid's close friends. April Kaminsky and I had testified against him too, along with a handful of others, but it was Sid's graphic and somewhat exaggerated eyewitness account that ignited the court, and for weeks afterward, the entire town. Harlan, I was sure, had not forgotten the incident. None of us had.

Andy cleared his throat. "Any enemies, Fran? Anyone you know of?"

I shrugged and shook my head. "I don't think so, at least not up here."

"Somewhere else?" Harlan asked. I detected a glimmer of relief in his voice.

"I'm not sure about her situation in Los Angeles. She wasn't keen to go home after the funeral because she was having problems with her boyfriend. I think he may have been abusive."

"Oh?" Harlan furiously recorded my responses in his notebook.

"I don't really know much more than that. Sid and I weren't real close. She didn't confide in me."

"Boyfriend got a name?"

"Deke. I don't know his last name." I sighed and struggled to keep my brain on track.

He looked at me and squinted. "Job? Phone number? Address?"

"At one point he was living in Sid's apartment, I think. But that was a while ago. I have no idea if he's still there. If not, maybe the landlord or neighbors can help." I told him Sid's phone number and address and pushed to my feet, determined to bring the interview to a close. "If that's it for now . . ."

Peter followed my lead and stood up. Andy and Harlan did too. For a moment I thought they would leave, but my optimism was premature.

"We'd like to see her things," Harlan said. "To see if there are any indications she was in trouble."

I wasn't surprised. It was all part of the thorough investigation promised by Dominick Carbone. I led the way to the guest room above the garage and sat as patiently as I could beside Peter on Sid's unmade bed while the cops rummaged through her belongings. She hadn't brought much with her from L.A., just what she could cram into an army surplus duffel bag. Her clothes were a wrinkled mess, but Harlan picked through them, piece by piece, pocket by pocket. He found nothing.

There was a scrap of paper on the nightstand beside the telephone. Andy snapped it up. "Hey, look at this. Uzis at GAMH. What do you think it means?"

"The Uzis are a rock group," I said before they could get too excited. "They're playing Thursday night at the Great American Music Hall in San Francisco. Sid wanted me to get tickets."

The stitches over Harlan's left eye jumped like a dancing centipede. "Did you?"

"Are you kidding? The Uzis?" I forced a wry smile. "Sid and I have very different tastes in music."

"Did she get the tickets herself?"

"I doubt it. She expected me to pay. Besides, she'd have no one else to go with."

Harlan studied the note and slipped it into his pocket. "Doesn't seem to me that a woman who was planning to kill herself would want tickets to a rock concert."

One more shovelful of dirt on my suicide theory.

They headed for the bathroom next. Harlan and Andy squeezed into the closet-size room while Peter and I watched from the doorway. There they found all sorts of good stuff. They confiscated Sid's fake leather cosmetic kit and her hairbrush and comb, which they deposited into white paper evidence bags. Then they scavenged through the wastebasket, adding a few bits of garbage to their collection.

Before leaving the guest room they flipped through the covers on the bed and checked under the pillow. It was almost nine-thirty by the time they finished. We trooped back to the living room and I dropped onto the couch.

"Look, guys, I've had a rough day. I'm hungry and tired and feeling a little sick. Do you think we could wrap this up?"

Andy grunted and dropped his handful of evidence bags onto the coffee table. "Goddamnit, Fran. It's clear you'd like to be rid of us, but your sister was murdered last night. We're here because we want to find out what happened to her. Don't you?"

I started to snap back, but a vision of April Kaminsky's dead body stopped me. The Black Bay police had investigated April's murder for nearly two years without success. The entire force had come under fire for failing to find her killer, and it was rumored that Andy had nearly lost his job over the case. Perhaps his frustration was justified.

"Of course I want to find out what happened. Let's continue."

Andy stared at the floor and dug his toe under the edge of the rag rug. Either he didn't know where to begin or he didn't have the guts to ask the tough questions. Once again, Harlan took over.

"You were fighting with Miss LaSalle last night," he said. It was a statement, not a question, so I didn't respond. I heard Peter suck in his breath.

"Is that correct, Mrs. Estes?"

"We argued."

"You came to blows."

Apparently Woody Hanks had told the police a bit more than just the location of Sid's car. I felt Peter's leg press against mine. He was sitting up straight and didn't seem to be breathing.

"Did you come to blows?"

"Maybe."

Harlan lunged toward me. "Maybe? What the fuck kind of answer is that?"

Peter scrambled to the edge of the couch and pointed an accusatory finger at Harlan. "Hey man, cool it. You've no right to speak to her like that."

Harlan pointed back. I had visions of them getting into a poking match, or worse. "You stay out of this, pal. Better yet, leave the room. Andy, take him into the kitchen. I want to talk to his wife by herself."

By now Peter was so angry his voice shook. "Frannie, you don't have to stand for this. You can call a lawyer. Call Sam Goldman."

"Maybe we should call Sam." I glared across the coffee table at Harlan, who calmed himself quickly at the mention of Sam Goldman's name.

"Of course you don't have to answer my questions without consulting your attorney," he said. "I'm beginning to wonder if you have something to hide. If so, you damn well better call a lawyer."

His tactic worked perfectly. "I have nothing to hide," I said. "I'll be happy to answer your questions, provided you behave like a civil human being and provided Peter can stay."

Harlan nodded, and we all took a deep breath. Peter obviously wasn't happy with the situation, but he kept quiet except to ask Harlan to hold off for a moment while he got me some ginger ale. This time he didn't offer anything to Harlan or Andy, although Andy was sweating like a pig and looked as if he would have loved a drink.

"Let's start again," Harlan said evenly when Peter returned with my soda and a handful of saltine crackers. "Did you and your sister engage in a physical altercation last night at the Seahorse Pub?"

I took a bite of a cracker and nodded. "I don't remember the details. We both had too much to drink and we got into an argument."

"A physical altercation."

"Yes."

"Did either of you draw blood?"

I thought of my bloodstained clothes and rolled my eyes. "Are you kidding?"

Peter let out a loud sigh. I felt his stare and understood the telepathic message. *Shut up,* he silently shouted at me. *Don't be a stubborn idiot. Call Sam.*

"I was angry at Sid for the way she acted while our mother was sick. We argued about it, and yes, we came to blows. I did not, however, kill her, if that's what you're insinuating."

Harlan leaned forward so his face was within several inches of mine. He planted his palms on the coffee table, displaying the ugly red scratches that covered his hands and wrists. "Did you hate her, Mrs. Estes?"

I could feel the heat rise up my neck and into my face, which I knew by now was beet red. I shrank back into the cushions of the sofa. "No. Of course not. She was my sister. I . . . I loved her."

"Do you know why she would say you hated her?"

"No." Two nights ago Sid and I had gotten into a shouting match during dinner. My exact words, in the heat of the moment, were, I believe, *I hate you when you act this way.* I wondered if she had told Woody Hanks about our spat the following evening at the Seahorse Pub and if he had repeated it to the police. No wonder Woody had been so aloof when I came into the bar.

Peter had heard enough. He stood up and said, "I think it's time for you two to leave. If we're not done you can come back in the morning, but right now my wife needs dinner and sleep. Her mother died two weeks ago and her sister was killed last night. Give the woman a goddamn break."

To my relief, Harlan stood up too and picked up his jacket. Andy did the same. I watched in silent appreciation as Peter ushered them to the door. "One more thing, Mr. Estes," Harlan said from the porch. "I understand your wife and her sister were alone last night. Where were you after, say, eleven o'clock?"

"I was at work."

"At midnight?"

"I work at the Day-n-Night MiniMart. I had the graveyard shift last night, from ten o'clock until six this morning."

"And you could prove that if it ever became an issue?"

Peter hesitated. "I suppose so. I wouldn't expect it to become an issue." He stepped back into the foyer and let the screen swing shut. "Good night, Lieutenant Fry, Andy."

I waited for the door to slam. Then I ran for the bathroom and threw up ginger ale and crackers.

* * *

Ten minutes after Andy and Harlan left, I joined Peter in the kitchen and watched him painstakingly assemble an enormous green salad. He jabbered while he worked, skipping from one mundane topic to another, obviously doing his best to keep my mind off Sid. I was too hungry to pay attention to what he was saying, but I didn't offer to help. We had long ago learned that my assistance in the kitchen was not conducive to good domestic relations.

I laid my head on the table and tried to be patient. Life had been less complicated when it was just Mom and me. It's not that I wasn't grateful to Peter for sacrificing his seventy-thousand-dollar-a-year job in San Francisco to be with us. I was. I unquestionably owed my sanity to his presence, especially during the final weeks before my mother's death. Still, in some ways things had been easier without him.

He was exuberantly tossing his beautiful salad when I noticed the light blinking on the telephone answering machine. "Somebody must have called while we were in Sid's room," I said as I reached for the play button.

Peter loaded my plate while the tape rewound. "It's probably Bobby Olson," he said. "He's finishing my shift tonight. I need to let him know if I want him to work for me tomorrow too."

"Hello, Frances and Peter." It was my father's deep monotone. Peter set the salad bowl down with a thud and we stared at the answering machine, our meal forgotten. "Just checking in to see how you're doing. . . ." I glanced at Peter and rolled my eyes. My father checking in to see how we were doing? That was a first. "I'll try you again tomorrow. I'm not in Texas, so you won't be able to reach me at home. Bye now."

"Bye now," Peter said to the machine. He pushed the erase button and turned to me. "That was odd. What do you think he wants?"

"Who knows? I wonder where he is."

My father had been living in Dallas for the past several years, shacking up with a string of girlfriends, most recently a skinny, suntanned thirty-five-year-old named Barb something-or-other. Barb had a big mouth, a Texas drawl, and Texas-size silicon breasts that stood out like melons under her tight sweaters. Dad had the poor taste to appear at Mom's funeral, uninvited, with Barbie doll on his arm. I didn't speak more than ten words to him, and Sid wasn't any friendlier, but Peter, to my extreme frustration, felt it his duty to be polite. After I calmed down, he told me that Dad had brought Barb because she had never been to California before and he wanted to show her the sights. It was just like my father to use Mom's death as an excuse for a vacation.

I tried to guess where Dad was now. At Disneyland, maybe, in a tour boat with his arm around Barbie doll's bony bronze shoulders, squeezing those plump pink melons while they floated through some attraction intended for eight-year-olds. He had never taken Sid and me to Disneyland. He had never taken us anywhere.

I pushed back my plate and silently cursed my father. It had hurt when he left us—I could still hear the cruel comments of my childhood playmates and feel the searing shame of our single-parent status—but it had hurt even more two decades later when I learned from my sister just how much better off we had been without him.

Peter waved his fork in front of my unfocused eyes. "Don't let him get to you, Frannie. He's not worth getting upset over. Remember what Dr. Fielding would say."

I nodded and stuffed a forkful of spinach into my mouth. My therapist would tell me to let go of the past, to move on with my life. Easy for her to say. She hadn't had a father like mine.

6

There is something strangely liberating about tragedy, when things get so bad they can't get any worse. The second morning after Sid's accident, as I had come to think of it, I awoke at ten o'clock in a remarkably tranquil state of mind, all things considered. Over the course of a good night's sleep, I had shed some of the burden of my recent troubles. My mother's painful struggle had come to a peaceful conclusion, and although my relationship with my sister had never been what I had hoped, there was nothing I could do about it anymore. I had only myself and my husband to be concerned with now and a powerful urge to let him take care of both of us for a while.

I slid over to Peter's side of the bed and nestled up against him. I fitted the front of my body into the curve of his back and inhaled the sweet familiar smell of his smooth skin. With my arm squeezed tight around his belly, I pulled myself in close. He groaned softly as he emerged from a deep sleep. I allowed my hand to wander lower, checking for signs of life, wondering if we would make love. It would be the first time in weeks—neither of us had been in the mood lately—but I thought this morning I could be convinced.

He groaned again and rolled onto his stomach, safely out of reach. It was not the reaction I'd had in mind but not a particularly surprising one either, his passion for me having dwindled to a meager flicker over the past several months. I pulled my hand away, resigned to doze a while longer.

Next I knew, he was stretching and gently pushing me aside so he could turn onto his back. I checked the clock. It was almost an hour since I last looked.

He leaned over for a kiss when he saw my eyes were open, tickling my chin with his silly little beard. "Hey, sleepyhead. How you doing?"

I let out a loud yawn. "Good. A lot better than yesterday."

"Sleep okay?"

"Like a rock."

"Really? You were talking up a storm."

I do that sometimes—talk in my sleep—although not as much these days as when I was a kid. Sometimes I wake the next morning with a vivid memory of my dreams, or all too frequently my nightmares, but more often I don't remember a thing.

"Hmmm . . . nothing's coming to me. What'd I say?"

He hesitated for not more than a couple of seconds, but long enough to pique my interest. "You sure you don't remember?"

"Uh-huh. Was I upset? Like I was having a nightmare?"

He concentrated a little too intently on the buckle of his watch, which he had pulled off the nightstand and was fastening around his wrist.

"Peter?"

"You mentioned Sid," he said haltingly. "You sounded . . . angry."

"Angry? What did I say?"

"I dunno. You were mumbling. It must not be a big deal if you don't remember."

He rolled out of bed and headed for the bathroom, leaving me to ponder what I might have said. I couldn't remember anything, no dreams, certainly no nightmares, which perhaps was just as well. From his behavior, I had a feeling I should drop it.

I didn't drop it, of course. That would have been too painless. I waited until he was in the shower and then followed him into the bathroom. I stuck my head inside the curtain, ignoring the spray of hot water that speckled my face. "What did I say?"

He stepped back and lathered himself with pine-scented soap. He kept his eyes on the white tile of the shower wall.

"Look, Peter—"

"Jesus, Frannie, can't you let it be? Can't you ever just let it be?"

"No, I can't let it be. Not after you've insinuated that I said something outrageous. I think I have a right to know.'' I had leaned into the shower and by now was practically as wet as he was.

He tossed the soap onto the plastic rack under the shower head and watched it slide off and land at his feet. I didn't need to ask again.

"You said, *Now we're even, Sid. This time I win and you lose.* There. Are you happy now?"

"Anything else?" I asked in a quiet voice.

"No."

I backed out of the bathroom and stumbled into the bedroom, where I collapsed onto the edge of the bed and stared at the polished wooden knobs on the drawers of my dresser, wishing I had let it be, as Peter said. When the wooden knobs transformed themselves into little brown buttons like the one I had buried out at Pirate Point the day before, I flopped backward onto the mattress and covered my eyes with my hands. Why the hell had I made that remark? *Now we're even, Sid.* I still hadn't the vaguest recollection of my dream. Peter said I was mumbling, but I suspected he had heard me clearly. Me and my goddamn big mouth.

After Peter finished in the bathroom, I showered and dressed while he made the bed. Neither of us said a word.

I was standing in front of the dresser, fighting to get a hairbrush through my tangled curls, when he finally spoke. "I have a suggestion," he said softly, his voice strangely timid. "Something I want you to consider."

I kept brushing my hair but I edged a few inches to my right where I could see his reflection in the mirror. Our eyes met for an instant, but he looked away and busied himself with a pillow sham.

I tried to sound upbeat. "So let's hear it. What's the suggestion?"

"I think you should start seeing Dr. Fielding again."

I didn't answer at first, although I could have. He was right. It was time for a sanity check. I hadn't seen my therapist in nearly nine months, but Elizabeth Fielding was still a good listener, a friend really, when I occasionally needed someone to talk to. I had called her several times since Peter had moved to Black Bay last March, mostly on Mom's bad days, but I hadn't wanted to commit to a weekly trek into San Francisco or the thirty-dollar portion of her hourly rate that wasn't covered by insurance.

Peter took my silence as an objection. "Think about it, Frannie. You've gone through a hell of a lot lately. Those things you said in your sleep last night, you wouldn't be talking like that if you weren't upset. There's nothing wrong with getting help."

*   *   *

Thankfully, we had finished our English muffins and read most of the morning paper before Andy Saybrook appeared on our front doorstep. Peter let him in, but his welcome was less than heartfelt. "Back again, Andy?"

"Sorry to bother you folks. I know this is difficult, but it's important, you know, to conduct a homicide investigation before the evidence deteriorates." He was holding his cap in his left hand, examining it as he had the day before when he first delivered the news about Sid. In his right hand he clutched a small brown lunch bag. He looked miserable. I believed he really was sorry to be bothering us.

Peter brought him into the living room. "We understand, Andy. Obviously we want to assist you in any way we can. Somebody killed Frannie's sister, and we want that person arrested and put away so he or she can't kill again."

Andy looked relieved. "I'm just here to follow up on a couple points and to ask you to identify some items." He held up the paper sack. "I'll be brief and get out of your hair."

He willingly relinquished the sack when I reached for it. I unfolded it slowly and peeked inside, fearing its contents would include a brown button made of marbleized plastic. Finding no button, I emptied the sack onto the coffee table. There were only two items: a black clog with a scuffed toe and worn wooden sole, and a triangular scrap of tie-dyed cotton, hemmed on one side, ragged on the other two. I picked them up one at a time, ran them through my fingers and placed them back on the table. Both were slightly damp to the touch. Both were unquestionably parts of the outfit Sid had been wearing Monday night. The final remains of my twin sister.

I looked up at Andy and nodded. He nodded back and scooped the articles into his bag—quickly, so I wouldn't have to look at them any longer than necessary.

"I have just a few questions," he said, blushing. "Nothing too tough."

I forced a smile. "How about a cup of coffee?"

Andy followed Peter into the kitchen and I trailed along behind, amused by his constipated expression as he eyed my husband's long hair, which this morning was pulled back in a stubby ponytail. He eased his bulky frame onto one of the four pine chairs around the kitchen table, gripping his cap so tightly I was tempted to yank it out of his fat freckled fingers and toss it into the sink. Peter looked on silently, but I could see the disdain in his pinched lips.

"How do you take it?" I asked.

He jerked up straight, as if I had sneaked up behind him. "What?"

"Your coffee. How do you take it?"

"Oh. Cream and sugar, please."

I wondered whether Andy was always this ill at ease or if it had to do with me. We had never really normalized our relationship after a brief, unmemorable series of dates in high school. We hadn't officially broken up—that would have been unnecessarily dramatic given the circumstances—but several times after we stopped seeing each other I caught him staring at me in class and once or twice I suspected he was following me in the halls. I ignored him and before long he quit paying me any noticeable attention. Now I wished we had talked things through and remained friends.

I poured three mugs of coffee and set out sugar, Sweet'n Low, and low-fat milk, but the phone rang before Andy posed his first question. He jumped at the sound, splashing coffee onto the table.

Peter and I exchanged an anxious glance. It was my father calling back. We knew it without answering. I handed Andy a napkin and picked up.

"Hello?"

"Frances?"

I nodded to Peter, who explained to Andy that I needed to take the call.

"Hello, Dad."

"How are you doing, Frances? Everything okay?"

"No, as a matter of fact, everything's not okay."

"What is it? Are you ill? You didn't look so good at your mother's funeral."

"No, I'm not ill, Dad. That's the way I look. I can't help it."

Andy's chair creaked as he searched for a comfortable position.

"What is it then?" My father sounded more impatient than concerned. Soon he would be yelling at me.

"It's Sid."

"What about her?"

"She's dead."

That shut him up. I waited for the news to sink in and then explained what had happened. He listened without interrupting and didn't respond for a moment, but when he finally spoke he had regained his icy composure. "Well, my goodness. That's terrible."

"Yeah, my goodness." I found it impossible to speak to my father without being sarcastic.

He cleared his throat, probably struggling to resist an urge to respond to my smart remark with one of his own. "Will there be a funeral?"

"No. Look, Dad, I need to go. This isn't a good time for me to talk."

"You know about the insurance?"

"Oh. Of course, the insurance." With an insurance salesman for a father we were a very well insured family.

"You remember. There's a life policy on each of you. With your mother gone, you're each the beneficiary of the other's policy. You're due some money, Frances."

As kids, life insurance had never been an exciting topic, but I did remember now. "How much?"

"Five hundred thousand dollars. You'll be quite a rich young lady. I think Sam Goldman has the policy in his safe. He can explain how it works."

"Five hundred thousand?" I tried to keep my voice steady so he wouldn't have the satisfaction of knowing how I really felt. Five hundred thousand dollars. We would be able to pay off the mortgage on Mom's house. Peter could quit the MiniMart and take his time finding a decent job in San Francisco, something that didn't require him to travel so much as his previous position with Intersoft. My hands were trembling and starting to sweat. It was too much to absorb so quickly, especially with Andy and Peter gawking at me from across the table. "I can't talk now, Dad. We've got the police officer here who's investigating Sid's, um, accident."

"Okay. I'll be in touch."

I wouldn't hold my breath waiting for the phone to ring. "Sure, Dad. Where are you, anyway?"

"Napa."

Napa? He was less than two hours away. He might just call. Worse yet, he might show up.

"Five hundred thousand dollars? You're getting five hundred thousand dollars?" Peter flew around the table and grabbed me by the shoulders. "Frannie, that's half a million bucks!"

I might have reacted the same way if Andy hadn't been there, but with a police officer sitting at our kitchen table, particularly one who might be sniffing around for clues that I had done away with Sid myself, I didn't think such unrestrained glee was appropriate.

"Yes, Peter," I said through clenched teeth. "That's right. How about we discuss it later, after we've answered Andy's questions?" I turned to

Andy with an apologetic half smile. "Now then, what do you want to know?"

Andy gulped down a mouthful of coffee, more than his throat could handle in one swallow. After he stopped choking, he said, "There was an insurance policy?"

The knot in my chest ruined my attempt at a nonchalant shrug. My father's timing had always been impeccable. Today was no exception. I nodded.

"You'll get five hundred thousand dollars?"

"Sounds that way. I didn't know about the policy until my father mentioned it just now."

Andy gazed into his mug and swirled his coffee like a wine connoisseur. I half expected him to put it to his nose to sniff the bouquet. "Is that so? It sounded like you did know about it from what you just said to your father, except you didn't know how much."

I hadn't given Andy enough credit. He wasn't very smart, but he had decent hearing.

"Well, yes, I guess that's right. Technically, I knew about the policy. I mean, I used to. Actually, I had forgotten about it until just now when my father reminded me."

"Oh." He didn't sound convinced. I couldn't say I blamed him. "You'll get five hundred thousand dollars in cash?"

"That's what my father said. The policy is in our attorney's safe. I'll know more after I read it." I glanced at my watch. It was after one o'clock. "Look, Andy, I was planning to go into work this afternoon and I know you didn't come here to talk about insurance."

"That's correct, but I'd like to take a look at the policy, if you don't mind."

I did mind, but I didn't think I should say so. "Fine. I'll get you a copy. Now what was it you wanted to ask me?"

"Was your sister about to leave Black Bay?"

"Leave Black Bay?" I was taken aback by the question.

"Go back to Los Angeles?"

"No. Not for a while. Eventually she would have gone home, but not immediately. Like I told you guys last night, she'd been having trouble with her boyfriend and didn't want to go back there right away. I expected her to hang around here another week or two. Why do you ask?"

"She told Tom Fredrickson she was going home."

"Who's Tom Fredrickson?"

"He works at the Shell station north of town, across from the Seahorse

Pub. Sid filled her car with gas Monday afternoon and had Tom check the oil and fluids. She told him she was heading for L.A. and wanted to be sure the car would make the trip okay. Tom wouldn't have remembered the conversation except her credit card was rejected and she didn't have cash, so he had to call his manager at home to get permission to take a check.''

"That's weird. She didn't tell me she was leaving." At least I didn't think she had. Maybe she'd mentioned it that night at the Seahorse Pub, sometime between the beer and the rum and Coke. Her travel plans buried my suicide theory a little deeper. Why get her car ready for a long trip if she was planning to drive it off a cliff a few hours later? I shrugged. "I had no idea."

"She told Tom she was leaving because the two of you weren't getting along."

So what else was new? Sid and I hadn't been getting along any worse than usual, but she sure enjoyed talking about it. She had always been that way. I smiled at Andy and put on my best innocent face. Beside me, Peter fidgeted and cracked his knuckles.

Andy took a swallow of coffee and wiped his mouth with his shirt-sleeve. "Tom said she told him she didn't feel welcome here."

"That's not true." I wondered if Peter had said something to Sid I didn't know about, but he looked as surprised as I was. "That's absolutely not true, Andy. She could have stayed until we sold the house. She knew that. Maybe she got lonely for her boyfriend. Maybe he called and they made up."

Peter nodded. "I bet that's it."

"Yeah, well, that's another thing. We haven't been able to locate the boyfriend yet. Deke Brenner. That's his name."

"You've tried Sid's apartment?"

"We have. He's not there. Landlord put us in touch with her neighbor, a woman named Sunshine Scott. Sid ever mention her?"

"No. I'd remember a name like that."

"They were pretty close, apparently. Miss Scott lives across the hall. She confirmed what you told us yesterday about Sid and Brenner having problems. Sid wanted to break things off and Brenner didn't. They had some pretty violent arguments, according to Miss Scott."

"Could he have followed her up here?"

"It's possible. Neighbor lady hasn't seen him in two weeks, so who knows where he is. We're getting a picture to show around. Would you recognize him from a photo?"

"No way. I've never seen the guy."

"Sid ever say what he looks like?"

"No. She and I didn't talk much about personal stuff."

"Can you think of anything she may have mentioned about him? Anything at all?"

I thought for a minute but came up blank. "Nothing," I said softly, wondering how I could have let this happen—how I could know so little about my twin sister, how we could have grown so far apart. The threat of tears burned in my eyes and nostrils.

Andy gulped down the rest of his coffee and pushed himself up from the table. "I guess that'll do it for now."

I took his mug to the sink. "Any other leads?"

"We should get the information on the tire tracks later today. That may give us something to go on."

"Any suspects?"

He flinched. They did have at least one suspect and we both knew it, but he was gracious enough not to rub it in. He flicked an invisible speck of dirt off his cap. "I'm really not supposed to discuss the investigation, Fran."

Not supposed to discuss it. Practically an invitation. I rinsed out his mug and set it on the counter. "You know, Andy, I've been thinking. There were two guys at the Seahorse Pub Monday night besides Woody Hanks and Sid and me. One was real big with black hair and a beard. The other was smaller, but muscular. Blond crew cut. They were playing p—"

"Chet Lee and Billy Pepper."

"*That* was Billy Pepper?"

"You know him?"

"I used to."

When I knew Billy Pepper, twenty years ago, he was a towheaded teenager who occasionally worked in our yard. I used to station myself at my bedroom window and pull the drapes shut except for a tiny crack through which I would peek out at him, dreaming about what it would be like to be Billy Pepper's girlfriend.

"Have you talked to him about Monday night?" I wondered if Billy remembered me and decided he did not. It was altogether possible he had never even been aware of my existence.

"Yeah, we talked to him. He told us he and Chet Lee were there when you and Sid left the bar. You remember Chet, right?"

"Never heard of him."

"Sure you have. He played football for Black Bay High. Quarterback. Same class as Billy. Same class as Harlan too. They hung out together. His junior year he stole a gun and held up Paulsen's Market. Wound up spending the next year in juvenile detention."

I shook my head. "I don't think I've had the pleasure of making Chet's acquaintance."

"Well, he knew you and Sid—although it seems he thought you were her and she was you."

"What did they tell you about Monday night? Did Billy say anything?"

"Not much. They didn't see anything unusual other than the two of you duking it out at the bar. They said you shoved each other around a bit and then staggered outside still fighting. They left a half hour later and don't remember seeing either of you or your cars, or anything else for that matter. I have a feeling they were pretty well pickled by then. Neither of them could recall seeing Woody Hanks's pickup either, even though he worked the bar till it closed at one o'clock and was parked right up against the side of the building."

"Could they be lying? What if they came out after I left and they found Sid still in the parking lot? Passed out in her car maybe. Maybe—"

"Yeah, maybe. We haven't found a shred of anything that says they could have been involved."

I pushed out a chestful of air. "Gee, why doesn't that surprise me? You haven't found anything on Harlan's buddies."

Andy wheeled around and headed out of the room without comment. I hurried after him with Peter on my heels. I had one more question and he wasn't getting away without answering it.

"Any indication what happened to Sid could be connected to April Kaminsky's murder? She and Sid were friends, you know."

He kept walking, but I beat him to the door. "Do you think it could be the same guy?"

"Hard to say for sure if we don't recover the body," he said stiffly. "Harlan's following up on that angle. He and Chief Carbone have been handling the Kaminsky investigation."

"What about you? Aren't you working on it too?"

My question hit a nerve, as I expected it might. Little red spots appeared in his cheeks and exploded like cherry bombs. Within seconds his whole face was on fire. "I'm assigned to Sid's case now, with Harlan."

Whatever it was that Andy had done wrong on the April Kaminsky case, it must have been pretty bad. As I recalled, the *Recorder* had hinted at a scandal but never got the whole story and eventually went on to other news. But, Jesus, to get Andy removed from the investigation and replaced by the chief of police? That was serious damage control. I wasn't surprised he didn't want to explain. He was out the door and hustling down the walk before I could ask another question.

Peter let the door swing shut and swept me into his arms. "Five hundred thousand dollars. Five hundred grand. Wow."

I wriggled free, dropped onto the couch, and glared at him. My usually unflappable husband was downright giddy at the thought of our impending windfall.

He bounced onto the cushion beside me. "Come on, Frannie. Smile."

I tried but ended up just gritting my teeth. He mimicked me and looked so ridiculous I finally did give him a real smile.

"That's better. Look, kiddo, I'm sorry about Sid, but we can't change what happened to her. We can use the money. Think about it. It'll pay for law school. You won't have to work, even part-time. You can keep your mom's house now if you want, pay off the damn mortgage, even if we get a place of our own in San Francisco."

I nodded. "You're right. It's great about the insurance. I just don't think it was such a hot idea to get so excited about it in front of Andy."

"Why not?"

"Jeez, Peter, wake up. Andy is investigating Sid's murder. He's got a short list of suspects, and I'm on it, probably right at the top. How does it look that I stand to make a big pile of money?"

He turned away. Neither of us was smiling anymore. "Not very good, I guess. Shit. I'm sorry."

We didn't speak for a couple of minutes, and it wasn't our usual comfortable silence. Peter settled back into the couch but he leaned away from me so we weren't touching. He stared at his hands and twisted his wedding band. Finally he said, "How come you never mentioned the insurance, Frannie? I guess you knew about it all along?"

I could feel my blood pressure climbing. "What is that supposed to mean?"

"Nothing." He glanced over at me but dropped his gaze when I caught his eye. "Look, I better get going. I'll be late for work."

I nodded and stood up. He grabbed my hand.

"Frannie?"

"Yes?"

"I love you. No matter what."

7

The first thing I saw when I pushed open the carved oak door at the top of the stairs was a glossy pink O on Millicent Trimble's surprised face. Millicent was on the phone when I arrived, but she hung up in midsentence, pulled off her bifocals, and rushed to greet me in a ninety-eight-pound whirlwind of pastel cotton and lilac perfume.

"Fran, dear. We didn't expect to see you until next week."

I let her drag me by the elbow to a burgundy velvet love seat across from her receptionist's desk. "I needed to get back to work, Mil. Something to get me using my head again."

She dabbed her peachy pink lipstick from my cheek with a bit of wadded tissue and brushed my bangs out of my eyes. Millicent was forever grooming me when I got within arm's reach. It drove me nuts until I realized it was a gesture of affection, like a mother cat grooming her kittens. I had since come to depend on her to keep me presentable.

"We certainly missed you. The boys will be thrilled to have you back, but don't push yourself on our account. You're still in shock, no doubt."

The "boys," as Millicent called them, were Samuel T. Goldman, age fifty-seven, and Robert M. Green III, age sixty-one, the Goldman and Green of Goldman & Green. Sam Goldman, my mentor and friend, was a business attorney who specialized in contract law, tax planning, and real estate. He had handled my parents' legal affairs over the years and had been a good friend to my mother after the divorce. His partner, Bob Green, was a trial lawyer and former judge.

I accepted Millicent's effusive condolences as graciously as I could and deflected her attempts to learn more about Sid's death. After ten minutes I nodded toward a closed door midway down the book-lined corridor leading off the lobby. "Sam in?" I asked. Bob's door across the hall was open, but his light was off, as usual when he was in trial.

"Yes, he's in there, on a conference call that started nearly two hours ago. He should be off soon." She took a last swipe at my unruly bangs. "Come along. Let's get you situated."

We stood up together and I followed her along the worn Oriental rug that led to the private offices. The air welcomed me home with the familiar scent of old books, furniture polish, and Millicent's flowery perfume. It was good to be back, good to be surrounded by the oak and old leather, the stained glass and the velvet. Even more, it was good to be back in Millicent's loving care.

She turned on the lights in my office, adjusted the thermostat, and gave the room a quick once-over with her eagle eye. Satisfied all was in order, she backed into the doorway. "I'll put water on for tea and let Sam know you're in. He'll want to see you immediately. We just got the news about your sister this afternoon. Bob called from the courthouse."

"They're talking about it at the courthouse?"

"He ran into Dominick Carbone. Mr. Carbone told him the police have some good leads and expect to solve the case quickly." She tried to smile but wound up just shaking her head. "Considering the source, I wouldn't get my hopes up."

I nodded and switched on my computer.

"And Fran, dear, just so you know . . . ."

"Yes?"

"There's been a reporter from the *Recorder* calling for you. Kevin Grant."

I winced. Grant had left a message for me at home, too, but I hadn't returned the call. I was familiar with his work and had no desire to be harassed. "If he calls again, tell him I have no comment."

After Millicent left, I leaned back against the worn brown leather of my man-size executive chair and surveyed the papers and files spread out in neat stacks across my desk. There were corporate filings for the North Coast Friends of the Whales, the Sanderson tax appeal, and several smaller matters. Everything seemed disconcertingly unfamiliar, as if I had been away six months, not six weeks. I picked up a pad and pen and started a to-do list, but it quickly turned into a string of questions.

Fortunately, Sam appeared at my door before I could panic. "Hello, Fran," he said with a warm smile that failed to hide the sadness in his soft gray eyes. He stepped across the room to give me a hug.

We stood behind my desk, silently holding each other until I pulled away and managed to speak. "I'm afraid I've forgotten just about everything I was working on before I left. You'll have to bring me up to speed. Guess I have a short memory."

"Or more important things on your mind." He took a seat across from me and placed a legal-size manila envelope on my desk. His quiet hands came to rest in his lap, lightly folded. "There'll be plenty of time for work later, Fran. First, let's talk about you. I heard about Sidney. I can't tell you how sorry I am. How are you holding up?"

"All things considered, pretty well. I'm afraid it hasn't really hit me yet. I've been trying not to think about how it happened. You heard that too, I suppose?"

"Nick Carbone told Bob. He said it looks like a homicide."

"Did he happen to mention that I'm a suspect?"

"Come now, that's ridiculous."

"Harlan Fry and Andy Saybrook don't seem to think so. They found out Sid and I argued Monday night before it happened. We had too much to drink at the Seahorse Pub and got into a fight."

Sam shook his head. "It's a far stretch from arguing with your sister to killing her."

"It gets worse. They've discovered I had a motive."

"Oh?"

"Money. Sid's life insurance."

"Yes, of course." He pointed to the manila envelope. "I pulled the policy. We should talk about it. If I remember correctly, you'll receive a significant sum."

"Five hundred thousand dollars."

His eyes widened and he reached for the envelope. "After all the trouble you've been through, it's good to know you won't have to worry about money anymore. It'll help, Fran. Now you can do something for yourself, get back to work on that law degree." He emptied the contents of the envelope onto the desk. "Let's have a look, shall we?"

Together we reviewed the relevant provisions of the policy. After Sam read the beneficiary paragraph another time to himself, he summarized it for me.

"The bottom line, as you know, is that you will receive five hundred thousand dollars. That's the simple part."

"And the hard part?"

"Not hard. Just a bit complicated. There are two identical policies. One on you and one on your sister. The policies are designed to benefit you and Sidney, your respective families, and your mother during her lifetime. Since Sidney died first and your mother is no longer living, it's straightforward. You collect on her policy. In the event you had prede- ceased her or had been otherwise rendered ineligible as a beneficiary, the policy provides a detailed designation of alternate beneficiaries. Your fa- ther devised an elaborate plan. He wasn't a man to leave anything to chance."

I rolled my eyes, but Sam didn't notice. My father left a lot to chance, just not insurance. "How does it work?"

"Okay, here goes. The designated beneficiaries under Sidney's policy, in order, are as follows: first, your mother if she were alive; second, you; third, if you had predeceased Sidney or were otherwise ineligible, her living children, if any, in equal shares; fourth, if Sidney had no living children, then your living children, if any, in equal shares; fifth, Sidney's living husband, if any; sixth, your living husband, if any; and finally, if there were no eligible members of the foregoing categories, then the pro- ceeds would be paid to any other living relatives according to state in- heritance law, including your father if he were to survive the two of you. The policy on your life contains an identical provision."

He set the papers back on the desk beside the manila envelope and removed his reading glasses. "I'll go over the rest of it later, to be sure there'll be no snags. We'll need to discuss how we approach the insurance company, and when. They can sometimes be a bit difficult in cases like this."

"Where the beneficiary is a murder suspect."

He gave me a noncommittal half nod. "That too, I suppose, but I was referring to the fact that the police haven't recovered the body. We may have to go to court for a declar—"

His words were cut short by a soft rap at the door. It slid open a crack to reveal Millicent's blue eyes and fluffy white curls. I expected her to slip in unobtrusively with a tray of peppermint tea and shortbread, but from the look on her face I could see that tea and cookies were not on her mind.

*   *   *

"It's the police. For you, Fran."

Millicent stepped into my office and closed the door behind her. She was wringing her hands and shifting her weight from one foot to the other like a nervous little bird. "I told the officer you were in a meeting, but he insisted I come for you."

I nodded and forced a grin. "He wasn't waving his gun and handcuffs, was he?"

"Dear Lord. Nothing like that. Oh my." She pressed a bony, age-spotted hand against her chest and threatened to burst into tears. "It's just that he was so terribly persistent. I told him you were behind closed doors with Mr. Goldman, discussing business matters, but he . . ."

"He what, Mil?"

"Well, he was very pushy. He said he was here on *more important* business. He said I should tell you that." She shook her head and lowered her voice. "He was very discourteous for a public servant, I must say."

Pushy? Discourteous? "Let me guess. Harlan Fry? Short, tough-looking guy with black hair and stitches over one eye?"

"That's him." Her jaw relaxed a bit. "Should I bring him back?"

I shook my head and started to get up. I'd be damned if I was going to invite Harlan Fry into my office.

Sam remained seated and motioned to me to do the same. "Tell him we'll be right out, Millie."

She disappeared, looking much better now that Sam had taken charge. It made me feel better too.

Sam waited for the door to click shut before he turned to me. Then he waited another moment before he spoke, as if to signal that I could take time to compose myself before I confronted Harlan. "Any idea why he's here?"

"No. He and Andy Saybrook have already questioned me pretty thoroughly."

He leaned across my desk and gazed into my eyes, as if he was trying to read my thoughts. "You okay?"

I nodded.

"Then let's go find out what he wants, shall we?" He stood up, straightened his tie, and ran a hand through his dark, silver-streaked hair. "And Fran . . ." He hesitated and smiled at me. "Don't blurt out anything you might regret later. We can confer in private if you're not comfortable with any of his questions."

"Right, boss."

I followed Sam's shiny black wing tips step for deliberate step down the hallway, grateful to have such a worthy ally and good friend. Harlan was alone in the lobby. Millicent had abandoned her receptionist post, probably in favor of the nearby pantry, where she no doubt was hiding with her ear to the door. Harlan stood at the far end of the room with his back to us, staring out the big bay window that overlooked Main Street, and fifty yards beyond, a vague shadow of the rocky coastline. It was another ugly gray day, made uglier by the presence of Harlan Fry in our offices.

He spun around at the sound of our footsteps on the polished hardwood floor and marched toward us with his hand outstretched. "Mr. Goldman, I'm Lieutenant Harlan Fry with the Black Bay Police. We've met before."

Sam gave no indication he recognized Harlan, but he reached out to shake the offered hand. I shoved mine into the pockets of my navy wool trousers lest there be any question about whether I was interested in doing the same.

Harlan nodded at me but addressed Sam. "I'm here to speak to Mrs. Estes regarding her sister's death. I'm sure she's filled you in."

"Yes, of course. We can use the conference room if you like." Sam pointed to an open door across the room.

"Actually, that won't be necessary. I've come to take a look at Mrs. Estes's car."

I could feel my face coloring with emotion, but my anxiety level fell. Perhaps this whole embarrassing episode was no more than one of the many meaningless details in the thorough investigation promised by Dominick Carbone. After our confrontation out at Pirate Point the day before, it wouldn't have surprised me if he had instructed his officers to make me personally aware of their diligence.

"I take it you don't have a search warrant, Lieutenant?" Sam asked.

"No, but I can get one, if need be."

"That won't be necessary," I said. "I have nothing to hide."

I led the way downstairs and around the side of Goldman & Green's restored Victorian office building to the gravel parking lot in back. I pointed to my mud-splattered red Cherokee at the far end of the lot. "There it is," I said. "Take a look."

Sam and I stood together, silent and stoic, while Harlan examined the exterior of the Jeep. The heavy afternoon mist had turned to drizzle, and the temperature couldn't have been much above fifty, but we stuck it out, too stubborn to go inside for an umbrella.

Eventually Harlan waved me over. "This headlight, how'd it get broken?"

With a lump in my throat, I inspected the headlight on the passenger side of the Jeep. The bulb was badly cracked and its chrome casing was scratched and dented. I attempted a casual shrug. "I don't know. Frankly, I didn't even know it was broken. I suppose it could have happened here in the parking lot or at Paulsen's Market or the Seahorse Pub. I'm sure I wasn't in the car at the time. Sid sometimes borrowed the Jeep. Maybe she did it. She wasn't a very careful driver." I was babbling, so I made myself swallow my next point.

"You were driving Monday night, weren't you?"

"Yes, briefly. Just to meet Sid at the Seahorse and then to go home again afterward."

"You didn't notice the headlight was out?"

"No, I didn't notice. Maybe it wasn't out. Maybe the damn thing just got broken five minutes ago, right here in this parking lot."

Sam stepped closer. I could feel his arm against mine. "Are you done out here, Lieutenant? If so, I suggest we get out of this weather before one of us catches pneumonia. I've already had my share of colds for the season and it's not even December yet."

"You're free to go inside, Mr. Goldman, but no, I'm not done out here. Mrs. Estes, may I have the keys?"

I tossed him my key chain, the one with the brass *D* for Dottie. It had been my mother's until two weeks ago.

He opened the driver's door and flipped the button on the armrest to unlock the others. Then he dropped the keys into the pocket of his windbreaker and began examining the Jeep's interior, conspicuously careful not to disturb any potential evidence.

"Feel free to check for fingerprints," I said. "You'll find plenty of mine and I'm sure some of Sid's as well."

He ignored me and kept snooping, finally working his way back around to the driver's door. "What's this?" He pointed at a dark smudge on the side of the seat. "And how'd it get here?"

I looked in and stepped back quickly, fighting to conceal my rising panic. Sam moved in between us to take a look.

Harlan had noticed a reddish brown stain, approximately a half-inch wide by an inch long. It looked like mud, but something told me it wasn't. I could take a pretty good guess how it got there. In my drunken clumsiness Monday night I must have brushed against the side of the seat as

I climbed in, wiping a bit of blood, Sid's blood, off my blazer onto the tan vinyl.

"I have no idea what it is or how it got there," I said evenly. "Looks like mud."

Sam completed his inspection and stepped back beside me. "That's right. Mud."

Harlan smiled. "Tell you what. You folks go back to your business. I'll lock up the vehicle and leave it here while I shoot over to the station and come back with the proper kit to take a sample. I'll bring the keys up to you when I'm done."

I glanced at Sam, feeling helpless to object, and he nodded at Harlan, no doubt certain the smudge was in fact nothing more than a harmless bit of mud. He took a firm hold of my arm as we trudged across the shadowy parking lot and around to the front of the building. I looked straight ahead so he wouldn't see the drops of wetness streaking down my cheeks. Whether they were raindrops, beads of sweat, or tears, I couldn't be sure.

Sam and I were soaked through and chilled when we straggled back into the office. My wool trousers, sturdy walking shoes, and cotton blouse would dry out just fine, but Sam wasn't so lucky. His custom-tailored suit and Italian leather shoes weren't intended as all-weather gear. His lips matched the violet paisleys on his rain-spotted silk tie.

Millicent spun into action when we stepped into the lobby. "I've got hot tea waiting. Come along, both of you, before you catch your death."

While we were out she had brewed a pot of cinnamon tea, which she'd laid out on the coffee table in Bob Green's office, along with china tea-cups, white linen napkins, and a plate of sugar-coated lemon bars. She had cranked up the antique wood-burning stove, so the room was toasty and fragrant with the scent of smoking cedar.

After assuring herself we were properly served, she scurried out of the room and reappeared with a beaded pink cardigan she kept tucked away in the back corner of the lobby coat closet. She ordered Sam to turn his head and handed me the lilac-infused sweater. "Here. Take off that wet blouse."

I did as she said, although the sweater, which hung loosely on Milli-cent's petite frame, was embarrassingly tight on me. Already I regretted my half-eaten lemon bar.

She looked me over with a satisfied nod and took a swipe at my wayward bangs. "It'll do." Then she dragged a spindly ladderback chair over to the stove and draped my wet blouse over it.

I patted the davenport beside me. "Thanks, Mil. Now sit down and join us." Before she could object I poured a cup of tea and held it out to her. I needed a break. I knew Sam wouldn't delve into personal matters with Millicent in the room.

The next forty minutes were almost pleasant. For a moment or two, I managed to think of something other than Sid or Harlan Fry or the bothersome brown smudge on the seat of my Jeep.

I was debating whether to finish off the last lemon bar when our tea party was interrupted by the door chime. "That'll be Harlan with my keys," I said as I pushed to my feet, feeling achy and stiff from my stint in the rain.

I heard Millicent fretting as I shuffled to the door, but she didn't come after me. She'd had enough of Harlan earlier that afternoon.

Sam started to follow, but I waved him back. "I'll be okay, Sam. Finish your tea."

"I'm here if you need me."

I marched across the lobby with my fists clenched, determined to retrieve my keys and fend off further questions. To my surprise and relief, Andy Saybrook's flushed face greeted me when I opened the door.

"Andy."

"Hello, Fran. Harlan asked me to bring these to you." He dropped the keys into my outstretched hand and shrank back, as if I had a contagious disease. His eyes fell from my face to the floor, catching for an instant on Millicent's too-tight pink sweater.

I opened the door wide so he could fit through. "Come in."

"No. I need to be going." He inched backward and grabbed the banister to keep from tumbling down the stairs.

I followed him onto the landing. He stepped down to the first stair to keep me at arm's length.

"Wait, Andy. Why is Harlan picking on me?"

"Picking on you?"

"Yes, picking on me."

"He's not."

"No? Then tell me, is he even open to the possibility, however remote, that maybe—just maybe—I didn't kill my sister? That somebody else did?"

"Of course he is, Fran. Be fair."

"Be fair? Damnit, you be fair, Andy. My sister's been murdered and you guys aren't even investigating. You're just trying to pin it on me."

"That's untrue and uncalled for. Harlan and I have been working this case nonstop since we got the call from Woody Hanks yesterday morning. We're looking into all kinds of possibilities."

"Is that so? How about those two guys at the Seahorse Pub Monday night, Billy Pepper and Chet what's-his-name? Have you followed up on them? Or are Harlan's buddies immune?"

"Nobody's immune. There's nothing to follow up with those guys. They didn't do it."

I rolled my eyes but managed to hold my tongue.

"Funny thing, Fran. The only consistent trail we've found leads straight to you."

"For Pete's sake, Andy, how can you say that? Sid and I got into an argument Monday night and my car has a broken headlight. So-fucking-what?"

He shot me the same look I used to get from my late Grandmother LaSalle. The *f*-word had not been a part of my vocabulary when Andy and I were in high school.

"What about the insurance, Fran? Or did you forget? You stand to make a bundle off your sister's death."

"Okay. And the insurance. I'd hardly say that's conclusive."

"Nobody said it was conclusive. But it is evidence, and frankly it's only part of what we've got."

"What else?"

He clamped his mouth shut and began fiddling with the zipper of his windbreaker.

"What else, Andy? You can't accuse someone of murder and not tell them why."

After an excruciating pause he responded haltingly, keeping his eyes on his zipper. "Well, first there's the fight Monday night and some things we learned from Woody Hanks, things Sid mentioned about the two of you not getting along and how you were acting real hostile toward her. Then the next morning Sid's car turns up on the rocks and we find tire tracks from what looks like a truck or a sport utility vehicle, like a Jeep or an Explorer. The tracks were pretty much washed out by the rain, but they look like they could have come from your Jeep. Then—"

"Whoa, Andy. There are hundreds of trucks and four-wheel-drives in this town. Couldn't the tracks have come from somebody else's? Like your Blazer? Or Harlan's? Or maybe Woody Hanks's pickup?"

"Maybe, but they also could have come from your Cherokee, which would explain why Woody remembers seeing a red Jeep on the highway on his way home that night, about an hour after you and Sid left the bar, more than enough time for you to have killed her and bumped her car over the cliff."

"Give me a break, Andy. Woody remembers every car he passes on the highway? That's a little far-fetched."

"I'm just telling you what he said. Seems he was about to turn onto the road out to his place, but at the last second he realized how fast the approaching vehicle was traveling, so he slammed on the brakes. The road was wet, and he skidded, nearly got himself hit. That's why he remembers that particular vehicle."

"It wasn't me."

"Yeah, well, now we discover your Jeep has a broken headlight. And you say you don't know how it got that way. And then there's the stain on your car seat. It's blood, Fran. Blood." He paused to let the words sink in. "I don't mind telling you, I had a heck of a time convincing Harlan not to impound that vehicle."

"That's still not proof, Andy. Just bits and pieces of circumstantial crap, no more than you could probably dig up on anyone else in town if you put your mind to it." I thought of the brown button I had buried in the mud. Thank God they hadn't dug up that too.

"I'm not done, Fran. Let me finish." His voice had an edge to it that I sensed was only partly due to the interruptions. "I'd be the first to admit we haven't got all the logistics worked out yet. We don't know how you got your sister to the edge of the point in the first place, whether she went there with you voluntarily or whether she was already dead. And, if she was already dead, we haven't figured out how you were able to get both her Volkswagen and your Jeep out there without being seen, if that's how you did it. But we're talking less than a mile, and you're in good shape. . . . That's all just details, far as I see it. We'd have those questions with any suspect."

"Great. You can't even prove it was physically possible for me to have committed the crime and you're writing that off as a *detail*?"

"All I meant was we haven't worked that part out yet. We will. Besides, there's also been things you've done after the fact, the way you've acted."

"The way I've acted?"

"Well, for one thing, you haven't seemed real upset about your sister's death."

"Give me a break, Andy. My mother died of cancer two weeks ago. I need a little time for this one to sink in."

"And yesterday morning when I first went out to your house to tell you what happened. All I said was that I'd come about your sister. You immediately guessed it was a car accident, like you already knew what happened."

"That's ridiculous. Sid and I got plastered the night before. We both had to drive home on a curvy, slippery two-lane highway. I'd say it was pretty natural for me to be worried she might have had an accident."

"Even your real estate agent, Beverly Topes—"

"Bev? Why would you talk to her?"

He shrugged his hulking shoulders and glanced down at his zipper. "It was Harlan's idea."

"See what I mean? He's picking on me. Why would he want to bother my real estate agent unless he's out casting around for dirt on me?"

"Beverly was just one name on a list of people. She's lived in Black Bay for fifty-some years. She's a good resource. She said you and she were supposed to have had a meeting yesterday morning to discuss selling your mother's house."

I tried not to let him see me cringe. I had slept through the scheduled appointment and hadn't called to apologize.

"She said you'd been all in a frenzy to get the house on the market as soon as possible because you couldn't afford the payments and the bank wouldn't lend you any more money. So she put together a marketing package for you to approve, but you never showed up."

"Come on, Andy. I got drunk the night before and I overslept. My appointment with Bev was for nine-thirty, but I didn't even wake up until you got to our house at eleven. With all the commotion, I simply forgot about Bev. It's rude, I agree, but it doesn't make me a murderer."

"Seems like maybe you knew yesterday morning you wouldn't be needing to sell the house after all."

"Damnit, Andy. That's not evidence. It's bullshit."

He shrugged. I doubted he could tell the difference.

"Andy, I'm not that dumb. If I *had* killed Sid for the insurance money, do you really think I would have blown off the meeting with Bev? I don't think so."

"Yeah, well, even your husband admits you and Sid were having problems."

"Peter? When did you talk to him?"

"This afternoon. When you weren't home, we stopped by the Mini-

Mart. He told us where to find you. He also confirmed that you and Sid hadn't been getting along. But according to him, it was Sid's fault. He said she'd been provoking you, that you were a good person, just distraught over the loss of your mother. He said Sid waltzed into town a couple weeks ago and started causing problems.''

''Are you saying my own husband thinks I killed my sister?'' I laid a shaky hand against the wainscotted wall.

''No. Peter backtracked fast when he realized he was doing you more harm than good. He swore up and down that you didn't do it, that no matter how bad things got between you and Sid, you'd never kill her.''

I felt a glimmer of relief, but Andy did his best to squelch it. ''Of course, a husband would say that, wouldn't he? Particularly one who stands to share in a half-million dollar insurance payoff.'' He let go of the banister and rested his hands on his hips in a tough policeman stance. I felt like giving him a shove.

''If that's the way you see it, I'm surprised you guys aren't trying to pin this on Peter too.''

''Oh, we checked on Peter. You bet. But unlike you, Peter's got an alibi. Lucky for him the Day-n-Night MiniMart has a history of armed robberies.''

''Lucky?''

''Couple years ago they installed a twenty-four-hour security camera. Peter's shift Monday night was on video. He was on camera the whole time except for one little bathroom break. So your husband's accounted for . . .'' His voice trailed off as a new idea came to him. ''Unless he was in on it with you. That's something we really haven't considered—yet.''

His tiny brain ticked away at full capacity and a joker's grin spread across his freckled face until he noticed my expression. ''Sorry, Fran. Just doing my job.''

''Gee thanks, Officer Saybrook. Thanks to you doing your job, I can look forward to having my hubby keep me company in jail.''

He shook his head in exaggerated exasperation and abruptly turned to leave. He was peeved at my attitude, I guess, irritated with me for not taking all this like a good sport.

''I don't think it's quite like that in the pen,'' he muttered from the stairwell on his way down.

The streetlight on the corner was out, so it was pitch black outside the window in my office when I switched off my computer at six-thirty. If this were July or August, the bulb would have been replaced immediately and beneath it bright bunches of red and blue petunias would spill out of a pair of white wicker baskets dangling from the cast iron lantern. But not in November. During the slow season, Black Bay reverts to its days as an isolated coastal village with not much to recommend it. In November in Black Bay there are fewer children with ice cream cones than there are rednecks with shotguns, fewer cocker spaniels tugging on leashes than scrawny strays digging in garbage bins.

I took my time undoing the pearly buttons of Millicent's pink cardigan, hoping I hadn't stretched it too badly. My own blouse was stiff and smoky, but at least it was dry. I tucked it into my wrinkled trousers and thought again about going home, but instead I sank into the embrace of my soft leather chair and stared at the depressing conglomeration of papers and files awaiting my attention, some patiently, others less so. The Sanderson tax appeal documents were at the top of the pile, but I was too consumed with my own problems to focus on anyone else's. Perhaps it was a mistake to be here at all.

My eyes gravitated to a photograph of my mother smiling back at me from the corner of my desk. It was a candid shot of her standing in the doorway of our house, one I had taken for a high school photography class, as part of an assignment entitled "A Study of Emotions." I picked up the photo and held it closer so I could examine the expression on Mom's face. She was laughing her lovable lopsided laugh. The right side of her face was animated and smiling. The left side drooped a little, as always, the souvenir of a long-ago car accident. I had labeled the photo HAPPINESS for the assignment. If I were doing it today, I'd name it COURAGE or maybe LONELINESS. It hurt to see her standing there, alone as ever, smiling in spite of everything.

The office was depressingly quiet now, dead silent without the low hum of my computer. The phones had stopped ringing by five-thirty, and Millicent had gone home at six. Now it was just me in my office and Sam next door in his. I gazed out the window at the lonely night sky and beneath it, the invisible black ocean. At some point the two met, but there was no distinct horizon tonight, just darkness blending into darkness. On starless nights like this it was easy to see how Black Bay got its name.

Sam's reflection on the windowpane brought me back into the room, and I turned to greet him. His rail-thin frame and hollow cheeks made him look older than his fifty-seven years and deceptively frail, hardly like a man who three months ago had run a marathon in less than four hours.

"Hi, Sam." I forced a smile, which he returned with one no less strained.

"Getting ready to call it quits?"

I nodded. Sam had encouraged me to go home two hours ago when Andy brought back the keys to my Jeep, but I had nothing to do at home and little desire to sit there, alone, speculating about what had happened to my sister and nursing a paranoid notion that the police were on the right track. The office provided a change of scenery if not an escape, so I told him I wanted to ease back into my old job.

He looked at his watch. "I've got tax regulations ricocheting around in my head. How about we walk down to the Wildflower Cafe? I'll buy you supper."

The quaint Queen Anne cottage that housed the Wildflower Cafe was five blocks from our offices, at the busy end of Main Street. We walked there fast along the slippery cobblestone sidewalk, neither of us dressed for the cold. Fortunately the rain had let up, but a bitter winter wind was gusting inland across the bay, the kind of wind Black Bay typically doesn't face until well after Thanksgiving.

We passed North Coast Hardware, the old Ben Franklin five-and-dime, the lavishly restored Victorian headquarters of Pacific Bank, and a colorful assortment of galleries, gift shops, and restaurants, but there was little activity in downtown Black Bay this time of day, this time of year. The Crazy Frog Saloon, Fritzel's Deli, and the Wildflower Cafe were the only establishments open. Everything else was closed for the day or for the season.

We saw just three other people on the street, all locals. Sally Webster, who worked in the bank, Jerry Fritzel, whose father owned Fritzel's Deli, and Beau Bohannon, my family's dentist. They each nodded a curt greeting and kept walking. Not one of them stopped to say hello or offer condolences for the loss of my sister. Nothing like the outpouring of sympathy I had experienced two weeks before, after Mom died. Black Bay had been seriously shocked by April Kaminsky's death. In some ways that tragic event had brought out the worst in our little town. It was too soon for another young woman to be murdered.

When we got to the Wildflower Cafe, we were welcomed by the aroma of fresh basil and rosemary and the sound of New Age woodwinds wafting from hidden speakers. We took a booth near the window and scanned the list of specials written in perfect looping script on a chalkboard mounted on the sponge-painted yellow wall. Our waitress was a buxom

redhead named Jeannette who had worked at the Wildflower for years
and was friendly, witty, and efficient. Tonight, though, she seemed more
efficient than usual and less friendly. She managed a quick hello, took
our orders, and disappeared into the kitchen. Only one other table was
occupied, but Jeannette gave the impression of being too busy to be
sociable.

I crunched on an ice cube and watched her hover near the kitchen door.
"Is it my imagination, Sam, or are people avoiding me?"

He answered with a sad smile. "You know how folks are in a small
town, Fran. They feel badly for you, but your problems make them uncomfortable. Don't take it personally."

I did take it personally. "They feel badly for me? Or they think I
belong in jail?"

"I know it's tough, but you'll be better off if you try not to worry
about what people are thinking. They don't mean to hurt your feelings.
It's just the way they are."

"Yes, but still . . ." I took a deep breath and let it out slowly. "I *am*
worried about what Harlan Fry and Andy Saybrook and Dominick Carbone are thinking. I know what they're thinking. They're thinking the
best way to wrap up this case nice and quick is to prove I killed Sid.
They're after me, Sam."

Between mouthfuls of lentil soup I described the evidence against me,
watching the muscles in Sam's neck grow tighter with each new point. I
did not mention my bloodstained clothes or the button I had found in the
mud at Pirate Point. Sam was a loyal friend, but he was also an ethical
man. I wasn't sure how he would feel about me concealing evidence.
Frankly, I wasn't sure how I felt about it either. I had once thought of
myself as ethical too.

He took his time responding. "Too bad about the broken headlight,"
he said finally. "I take it they've determined Sidney's car was pushed
over the cliff by another vehicle?"

"I guess, but that junker was already so beat up I don't see how they
can distinguish new dents from old."

He picked up a breadstick and took a bite, chewing slowly and thought-
fully.

"It doesn't make sense, Sam. Who would kill Sid? She'd been away
from Black Bay for ten years. She couldn't possibly have had any enemies around here, not anymore."

"It's not always an enemy, Fran. Remember April Kaminsky."

"True."

We shared a moment of silence, thinking of April. The police's current theory was that my sister's friend had been the victim of a psychotic drifter passing through town on the coast highway. He saw a pretty young woman, so he hung around and stalked her. When he was ready to move on, he raped and murdered her, then got in his car and drove off.

I took a swallow of Diet 7UP and held the icy glass in my hand, mesmerized by a column of bubbles rising up and bursting through the surface of the liquid. "Could be the same thing happened to Sid as April. Maybe it's even the same guy."

Sam nodded. "I was thinking the same thing. I'm sure the police are too."

"I wouldn't bet on it." I took another sip of 7UP, but had trouble getting it down. "You know, Sam, if we find out Sid was butchered like April . . . that would be . . ." I pressed my fingertips against my lips to stop them from trembling.

It would be horrible. But it also would establish my own innocence. Was that, deep down, what I was hoping for? That my sister's body would be recovered and we would learn that she had been raped and mutilated by the lunatic who killed April Kaminsky?

8

I slid out of bed Thursday morning when the first gray pinstripes of light filtered through the slats of our venetian blinds. Peter grunted and turned over when I kissed him, happy to be rid of me. I hadn't gotten much sleep the night before and consequently neither had he.

My jeans and turtleneck hung in their usual spot on the arm of a slouchy stuffed chair near the foot of the bed. I gathered them up, slipped into the hallway, and dressed quickly without bothering to shower. Downstairs, I put a kettle of water on the stove and pulled on a pair of heavy-duty hiking boots, a fleece pullover, and my rain slicker. The water wasn't even close to boiling when I poured it over a Lipton tea bag in my thermos, but it would have to do. I wasn't in the mood to wait.

With the thermos in one hand and a wet paper towel in the other, I grabbed my keys from the clay dish on the shelf in the hallway and hurried out to the garage. Before climbing into the Jeep, I tossed the thermos onto the passenger seat and used the paper towel to wipe away what was left of the brown smudge on the side of the driver's seat. Why the hell hadn't I noticed the smudge before Harlan Fry got to it? I wadded the towel and threw it into the garbage can where two days ago I had disposed of my bloodstained clothes.

Five minutes later I veered off the highway into the turnoff at Pirate Point. The yellow police tape was gone, so I drove to a spot several yards off the paved road where the trees would shield the Jeep from the view of passing motorists. I turned off the engine, gulped down a few mouthfuls of lukewarm tea, and climbed out, leaving the thermos on the car seat.

It was damp and cold outside, but it wasn't raining, not yet anyway. A gusty morning wind had prevented the fog from taking hold, so the visibility was better than the last time I'd been out here. I slogged through the mud, dodging puddles that looked deeper than the rubber soles of my boots. As I approached the end of the point, the trees and other vegetation gave way to a barren rocky plateau and the temperature dropped five degrees. I stopped a few feet from the boulders at the edge of the cliff and searched for the spot where I had buried the button two days before. The previous day's rain had washed away any distinguishable footprints, so it wasn't as easy to find as I had expected.

A knot took hold in my stomach as it occurred to me that the spot would look different if the police had found the button and dug it up. Perhaps they had been more observant than I thought and had seen me press it into the muck. Maybe at this very moment they were searching for an article of clothing missing a little brown button. I fell to my knees and clawed at the mud until it covered my hands like a pair of cold wet gloves. If the button was still here it would be camouflaged by the soggy brown earth, so I searched by feel rather than by sight, praying my frozen fingers would be sensitive enough to tell the difference.

Thankfully, it took me only a few minutes to find the button. It popped out of the mud like a gold nugget. I wiped it off as best I could, crammed it into the pocket of my jeans, and with a hasty glance over my shoulder to make sure I had no witnesses, replaced the chewed-up soil and smoothed it with my hands and feet.

When I was satisfied I had left no telltale trace of my activity, I turned back to the rocks. The ledge at the tip of the point looked cold and slippery and uninviting, but I hoisted myself onto the first boulder and began picking my way toward the edge. It was gustier than usual for this time of day, so I kept low to the ground as I crept along, praying a sudden squall wouldn't send me sailing. Two days ago I had scrambled across these rocks the way I used to when I was a kid. This morning I wasn't sure I could do it.

Several feet from the edge I stopped to stretch my back muscles, which had cramped up from the damp cold and my hunched posture. With my feet planted firmly on two smooth boulders, I straddled a foot-wide crevasse, straightened up, and leaned first to one side, then to the other. It was then that I heard something behind me. I pivoted to see what it was, moving my left foot across the crevasse to the boulder where my right foot was anchored. As I did so, I lost my footing on the slick rock and went down hard. I tumbled backward into the crevasse and smacked my head on the rock where I had been standing.

Pain shot up my spine like a bottle rocket and ended in a grand display of fireworks. After the sparks subsided, it took me a minute to remember where I was and what I was doing, and even longer to determine that although I was badly bruised, I probably was not seriously injured. I suspected I had broken my wrist, but I also was fairly certain I had not broken my back.

I scrambled to my knees but thought better of trying to stand up. My numb fingers gravitated to the back of my head, where I had whacked it on the rock. It was wet. I pulled my hand away and wiped it on my jeans without looking to see the blood.

Reluctant to straighten up for fear I would wind up back in the crevasse, I crouched in place and scanned the terrain behind me in search of the source of the noise that had sent me flailing. I saw nothing unusual on the barren approach to the point, just rock and mud and scrub. Farther off, the redwoods blocked my view of the Jeep and the highway. Was someone lurking there, in the cover of the trees? Or back at the Jeep? Someone who had followed me out here, perhaps, and watched me dig up the button? Someone who had seen me fall and knew I was hurt? Frozen in place by a combination of sheer terror and the bite of the wind and the ice-cold boulders, I remained on all fours for what must have been five minutes. Eventually I managed to convince myself that the noise had been the squawk of a seagull or tires squealing around a curve on the highway.

Before heading back, I made myself crawl to the edge of the cliff. When I got to within a few feet of the drop-off, I sprawled forward onto my belly and locked my feet between two boulders, the way I had done two days earlier. I took a quick look over the cliff, down to the rocks where Sid's car had been. I felt the same queasy dizziness I had experienced the other day, so I shifted my view to the horizon. This time I saw what I had come for.

I stared northward across the cove toward the bluff where Woody Hanks had been walking his dog when he discovered Sid's car two days ago.

Unlike that morning, when the bluff was barely visible in the heavy fog, today it loomed in the distance. Slowly my chilled lips stretched into a wide smile. A lot of things were clearer today.

As I had suspected, Woody Hanks's story didn't hold up.

If Woody had been standing on the edge of the bluff and looking due south, there was no question he would have had a direct line of sight to the tip of Pirate Point and the rocks below, including the spot where Sid's car had been found. His view would not have been very sharp because the fog had been so thick, but I could believe it had been good enough. Oftentimes the fog around Black Bay lingers over the land long after it has burnt off over the water, so it was possible the bright yellow of Sid's car had been visible against the dark background of rock and water despite the opaque gray blanket that had shrouded the point itself. The question I had for Woody was, how the hell had he gotten himself out to the edge of the bluff in the first place? And why? From what I could tell looking back from Pirate Point, it was highly unlikely anyone would just happen to be out there, dog or no dog.

Unlike Pirate Point, which was barren and rocky, the bluff to the north was covered with thick brush. Parts of it were passable, but only in the interior, which was less densely overgrown than the perimeter. I had been out there as a kid but not often, since there really was nowhere to hike and very little to see. Unless one battled one's way through prickly bushes six feet high and at least as thick, there wasn't a view of the water. Or of Pirate Point. If Woody had seen Sid's car from the bluff, he was doing more out there than taking his dog for a walk.

Mission accomplished, I turned back, anxious to be in my Jeep with the heat blasting. I was woozy and sore from my fall, and there was a cold spot where the wind hit the gash on the back of my head. I scanned the point again to confirm I hadn't been followed and then scrambled back across the rocks, suddenly overwhelmed by a desire to get as far away from Pirate Point as possible. Although I had seen no one, I couldn't shake the feeling I was not alone, that the sound I had heard minutes earlier was not an innocent bird or passing car.

By the time I clambered off the last boulder, my apprehension had boiled over. I hit the soggy ground at a gallop. While I ran, I pulled my keys from the pocket of my rain slicker and wove them through my fingers the way I had been shown in a self-defense seminar in college. Not much protection perhaps, but at least it was something.

The sloppy rutted surface of the roadway back to my Jeep made for a less than ideal running track, and my clunky hiking boots were hardly a pair of Nike trainers, but I charged ahead, full tilt. Predictably, I covered no more than a few dozen yards before the muck grabbed my ankle and sent me stumbling to my hands and knees. I scrambled to my feet and kept running, ignoring the pain in my wrist and back and now in my ankle.

When I got to the Jeep, my fingers were filthy and frozen and my keys were covered with mud, so it took me a frenzied minute to unlock the door and start the engine. Without taking time to think, I punched the Jeep into gear and floored the accelerator, spitting up a plume of mud and stones as I spun toward the highway. A few hundred yards later I veered onto the shoulder, fearful I would kill myself or someone else if I didn't slow down. I kept the engine running, the heat blasting, and doors locked while I examined my tender swollen wrist and squeezed my stinging fingers as they thawed. In the safety of my warm vehicle, I calmed down quickly. I had let Pirate Point spook me, but now I needed to get a grip on myself and determine what to do next.

I took a long last swallow of tea and tossed the empty thermos onto the passenger seat. I knew exactly what I *should* do. I should go home. It was only eight o'clock, so Peter would probably still be sleeping, but he would be worried if he woke up and I was gone. I should let him know I was okay and then get cleaned up and put some ice on my wrist and ankle. Then I should drive into town and tell the police what I had found out about Woody Hanks. But the prospect of relating what little I had learned didn't grab me. Excited as I was about my discovery, I suspected it would fall flat when I reported it to Harlan and Andy. What did it really prove, after all? Not much, especially if Woody was able to come up with a plausible excuse for why he had been prowling around in the bushes at the edge of the bluff.

Sore as I was, I had still a bit of detective left in me. I pulled back onto the highway heading north.

The bluff warranted neither a name nor a turnout off the highway. It was not a *point* per se, although it stuck out far enough into the ocean to provide an unobstructed view back to Pirate Point. I parked on the side of the road and hiked in, trying as best I could to keep my weight off my twisted ankle. As I remembered, the area was overgrown with dense prickly bushes. *Thistle brush,* we used to call it as kids. It was thick nasty stuff, full of tiny thorns that in my experience had always been able to get imbedded in my skin if I came within three feet. There was a path, if you could call it that, leading to the cliffs. By comparison, it made the muddy drive out to the end of Pirate Point seem as smooth as the slick tar streets of Black Bay after a recent repaving. It was rocky and rutted and sloppy with mud, but I followed it without hesitation. By now I was such a mess I didn't bother to avoid the puddles. I limped along at a determined pace, anxious to see what I had come for and be back within the warm safe confines of my Jeep.

There were vague footprints along the path, and paw prints. Woody and his dog, I figured. If I had a dog I sure wouldn't take it for a walk out here. The farther I went, the worse the terrain became. Back near the highway there had been an open area several yards wide flanked by solid walls of thistle brush, but the clearing soon narrowed to no more than four feet across. The bushes were so thick and thorny it was inconceivable that anyone would innocently venture into them. I hugged my slicker tighter around me and pulled up the hood, determined to keep the thorns from snagging my exposed skin and desperate to retain what little body heat I had left.

Near the end of the trail there was a gap in the brush. Not much of an opening, really, but a spot where it looked as if the bushes had been disturbed and the weeds trampled. I pulled my hands inside the rubberized sleeves of my slicker and used my forearms to push apart the bushes. I got a better look, but the view didn't change much. Mostly more brush, although I did see what might have been a path into the bushes, including a distinct depression in the mud that could have been a footprint. I would have gone deeper into the brush, but to proceed farther would have been like barging into a roomful of porcupines. The thorns had already nailed my legs, right through my jeans. Besides, I could see all I needed to see right from where I was. This surely was the spot from which Woody Hanks had sighted Sid's car, and it just as surely was not a spot he would visit on an innocent walk with his dog.

I checked my watch and turned to leave, satisfied with what I had learned and anxious to be home. It was just past eight-thirty. By nine o'clock I hoped to have my chilled and aching body submerged in a steaming cloud of lavender-scented bubbles.

I heard the growl first, a low throaty rumble. Then I saw the teeth, two rows of snarling serrated fangs.

I jerked backward into the thistle brush, barely aware of the thorns that grabbed at my legs and exposed hands and face. The animal kept growling, but it didn't advance. I took another step back.

I was two feet into the thorns before I saw Woody Hanks. He looked no more friendly than his dog, a husky and shepherd mix masquerading as a wolf.

"Jesus, Woody, call him off."

He looked at me and then at the dog, apparently deciding whether to call him off or order him to attack. Finally he said, "Down, Rocky," and the monster dropped to his haunches, still growling. "Rocky, quiet," he said. The dog obeyed, but he continued to eye me like a slab of raw beef.

Woody watched me too, with a not entirely dissimilar expression. I didn't move, not even to push away the barbed branch scratching my face.

"What the hell are you doing out here?" he asked. His tone did nothing to comfort me.

Dumb as he was, I figured Woody knew exactly what I was doing— and why. I couldn't begin to guess what he was doing, but he looked well prepared for something. He was decked out in a leather jacket with a turned-up collar, drab green rain pants, and a black wool cap with earflaps. A pair of leather gloves was sticking out of the pocket of his jacket, and he had a beat-up canvas backpack slung over one shoulder. I stared at him, speechless and paralyzed. He stared back.

Our silent confrontation rapidly escalated into a full-fledged staredown. I blinked first, hoping to diffuse the tension. "Help me out of here," I said, extending my hand.

The dog's ears perked up and his fangs came out. He emitted a low growl, but he didn't move. Neither did Woody. I climbed out of the bushes on my own.

"You've no business out here," Woody said.

"And you do?"

"I'm taking my dog for a walk."

"My ass, you're taking your dog for a walk. You look like you're dressed for combat. What gives, Woody?" My voice was loud and deceptively steady, but I couldn't resist a furtive glance at the path behind him. I wanted to be prepared for a quick exit if it became necessary.

He took a step toward me. I moved to the side, careful to stay out of the brush. I would have made a run for it right then if it hadn't been for the damn dog.

"I'm dressed to keep warm and dry," he said. "Now I'm asking you for the second time. What're you doing out here?"

I stalled for a moment, but no plausible excuses came to mind. "I was looking for evidence relating to my sister's murder," I finally admitted. "But I didn't find anything."

"What'd you think you were gonna find?"

I shrugged. "Who knows? I wanted to get a better angle on the spot where her car went down, but I couldn't see much."

"Uh-huh." He spat a brown wad of tobacco in the general direction of my feet.

"How'd you happen to see her car, Woody? There isn't much of a view through the brush as far as I can tell."

He hesitated. As I suspected, he didn't have a good answer. His eyes darted from mine to the bushes behind me and then to Rocky. My heart stopped when he nodded at the dog. "Rocky went in there," he said. "Chasin' a rabbit. I had to go after him. That's when I spotted the car."

I nodded and pretended to believe him.

He leaned toward me and squinted. He wasn't wearing the wire-rimmed glasses he'd had on Monday night at the Seahorse Pub. His pupils were dilated. "You look just like her, you know? You got a little more meat on your bones, but other than that you could be her."

"Yes, I know. We're—we were—twins."

"I knew that." He smiled for the first time, still squinting, scrutinizing me like a mad scientist examining a half-dissected frog. "What do the cops say about what happened to her?"

I attempted to smile back but couldn't summon more than a flash of gritted teeth. "Frankly, Woody, after talking to you, they think maybe I killed her. It seems that whatever it was you told them, it made me look pretty bad."

He shrugged. "Didn't tell them nothing that ain't true."

"You told them I hated her."

"No I didn't."

"No?"

He pulled his gloves out of his pockets and slipped them on. My own scratched-up hands were stinging from the cold. My sprained wrist was throbbing.

"I told them she *said* you hated her. There's a difference." He chuckled at his clever response. I noticed his eyes again. They were bloodshot and unfocused.

"You realize how it looks for me, Woody?"

"Maybe you shoulda thought of that before."

"Before what?"

"Before Monday night."

"You're an asshole, Woody. Let me by." I made a move to walk past him, but he didn't get out of the way.

"You gonna tell the cops you were out here?" He took a wobbly step in my direction, and I took one to the side. Rocky kept his beady black eyes on my neck. He was licking his chops.

Goddamn dog, I thought. I could shove Woody aside and have a good shot at getting past him, but I could never outrun the dog. He'd have me for breakfast.

"I'm not going to the police. I have nothing to report. Now if you'll let me by, I'm going home."

He didn't move.

"Woody, please." I hated to beg, but I couldn't help it. "I just want to go home. I haven't found anything to tell the police. Let me by. Please."

"And if you decide to go to the cops?"

"I won't. I have no reason to."

He stepped aside to let me pass. "You better not."

I half walked, half stumbled the first several yards and then broke into a jerky run. Woody didn't follow. Neither, thank God, did Rocky.

9

Peter heard my Jeep pull into the garage and met me at the door. His face was fixed in an all-too-familiar frown that made railroad tracks across his forehead.

"Frannie, where have you—"

His scowl gave way to a look of shock when he registered the shape I was in. I was covered with mud, as if I'd been swimming in it, and my face and hands were scratched and bloody from the thistle brush.

"What the hell? Look at you, Frannie. Where have you been?" He spoke in a loud frantic whisper.

"Pirate Point," I whispered back. "Why are we whispering?"

I saw the answer before he could respond. Planted on the threshold immediately behind him were two thick-soled black ankle boots and a pair of bulging calves clad in cop-colored khaki. I pushed back my hood so I could take in the rest. Harlan Fry loomed two steps above us in the open doorway, looking larger than life in a shirt so tight he was liable to pop a button if he puffed out his chest any farther.

"Delighted to see you, Mrs. Estes. Come in." He stepped back into the hallway and with a sweep of his arm invited Peter and me into our own house.

Peter grabbed the back of my slicker to keep me from following Harlan. "I'd like moment alone with my wife, Lieutenant." He kicked the door shut, grabbed my injured wrist and dragged me to the far corner of the garage, safely out of earshot if Harlan thought to listen at the door.

I twisted out of his grasp and cradled my wrist in the crook of my healthy arm. "Watch it, that hurts. What's going on? Why is he here?"

"You tell me what's going on, Frannie. Jesus, look at you. What've you been doing?"

"I went to Pirate Point to have a look around."

"You went there *again*, you mean."

"Okay, I went there again." I rolled my eyes at his dramatics. No doubt I was in for a lecture after Harlan left. "I saw something Tuesday afternoon that didn't seem right, so I went back to see what it was."

"And?"

"I climbed out on the rocks and looked back to where Woody Hanks spotted Sid's—"

Harlan burst in before I could finish. "That's enough," he said. "You two can have all the time alone you want *after* Mrs. Estes answers my questions."

Peter squeezed his eyes shut and nodded. "Go ahead, Frannie."

I led the way to the living room, but my clothes were so filthy I didn't want to sit down. "I'm going to take off these muddy things," I told Harlan. "I'll be back in ten seconds." I hobbled off toward the stairs before he could object. "Peter, could you fix me an ice pack? I think I sprained my wrist." My ankle was stiff and sore too, but it would have to wait. So would my bruised back and the throbbing gash on the back of my head.

I traded my mud-caked clothing for a sweat suit and slippers and splashed hot soapy water on my face. The soap stung the cuts on my hands and forehead, but I didn't take time to be gentle. When I got back to the living room Peter was waiting with a plastic bag of crushed ice and a mug of black coffee. He'd brought coffee for himself too, but nothing for Harlan.

We sat side by side on the couch, across from Harlan, who had commandeered my mother's platform rocker, the same as he had when he'd grilled me Tuesday night. His hostile stare warned me that this morning would be no more pleasant.

Peter helped me balance the ice bag on my wrist, which by now had swelled to nearly twice its normal size. He thrust the coffee into my other hand. "Here. Drink this. Your lips are blue."

I wrapped my fingers around the warm mug and took a grateful sip. "You have some questions," I said to Harlan.

"I do indeed." He pulled out a pocket notebook and a pen, taking time to clear his throat and run his fingers through his slick black crew cut. "First of all, tell me, Mrs. Estes, what were you wearing Monday night?"

His question knocked me back and sent my coffee sloshing onto the couch.

Peter took a distracted swipe at the spill with the sleeve of his flannel shirt and set his own mug on the table. "He asked me the same thing," he blurted out before I could concoct an inconsistent story. "I said I thought you were wearing jeans and a white blouse and your tan bl—"

"Let her answer for herself," Harlan snapped.

I forced down a mouthful of burning coffee and nodded. "Peter's right. That's what I was wearing."

"Care to show us? Your husband couldn't seem to find anything you had on that night."

The path of my gaze crossed Peter's, and we both looked away. Mr. Helpful. Mr. Let-me-tell-you-what-I-know. Why did he have to be so damn forthright?

"I looked upstairs and in the laundry room," he said softly, his earlier anger replaced by humility. "But I couldn't—"

"That's okay, Peter." My voice was calm, but somewhat too loud to be natural. "Actually, I threw those clothes out Tuesday morning."

Harlan nearly slipped off the edge of the rocker. "You threw them out?"

"Yes."

Peter grabbed for my hand and knocked the ice bag to the floor. Neither of us bothered to pick it up.

"May I be so presumptuous as to ask *why* you threw them out?" Harlan asked.

I stared at a wet spot on the thigh of my sweatpants where the ice had been. The nape of my neck felt warm and moist where the blood oozing from the cut in my head had soaked into the collar of my sweatshirt. "I drank too much the night before. I got sick on myself."

"You got sick on yourself? So you threw your clothes away? It didn't occur to you to wash them? Or take them to the cleaners?"

I didn't answer. My eyes were glued to the wet spot on my thigh.

"I'm surprised you'd be so wasteful, Mrs. Estes. Correct me if I'm wrong, but I understood you and your husband were short on cash these days."

Peter had heard enough. "For Chrissakes, man. If you have questions, ask them. You've no cause to harass her."

"Fine. I'll try again. Mrs. Estes, why did you throw your clothes away instead of taking them to the cleaners?"

"Like I said, I got sick on them. I guess, well . . . I didn't want Peter to find out." *Or anyone else, not without a better explanation for the bloodstains.*

Peter dropped my hand and fell back into the couch. I had no idea what thoughts were going through his head, nor did I care to guess.

"Why do you care about my clothes, Lieutenant?"

Harlan's lips stretched into a mean grin. "I'm glad you asked that question. I care because the blood we found in your Jeep is consistent with a sample from a Band-Aid we found in the bathroom above your garage."

A hot, tingling sensation rushed up my neck and into my cheeks. Harlan knew Sid's blood was on my clothes. He knew it without even seeing them.

"If I remember correctly, Mrs. Estes, you told us no one but Miss LaSalle had been in that bathroom since she arrived for your mother's funeral. Naturally, we concluded that the blood on the Band-Aid must be hers."

I met his stare with feigned confidence. "For your information, Lieutenant, Sid and I were identical twins. Our blood is the same. If the smudge in my Jeep matches Sid's blood, it also matches my own." *So there.*

"Then you won't mind taking a test."

"Of course not. I'm happy to prove my point."

"Fine. I'll set it up."

"Fine."

He rocked back with a satisfied smile. "So that's why I'm here this morning. You see, I think the blood in your vehicle is your sister's and I'm betting it might have gotten somewhere else too, like on your clothes. It's rather inconvenient that you saw fit to dispose of those clothes so hastily, wouldn't you agree?"

I looked him hard in the eye. "You're barking up the wrong goddamn tree, Lieutenant." As I spoke, I calculated the number of days since North Coast Disposal had picked up our garbage, wondering if my clothes were still sitting at the town dump, intact, waiting to be dug up by some rookie cop. If they were found, I would have to claim the blood was mine, that

I'd been the one with the bloody nose. Before long I would be drowning in a sea of lies.

Harlan shrugged and reached into his pocket. He pulled out a photograph and handed it to Peter. "Recognize him?"

Peter examined the photo and shook his head. "No."

Harlan took the photo back and handed it to me. "Mrs. Estes?"

It made no impression at first. It was a slightly out-of-focus black-and-white snapshot of a man in his late twenties or early thirties leaning against a brick wall, holding a shovel. He wore soiled khaki pants and a dark T-shirt with a pack of cigarettes bulging in the sleeve à la James Dean. He was solidly built, like a weight lifter, and tall, definitely more than six feet. Good-looking, but not nice-looking. The kind of guy who's long on muscles but short on brains.

I started to say I didn't know the man, but stopped to take a second look. I was an avid amateur photographer myself and something about the photo fascinated me. Oddly, even though the shot was in black and white, it was the color that spoke to me. The man had pale almond-shaped eyes, darkly tanned skin, and shaggy bleached-out hair, almost white. The overall effect was like a negative. Everything that should have been dark was light and everything that should have been light was dark.

The longer I studied the photo, the more convinced I became that I had come across the man somewhere before, sometime in the recent past. But where? I frowned and handed it back to Harlan. "I can't place him, but I've seen him before. He's not someone I'm personally acquainted with."

Harlan nodded and slipped the photo back in his pocket.

"Who is he?" Peter asked.

Harlan seemed not to have heard. He pulled on his jacket and started for the door.

"If you tell us who he is, maybe I'll remember where I've seen him," I said.

Without looking back, he said, "Your sister's boyfriend. Deke Brenner."

Peter stomped into the house and slammed the door. "Jesus, Frannie, if you've got any more surprises, you better fill me in."

"Peter—"

"I saw the look you gave me when Harlan asked about your clothes, like I told him something I shouldn't have. You gave me that same look yesterday when Andy asked about the insurance."

"You don't underst—"

"Goddamn right, I don't understand. I have no idea what's going on with you, Frannie, and I'm tired of feeling stupid. I feel like every time we talk to the cops I'm giving away some deep dark secret." He marched past me and disappeared into the kitchen.

Deep dark secret? Did Peter actually suspect I had killed Sid myself? I couldn't believe it—and yet in a way I could, since I hadn't entirely ruled out the possibility myself. I fell forward and hugged my chest against my thighs, willing myself not to cry. What the hell had happened after Sid and I left the Seahorse Pub that night? Had I blacked it out because it was too terrible to remember? I squeezed my eyes shut and tried to bring it back, fearful of what "it" might be. I remembered Sid and myself fighting in the parking lot . . . and rain . . . and mud . . . God, I was so angry . . . Sid screaming . . . Sid on the ground, in the mud, not moving. . . .

I jerked upright and opened my eyes. The picture of Sid was gone, a fleeting glimpse. Memory or imagination? I didn't want to bring it back.

I spent the next twenty minutes on the couch practically hyperventilating while Peter camped out in the kitchen with the morning paper and the remains of our coffee now gone cold. When I heard him put on a fresh pot and return to the kitchen table, I gave up. I limped upstairs and took my muddy clothes into the bathroom. Like a junkie hiding her habit, I pulled the door shut behind me and locked it before I dug the mud-caked brown button out of my pocket. I rinsed it off and examined it more closely. I couldn't be certain it was the same as those on my tan blazer, but it did look depressingly familiar.

Determining what to do with the button was more difficult than I had anticipated. My first thought was to flush it down the toilet, but my conscience stopped me short of doing something so irrevocable. I considered burying it in our backyard or hiding it at the bottom of my underwear drawer, but neither seemed safe enough. After several minutes of indecision, I opened the bathroom door a few inches and peered out to confirm that Peter was nowhere in sight. Then I hobbled down the hall as quickly and quietly as I could on my twisted ankle. I found my mother's sewing box on the top shelf of the linen closet and inside it a recycled cookie tin filled with assorted buttons she had accumulated over the years. I pried the lid off the canister, dropped the button inside, and gave it a good shake to mix the new button in with the old. Then I returned the box and canister to the shelf, pulled a stack of towels in front of them, and headed back to the bathroom.

An hour later, lavender-scented and clean but no more relaxed, I ventured downstairs. Peter hadn't budged from his spot at the kitchen table and he didn't look up when I walked into the room. The newspaper lay before him, still in the clear plastic bag it came in during the rainy season. I poured myself some coffee and stood at the counter, waiting for him to speak. He didn't. Neither did I, despite the voice inside my head screaming at me to defend myself, to tell him about the thistle brush and Woody Hanks and Rocky. After five minutes I abandoned my full mug and wandered into the living room, wondering whether the police would search the town dump, and if they did, whether they would turn up the plastic bag containing my bloodstained clothes.

Finally Peter came into the living room. He took a seat across from me on Mom's rocker, in Harlan's spot, and said, "We need to talk." His gaze was fixed on a lime green pottery bowl filled with butterscotch candies in the center of the coffee table. His voice was flat.

"I agree. This whole business is getting totally out of proportion."

"Out of proportion? Your sister has been murdered, Frannie. I'd say it's hard to get more out of proportion than that."

I started to tell him what had happened that morning out on the bluff, but he cut me off.

"I want to ask you something, Frannie, and I want you to answer truthfully."

I bit back an angry retort and nodded.

"You promise? The truth?"

I held up my right hand. "The truth. I swear on a stack of Bibles. Now ask, so I can finish telling you about Woody."

"Your clothes from the other night, was it just vomit?"

I sank my teeth into my lower lip. I didn't trust my voice, so I nodded.

He stared at me, saying nothing, giving me a chance to change my answer. I could feel my nose growing longer.

"That doesn't make sense, Frannie."

"Why not?"

"The blazer you were wearing was the one I gave you last Christmas. You know damn well how much it cost. You wouldn't have just thrown it away."

"Like I said, I threw up on it. It was ruined."

He pulled on his beard and looked at the candy dish. Neither of us spoke while he considered what I had said. My face felt hot. I was humiliating myself.

"Frannie, remember a few months ago when the chemotherapy made your mother so sick?"

"Of course I remember."

"And the time she threw up on her nightgown? I thought it was ruined, but you said it would be fine if we took it to Cypress Cleaners?"

I nodded. We had taken the satiny pink nightgown to the dry cleaner, and it had been fine. Mom was wearing it the day she died.

"So how come you threw away your blazer? If it was just vomit, it would have come out."

There was nothing for me to say, except to admit I had lied, so I said nothing.

"I've been thinking, Frannie. I have an idea."

"What?"

He paused to take a deep breath and crack his knuckles. "What if, well . . . what if we happened to find a suicide note? You know, one we'd somehow overlooked until now?"

I heard a choking sound coming from my throat, something between a laugh and a whimper. My husband, Mr. Forthright, was suggesting we lie to the cops. He was no better than me. "I didn't kill her," I whispered.

"Think about it, Frannie. What if Sid had left a note on the desk in the den? We never go in there. It'd be logical we wouldn't have found it right away."

He reached for me, but I jerked away. "That's absurd."

"It's an alibi."

"It is not an alibi. Jesus. The police know Sid didn't commit suicide. They'd never in a million years believe us. It would only make me look guiltier than I already do—and you'd look guilty too, like you were in on it with me. I didn't kill her, Peter. There's no way they'll find evidence that proves I did."

"And justice will prevail? How can you be so naive?" His voice was low and tense. He pulled his fingers through his hair and let it fall in his face. "Damnit, Frannie, they already have evidence that says you did it. You were fighting with her Monday night. They know the two of you hated each other—"

"We didn't hate each other, Peter."

"But it sure looks like you did. And they know you need the money. You think they haven't figured out by now how badly you want to keep this house and how hard you've tried to get another loan? Half the town was talking about it at your mother's funeral."

I tipped my head back and stared at the ceiling. "Goddamn insurance."
It was the insurance that made Peter think I was guilty. I had seen it in
his face the day before when my father told me about the policy. Shock,
elation, and finally, realization.

"Now this thing with your clothes. They'll find the clothes, Frannie.
They're probably sitting right on the top of the town dump. If Harlan's
right and they have blood on them, you'll be in big trouble."

I closed my eyes and grabbed the edge of the couch. "Sid and I did
get in a fight Monday night. I think I may have given her a bloody nose."

"There *was* blood on your clothes?"

"I didn't kill her, Peter. I'm not sure what happened after we left the
Seahorse, but I couldn't have killed her. I just blacked out, you know? I
wasn't in any condition to get Sid and her car to the edge of the cliff and
push her over. I know I didn't do it." I gripped the couch tighter. I was
shaking now and light-headed. Holy Jesus. I couldn't have killed my
sister. I couldn't have.

Peter twisted his wedding band and cracked his knuckles. He kept his
eyes on the floor. "I have another idea. It kind of defeats—it would mean
giving up the insurance money—"

"It defeats what, Peter? My purpose for killing Sid in the first place?"

"Listen to me, Frannie. We don't need that money. We don't need this
house either. We're moving back to San Francisco and you're going to
finish law school. I'll get a job with a good company and probably end
up making even more than I was at Intersoft. The insurance money would
be great to have, but we'll do just fine without it."

"What are you saying?"

"Look who we've got investigating this case. Harlan Fry and Andy
Saybrook. And look what happened to the April Kaminsky case. It never
got solved. They could do the same with Sid."

"Jesus, Peter, are you suggesting we bribe them?"

"Five hundred thousand dollars would be a hell of a lot of money to
those guys."

"You're insane."

"You don't think they'd do it? Harlan Fry? He'd take the money in a
heartbeat. The guy's a total sleaze. And Andy? Have you noticed the way
he looks at you? He's nuts about you, Frannie. He doesn't want to arrest
you."

"Bullshit. Andy's my friend. He's not a crook." *And neither are we,
Peter.*

"It's not bullshit. I'm a man. I see the way Andy looks at you, the way he acts around you. He's dying to find a way to help you. He'd do it, Frannie."

"Well, I won't do it, Peter. I won't even consider it."

He took my hand and pulled it to his cheek, holding it there like a child. "We've got to do something," he said softly, his eyes shining. "I don't want to lose you, kiddo. I love you too much."

10

With the help of some leftover Percodan from my mother's medicine cabinet, I dozed much of Thursday afternoon. I popped two tiny yellow capsules after Peter left for work at two o'clock and was too groggy to hold my head up straight a half hour later when I drew the blinds in our bedroom and crawled under the covers.

As I lay quietly in the darkness, my imagination took off. Over and over again, I watched Sid's Volkswagen plummet from the cliffs at Pirate Point and hit bottom with an explosion of steel and rock. Then I watched the stormy surf slam her limp and lifeless body against the rocks and sweep it out to sea. I couldn't see what—or who—set the incident in motion, but my imaginary vantage point was that of someone standing on the edge of the cliff looking down at the destruction. It was the same view the killer would have had. I woke to the sound of my own muffled scream. I was drenched in sweat.

At seven-thirty I forced my sluggish body out of bed and limped downstairs to the kitchen. My head was spinning from the Percodan, and my bruised lower back had cramped up tight. We had gotten a call while I was sleeping, but I hadn't even heard the phone ring. I pushed the play button on the answering machine.

"Frances, this is Cliff LaSalle . . ."

My father. He was wasted.

"I want to talk to you about your goddamn sister . . ." He babbled on, but I could hardly make out the words—except that they grew progressively more profane and less coherent.

Disgusted and shaken, I erased the message. He hadn't thought to leave a number, so I couldn't call him back if I wanted to, which I didn't.

I made a pot of espresso-strength coffee and scalded my throat forcing it down. Then, knowing it would only make me feel worse, I went for the double fudge ice cream Peter kept in the freezer. Determined not to think of my father, I ate heaping spoonfuls straight from the carton and focused on Harlan's snapshot of Deke Brenner. I had seen Brenner somewhere before. He hadn't been introduced to me as Sid's boyfriend, I knew that much, but I was convinced I had seen him, and not just in a photograph. I also was sure we had talked, for I knew exactly how his voice sounded—curiously high-pitched for such a bruiser of a guy.

In the dead silence of our kitchen, I concentrated on the sound of Brenner's voice. Where had I heard it before? What had it been saying? My half gallon of double fudge sat forgotten on the counter, turning to chocolate soup, while Brenner's words hovered teasingly on the edge of my brain. I closed my eyes and listened, but I couldn't bring them back. What I heard instead was much more immediate—and much more disconcerting. I heard twigs crunching. The sound of nearby footsteps.

I bolted to the window, but it was pitch black outside, and we had no lights on the south side of our house. A car zipped past on the highway, briefly illuminating the row of pines that separated our yard from the Olsons' property next door. Was someone prowling around out there? Hiding in the trees, maybe? Or peeking in the window? I listened again but heard nothing except a dog barking in the distance.

With one hand pressed against the small of my aching back, I ran for the phone and dialed Peter at work. "It's me. Someone's outside."

"What? Are you okay? Where are you?"

"I'm okay. I'm in the kitchen. I think I heard someone outside the window."

"Jesus Christ."

"I'm—"

"Listen, Frannie. The second we hang up, I want you to go straight to the garage, get in the Jeep, and drive to the MiniMart. Don't go outside. I'll call the police."

In less than five minutes I was in Peter's arms and Andy Saybrook was on his way to our house. Forty-five minutes later, Andy called us at the store.

"I'm not saying you were hearing things, Fran, but there was nobody there when I arrived and no sign anybody'd been there before that."

"You're right. I probably was hearing things."

"Raccoon maybe."

"Yeah, maybe."

"Well, like I said, ain't nothing there now. I'll have a look around tomorrow morning, but you might as well go on home tonight."

I was happy for the all-clear sign, but I had no intention of going home alone. I climbed onto a stool beside Peter and announced that I was staying until the end of his shift.

"Great. You can keep me company," he said. "We need to talk."

I was struck by his tone. "I don't want to talk about your *ideas,* Peter. The answer is still no. No suicide note. No bribe. I've thought about it enough."

He stared at me, chewing his lip and pulling at his beard. "Okay. The choice is yours. I'll stand by you no matter what. I won't mention it again." His voice was clipped and strained.

"Thanks, Peter. I appreciate your support." I reached for his hand and gave it a quick squeeze. "I'd also appreciate your trust. I didn't do it."

He smiled and squeezed back, but the look on his face said he didn't believe me. "I have one more suggestion. This one is nonnegotiable."

My jaw tightened. "What?"

"I want you to see Dr. Fielding, like we talked about. Sooner rather than later."

I stared at a shelf crammed full of bleach and detergent and scouring powder. "I guess it's time," I said quietly.

What I wanted to tell him was that I didn't need to see a therapist so much as the two of us needed to see a marriage counselor. Peter had been a rock during my mother's illness, especially in the first horrible weeks after we learned she had cancer. Despite our problems, he had been the one thing in my life I could count on, and I had tried to be there equally for him. Although our relationship had grown undeniably and increasingly strained since he moved to Black Bay last March, I thought we had come through the hard times intact, if not entirely un- scathed. But this latest incident had changed him. He'd lost faith in me. I had seen it in his eyes the previous morning when we found out about the insurance, and he confirmed it when he suggested we forge a suicide note or bribe the police. How long would Peter respect some- one he thought was a murderer? And how long would he love a wife he didn't respect?

I fled to the rest room before he could make another comment about my state of mind. I had enough troubles without adding Peter to the list.

I stayed with Peter for the remainder of his shift, presiding over a kaleidoscope of modern Americana from our high wooden stools behind the cashier's counter. From where we sat, facing the snack food aisle, I counted nine different kinds of potato chips—barbecue, sour cream and onion, vinegar and salt, cheese, jalapeño, low-salt, low-fat, with ridges and without. There were dozens of varieties of soft drinks and beer and cigarettes, and an entire aisle of candy and gum. The far end of the store was a wall-to-wall freezer case filled with ice cream and pizza and egg rolls. A single aisle was devoted to less interesting items like bread and rice and canned vegetables. The MiniMart definitely was not a grocery store and didn't pretend to be. That my husband's career had come to this, even temporarily, was too depressing for words.

I knew Peter regretted not taking the time to find a better job when he first joined me in Black Bay, but neither of us had dreamed his stay would stretch to eight months. He rarely complained about the situation, but clearly it bothered him to have given up his high-paying job in San Francisco after he had worked so hard to establish himself. It bothered me too. And it bothered me even more that we never talked about it. I guess he thought he was doing me a favor by keeping up a happy front. I wasn't so sure.

"It's a store policy," he said when I asked him if anyone ate Twinkies anymore. "We stock nothing with a shelf life of less than fifty years. Those Twinkies have probably been here since you were ten."

At the rate of business the MiniMart did that night, it would take more than fifty years to turn the inventory one time. Not a single customer came in during the two hours I was there. As the clock approached quitting time, we were both struggling to stay awake.

I slid off my stool and stretched from side to side and then straight forward, reaching for my toes. "How does this place stay in business?" I asked. "Every time I'm here it's empty. Tonight they paid you to sit here for the past two hours and not a soul came in, other than me, and all I bought was a five-cent mint."

From my folded-over point of view I couldn't see Peter's expression, but the tone of his voice suggested I should have kept my mouth shut.

"Twelve whole dollars for sitting here all this time and I'm not even worth that much."

I cringed and stood up, holding the edge of the counter to steady myself. The gash in the back of my head was bleeding again. I could feel the wet spot. "I'm sorry, Peter. I didn't mean it that way. I just don't understand the economics of operating a convenience store on a deserted highway in the middle of the night. Last time I was here it was the same way. I think you had one customer the whole ti—" I grabbed his arm and nearly pulled him off his stool. "Peter! It was *him*."

"What are you talking about?"

"Sid's boyfriend. Remember? I stopped by while you were working last weekend, and that guy came in to ask where he could get a cheap room. It was Deke Brenner, the guy in Harlan's photo."

It had been late Sunday night. Peter was working the graveyard shift and I was at home, foraging through a year's worth of negatives in search of a shot or two of my mother that might be good enough to frame. Sid had eaten an early dinner in front of the TV in the den and retreated to her room above the garage, having declined an invitation to join me. Around midnight I drove to the MiniMart in search of microwave popcorn and conversation. Shortly after I arrived, a tall blond man came in to ask about accommodations. Most of the inns around Black Bay were closed for the season and those that weren't cost well more than the thirty dollars he wanted to spend, so we sent him up the road to Milton and Orcas Cove, where there were plenty of cheap motels open year-round. He thanked us, bought a pack of cigarettes, and left.

Peter squinted at a plexiglass case full of donuts and shook his head. "I remember some dude asking about motels, but I don't remember him being the guy in Fry's photo. The guy in the photo had really light hair and freaky washed-out eyes. You sure the one who came in here last weekend looked like that?"

"Absolutely. He had long blond hair, almost white, and pale gray eyes. He kept flipping his bangs out of his eyes. That's why I noticed the color, kind of silver, like ice."

I could picture the man perfectly, especially his eyes, but not entirely for the reason I mentioned. He had grabbed my attention the moment he walked into the store, in a way I couldn't quite explain, at least not to Peter. He had a haunting, sexy air about him, and I had found myself wondering who he was and how he had come to be in Black Bay. He had looked at me strangely at first too, as if he thought for a moment that he knew me and then decided he didn't. I found the intensity of his stare flattering, but also a little frightening. At the time I had thought perhaps he had been as intrigued by me as I was by him. Now I realized it must have been because of my resemblance to Sid.

Peter raised his eyebrows and shrugged, not the least bit fooled by my act. "I guess you'd know better than me. Seems you checked him out pretty good."

"I wouldn't say I *checked him out*, Peter. The guy gave me the creeps." I scrambled to squelch any budding suspicions. "Remember his squeaky voice? Very odd. Remember?"

Peter shook his head. "You work at a place like this too long and everybody blends together."

"I hear you, but Jesus, Peter. *That* was Sid's boyfriend?" I threw in an emphatic shudder for good measure.

"I'll tell you one thing. If it was Deke Brenner, the guy's got some explaining to do. Like why the hell was he in Black Bay and we didn't know about it?"

"I wonder if Sid knew." And more than that, I wondered if he had killed her.

11

The Northern California coastline warms slowly on overcast November mornings. Sometimes, especially if the fog hangs on, it doesn't warm at all. The thermometer hovers around fifty all day, but it feels ten degrees colder because of the dampness. Friday was one of those days. I was standing at the living room window when Andy Saybrook pulled into our driveway at eight o'clock, but the fog was so thick I heard his door slam shut before I realized he was there. It wasn't until I stepped outside that I was able to distinguish the hazy outline of his Blazer just five yards in front of me.

As promised, Andy had come to check for signs of the prowler I had reported the night before. I hurried to the hall closet to get my boots and slicker so I could join him, but by the time I maneuvered my swollen ankle into my tight boot and hobbled out to the porch, he was already reemerging from the whiteout, his inspection completed.

"Nothing there, Fran. Like I said last night, you probably heard a raccoon in the woods."

What I had heard had not been in the woods. It had been right outside our kitchen window. But I didn't challenge him. The local raccoons were known for coming up close to houses in search of garbage.

I backed into the house and held the door open. "Come have a cup of coffee, Andy. I have something to tell you about Woody Hanks."

He checked his watch. "Sorry, Fran. I'll have to take a rain check. I'm due at the station at eight-thirty, and it's bound to be busy with this blame fog. Folks around here ain't got sense enough to slow down when they can't see where they're going."

He had followed me far enough into the foyer that I was able to push the door shut behind him. I stepped in between to block his exit. "I'll talk fast, Andy, but this is important. I went back out to Pirate Point and to the bluff where Woody Hanks was when he spotted Sid's car. Have you gone out there?"

"No."

"Well, you should. You'll see that there isn't a view back to Pirate Point from that bluff because of the thistle brush. There's no way Woody just happened to notice Sid's car from out there, not unless he already knew to look for it."

Andy reached around me for the doorknob. "That's interesting. I'll check into it."

"Hold on. There's more. Woody was out there yesterday morning. I ran into him and his dog. He was acting real suspicious—"

"Suspicious? What makes you say that, Miss Marple?"

"Don't be an asshole, Andy. Woody got totally bent out of shape when he found me out there. He warned me not to tell the police I'd been there, as if he didn't want me to attract attention to the fact that there's no friggin' way he could have seen Sid's car like he said he did."

"So Woody doesn't want us checking out his story?" Andy shook his head, but he looked more amused than concerned. "I'd better have myself a little chat with the guy."

"Great, Andy, especially after he specifically warned me not to talk to you. Be sure to tell him I'm the one who squealed on him."

"I promise to keep your name out of it, Fran." He gave me a patronizing little smile. I half expected him to pat me on the head like a lost child. "I wouldn't be too worried about Woody. He's a harmless old coot."

"You might not think so if you'd been the one out there getting backed into the brush by that attack dog of his."

"I expect that's true. Damn nuisance, that dog." He checked his watch again. "One last thing, Fran, and then I really do have to be on my way. You take this for what it's worth. Harlan was none too happy about you showing up out at Pirate Point while we had the scene cordoned off last Tuesday. He's going to be pissed to hear you went back out there yesterday. He figures you could be looking to tinker with the evidence.''

I thought of the button I had stashed upstairs in my mother's cookie tin and swallowed hard. ''That's bullshit, Andy, and you know it.''

''Maybe it is, maybe not, but Harlan wants you to keep out of the way.''

''And you agree?''

''I think if I was you and if I had killed my sister, I'd sure be doing whatever I could to keep the police from figuring it out.''

''Listen to you. *If you were me and you had killed your sister.* I *didn't* kill my sister, Andy. That's the whole point.''

''I said *if,* Fran. I didn't say you did it. Now look, I hate to be short with you, but there's sure to be trouble with this blasted fog.'' He squeezed past me and opened the door.

I followed him onto the porch. ''Will Harlan be on duty today?'' Unpleasant though it was sure to be, I figured I would be better off talking directly to Harlan about Deke Brenner and how I suspected I had seen him at the MiniMart the previous weekend. Andy clearly was too worried about road conditions to be interested.

He answered from the steps without looking back. ''No. He'll be back tomorrow.'' If he wondered why I cared about Harlan's schedule, he was in too big a rush to ask.

Andy was right about the fog. Shortly after he left, I headed into town for the blood test Harlan had arranged the day before. I inched along, doing no more than twenty miles per hour, feeling my way along the invisible highway. I saw no other cars until I crested the last big hill before town and found a four-car pileup on the downslope. I pumped my brakes and swerved onto the shoulder, narrowly avoiding adding my Jeep to the mess. In the process I came within inches of running down Andy, who was marching along the side of the road with a handful of flares. He dove out of the way and rolled into the ditch, spewing flares and obscenities.

I skidded to a stop and fumbled with the car door, but he was on his feet and staggering toward me by the time I got it open.

''Andy—''

''I don't want to hear it, Fran. And don't get out of that Jeep. Just drive on out of here, real slow. We've got too many folks stopped here as it is. But, Christ Almighty, slow down. You could kill someone.''

I nodded and swung my legs out of the way of the door, which he shoved back at me. It slammed shut with a loud thud, but not before I heard one of the other drivers say, "Kill someone? I hear she already has." I recognized the voice as that of Bert Fisher, owner of the local Dairy Queen and a member of the town council. I was pleased to see his late-model Saab smack in the middle of the pileup with steam coming out of its hood.

12

They found the body Friday.

Andy Saybrook appeared on our doorstep at four-thirty, but didn't want to come in. He gave us the news outside on the porch, in the rain.

"A woman's body has been recovered off the coast of Jenner. Brown hair, medium build. A shark got it, ripped it up real bad. What's left is bloated and discolored from the water. I haven't seen it yet, but apparently it's not a pretty sight." He kept his head down and his hands buried in his pockets. He spoke in a rapid monotone, as if he were reading from notes.

I closed my eyes and leaned back against the wet railing of the porch, my mind wandering in a drug-induced haze caused by the double dose of Percodan I had taken twenty minutes earlier. "Oh."

"They're sure it's Sid?" Peter asked. "Jenner's a long ways down the coast."

Andy shrugged. "It's likely to be her, but we do need to make a positive identification. A seventeen-year-old girl went missing from up by Redding a month or so ago. Repeat problem. She's run away before and always turns up, usually in San Francisco. I hate to bother her family with this if we don't have to."

Peter nodded. "We understand. Where's the body?"

"County morgue in Santa Rosa. I'm heading there now. One or both of you should come too—get her IDed so the coroner can get on with the autopsy. I've got to warn you, though. Whatever you're expecting, it'll be worse.''

Peter put his arm around my shoulders. "It's got to be done, obviously. Frannie, you up for this?''

I tried to nod. This was a good thing, of course, the break we'd been praying for. Now we would learn once and for all what had happened to Sid.

''Frannie?''

When I didn't answer, Peter let his arm fall from my shoulders and said with less than total enthusiasm, ''I'll go, if that's what you want.''

From the tone of his voice it was clear that I was supposed to insist on going myself, but I didn't insist. Maybe it was the Percodan. Maybe it was the fear of what I would see, what had been done to Sid's body—or what had not been done. I just looked at him and nodded.

Andy gave Peter directions and left immediately. Peter changed clothes, fixed me some toast and warm milk, and departed a half hour later. I ate the toast and dumped the milk down the drain. Regretting the overdose of painkillers, I limped upstairs and descended into a dreamless, deathlike sleep.

Next I knew it was ten o'clock and Peter was shaking me awake. ''Frannie—''

I squinted up at his pale thin face, its features lost in the shadows of the dark room.

He leaned over me and brushed my matted bangs off my forehead. ''It was her,'' he said softly.

I pulled myself up and kicked off the covers. The shock of the cold air raised goose bumps on my damp skin. My T-shirt and the sheets were soaked with perspiration. I rolled to the side of the bed and huddled beside him, clutching my hands in my lap, thanking God my mother wasn't alive to go through this.

''How did she look? Could you see if she'd been . . . like April?'' My voice was barely a whisper.

He shook his head and picked at the nubbles on his wool sweater. ''Couldn't tell. The shark tore her up so bad you could hardly tell it was her. Took off most of her face and the entire lower half of her body. She didn't look good, Frannie.'' He bit his lip and pulled his fingers through his hair.

"Will they be able to tell us how she died? If she was raped?" I prayed for some bit of evidence that would establish I was not the killer.

"I don't know. They don't know. The coroner's looking her over now, but he wasn't optimistic. The shark did a lot of damage. So did the water."

He reached into his pocket and handed me a small plastic bag. Through the clear plastic I could see an earring. Two interlocking rings, one silver and one gold, with a small triangular black onyx set in the center. It was Sid's. She had been wearing it Monday night at the Seahorse Pub.

I removed the earring and let the bag fall to the floor. "Where's the other one?"

Peter shook his head. "Gone. Along with her left ear. Her face and head took the brunt of the attack."

I made a fist around the earring, squeezing it so tight the silver post punctured my skin. When I opened my hand a tiny drop of blood formed in the center of my palm. It was official now. Like this little earring, I was no longer one of a pair.

Peter hugged his jacket closer about him. "You're shaking, Frannie. It's freezing in here. Why don't you put on your robe and we'll go downstairs and have a cup of hot tea? Or a drink. Would you like a drink? I could fix us something." He sounded as if he needed it more than me.

"Maybe a glass of wine," I said, wondering if it was a good idea to mix alcohol and Percodan.

He helped me out of my T-shirt and into my robe. I followed him downstairs to the living room couch, where I waited while he went for the wine. He filled two glasses and set the open bottle on the coffee table.

We sat in silence for several minutes. Peter finished his wine and poured himself another glass. I took one sip of mine and had trouble getting it down. It tasted sour, as if it had turned, but Peter didn't seem to notice.

"You need to decide what to do about the body, Frannie. The coroner suggested we have it cremated in Santa Rosa and have the ashes brought home next week. He gave me the name of a funeral parlor. If you want, I'll call tomorrow and make the arrangements."

I nodded.

"You can decide later what to do with the ashes. We could bury them beside your mom if you want. Or we could scatter them somewhere. Or . . . whatever. Frannie? You okay?"

The room suddenly felt unbearably hot. I pushed up from the couch and staggered to the front door and outside to the porch, where I leaned out over the railing, struggling not to throw up. The wind whipped my hair and sprayed my face with a steady drizzle.

I should have gone with Peter to see Sid. If it had been my mother I would have gone, no matter what condition the body had been in. I would have wanted to touch her hand one last time, to say good-bye. But I didn't do that for Sid. I made Peter go alone. Peter, who had not been a significant part of Sid's life—who hadn't even particularly liked her—was the only one who went to bid her a final farewell.

Within minutes my robe was soaked and my teeth were chattering, but I didn't go inside.

I should have done more for Sid while she was living. I could have done more at her death. What I *would* do was find her killer. That much at least I could pledge to my dead twin sister.

13

After two weeks of unrelenting gloom, the sun came out Saturday. A true California sun that burned like white gold against a bluer-than-blue California sky. Peter and I slept late, ate a big breakfast, and spent the remainder of the morning on the front porch, pretending the cloud of tension that had been hanging over us for the past four days had cleared up with the weather. But pretending didn't make it so, and Peter's experience at the county morgue the night before hadn't helped.

We suffered through two hours of clumsy off-and-on chitchat before I struggled out of the porch swing and stepped lightly to the front door, hoping Peter wouldn't notice how badly I was limping. I told him I was going to Salt Point State Park to take photographs. He didn't object. He looked relieved.

By one o'clock I was on the road, my canvas carryall beside me on the passenger seat, filled with the usual provisions—my Nikon camera and assorted lenses and filters, three canisters of film, an extra wool sweater, water, and a Ziploc bag filled with trail mix. Predictably, I had driven less than a mile before I pulled out the plastic bag and began fishing for the chocolate chips.

Without taking my eyes off the double yellow line in the center of the highway, I sped past Pirate Point and the bluff to the north where I had encountered Woody Hanks and Rocky two days earlier. To my left the restless Pacific stretched out to the horizon, blue as sapphire velvet studded with a million diamond white waves. To my right a brigade of weathered fence posts marched along the winding road like drunken soldiers guarding the golden hillside. Every quarter mile or so I came upon another vista that begged to be preserved on film, but I didn't stop. For all my preparations, I had no intention of taking pictures.

The sign for the BelAir Motel and Cabins was my first indication I was coming into Milton. VACANCY—HEATED POOL—CABLE TV. The words accosted me in chartreuse neon. The BelAir was the first in a strip of tourist motels and RV parks that started at the south end of Milton and ended ten miles up the highway at the north end of Orcas Cove. Unlike Black Bay, where a hostile planning department had excluded all but a handful of pricy little inns and the historic Black Bay Hotel, the two towns to its north catered to travelers on a budget. This was where Peter and I had sent the man who came into the MiniMart the previous Sunday night looking for a room, the man I was convinced was Deke Brenner.

I pulled into the asphalt lot and up to the motel's main building, but the office was empty and locked. A sign in the window said PRESS BUZZER FOR SERVICE, so I did. When no one appeared after a few more tries I gave up, figuring I could stop back at the BelAir on my way home if I hadn't picked up Brenner's trail elsewhere. I was backing out of the lot when a stocky fellow in overalls emerged from the office and jogged toward me.

I rolled down my window and pulled closer. "Do you work here?"

"Sure do. I was in back, taking a nap. Heard your car door slam."

"You heard my car door but not the buzzer?" I pointed at the front door.

"Darn thing's broke. I keep meaning to take the sign down."

I resisted the urge to tell him that would be a good idea and instead launched into my story. "I have a friend who stayed here last weekend, a big blond guy in his early thirties. I wonder—"

He was shaking his head. "Didn't stay here. We've been closed. Been in Maui for the past two weeks."

I thanked him and pulled back onto the highway, heading for the next motel on the strip. One down and a dozen to go.

I had no better luck at my second stop. The Redwood Motel had no record of anyone matching Brenner's description. Neither did the Milton Overnighter nor the Land's End Best Western. That was it for Milton. The town's other motels were closed for the season. I continued northward, feeling decidedly less confident than before. If the motels in Orcas

Cove produced no leads, I would have to hit the bars, convenience stores, and gas stations on the drive back to Black Bay.

The Oceanside Motel came upon me suddenly as I rounded a blind curve a mile out of Orcas Cove. I couldn't see the motel from the highway, just a smallish white billboard with green letters and a red arrow that directed me through a ten-foot-wide gap in a thick wall of Scotch pines.

The driveway was steeper than I had expected, and I was traveling faster than I should have been going into a ninety-degree turn. I dropped over what seemed like the ledge of a cliff, slammed on the brakes, and fishtailed down the gravel hill. The sound brought the motel's silver-haired manager scurrying out the screen door from the office. She was plump and pink-skinned but not unattractive in her floral print dress and ruffled white apron. Had she been smiling, she might have looked like someone's grandmother.

"This is a family motel," she informed me as I climbed out of the Jeep. "There could be children about."

"Sorry. I nearly missed the turn."

"Obviously."

I glanced around. There was no one in sight other than the two of us, certainly no kids. My Jeep was the only vehicle in a parking lot that stretched the length of the motel, which I was surprised to see was not as tawdry as most of the places in Milton. There were a dozen units in a long single-story building clad in clean white aluminum siding. The place looked neat and well-kept, but decidedly deserted.

"I really am sorry." I gave her my toadiest smile. "It's so beautiful around here I guess my mind was drifting."

After a moment's hesitation, she smiled back, and I saw that I was right. She did look like a grandmother. "Welcome to the Oceanside Motel," she said. "I'm Rose."

She led the way into the motel's tiny office and took her place behind a counter plastered with postcards under a sheet of green-tinted glass. "Do you need a room, Miss—?"

"Fran. No, actually I don't."

"Well then, Fran. How can I help you? Do you need directions?"

"It's about someone who stayed here last week. My husband and I referred him to your motel."

"How kind of you to think of us. What's his name?"

"Deke Brenner."

"Let's see." She opened her register with one hand and used the other to slip on the pink cat-eye glasses that dangled from a beaded chain around her neck. "What night did you say?"

"Sunday."

She flipped back to the previous week and ran her finger down the page. "We have no record of a Deke Brenner. I wonder if Mr. Brenner didn't take you up on your recommendation."

I leaned over the counter to get a look at the entries. "Maybe I have the wrong date."

"To be quite honest, dear, this is a very slow time of year for us and the wretched weather has been making business even worse than usual. Things'll pick up next month when we start getting the whale watchers, but lately it's just been terribly quiet. . . ."

I gently pried the register from her grip and twisted it so I could read the names. There weren't many. She was right. Business hadn't been good. I saw only four rooms booked during all of the previous week, and not one of them was registered to Deke Brenner. I looked at the entries for Sunday night. Wade and Sandy Henderson in room two. Don Brown in room three.

Before leaving, I tried one more idea. "Gosh, Rose, did I say Deke Brenner? I meant Don Brown, his bro—his cousin. And I do see Don's name here."

"Oh, of course, Mr. Brown. Quiet young man." She wrinkled her forehead when she said the name. Evidently something about Don Brown troubled her.

"Big guy with light blond hair?" I asked.

"Yes, that's him. He looked like one of those surfer types. We get our share, even in winter. Bunch of yahoos. They ruin the furniture with their wet suits and surfboards." She paused for a moment, frowning at the register. "As far as I could tell, though, Mr. Brown wasn't here to surf. Has something happened to him?"

"Oh no, he's fine, except he called the other day to say he thinks he left his jacket in the room Monday morning. He asked if I'd check for him."

She shook her head. "No jacket. We didn't find anything. I'm quite sure of it. I was the one who cleaned his room after he left. I'm a one-woman show November through March." She pushed her glasses up on her nose and examined the register. "Your friend stayed more than one night, you know. Came in late Sunday night and left sometime Tuesday. Didn't even check out, just left. Oh, it was okay, him leaving like that and all. He didn't cheat us out of any money. In fact, he prepaid in cash for three nights, so we owe him a refund. It's our policy, you see, when folks don't use a credit card they have to pay in advance. That way we have a deposit, in case there's damage. . . .''

I bobbed my head and rubbed my hand across my cheeks and jawline in hopes of concealing the smile that had swept across my face.

"But Mr. Brown didn't damage anything. He barely used the room."

"Oh?"

She pursed her lips and pulled off her glasses. "It's unusual these days that folks don't pay with a credit card. I'm surprised the rental car company would rent to him without one. They usually insist on it. Plastic, you know, is the thing these days. Maybe that's why he had to go to Golden Oldie Rentals."

"Golden Oldie Rentals?"

"I'd never heard of it either, but I noticed the sticker on his pickup. He said he rented it in San Francisco. Didn't look like much of a truck to me, and I told him so, but he said it was less expensive than Hertz or Avis. Golden Oldie Rentals. What will they think of next?"

"Anything to save a buck, I guess."

"Speaking of which, if I give you the twenty-five dollars Mr. Brown overpaid, would you be so kind as to return it to him? He didn't leave a phone number or address, but I do feel guilty overcharging anyone these days, especially a young person trying to save money."

I shook my head. "Don does okay, ma'am. I'm sure he won't miss the twenty-five dollars."

She lit up like she'd won the lottery and was still beaming five minutes later when I wished her a good day and drove slowly and carefully up the steep gravel hill to the highway.

When I arrived home after my visit with Rose at the Oceanside Motel, I found a note from Peter taped to the door.

F: Call me at work. ASAP! P.

I dropped my carryall and jacket in the hall and stumbled over them in my dash to the phone, sending peanuts and raisins skittering across the wood floor. As it turned out, Peter wanted nothing more than to confirm I had gotten home safely and to tell me there was rice and tomato casserole in the refrigerator. Nothing remotely urgent, nothing even interesting. Just rice and tomato casserole, which he knew I didn't like. No news about the investigation, no prowlers, no surprise visits from the

police. He had to get back to work before I got a chance to tell him about
my afternoon in Milton and Orcas Cove.

After we hung up, I swept up the mess in the hall and wandered into
the living room with a can of Diet Coke. The big blond fellow who had
come into the MiniMart Sunday night *had* taken our advice about where
to stay. But was he Sid's elusive boyfriend Deke, sneaking around the
North Coast under an assumed name? According to Rose, the man who
called himself Don Brown had been in the area Sunday night through
Tuesday afternoon. Perfect timing for him to get his bearings on Monday,
murder Sid that night, and hit the road the next day. It fit. The police had
not found anyone who had seen Brenner in Los Angeles within the past
two weeks.

On an impulse, I went back to the phone in the kitchen and called
directory assistance for L.A. I got the number for an S. Scott on Victoria
Way and dialed, not quite certain what I would say if Sid's neighbor
answered her phone.

After five rings, I expected to get an answering machine, so I was
taken aback when the singsongy "Helloooo" was not followed by a
recorded greeting.

"Hello," the voice said again. It was deep and throaty and androgy-
nous. "Hello, hello?"

I recovered my wits before she—or he—could hang up. "May I speak
to Sunshine Scott, please?"

The person's tone changed at the sound of my voice. Definitely female
now. "If you're peddling long-distance service, there ain't nobody here
by that name. Miss Scott died last week."

"Died?" My stomach did a somersault. "What happened?"

The woman hesitated. "Let's just say it was tragic causes. Now, if you
don't mind—"

"Was she murdered?"

"Murdered? Who the hell is this?"

"My name is Fran Estes. I'm the sister of Sid LaSalle, Miss Scott's
neighbor—er, former neighbor."

"Oh, for goodness sakes, this is Sunshine."

"You're Sunshine Scott? And you're not dead?"

"Alive and kicking. That's just what I tell those damn solicitors. Otherwise they never leave you alone. If it's not MCI or AT&T, it's Visa or
American Express. Preapproved credit, my ass. I used to tell them I was
out of town, but then they keep calling back. Now I say I'm dead so they
take my name off their damn list."

"I see . . . good idea."

"So you're Sid's sister? Shit. I didn't know the girl had a sister."

The comment, innocently made, hit me like a rock between the eyes. This was one of Sid's closest friends, and she didn't even know Sid had a sister? "Yes, well, she does—she did, that is."

The significance of my words flew right by her. "When's that girl coming home? I'm sick of watering her plants. I'm sick of Mr. Soo too."

"Mr. Soo?" I almost didn't want to ask. "Who's that?"

"Parakeet—parrot—whatever. Green bird. Goddamn noisy little shit. I'm half tempted to open a window and see if he can fly. . . .''

I figured I'd better be more direct. Clearly she wasn't going to inquire about my sister's health.

"Now, I'm no bird-hater, mind you, but Mr. Soo is such a goddamn little turd factory. Stinks up the whole—''

"Sid's dead."

"—apartment. . . . What did you say?"

"Sid's dead. It happened a few days ago. We think she was murdered."

"Sweet Jesus in heaven. Murdered?"

"Her car was pushed over a cliff."

"Murdered. Dear Lord God." Her voice faded to a husky whisper. "Now why would somebody go and do that? Sid wasn't no harm to anybody, not anybody other than herself. They know who did it?"

"Not yet. They don't have much to go on. That's why I'm calling, actually, to see if you might know of anyone down there in L.A. who had reason to kill her."

She was too stunned to hear my question, let alone answer it. "So that's why the cops were in her apartment Tuesday night. They were asking all sorts of questions, said she was missing and then got all evasive when I asked what the hell they meant by that. They never said she was dead, not in so many words. Shit. I thought the girl was about to get busted for some stupid deal that loser D.B. got her mixed up in."

"D.B.? As in Deke Brenner?"

"Yeah, Deke. You met him?"

"No, but Sid told me all about him." I figured Sunshine would be more talkative if she didn't know the sad truth about my relationship with Sid.

She took a deep breath and exhaled slowly. When she spoke again her voice was stronger than before. "Born loser. Sid should never have gotten involved with him in the first place. Oh, he was loopy for her, I'll grant

you that, but that's the only good thing I've got to say for the guy. Deke
Brenner was trouble from the get-go, and I told her so. Does he know
yet?''

''No. I was hoping you could help me contact him.''

''I ain't giving him the bad news, hon. You'll have to find some other
sucker for that.''

''No, no, I'll tell him. I just thought maybe you'd know where he is.
He's disappeared.''

''Disappeared?'' She let out a gravelly half laugh. ''What's your def-
inition of disappeared?''

''The police can't find him. It's their word, not mine. They can't find
anybody who's seen him in the past two weeks. Do you know where he
is?''

She didn't answer.

''Sunshine?''

''Look, hon—what'd you say your name was?''

''Fran.''

''Look, Fran, I'm one to mind my own business, you know? If the
cops are looking for Deke Brenner, that's his problem, not mine. That's
really all I can tell you.'' Her voice was colder now, as if she would
prefer to end our conversation.

I struggled to keep the frustration out of my voice. ''I hear you, Sunshine, but if you had to guess where Deke Brenner is right now, where
would you say?''

''I wouldn't. There's nothing I can tell you about Deke Brenner. I got
nothing to do with the guy. If the cops want D.B. they can damn well
find him themselves.''

''I think you're misunderstanding me, Sunshine. I'm the one who's
trying to find Deke. And I'm Sid's sister, for Chrissakes, not a cop. As
far as I know, the police aren't even looking for him anymore.'' I waited
for her to respond. She didn't. ''Deke was Sid's boyfriend, Sunshine. I
just want to talk to him. I want to meet the guy and tell him what happened.''

''*Boyfriend?* I'd say you're about a year out-of-date.''

''Sid wasn't seeing him anymore?''

''Yes and no.''

''Yes and no?'' What the hell did that mean?

''Seeing him, yes. Dating him, no. They had unfinished business, if
you catch my drift.''

"I'm not sure I do, actually." I wasn't sure I wanted to, either.

"Pharmaceuticals." She clicked her tongue like a disapproving school-teacher. "Asking for trouble, they were. Begging for it."

I nodded slowly. For Sunshine's benefit, I softly said, "I understand."

"Sid had been giving D.B. the big see-ya signal, but he didn't want to believe it. He kept hanging on, like a goddamn terrier with an old sock."

"I'd like to talk to him, Sunshine. I think I should tell him what happened."

"That'd be up to you."

"I need to find him first."

"Look, I don't keep track of the guy. He was your sister's problem, not mine. Only way I'd know where to find him is if he showed up at Sid's place, which I wouldn't count on."

"Why not? Won't he eventually come looking for her?"

"Let's just say she gave him a good talking to before she left. Read him the riot act, and he didn't take it so good. Turned into more than a polite conversation."

"He beat her?"

"Beat her? Nah. Pushed her around is all. Sid's a tough girl. Or she was, anyway. Shit." Her voice quavered, and she paused for a breath. "She started it. Threw a lamp at him. Cut up his neck pretty good, she told me later. She thought it was a hoot."

I tried to picture the man I had seen the previous Sunday night at the MiniMart. I didn't recall noticing any cuts on his neck.

"Do you think he might have come up to Black Bay to find her?"

"And kill her, you mean? I said the guy's a loser, but you're not going to get me to say he's a killer." She sounded annoyed.

"I need to find him, Sunshine. Can't you think of anything?"

I could see her shaking her head even before she told me no.

"A woman has been murdered, Sunshine."

"Welcome to the real world, girl. People get killed every damn day."

"This one was your friend."

"I've lost friends before."

"So that's it? Even if you knew how to find him, you wouldn't tell me? I'm real glad to know my sister had a friend like you, Sunshine. No wonder she's dead. Thanks for nothing."

I had the receiver halfway hung up when I heard the boom of her deep voice. "Goddamnit. Don't you be laying no guilt trip on me.

Sid's gone and there ain't nothing you or I can do about it. Life sucks, but that's just the way it is. If you really want to find D.B., you'll haul your ass down here and look for him yourself. You call me if you're coming, and I'll see what I can do. Otherwise, don't be bothering me no more.''

14

Sunday morning I woke at six-fifteen to the familiar grinding and sputtering of our old Volvo pulling into the driveway, followed by the click of the front door. Peter had worked from two in the afternoon on Saturday until ten that night and then covered the graveyard shift for a sick coworker. Sixteen lousy hours without a break.

When he slipped into bed thirty minutes later, I pretended to be asleep. I didn't feel like conversation, and Peter deserved the rest. I rather wished he would snuggle up next to me, but he kept to his side, careful not to disturb me. By seven o'clock his rhythmic breathing had turned to a soft snore that meant he was out for the next few hours.

Softly, so as not to wake him, I slid closer and reached out to touch his sleeping face. I pushed aside his scraggly bangs and traced my fingertips across the ridge of his forehead, struck by how old he looked. He was only thirty-four, but he had worry lines across his forehead and a deep vertical crease between his eyebrows. This was not the face of the man I married three years ago. In San Francisco, Peter had been the prototypical yuppie—hardworking and ambitious, but essentially carefree. Today he was a different person, burdened by a thankless, mindless job and his wife's endless problems. With his long hair and goatee, I hardly recognized him anymore.

Shortly after seven I rolled out of bed, pulled on my robe and slippers, and padded downstairs. The morning paper lay open on the kitchen table, greeting me with a front-page story about homeless children. I didn't have the heart for bad news, so I found a pencil and flipped to the crossword puzzle.

Before long I was thoroughly frustrated. I had gotten that *defeasible* was a ten-letter word for capable of being annulled, and that *chestnut* was an eight-letter word for a callus on the leg of a horse, but who the hell knew—or wanted to know—a five-letter word for the liquid portion of a fat? I was glad when the phone rang to put me out of my misery.

"Hello?"

"Frances."

"Hi, Dad." Why hadn't I let the answering machine get it?

"Hello, Frances."

"Hi." I wondered if he would say hello again. We could go back and forth indefinitely.

"I'm at a pay phone at a place called the Wildflower Cafe."

Damn. He was back in Black Bay.

"Care to meet me for breakfast?"

"No thanks."

"Barb's sleeping in this morning. I thought you and I could get together." No mention of his drunken message three days ago. He probably didn't remember it.

"Where are you staying?"

"Little place called the Bayview Inn. Heard of it?"

"Sure. Very nice."

"Pricy too." Lest I forget what a tightwad he had always been.

"Nothing but the best for Barbie doll."

"Now, Frances. Barb's never been to California. The least I could do was find us a decent place to stay. I don't suppose we'd be welcome at the house."

"No, I don't suppose you would."

He paused to clear his throat. "How are you doing?"

"I'm fine. How are you?"

"I'm still a little shocked by the news about your sister, to say the least. I do wish you'd come to breakfast. I'd like to talk to you."

"Talk on, Dad. You've got my undivided attention." I picked up my crossword puzzle and tried to think of a nine-letter word for self-possession.

"Goddamnit, Frances, I can't order you to see me, I know that. I'm asking. I take it you know where the Wildflower Cafe is located. I'll expect you in fifteen minutes.''

By the time I got to the Wildflower, it was twenty minutes past the fifteen-minute deadline my father had given me, but he was still there and he hadn't ordered. He knew I would come.

I slid into the booth across from him, ignoring his proffered cheek. ''Hello, Dad.''

''Hello, Frances. Thanks for coming.''

''I was hungry.''

He made a sorry attempt at a smile and pushed my menu toward me. ''Let's order then. I'm hungry too.''

I stared at the menu and he stared at me for an uncomfortably long time before our waitress came. I ordered a mushroom and avocado omelette with dry nine-grain toast and fruit salad. He said he'd have the same, to irritate me in some small way, I figured. We both knew he would prefer fried eggs with bacon and hash browns.

I sipped my coffee and tried to look disinterested. ''You said you had something you wanted to talk about.''

''Yes.''

''What? I haven't got much time.'' I had all day, but he didn't need to know that.

''I don't think we're getting off to a good start, Frances.''

I leaned back against the smooth vinyl upholstery of the booth and folded my arms across my chest. I would regret my behavior later—I always did—but the anger took over. ''No? Then tell me, Dad, what do you want with me? Why the hell are you here?''

''Watch your mouth, Frances. I'm still your father.''

''I know that. Why are you here?''

''As I told you before, Barb and I are touring Northern California. Would you like to hear where we've been?''

I clenched my teeth and managed a noncommittal shrug. Might as well let him talk.

He droned on for ten minutes and I struggled to pay attention. I ran out of patience when he mentioned that he and Barb had stayed at Auberge du Soleil in the Napa Valley because she had read about the place in *Town & Country*.

''I'm impressed,'' I said. ''She can read.''

His face turned the color of the geraniums in the window box beside our table. "That was uncalled for, Frances. You sound more like your sister every damn day. You look more like her too, you know. Unhealthy."

"Dad, why are you here? To talk about your vacation and criticize me? I don't think so. Why don't you get to the point? Or, better yet, why don't you do us both a big fat favor and leave me alone?"

"Your mother and sister are dead, Frances. You've got no family left, other than me."

"I've got Peter."

"I meant blood relations."

"Since when did blood relations become so important to you? Where were you when your blood relations needed you?"

"Frances—"

"Sid doesn't need you anymore, and neither do I."

He grunted an indiscernible obscenity and pounded the table. "You think I didn't provide for you? You're wrong, young lady, dead wrong. Who do you think is responsible for the five hundred thousand dollars you're about to collect? And who do you think is responsible for the policy that paid your mother's medical bills? I'll tell you who. Me. That's who. I've had some hard times over the years, but I never stopped paying the premiums on those policies."

He shut up before his voice cracked, but just barely, and without claiming credit for lending Sid the fifty thousand dollars Peter had overheard Barb complaining about at the funeral. I wondered if maybe he didn't want me to know about that. By now he had worked himself into such a state his hands were jerking too violently to grip his coffee mug. He was sixty years old this year and apparently going through some sort of psychological crisis. I almost felt sorry for him.

"I didn't come here to fight, Frances."

"I didn't either."

"What's the word from the police about your sister? Any leads?"

"Her name is Sid, Dad."

"I know her name. I asked if the police have any leads."

I shook my head. "They have very little to go on. It was raining that night and the next day, so any physical evidence was washed away. They found her body down by Jenner two days ago, but there wasn't much left of it. A shark got it. She'll be cremated tomorrow and they'll deliver the ashes out to the house on Wednesday."

"They have no leads? Nothing at all?"

"No, Dad. Nothing." He had every right to be interested in the investigation of his daughter's murder, but his concern, like everything else about him, struck me as less than genuine.

"No suspects?"

Yes, Dad, they have a suspect. Me. And for all I know, they could be right. "Remember April Kaminsky?" Of course he remembered April. She had been his least favorite of our childhood friends. She had him pegged as an asshole from the day she met him twenty-five years ago, and he liked her no better, thought she was a strange child.

"Yes. I heard what happened to April. Tragic."

"That's your suspect. Psychotic drifter. Same guy who killed April may have come back for more. Only they can't say for sure because the body was in such bad shape."

His stony face absorbed the information without the slightest change of expression. "I see." The waitress delivered our plates, and he began poking his omelette with his fork, as if he could tell he didn't like it even without tasting it. "That's the only suspect? There's nobody else?"

"That's right. Like I already told you, there's nobody else. *N-O-B-O-D-Y*. Nobody. Got it?"

He glared at me and slammed his fork onto the table. "There's no reason you and I can't get along, Frances, now that your sister is gone. The past is the past, for Chrissakes."

"The past is the past? You make it sound so simple."

"It is simple."

Not to me, it wasn't. My memories of my father were in the present, not in the past. I remembered a critical, short-tempered man who was too busy chasing his next insurance sale to be bothered with his wife and kids, a man who spent most days alone in his office above the garage with a pilfered DO NOT DISTURB card hung on the doorknob. I remembered a man who barely knew I existed and who cared even less. Sid's memories, I suspected, were significantly worse.

I watched the motion of his square jaw as he chewed a mouthful of fruit salad. When the waitress stopped at our table, he barked at her for more coffee and for new toast because the first order was cold. She served him with a pleasant smile that disguised what she must have been feeling. He didn't even say thank you.

I gritted my teeth as he smeared his toast with butter and strawberry jam, the way I would have loved to. He was in good shape for a man of sixty. Straight and solid as a thick wooden plank. Compact. He claimed to be five foot nine, but I doubted he was any taller than my own five seven. His cropped hair was steel gray and only just starting to recede.

His neck was muscular, his lips tight and thin. He would have made a good Marine.

"Frances?"

"Yes?"

"You're not listening."

"Oh. What were you saying?"

"I asked how much contact you had with your sister this past year."

I shrugged. "Some. Not much."

"She spoke to you of her financial problems?" *Here it comes.* He was about to disclose the fifty grand. It must have been eating him alive that Sid had the audacity to get herself killed before she could pay him back.

"She asked Peter and me for money, but we didn't have much to spare."

"You know she came to me too?"

He asked the question casually enough, but his twitching hands gave him away. Suddenly a lot of things became clear, including his reason for insisting on seeing me.

I picked up my fork and began hacking the remains of my omelette into little bits. "Oh, really? She came to you too?"

"Yes, really. She said you told her to. She said you assured her I had plenty of money."

I wondered what else Sid had told him. I had an idea her discussion with Dad hadn't stopped at a simple loan request. Sid had a way of creating leverage against people and using it ruthlessly. Now, even after her death, he was still stewing about it.

I dropped my fork into a mound of minced egg and avocado and looked him in the eye. "That's why you're here, isn't it? To talk about Sid wanting money. She threatened you, didn't she?"

"Don't be ridiculous. I don't know what she told you, but I'm sure it was a lie." He sat up straighter and wiped his pinched lips. After a moment of tense silence, he tossed his napkin onto his mostly uneaten omelette and waved for the check.

Without another word, he paid the bill, left a chintzy tip, and pulled on his jacket. "I should get back to Barb," he said as he slid out of the booth. "I've taken enough of your time."

"Yes."

I followed him outside and watched him climb into a shiny green Ford Explorer. He didn't look happy. I didn't care.

15

What is it about being forbidden to do something that creates such a compelling urge to do it? When I casually suggested to Peter that I might fly down to Los Angeles to clear out Sid's apartment, he immediately saw what I had in mind. He didn't just say *no*. He said *hell no*. He wasn't going to hear of it.

"Damnit, Frannie, let the police do their job. You're not qualified to go running around like a goddamn detective."

"I'm not running around like a detective, Peter." He knew I had gone out to Pirate Point twice since Sid's car was found and about my encounter with Woody out on the bluff, but nothing more. I had not yet told him about the button I'd dug up by the rocks, or my trip to Milton and Orcas Cove, or my conversation with Sunshine Scott—nor would I, if this was to be his attitude.

"Why are you doing this, Frannie? It's dangerous. It's nuts."

"Because I want to know who killed my sister, Peter." *I want to know it wasn't me.*

"Well, I know why you want to go to L.A., and it's not to clear out Sid's apartment. It's to look for her boyfriend, that guy in Harlan's photograph. What if you find him? Have you thought about that? Have you forgotten why Sid stayed in Black Bay after the funeral? She was scared to go home, scared of what that guy would do to her. This is something for the police to investigate, not you.'' He put his fingertips under my chin and lifted it so our eyes met. "Promise me you won't go down there, Frannie. Promise.''

Reluctantly, I promised. Then I devised a new plan.

I left for San Francisco early Monday morning, well in advance of my afternoon appointment with my therapist. Peter had worked late again the night before, so I slipped out of the house without waking him. These days we were like two planets on different orbits. What little time we had together was spent largely in silence or, more and more frequently, arguing.

Monday offered a welcome change. I was happy to be speeding southward out of Black Bay and happier still three and a half hours later when I passed into the sweeping red arms of the Golden Gate Bridge. The breezy air was fresh from the recent rains, and there wasn't a trace of fog. Beneath me, the bay was dotted with white-winged sailboats flitting across the waves like tiny butterflies. Beyond the water, the city spread itself gracefully over its famous hills, a fine mosaic of pale stucco and shining steel. The top of the Transamerica Pyramid poked up out of the distant Financial District like a giant party hat.

The off-ramp from the bridge dumped me into the Marina District, where not so long ago Peter and I had shared our first wonderful little shoe box of an apartment in a 1920s art deco building on Beach Street. I turned up Scott Street and took a detour past our old place, wondering who lived there now and whether they were as happy as we had been.

On Lombard Street I pulled into a Shell station and headed for the phone booth while the Jeep guzzled a tankful of unleaded. The Yellow Pages ad for Golden Oldie Rentals gave an address on Bayshore Highway in South San Francisco, near the airport. I had time to make the half-hour drive and get back for my two o'clock appointment with Dr. Fielding, but not a lot to spare, so I headed straightaway up the Fillmore Street hill toward Highway 101 South. My route took me through a microcosm of the city's best and its worst, from the tony mansions and foreign embassies in Pacific Heights and the chic Fillmore Street shopping district to the crime-ridden housing projects on the other side of Geary, home to a population that didn't participate in the San Francisco fairy tale.

Traffic was light. It took me just twenty-five minutes to get to the address I had found in the Yellow Pages. I pulled into an asphalt lot surrounded by a chain-link fence topped with barbed wire. The lot was packed full of the sorriest bunch of rental cars I had ever seen, most of which looked as if they belonged more appropriately in a junkyard than in a rental car lot. I parked next to a Honda Accord with a cracked windshield, blistered silver paint, and a deep depression in the passenger door. It hardly looked driveable, much less like something anyone would pay money to rent.

I picked my way across the buckling pavement to a trailer sporting a crude sign with the words GOLDEN OLDIE RENTALS in big black unartistic letters. Access to the trailer's dented aluminum door was by way of a plywood plank that sagged and creaked when I walked on it.

Needless to say, I was not greeted by a chorus line of fresh-faced clerks in red polyester smocks smiling out at me from behind a row of computer terminals. Instead there was a single attendant in a grease-stained green jumpsuit sitting on a stool behind the dirty counter. He was a stout swarthy fellow about my age with curly black hair and a wide grin that made a matched pair of dimples in his chubby cheeks. His name was Mike, according to the stitching on his pocket. I smiled as I approached. Mike was my man. I knew he was going to take care of me.

"Why, hello there, ma'am. C'mon in," he said with enthusiasm that bordered on absurd. "What can I do for you? Need a vehicle?"

I shook my head and produced another silly little smile. "No, actually I don't. I'm here on behalf of a friend of mine. Two friends. They rented a pickup from you last week."

"Oh-oh. Was there a problem?"

"No problem with the truck, but one of them left his camera under the seat—at least he thinks he did."

"Bummer."

"Yeah. I wonder if you could check?"

"You bet."

He stooped behind the counter and emerged with a large cardboard box, which he spilled out before me. There were several pairs of sunglasses, a cheap calculator, an umbrella, a pair of tennis shoes, and an assortment of other lost or abandoned items. No camera.

"Doesn't look like it's turned up. It'd be here if it had."

"Damn." I tried to look disappointed without overdoing it. "My friend said he stuck it way back beneath the seat. I wonder if it's still in the truck."

He produced a three-ring binder from under the counter. "What's the name?"

"Could be either of them. Deke Brenner or Don Brown."

"Date they took the vehicle out?"

"I'm not sure. Maybe last Sunday. Maybe before."

While he flipped back a few pages in the binder, I all but climbed onto the chest-high counter to get a look at the list of semilegible scribbles. He glanced up at me, amused. "I'll find it if it's here, ma'am."

"Name's Fran," I said. "I'm sure you will. I'm just nervous, that's all. It was an expensive camera."

He pushed the register across the counter so I would have a better view, but he found the name first. "Here it is. Deke Brenner."

I nearly leapt over the counter and kissed him.

"Clocked out last Sunday night at eight. Back in Tuesday at five-thirty. Black '89 Chevy pickup. Hopefully she's on the lot."

"Can you check, please?"

He grinned and winked. "If you'll keep an eye on the office. We're here alone, Fran."

I nodded and placed my left hand on the counter, making sure he couldn't miss my wedding ring. "I'd appreciate it. And one more thing while you're out there. Deke mentioned being involved in a bit of a fender bender. The driver in front of him stopped short and he rear-ended the guy. I wonder if you could check for damage, anything Deke should be responsible for fixing."

"Nah, don't worry about that. I know that old Chevy he rented and she's so banged up already, there's no way we'd try to collect for a few more dents. Besides, we got insurance that'll take care of anything that needs fixing."

"But could you take a look, anyway? See if you notice anything new?"

He winked again and reached over the counter to give my hand a reassuring pat. "You got it, Fran. Anything you say. Now, wait right here, and I'll be back in a flash."

He came out from behind the counter, grinning. I looked away but felt his eyes on my butt. The minute the door closed behind him, I grabbed the register and found Deke Brenner's name, address, and driver's license number.

I spent fifteen minutes searching for a parking space within walking distance of Elizabeth Fielding's office on Laurel Street in San Francisco's prestigious Presidio Heights. The streets were lined with big houses, big trees, and big cars. No big parking lots. Fortunately, I had accomplished my business at Golden Oldie Rentals quickly, so I had plenty of time to circle the block.

Mike the car rental clerk had come through for me, although his inspection of Deke Brenner's pickup turned up nothing—no camera and unfortunately no front-end damage. A big dent in the front fender with plenty of yellow paint chips traceable to my sister's VW would have been nice, but I was content to settle for the scrap of paper with Brenner's address I had stuffed safely in the pocket of my wool coat.

After several trips around the block, I parked illegally at the corner nearest the grand old mansion where Dr. Fielding leased space with a dozen other therapists. The three-story Victorian was painted the palest pearl gray and draped with lacy white filigree, like butter-cream trim on a wedding cake. I passed through a pair of Corinthian pillars stationed on either side of the black and gold double doors and let myself into a communal waiting room, where I flicked a switch to turn on a small red light inside Dr. Fielding's office and took a seat on a green leather wing-back chair. The room was softly lit by a matched set of Tiffany table lamps. Pachabel's Canon in D Major played over the intercom.

At precisely two o'clock Elizabeth Fielding appeared from behind her closed door, looking smart and proper in a navy gabardine suit and smelling faintly of herbal shampoo. Her chestnut hair was pulled back, as always, in a simple bun that showed off her delicate features and powdery complexion. She motioned me into her office and shut the door behind us. I settled into one of two antique easy chairs, and she took the other, facing me across a small rosewood coffee table. We stared at each other for a long moment, part of our routine, each waiting for the other to speak. As usual, I outlasted her.

"How have you been, Fran?" Her velvety voice was calm and caring.

"Well, for starters, my mother died three weeks ago."

She nodded and told me how sorry she was. Elizabeth Fielding knew better than anyone how much my mother had meant to me, better than Mom herself, I was afraid.

Before she could ask how I was coping, I blurted out my other news. "Sid was murdered a week ago and the police think I did it."

I had seen Dr. Fielding off and on since my father had left us twenty-two years before, but in all those years of divulging to her the most personal and at times traumatic events in my life, I had never seen her register such manifest emotion as she did at that moment. But it was sadness, not surprise, that I saw. She squeezed her eyes shut, managing a barely perceptible nod. For an instant she looked all of her fifty-some years, more like a middle-aged spinster than a successful psychologist. She reached out, as if to take my hand, but instead she went for a Waterford pitcher in the center of the table and filled a goblet for each of us.

A sip of ice water restored her professional demeanor and she nodded again, this time more forcefully. "I know," she said, cool as a frosted glass window in February.

"You know?"

"Peter called this morning. He wanted to—"

"Peter? Why would Peter call you?"

"As a matter of fact, I'm still trying to figure that out myself. It was an odd conversation. Obviously, he's very concerned about your emotional well-being, Fran, and his own, I'm afraid. He knows that my sole purpose is to protect your best interests, and, of course, because of our doctor-patient relationship—"

"You can't be called to testify against me in a trial."

"If it were to come to that."

"What did he say?"

"Not much. We didn't talk for more than a few minutes. I informed him immediately that you are my patient and I can't have conversations about you with anyone, including him, without advising you fully of what is discussed, and of course I can't divulge to him or anyone else any portion of any discussions between the two of us, or any analysis I may make of them."

"And?"

"He said he understood and agreed it wasn't appropriate for us to continue talking. He also told me, *off the record,* as he put it, that he loves you very much. He said he thinks you may be in trouble, but you won't admit it or ask for help."

"I'll admit I'm in trouble, all right, thanks to all the people like him who have jumped to the conclusion that I killed my sister. I feel like a rabbit trying to outrun a pack of hounds."

"Would you like to tell me about it?"

I would indeed. I gave her a thumbnail version of what had gone on the past week, including a summary of the evidence the police had against me. Then I took a long drink of water and told her about my bloodstained clothes, the brown button I had found out at Pirate Point, and the strange things I had said in my sleep.

I watched for her reaction, but she didn't so much as blink. When it was clear I had nothing more to add, she said calmly, "So you're thinking maybe you killed Sid yourself?"

I set my water on the coffee table before I spilled it. "The police think so. Peter does too."

A knot formed in my throat and swelled into a fist-size lump that threatened to cut off my air passages. Why hadn't I tried harder to get along with Sid over the years? Why hadn't I loved her more?

Dr. Fielding placed her goblet on the coffee table beside mine and pulled off her tortoiseshell glasses. "Would you like to know what I think?"

I nodded. It was highly unusual for her to divulge anything she was thinking.

"I think you're jumping to conclusions, just like Peter and the police. Don't do it, Fran. Let the others sell you short, but don't do it to yourself. The Fran Estes I know has brains, tenacious curiosity, and a keen sense of justice—and whether she admits it or not, the self-confidence to recognize those traits and the strength of character to stand up for herself. You haven't told me anything that makes me think you killed your sister. I suspect you know that."

I blinked back tears. A vote of confidence, at last. I forced a grim smile and changed the subject.

"My father showed up for Mom's funeral."

"How did it feel to see him again?"

"Fine at first. I was on sedatives. Barely noticed he was there. But he stayed on in California afterward, with his girlfriend. We got together for breakfast yesterday." I took a deep breath and exhaled slowly, keeping my eyes on the large oval-cut ruby glittering on the ring finger of her left hand. "I think Sid may have been blackmailing him."

"Oh?"

"What do you think of repressed memory syndrome, Doctor?"

Without batting an eye, she slipped her glasses on and said, "I think it occurs in rare cases. Extremely rare cases."

"Several months ago, almost a year now, Sid told me our father physically abused us when we were kids. She got into a fight with her boyfriend and had a flashback of Dad beating us."

I closed my eyes and slumped back in my chair. The afternoon of Sid's revelation was still fresh in my mind. It was shortly after I suggested she approach Dad for a loan. One day, totally out of the blue, she telephoned me at work to announce that she remembered him abusing us. She rattled off a list of horribles, the details of which I refused to let her describe. According to her account, the trouble had started when we were toddlers, probably two years old. It tapered off when we started kindergarten and stopped completely by the time we were in second grade.

Repressed memory syndrome, the latest legal fad. I assumed Sid had read about it in the paper, and suddenly, lo and behold, she had it herself.

She wanted me to corroborate her claims, but I couldn't. I had no recollection of being beaten and no desire to try to dredge something up,
especially with Mom so sick. That had been that. She had been annoyed
with me for not cooperating, but she dropped it, and I had been relatively
successful at banishing the whole dreadful business from my mind. I
didn't like to think about my father anyway, abuse or no.

I spilled out my story through a stream of tears. When I finished, Dr.
Fielding handed me a tissue and waited for me to blow my nose.

''Do you share any of Sid's memories?'' she asked softly.

I resisted the urge to respond with a knee-jerk no, but by the time I
was ready to answer, I couldn't. I stared mutely into the lenses of her
glasses, gripped by the reflection of my father's cold eyes staring back
at me. Instinctively, my hands rose to my burning cheeks. I could still
feel the sting of his palm.

16

I squealed up to the curb at the main entrance to the law school, abandoned the Jeep in a red zone, and sprinted for the registrar's office. According to the clock on the wall inside the clear glass door, it was two minutes after five. The door was locked and the office was dark.

I wandered back outside and plopped down on the cold concrete steps, elbows on my knees, chin in my palms, like a kid whose scoop of orange sherbet has toppled off its cone. From my perch at the top of the stairs I searched the crowded sidewalk, but it was dark out now. I couldn't find a single person I recognized, just lots of vague faces that mostly seemed too young to be in law school. I was invisible above them, an anonymous figure huddled on the stairs.

After ten minutes I relocated to a park bench in the grassy quadrangle across the street from the law school. I sat there, waiting and watching, hoping my friend and former classmate Barry Stein still went for his daily run before dinner. I was about to give up when I saw Barry's powerful frame loping toward me. I jumped up to intercept him. He was drenched in sweat and smelling of overtaxed deodorant.

Like me, Barry was older than most of the other law students, having gone back to school in his thirties; in fact, that's probably why we became such good friends. He had been number one in our class after our first year, and although he wouldn't acknowledge it, I knew he'd been number one after his second year too. He was an all-American Chicago boy with a mop of curly brown hair and a goofy smile that had no business on the face of someone so brilliant. His glittery brown eyes were flecked with yellow, and one was noticeably larger than the other. He had a roller-coaster nose that you'd swear had been broken more than the single time he remembered and a wide gap between his chipped front teeth. I found him incredibly, breathtakingly sexy.

He held me close for a long moment, squeezing so tight I could feel his heart pounding against the side of my head. When he released me, I was wet from his sweat and hot from the feel of his hard body pressing against mine. I felt color fill my cheeks, betraying the exhilaration of forbidden sensations.

"If you don't mind a sweaty bod in that fancy vehicle of yours, you can take me home and stay for dinner," he said when I told him I would be in the city that night with no plans for the evening. I had a room booked at the Airport Budget Inn and a ticket for an eight o'clock flight to Los Angeles the next morning, but no thought about what to do for dinner.

We climbed into the Jeep and pulled out of the parking lot, heading toward the one-bedroom flat on Twin Peaks where Barry lived with his wife, Sheila. When we came to the first corner I flipped on the blinker to turn left, but he told me to keep going straight.

"Where are we heading? You guys move?"

He paused before answering. "One of us did."

I veered into the parking lane and stopped just short of plowing into a pedestrian. "What happened?"

"Two years of law school was more than our marriage could handle, I guess. I clerked for Davis & Allen in Chicago last summer. Second week of August, Sheila informed me she wasn't coming back to San Francisco."

"But you're still together. I mean, you'll get back together when you graduate and move back to Chicago, right?"

"I'm afraid not. Sheila had an affair with the partner I was assigned to. They're living together now."

"Oh, Bear." I took hold of his hand. "What can I say?"

"You can start with, life goes on. Because it does." He squeezed my hand and laughed. "Hell, it hasn't been five months yet, and I'm already over the suicidal phase."

"Suicidal phase?" I blinked back a sudden threat of tears. Barry Stein, of all people, did not deserve such problems.

"That was a joke, Frankfurter. I see you still have your keen sense of humor."

"And yours is still as sick. Seriously, are you okay, Barry?"

"I'm fine. I wouldn't have wanted Sheila to stay with me if she didn't love me." He slid his hand out of my grip and placed it lightly on my shoulder, almost touching the back of my neck. "The last thing any man wants is to be with a woman who's in love with someone else." He was smiling, but his voice was low and serious. His eyes seemed to be saying more than his words.

Uncertain how to respond, I checked for traffic in the rearview mirror and pulled back into the street.

He gave my shoulder a quick pat and pulled his hand away. "I'm being selfish. You're the one who's been through some real shit lately, and here we are talking about my failed love life."

"I don't want to talk about me."

He nodded. "I'll be here when you do."

Barry juggled two bags of Chinese takeout and shoved open the door to his apartment. "Welcome to the bachelor pad," he said as he stepped aside so I could enter first. "You're my first guest."

I looked in and laughed. I had been expecting black Naugahyde and chrome with dim lighting, or maybe a few pieces of broken-down furniture drowning in empty Coke cans and pizza boxes, but the apartment was neat and bright and decorated in the lavender chintz furniture Barry had shared with Sheila. "Bachelor pad? Very macho, Bear."

"Sheila didn't take time to pack."

I wandered into the tiny kitchen and opened a bottle of Chianti while he showered and changed. The room looked so perfectly tidy I couldn't resist a peek in the refrigerator. As I expected, it was well stocked with beverages, but that was about it.

"I see you spend a lot of time here," I told him when he reappeared, looking clean and wholesome and very sexy in loose-fitting Levi's and a blue and white striped oxford shirt. "You've got everything you need: Heineken, Coke, orange juice, and Gatorade. And, in case you're hungry, you've got ketchup, mayo, and three kinds of mustard. Very impressive, Barry. I didn't realize you were such a gourmet."

"Hey, little shit, are you going to pour that wine, or not?" He handed me two fancy wineglasses. More souvenirs of Sheila, no doubt.

I gave him back a full glass and touched mine to his. They resonated with the ping of fine crystal. Sheila had good taste. "Cheers."

"Cheers, Frankie. Here's to . . ." He paused. "Here's to good friends."
I took a sip and smiled. "To good friends."
"Come with me. I want to show you something. Bring your wine."
He took my hand and led me to a small deck off his bedroom. The view back to the city sparkled with a million tiny lights.
"Oh, Bear. It's gorgeous. Like a carnival."
We stood there for several minutes, enjoying the view in compatible silence. The night was breezy and cool, and we weren't wearing jackets, so Barry put his arm around my shoulders and pulled me close to him. I wanted to put my arm around him too, but I didn't dare.
Later we ate kung pao chicken and potstickers straight from the take-out containers. We talked about my mother's death and about Barry's father, who had died when he was in high school. We spoke of our grief, but also of the healing process and of happy memories. I told him how Mom and I used to go hiking together in the woods behind our house in search of wildflowers to photograph, and how she'd known the names of all the birds and could find them for me in the thick old Audubon book she kept on the nightstand beside her bed. Barry told me about sunny spring days when his dad would call his school principal to say he was sick so they could go fishing or watch the Cubs play at Wrigley Field.
How long had it been since I had laughed out loud as I did when Barry told a joke? I couldn't remember the last time I had felt so relaxed or so comfortable in the company of a man, Peter included. Like it or not, and I didn't, I was as attracted to Barry as ever, only now I suspected it might be dangerous to admit it, even to myself. He no longer wore a protective shield on the ring finger of his left hand.
After dinner, feeling guilty and a little drunk, I called Peter to tell him I wouldn't be home until the following evening. I said I was spending the night at the Steins' and getting together with other law school friends the next day. I did not mention that Barry was the only Stein living at the Steins' these days.
Peter was happy to hear I was having a good time and glad to have me extend my trip an extra day, but he fell silent when I asked if anything was up at home. I could see him sitting at the kitchen table with the phone balanced between his ear and shoulder. The faint pop of a cracking knuckle annoyed me, even 150 miles away.
"Peter?"
"I wasn't going to mention this, but I suppose I should tell you."
"What? What's happened?" I felt Barry's curious eyes and wished I could ask him to leave the room.

"It's Harlan Fry and Andy Saybrook. They came by the house this afternoon, looking for you."

"What now?"

"They got back preliminary results from the autopsy. Totally inconclusive. The shark mauled her so bad the coroner couldn't tell what happened before that."

"No sign she was raped?"

"They didn't find any semen, but the coroner didn't completely rule out a sexual attack. He just couldn't tell one way or the other."

"Is that it?"

"No. They got back your blood test too. The blood in the Jeep was Sid's, not yours. They say they can tell the difference."

"I don't believe it. They must be trying to trick me." I waited for him to agree, but all I heard was another knuckle cracking. "Our blood matches, Peter. I know that for a fact."

"Well, Harlan doesn't agree."

I squeezed the phone and pressed it hard against my ear. *Fuck Harlan.* "Thanks for the support, Peter." I hung up before we could get into an argument.

Barry slid up beside me on the couch and took my hand when I set down the receiver. "You okay, Frankfurter?"

"I'm fine, thanks. Just tired."

He nodded and smiled sadly. "Let's get you to bed then."

I tried to insist that I would stay at the motel out by the airport, but he wouldn't hear of it.

"You're staying right here, Frankie. It won't take you more than an extra fifteen minutes to get to your flight. The bed's comfortable, the coffee's free, and it's bad karma to waste a parking spot right in front of the building." Without waiting for my response, he headed for the linen closet and pulled out fresh sheets. "You, my dear, are sleeping in my bed, and I'm taking the couch. I'll even let you use my favorite pillow. And I promise, no matter how much I want to, I won't climb in with you. You can lock the door."

I agreed to stay and I didn't lock the door. If Barry had climbed in with me, I don't think I would have sent him away.

17

"Hey, girl! Hellooo. Over here."

I scanned the crowd milling around the Southwest Airlines baggage carousel, searching for . . . what? I wasn't quite sure. There could be no mistaking Sunshine Scott's voice, but I had no idea what she looked like.

"Hey, Fran, hon! It's me, Sunny."

I saw her waving at me from the other side of the carousel. Whatever I might have expected, it sure wasn't what I got. Sunshine was a bone-thin black woman with ebony skin and a shaved head covered with black fuzz. She was incredibly tall, probably close to six feet without shoes and four inches more in her outrageous black patent-leather spike-heeled sandals. She wore a black leather jacket and matching skintight cigarette pants. Her long skinny legs looked like black lacquer chopsticks as she clickity-clicked toward me across the slick tile floor and swept me into her wide wingspan.

"Lordy, Lordy. If I didn't know better, I'd say you were the girl herself. Goddamn spittin' image." She held me at arm's length and examined me through teary eyes.

I stared back at her, awestruck. Her full lips were the color of red wine, the same shade as her inch-long nails, which were digging into my arms. She smelled of spicy oriental perfume and new leather. She was gorgeous in a wild exotic way, although at close range I could see she wasn't exactly a youngster, probably the other side of forty.

She snapped up my carryall with one hand and kept hold of my arm with the other, not waiting for a response. "C'mon. I'm double parked."

We headed for a gleaming black Porsche Carrera that was blocking the crosswalk immediately outside the automatic double doors. The license plate said HOT 1. A grim-faced cop was scribbling a ticket.

"Watch this," she said under her breath as she passed me back my carryall, eyes focused on her prey like a hawk soaring over a field mouse. She sauntered over to the cop and reached for his pen with a red-clawed hand. He jerked away without looking at her, but she slid in closer, into his peripheral vision. He kept his eyes fixed on his ticket pad, but I saw them widen. She said something I didn't hear and he started to blush, then to smile. A minute later we were on our way. No ticket, not even a warning.

Sunshine drove like Mario Andretti, which by now I was expecting. When she noticed me gripping my seat belt, she reached over to pat my leg. "Don't worry, hon. This car handles best at high speeds."

I managed a meek smile and gradually let go, first of the seat belt, then of my fear. Considering the Porsche's speedometer registered more than eighty, it felt as if we were barely moving. The car's solid mass smoothed out the rough spots in the highway until they were no more than quiet clicks.

I settled into the fake leopard skin that covered the contoured bucket seat and drifted off to semiconsciousness, tranquilized by the warm wind whipping my face from the open sunroof. I hadn't slept much the night before at Barry Stein's, partly because I was in his bed and he was just beyond the closed door in the living room, and partly because I never slept much anymore, not since Sid's death. My adrenaline had sustained me so far, but I wondered how much longer I could operate on just a few hours of sleep a night. The vicious combination of insomnia and nagging self-doubt was wearing me down.

We flew along in comfortable silence until the sound of squealing tires brought me back to L.A. I grabbed for the dashboard with one hand and the edge of the seat with the other. We were off the expressway now, drawing stares as we careened through the one-way streets of a dreary residential neighborhood. Sunshine appeared not to notice the attention. No doubt she was used to it.

She glanced over at me like a mother with a restless child. "Almost there, hon. You doing okay?"

I nodded.

She turned her eyes back to the road and said, "Want to talk about it? Sometimes it helps to say what's on your mind."

I shook my head and peeled my fingers from the dash. I was beginning to appreciate this woman. We hadn't gotten off to a great start in our first telephone conversation three days ago, but she had been a different person when I called back the next afternoon to tell her I was coming to Los Angeles. Deke Brenner still hadn't turned up, she told me, and she was starting to wonder herself what was going on. Provided I didn't get the cops involved, she would be willing to help me find him. I was surprised by the turnaround, but happy to have an ally.

We jerked to a stop in front of a less-than-deluxe, four-story apartment building in the middle of a block of similar nondescript buildings. Sunshine swung her door open and popped her spider legs out of the car. "Here we are. Home sweet home."

The building had been built in the 1960s and had all the character of the era—big-box architecture with no detail, metal frame windows, and a shade of paint straight from a first-grader's crayon box, in this case classic carnation pink. The yard was covered over with weed-infested wood chips, but it boasted two proud palms nearly three stories tall. Overall, the effect wasn't impressive, but I had seen worse. In fact, I had expected worse.

I took two steps for each one of Sunshine's as I followed her along the cracked cement sidewalk. When we moved into the cool gray shadow of the building a creeping melancholy began to fill my chest. My twin sister had lived at this place for seven years. It took her death to bring me here for a visit.

Sunshine unlocked the door and stepped aside. "This is it. Brace yourself."

I pushed the door open and peered inside, reluctant to cross the threshold. The air was warm and stuffy and stank of stale cigarettes and incense. Ribbons of late-morning sun slipped through cracks in the crooked aluminum blinds, providing just enough illumination for me to get the rough layout of the studio apartment.

The room was sparsely furnished and messy. On first glance, nothing about it felt familiar. Other than the smell of cigarettes, nothing reminded me of Sid. I stood in the doorway looking in, wishing I could turn away.

Sunshine's throaty laugh helped, but not much. "Go on, hon. I'm right behind you. Mr. Soo'll be wanting his breakfast."

From the sound of the bird's squawks, I guessed she was right. I took a tentative step forward and found the light switch.

Sunshine marched to the center of the room and pulled me with her. "Why don't you open a window? Clear out some of this stinking smoke. You'd think with Sid gone now almost three weeks it'd start to fade."

When I didn't move, she draped a bony arm across my shoulders and gave me a moment to survey the room in silence. There wasn't much to it. A mattress with a jumble of white sheets—no box spring or bed frame—a small chest of drawers, a card table with four folding chairs, three vinyl-covered beanbags. That was the extent of the furnishings, except for a pair of shaggy green ferns and Mr. Soo's ornate brass bird-cage, which seemed wildly out of place in the bleak apartment.

"Your sister wasn't much of an interior decorator," Sunshine said.

I tried to laugh but nothing came out. "It hardly looks like she was living here."

"Oh, she was living here, all right." Sunshine pulled her arm off my shoulders so I wouldn't feel her shudder. "Look at this." In three long-legged steps she crossed the room and opened a closet door. Inside were Sid's clothes, lots of black and denim and batik. On the floor was a wooden crate the size of a miniature refrigerator partially hidden beneath a square of black velvet. Sunshine flipped up the velvet and motioned to me to look inside, but her solemn expression warned me I was not going to like what I saw.

The crate was heaped full of what at first looked like a bunch of junk. It took me a moment to see that the junk consisted exclusively of stubby black candles and crosses, dozens of each.

In what felt like slow motion, I dropped to my knees on the soiled beige carpet and pulled off the velvet drape. I reached into the crate and picked out a fake wooden cross about the size of my hand with a painted plastic Jesus. It was missing half of its crossbar, which I found nearby on the top of the pile. I joined the two parts like pieces of a puzzle. They fit together perfectly, except that Jesus' right arm had broken off the smaller piece. I sifted around in the crate but didn't find the arm. What I did find was that all the crosses were broken. And all the little Jesuses were missing limbs.

After a moment I felt Sunshine gently pulling me away from the crate. "C'mon back from there, hon. I don't know that you want to be touching that stuff."

"What is all this?"

She shook her head slowly. "That sister of yours had some real weird interests, you know?" She headed across the room to the window. "Put that stuff back in the box and cover it up. We've got other business here today."

She pulled up the ratty metal blinds and struggled with the window. I stayed where I was, squinting at her lean black figure silhouetted against the glass.

The window slid up with a screech and Sunshine turned back to me, wiping dust off her hands. "Now then. Let's get down to it, shall we?" She stepped over to the birdcage and reached inside for two small plastic dishes.

"Want a doobie?"

I spun around at the question. It was Mr. Soo asking, not Sunshine. I didn't know birds, but I figured he was a parrot. Electric green body with bright red, yellow, and blue trim. I forced myself up off my knees, draped the black velvet over the crate, and went to have a look.

He gazed back at me and cocked his head. "Want a doobie? Want a doobie?"

"Shut up or I'll stuff you with Styrofoam and hang you on the wall," Sunshine shouted from the kitchen where she was rinsing his water dish.

When she placed the fresh water in his cage he pounced on it, as much as a large bird in a small cage can pounce. She nearly knocked him off his perch when she replaced his food dish, now filled with tiny brown seeds.

"Want a fuck?" he asked her.

My laughter broke the spooky spell of the apartment. "That's Sid's bird all right." I took a deep breath of musty air and headed for the chest of drawers. "Let's get through this and then go find Deke Brenner. I already have his address, so we don't need to look for that here."

Sunshine latched the tiny brass door of Mr. Soo's cage and came over to join me. "You got his address? How?" Her surprised voice was an octave lower than usual.

"Long story." I figured I could tell her about the Oceanside Motel and Golden Oldie Rentals later. "He lives at 5801 South Maxwell Street. Know where that is?"

"Maxwell's a ways from here. Twenty-minute drive, at least. It's not a stellar neighborhood, not the kind of place a girl like you belongs." She paused to let me consider the implications of heading into a tough L.A. neighborhood to track down the man I suspected of murdering my sister. "D.B. can be a rough character, Fran. You sure you want to be going after him like that? I mean, he'll probably show up on his own eventually, and when he does I can give him a message to call you."

I pulled the top drawer out of the dresser and dumped its contents onto the floor. "Seeing Deke is the whole reason I came down here, Sunny; I've got to talk to him, with your help or without it." I could feel her eyes drilling me in the back, but I didn't turn around. After a minute she went to work on the second drawer, leaving me to wonder if she would call my bluff. There was no way in hell I would head out after Brenner without her, not after what she'd just told me.

"It don't feel right, going through someone's stuff like this," she said finally, breaking an increasingly awkward silence. "You sure you want me doing this? I mean, I ain't family or anything."

"You were Sid's friend, Sunny. That's as good as family."

She grunted. "I tried, you know? I thought the girl could use a friend, a *female* friend. It ain't healthy hanging out alone or with men all the time. But Sid wasn't big on the buddy thing, you know?"

"I know. She wasn't big on the sister thing either."

We found little of note in Sid's dresser, just underwear, makeup, and assorted odds and ends, until I emptied the bottom drawer. It contained a few old issues of *Vogue,* a science fiction novel, and a photograph album I had given her years ago for Christmas. She had filled it with pictures of the two of us.

With shaking hands, I dropped the album into my carryall and staggered into the kitchenette to splash cold water on my face.

Sunshine watched me from the floor. "You okay, hon?"

"I'm fine. It's just . . . difficult."

"You want to go to my place and lie down for a while? It's nicer over there, and it doesn't stink of cigarettes."

"No. I want to finish here and then go to Deke's. I'm hoping you'll come with me, Sunny. Otherwise I'll have to rent a car so I can go on my own."

She didn't respond. She had to know I wouldn't really go without her. "How about it?"

She reached for her shoulder bag, pulled out a cellular phone, and dialed. I waited and listened, holding my breath and wondering if she was calling Hertz.

"Reginald? It's Sunny. . . . At Sid LaSalle's apartment with Sid's sister. She's down here from up north to go through Sid's things. . . . Not as far as I can tell. . . . Well, Fran here wants to pay a visit to Deke

Brenner, see if he knows anything about what happened to her sister. . . . You got it. . . . Could you? Maybe it's a good time to settle up with the guy." She held the phone to her chest and turned to me. "Give me that address again." I told her and she went back to the phone. "It's 5801 South Maxwell. . . . Yeah. . . . Let's see. . . ." She looked at her watch and paused to calculate. "How about three o'clock? . . . Hey, Reginald? . . . You're the best."

She folded the little phone and dropped it into her bag. "We're all set," she said to me. "I got a friend who'll meet us there, in case D.B.'s not ecstatic to see us. We've got time to finish up here and grab something to eat before heading over."

I grinned at her. "Hey, Sunny?"

"What?"

"You're the best."

She didn't laugh. She didn't even smile. "You may not be saying that later, girl. Reginald can only do so much."

I nodded and leaned back against the kitchen counter. "Well, I appreciate it."

"Yeah, that's great. Now, if you're done in here, I'm starving."

"Ten minutes more. Help me check the kitchen."

We rummaged through the cupboards but found nothing interesting until I came upon a small plastic bag tucked away behind a stack of chipped ceramic plates. It was empty except for a trace of white powder. With it were a square, frameless mirror and a package of razor blades.

I held them up for Sunshine to see. "Look."

"Flush it down the toilet," she said, turning away. "I ain't never used the stuff and I don't need the temptation to start now. I don't think you better have it either."

"There's nothing to flush. The bag's empty." I dropped it into the garbage can and continued my search.

After the kitchen, we went through the bathroom and a small coat closet. We found no sign of Deke Brenner or of any other male companion. In fact, we found very little evidence of Sid herself, not even the one thing I was hoping we would find—an engraved silver cigarette case our maternal grandfather had given her the year before he died. Because it had been special to Sid, it was the one keepsake I wanted to remember her by.

When we'd exhausted the possibilities, I collapsed into one of the bean bags and stared across the mess at Sunshine. "Jesus. Sid lived here for seven years, and this is all she accumulated?"

"She used to have more. There was an iron and glass dinette and a fancy stereo, but she got rid of those."

"When?"

"Who knows? I didn't spend much time in this place. Sometime within the past year, I'd say."

Suddenly the emptiness of my sister's apartment made sense. "Sid needed money. She must have started selling off her belongings." I wondered if Dad had come up with less than the full fifty grand. "Somebody probably gave her a lousy twenty bucks for a silver cigarette case worth hundreds. It was the one thing that meant something to her, Sunny—" My voice cracked. "Shit. Let's get out of here."

As we prepared to leave, Mr. Soo realized he was about to be left alone again. "Want a doobie?" he asked. I sensed a tinge of desperation in his squawk. "Want a doobie? Want a fuck?"

Sunshine went over to his cage and spoke to him softly in her deep soulful voice. "No we don't want a doobie and we don't want a fuck, you foul-mouthed piece of shit. But I am thinking of having poultry for dinner tonight. Mashed potatoes and fried parrot. You're invited."

Before we left she refilled his water dish and scattered a handful of sunflower seeds on the bottom of the cage. I took one last look and closed the door behind us.

The colorful stucco of Sid's middle-class neighborhood gave way to gray concrete and peeling paint as we drove toward Deke Brenner's South Maxwell address. Although it was barely two-thirty, the weak early-winter sun had already begun to fade and a chill had taken hold. The streets were narrower here than in Sid's neighborhood, the buildings shabbier, and the smell of exhaust stronger. There was a liquor store or gas station, or both, on nearly every corner. None of the Hollywood glitz I naively associated with Los Angeles.

"Like I said, D.B. don't live in the classiest part of town," Sunshine said as she downshifted and squealed onto Maxwell Street three blocks from the address I had gotten at Golden Oldie Rentals. It occurred to me that for someone who claimed not to know where she was going, she had done a fine job of driving straight to the right place.

When we came to Brenner's block, she slowed to within the speed limit for the first time since I had been in the car with her. We rolled to a stop in front of a dilapidated split-level with an exposed cinder-block foundation and dirty green siding. The number 5801 was painted on the curb. I made no move to get out of the car.

Brenner's house had a dark lonely look to it, like the low-end vacation rentals in Milton after the summer people have gone home. The oil-stained driveway was empty, and the shades were pulled down tight. The rotting wood porch was bare.

I wiped my sweaty palms on my slacks and silently cursed Sunshine for driving so fast. Reginald wasn't due for another fifteen minutes. "Looks like a wasted trip, Sunny. The place is deserted."

She pressed a button and the Porsche's sunroof slid shut with a hum and a thud. "I don't think it's deserted, hon. That heap of scrap metal parked across the street belongs to D.B."

I followed her eyes to a rundown blue pickup. Heap of scrap metal was a good description. It looked worse than the junkers at Golden Oldie Rentals.

By the time I turned back, Sunshine had gotten out of the car and was waiting for me on the sidewalk. I leaned into the Porsche's heavy leather-clad door, pushed it open, and climbed out, feeling vulnerable outside our big black tank. As we approached the house I took her arm to steady myself. Sunshine knew Brenner, after all, and she should have known if there was anything to be afraid of. She also knew Reginald and hopefully was justified in depending on him to back us up.

We rang the doorbell and waited, but no one came. Nor was there any sign of Reginald. We rang twice more, but still there was no response.

I was a little disappointed but more than a little relieved. I turned to go. "Not home."

Sunshine opened the screen and banged on the door with her fist. "Hold on. He's probably sleeping."

She was right. Seconds later we heard a muffled shout from inside. "Yeah? Who's there?" Even distorted by sleep, it was recognizable as the high-pitched voice I had heard nine days ago at the MiniMart.

Sunshine nodded and mouthed that it was him. "D.B.? It's Sunny Scott. Open the door."

I heard a chain rattle and a lock click. Suddenly we were face-to-face with the sleepy blond brute himself, the guy who more than likely had killed my sister and who probably wouldn't hesitate to do the same to me should he determine it necessary. Deke Brenner was a large man, more so than I remembered from our brief meeting in the MiniMart or from Harlan Fry's photograph. He was as tall as Sunshine in her four-inch heels and probably twice her weight. He had the sun-tanned skin and bleached blond hair of a beach bum, and the haunting silver-gray eyes I remembered. Even puffy with sleep, they were beautiful. He wore dirty blue jeans and a faded gray sweatshirt that matched his eyes.

He yawned and reached out to Sunny, but he jerked back when he noticed me cowering behind her. "Jesus. You're not—who the hell are you? What's going on?" He looked like he'd seen a ghost. The ghost of his dead girlfriend.

"No, I'm not Sid," I volunteered. "I'm her twin sister." I stuck out my hand, but he didn't take it. I felt a little better now. He seemed too groggy to be dangerous. I took a step toward him and could smell the pot. He reeked of it.

"What the hell are you doing here?"

"You know Sid is dead?"

"What? Dead? God, what happened?" He stuttered the obligatory exclamation, but I could tell he was more surprised by my presence on his doorstep than by the news of Sid's death. His healthy brown complexion had taken on a distinctly unhealthy florid undertone.

"That's what we're here to talk about, Deke. I'm hoping you can help."

Without looking at Sunshine, I could tell she was glaring at me. She stepped between Brenner and me and placed a hand on each of our shoulders. "Let's start with a proper introduction, shall we? D.B., this is Fran Estes, Sid's twin sister. Fran, this is Sid's friend Deke Brenner." She said it like a hostess introducing two guests at a cocktail party. "D.B., we have bad news, like Fran said. Sid's been killed. It happened last week up north. Her car went over a cliff. Fran came down to L.A. to see if she can get some information about what might have happened. Since you and Sid were close, she hoped you'd be kind enough to talk to her, in case you have any ideas that could be helpful."

"Sid's dead? Holy shit."

I averted my eyes so he wouldn't see the disgust.

"Yes, she's dead," Sunshine said. "It's a shock to us all, D.B. Can Fran and I come in to talk about it?" The tone of her voice left no doubt about the nature of our visit. This was to be a business meeting. No sentimentality would be tolerated.

Brenner stepped aside to let us enter, but there was no way in hell I was going into an empty house with the man I suspected of murdering my sister. I grabbed the back of Sunshine's jacket as she moved toward the door. "You know, guys, really, that's okay. I don't want to intrude. Let's just talk out here on the porch, outside." We weren't particularly safe on the porch either, I knew, but at least there would be the comfort of an occasional passerby—and Reginald, if he ever bothered to show up.

Sunshine shot me a strange look and zipped her leather jacket. "Up to you, hon. Guess you northerners like the cold."

I nodded.

Brenner jumped to the defensive immediately, as I expected he would. "I hadn't seen Sid in weeks, you know? I knew she was out of town, but I didn't even know where she was. We weren't going out anymore. We were just friends, you know?"

I figured I should play it safe and go along with his innocent act, so I smiled at him and nodded sadly. "I understand. But I know you meant a lot to Sid. I thought you might know if she was in trouble."

"Trouble? What kind of trouble?" He wagged his head, trying to look confused. All he looked was guilty.

I scrambled for a better leading question, something to warm him up, but all I could do was stare at his shining silver eyes and wonder if I was standing two feet from a cold-blooded killer. He looked as nervous as I was, maybe more. Out of the corner of my eye I saw Sunshine watching us. Her face was fixed in a tense tight-lipped smile.

Brenner's eyes locked on mine and his mouth dropped open to speak. For a fleeting instant I thought he was going to open up, but instead he let loose a barrage of obscenities and lurched toward me.

I jerked away from Brenner reflexively, but before my flustered brain could transmit a flee signal, a car door slammed in the street behind us. I turned to look.

Leaning against the driver's door of a pristine white Jaguar sedan with his arms folded casually across his chest, was a scrawny black man in a double-breasted business suit the color of French's mustard. This would be Reginald, our bodyguard. I had expected someone more menacing, someone larger at least.

Brenner, however, saw him and froze. "What's he doing here?"

Sunny laughed. "What do you think, man?"

"First Sid's sister and now your fucking pimp? You planning a party?" He bared his teeth in a poor attempt at a grin.

"Fuck you."

While they sparred, I took a closer look at Reginald. What the man lacked in size he made up for in style. He wore his yellow suit with a black V-necked sweater and a thick gold chain. His shoes were so shiny they might have been patent leather.

"So, Deke," I said with a newfound confidence. "Where were we?"

"What do you want from me?"

"First of all, I want the truth. You knew Sid was dead. You were in Black Bay when it happened." I had planned to be a bit more delicate, but the words spilled out.

"I was not," he squeaked.

"No? Let me tell you what I think. I think you flew into San Francisco a week ago last Sunday and rented a pickup out by the airport. Then you drove to Black Bay and stopped at a convenience store to buy cigarettes and to ask about a cheap place to spend the night."

He was breathing hard now and his eyes had grown wide with panic, like a deer caught in the headlights of an oncoming truck.

"Remember me? My husband and I sent you up the road to Orcas Cove, where you spent the night Sunday and again Monday, the night of Sid's death. Then Tuesday you drove back to San Francisco, returned the pickup, and flew home. The only open issue is what you were doing Monday night when my sister was killed."

"I didn't do it. I swear I don't know anything about that."

"Then why did you go to Black Bay? Sunny said you had unfinished business with Sid."

He shot Sunshine a look of desperation, but she didn't step up to defend him.

"What business, Deke?"

Still no response.

"Something worth killing her over?"

His silver eyes narrowed to steely slits. "No way, bitch. I told you I didn't kill her."

I made a point of glancing back at the street, as much for Brenner's benefit as for my own. Reginald hadn't moved. I turned sideways so I could keep him in my peripheral vision. "What business did you have with her, then?"

"Fuck you."

"You came to Black Bay for a reason, Deke. If it wasn't to kill Sid, what was it? Drugs?"

He didn't answer.

"That's it, isn't it? Drugs."

After a long silent minute the corners of his lips quivered upward and his eyes flickered. I got the impression he was holding back a smirk, but when he finally met my eye he looked contrite. In a barely audible voice he said, "We got in over our heads, or Sid did anyway. I was trying to help her, and now I'm in it too." He paused, either to make up the rest of his story or because he was reluctant to tell it, I couldn't say which. "It started more than a year ago. Sid met this guy who wanted heroin, lots of it, and I knew a source, so she agreed to be a go-between. It was a big deal."

"How big?"

"Total price was seventy-five thousand. Sid got to keep three grand for her fee. Twenty-five hundred for her, five hundred for me, for the referral. So she gets the stuff and delivers it to the buyer, this guy called Monty. He pays her the seventy-five grand and she turns over seventy-two to the supplier. . . ."

I was nodding along, but by now he needed no encouragement.

"Two days later Monty shows up wanting his money back. Turns out Sid hadn't inspected the stuff like she said she had. My guy told her it was real good shit, and she took his word for it, but the sonofabitch gave her nothing but worthless white powder. By the time she found out, he was long gone with the cash."

It struck me as uncharacteristic of Sid to have paid for the drugs without confirming she was getting the real thing. She wasn't the trusting type, nor did I think she was that stupid.

I looked over at Sunshine. "Any of this sound familiar?"

She rolled her eyes and shrugged.

"Okay, Deke. Let's assume it happened the way you say. Sid finds out she's been screwed. What'd she do about it?"

"What could she do? She gave back the three grand but that's all she had. Monty kept pushing her to fork up the rest, threatened to send one of his boys after her. That's when I got involved."

He paused for a breath and smiled to himself. I suspected he might be getting swept up in his imagination.

"I didn't do anything serious, just got on his ass for a while. Pulled up beside his Beemer on the freeway and nudged him a little bit, barely touched him. Then I shot out his tires. Really scared the fucker."

"You think it was Monty who killed Sid?"

He bobbed his head like a hungry child who's been offered a chocolate bar. "Yeah. It was him. It had to be."

"Do you know how to find him?"

"No way. The only time I saw him was that one time in the car. He came to see Sid about the money and I followed him from her place."

"When was that?"

"Last winter sometime, maybe February."

"That was nearly a year ago. Had he been in contact with Sid since?"

He shrugged. "She told him she needed time to come up with the cash, and eventually he just kind of disappeared. I figured he understood the situation. Fuck, that guy has so much dough, he didn't need another seventy-two grand from Sid."

"But she was trying to raise the money."

"I suppose. She quit talking about it, at least she quit talking to *me* about it. I figured she was planning to earn it back dealing. There was a time we were talking about going into business together—partners, you know? But lately she'd been giving me the cold shoulder, like she thought she was too good for me."

"What kind of business? Dealing heroin?"

"No. Cocaine eventually, but not at first. We didn't have the resources or the connections. Sid thought pot was a good way to get started. Wider appeal, cheaper product."

Marketing 101. My sister, the entrepreneur.

"She said the really prime stuff was from up north, the stuff she used to get in high school. So when she told me she was going to Black Bay, I figured it was to get a line on some product. She never said why she was going." He kicked at a rotten porch rail with his bare foot, hard enough so it had to hurt, but he didn't flinch. "Shit. She didn't tell me her mother died. I didn't find out about the funeral till I was already up there." He shook his head and looked at me like an abandoned puppy. "I'm real sorry about your ma, you know? My own mum died when I was twelve."

I forced my eyes away from his and focused on his filthy bare feet. The big toenail on his left foot was mottled green and black and seemed to be pulling off the toe. Despite his elaborate story, Deke Brenner quite possibly had killed Sid himself. I could always take pity on him later if he turned out to be innocent.

"I still don't understand why you came to Black Bay, Deke. For pot? Or for Sid?"

"Both, I guess, but I was nervous about showing up, you know? Sid was pretty firm about not wanting to see me anymore. She had a new guy."

"Really? Who?"

Brenner's jaw tightened. "Never saw him. She knew enough to keep him out of my reach."

"I saw him a couple times," Sunshine said, breaking her silence. "He used to come over to Sid's place when they first got together, must have been almost a year ago.''

Brenner looked like a man betrayed. ''Who is he?'' he asked.

''Don't know. She never introduced us. I thought maybe she was ashamed of him or something, cause she sure wasn't interested in showing him off. I passed them in the hall by her apartment once, but she acted like she didn't know me. One other time I saw them drive up in her car, but they just went on by without stopping. It wasn't until later I realized she was dating the guy. I asked her about him once, but she said he was nobody, so I dropped it. I ain't no busybody. Her life is her life, you know?''

''What'd he look like?'' Brenner asked.

She shrugged. ''Real average. Nothing like you. Kind of mousylike, nondescript.''

''Can you think of anything else you noticed about him?'' I asked. ''Or anything Sid might have mentioned?''

She shook her head. ''Hell, I haven't seen the guy for months. I doubt they were still together.''

I looked at Brenner. His face was drawn in a dark scowl. ''Do you think she was still seeing him?''

''If she wouldn't tell Sunny, she sure as shit wouldn't tell me. All I know is she wasn't seeing me.''

I pulled my jacket around me and stamped my feet to get the circulation going. The clouds had rolled in, and the wind had picked up, threatening a storm. ''You never said what you did in Black Bay, Deke. Tell us about the period between Monday morning and Tuesday afternoon.''

He tugged at the neck of his sweatshirt and glanced over at Sunny, who was glaring at him. ''I didn't kill her. I swear it.''

''Then you should be able to tell us what you did do. Let's start with Monday morning.''

He hesitated. I could see him casting about for a lie, but he wasn't quick enough to come up with anything. He let out a chestful of air and said, ''I found Sid. We talked.''

''You saw her?'' I was shocked Sid hadn't mentioned it to me that night at the Seahorse Pub. I wondered if maybe she had, but I'd been too drunk to remember.

''I found her at your house. We went for a walk. We argued. She told me to get lost. Simple as that.''

''You argued? Meaning you beat her up?'' I tried to remember whether Sid had any fresh-looking bruises that night at the Seahorse.

"Fuck you. She told me to get lost, and I did."

"But you didn't go home."

"I figured I might try to talk to her one more time. I thought maybe I could convince her to do some business, since we were both up there anyway, you know?"

"Pot business."

"Yeah. She gave me the name of a guy who supplies the local kids."

"Who is he?"

He shrugged. "I never got to talk to him. Some bartender. Hank something."

Woody Hanks. I wasn't surprised.

"Did you see Sid again before you left?"

"No. The next morning I went to look for her. I was on my way to your house, but the cops had the road blocked. I stopped to ask what the problem was. . . ."

"And, gee, what do you know? The problem was your ex-girlfriend, who blew you off the day before. Only now someone's blown *her* off, permanently. Surprise, surprise."

"Fuck you. You got the wrong guy, smart-ass. I didn't kill her. I was on my way to see her until the cops told me some babe in a VW convertible had gone over the edge."

"So you hightailed it out of there, like a man on the run."

He slumped back against the screen door. Its aluminum frame was battered and dented, as if someone had tried to kick it in, maybe the same person who had put the softball-size hole in the screen. I was wearing Brenner down. He was two inches shorter than he had been when we first arrived.

"I wasn't on the run," he said in a hoarse voice that threatened to crack. "Fuck, man, how would it look? Me coming up Sunday night and her getting killed the next day? Nobody knew I was there anyway, so I just went home."

"But you didn't go home. When the police came to find you, nobody knew where you were."

"I needed to chill. I stayed at a friend's place for a few days."

"Your friend can vouch for that?"

"He wasn't home."

"Did he know he had a houseguest?"

"No. I take care of his garden. I have a key to his carriage house, where I store my tools and shit. He travels a lot, so sometimes I stay there while he's out of town. He doesn't know, but he wouldn't care."

"So nobody can vouch for where you were?"

"No. What the fuck does it matter? Sid was already dead."

I didn't want to believe Brenner, but I felt myself wavering. I pulled a pen and a scrap of paper from my bag, jotted down my phone number, and pressed it into his hand. "I'm going to give you the benefit of the doubt, Deke. Will you call me if you think of anything that could be relevant?"

He didn't say he would call, but he stuffed the paper into his pocket. Without another word he disappeared into his house and locked the door behind him.

When Sunny and I turned to go, I was surprised to see Reginald strolling up the sidewalk toward us. Sunny grinned at him as we passed. "He's all yours, man," she said in a low voice. "Have at him."

18

I sat on a metal folding chair and stared at the linoleum floor in the public waiting room of the Black Bay police station. The room was drafty and dimly lit with cracked tan walls, gray metal furniture, and a hissing radiator that threatened to explode at any moment. It wasn't a place where the summer people spent much time. If it had been, it wouldn't look like it did, and they might install some ventilation so it didn't smell so bad.

I was alone except for a sallow-faced receptionist seated nearly out of sight behind a high counter. Her name, according to the plastic tag pinned to her beige cardigan, was Miss Beasley. She had yellow hair pulled back so tight it made her round head look like a giant onion. From my seat I could see only the very top of the onion, but I could hear her nimble fingers pecking away at a computer keyboard. When I arrived a few minutes earlier, Miss Beasley had taken down my name with icy efficiency and immediately resumed her work, too preoccupied to smile. To her credit, though, she did offer me coffee when she peered over the counter to inform me that Officers Fry and Saybrook were running late. I accepted the coffee and wrapped my hands around the steaming paper cup, but the smell of cigarettes and chemical cleaning compounds had made me queasy, so I didn't dare take a sip.

It was quarter after ten when Harlan stuck his head into the waiting room and summoned me with a curt nod. He said nothing, not so much as a simple "hello" or "good morning," let alone an apology for keeping me waiting almost an hour. I followed him down a narrow corridor, past a series of closed doors, into a windowless room the size of a walk-in closet. In the room were three folding chairs, a small rectangular table, and Andy Saybrook, who was sitting on one of the chairs, staring at a notebook lying open on the table. He gave no indication he noticed we had joined him.

Harlan sat beside Andy and directed me to take the chair across from them. He still had not said a word.

I looked from one to the other. "What's going on? Why the silent treatment? Am I under arrest or something?" I squeezed out a weak laugh that was intended to be sarcastic but fell pitifully short of the mark.

Andy looked up from his notebook, but he didn't meet my eye. "No, you're not under arrest," he said softly.

"Not yet," Harlan said.

"Is there more information from the autopsy? Peter told me the preliminary results were inconclusive."

Harlan shook his head. "Nothing else. They've wrapped it up. Fucking senile coroner didn't give us a goddamn thing."

"Then what's this about? Why am I here?"

"We have a few more questions for you, Mrs. Estes, and we'll get right down to it. We've got another appointment at eleven, so we'll have to skip the chitchat."

"By all means, let's skip the chitchat, Lieutenant. I assure you I'm just as anxious as you are to get this over with. Besides, I have some news for you. I found Sid's boyfriend."

"That's lovely, Mrs. Estes, but it'll have to wait."

"Did you hear what I said? I found Deke Brenner."

By way of response he pulled a worn three-by-five card from his breast pocket, cleared his throat, and read me my Miranda rights.

I listened in stunned silence. When he finished, I turned to Andy. "I thought I wasn't under arrest."

Harlan answered for him. "You're not. But you are a suspect, and as such you're entitled to know your rights. Now, if you're willing to talk to us without your attorney present, I'd like to begin."

He looked up, and I nodded. If things got bad I could always call Sam Goldman, but I hoped I'd be able to handle it on my own. I hated to have Sam see me in this situation.

Harlan held his hand out to Andy, who passed him a plain manila folder. He pulled out a single sheet of light blue paper and waved it under my nose. "The results of your blood test, Mrs. Estes. You failed."

"What do you mean, *failed*?" I looked at Andy. I knew he could feel my eyes pleading for support, but he didn't look up.

"Officer Saybrook can't help you, Mrs. Estes. The blood in your Jeep was your sister's. It matched the sample from the Band-Aid we found in her bathroom and it did *not* match the sample Dr. Neeley took from you last Friday."

"Something must be wrong with the test." My voice was shaking. "Identical twins have identical blood."

"Not when one of them's had hepatitis, they don't."

Shit.

He tilted his chair back, adding another black mark to the line of scratches that ran along the wall behind him. "Dr. Neeley was kind enough to assist us with the analysis. He pointed out that since your sister once had hepatitis, the hepatitis antibody was present in her blood—would be forever. You've never had hepatitis, so your blood doesn't contain the antibody. With a simple test he was able to distinguish each of the samples."

I glanced at Andy. He was sweating profusely and shifting in his chair as if he couldn't find a comfortable position.

Harlan grinned. He was in asshole heaven. "Let's move on. We're running short of time and we have another important matter to discuss with you."

He must have meant the royal "we," since Andy was taking no part in the discussion.

"What matter is that, Lieutenant?"

"A light brown blazer, a white blouse, and a pair of faded jeans. We found them at the town dump." He nodded at Andy. "Get the bag."

Without looking at me, Andy pushed up from the table and left the room. He returned seconds later, carrying a white plastic garbage bag.

"Recognize that bag?" Harlan asked.

I nodded.

"Tell me if the clothes inside it are yours."

I opened the bag and glanced inside. In a small voice I said, "They're mine."

"Those are the clothes you were wearing Monday night, the night your sister was killed?"

"Yes, but I didn't—"

"And they are the clothes you swore to us were soiled with vomit but not with blood?"

"Yes, but—"

"Take a closer look, Mrs. Estes." He picked up the bag and dumped the clothes onto the table, filling the little room with the stench of vomit.

Andy jerked back and buried his nose in his sleeve. Had I eaten breakfast that morning I would have lost it.

Only Harlan seemed impervious to the smell. He pulled my blazer to the top of the pile. "There's vomit. You were right about that. But there's blood too. And lookie here, there's even some soap. Looks like somebody tried to wash out the spots but didn't have a very good go of it." He pointed to a large reddish brown splotch on the front of the blazer. "This, Mrs. Estes, matches the stain on your car seat, which in turn matches the spot on the Band-Aid from your sister's bathroom. Looks like we've got us a trail of blood here. Your sister's blood."

I forced myself to look him in the eye. "I've already admitted that Sid and I got in a fight that night. I must have given her a bloody nose."

"And then you killed her."

"No."

I reached for the blazer, intending to flip it over to see if either of its sleeves was missing a button. My shaky hand came to rest on the collar, but before I got the nerve to take hold of the fabric Harlan scooped up the clothes and stuffed them back into the plastic bag.

He nodded at Andy, who pushed his chair back. "That will be all for now, Mrs. Estes."

Peter saw me coming and rushed through the MiniMart's double glass doors to greet me. He opened the door of the Jeep, and I stumbled into his outstretched arms. We stood clinging to each other in the parking lot, in full view of anyone who happened to drive by.

Eventually he broke away. "C'mon inside, Frannie. Tell me about it."

I climbed onto a stool behind the counter and watched him sell a six-pack of Foster's Lager to a couple of teenagers. They were obviously underage and belonged in school, probably junior high, but he hustled them on their way without bothering to check their fake ID.

He pulled up a stool beside me and rested his hand on my knee. "What happened, pal?"

"They found my clothes."

"I figured they would."

"The blood was Sid's."

He nodded.

"They read me my rights. It was an official interrogation this time."

He busied himself with the cash register tape while I summarized what I had just been through. I sensed he had come to the same conclusion as Harlan and was fighting off a wave of revulsion. "You going to work this afternoon?" he asked when I was finished.

"Yes. After I talk to Andy. He said he'd meet me for lunch and tell me where I stand."

"I think you should speak to Sam Goldman about legal representation. You need a lawyer, Frannie. You should have called him this morning when they read you your rights, before you answered their questions."

"Sam isn't a criminal lawyer, Peter. He negotiates contracts, not plea bargains."

"What about Bob Green?

"Bob doesn't do criminal work either." I thought of Barry Stein, who had applied for a job at the public defender's office in San Francisco. I wanted desperately to call Barry, to put myself in his care.

"Talk to them, Frannie. Maybe they can recommend someone. Promise me you'll talk to them."

I nodded and watched him try to straighten the candy and gum display on the counter. His shaking hands caused more of a mess than was there before he started.

"Peter? You okay?"

He gripped the edge of the counter to steady his hands.

"Peter?"

He took a deep breath and stared at the candy bars. "You were talking in your sleep again last night, Frannie. This morning, actually. At five-thirty when I got up for work."

"What did I say?" I didn't want to know.

"You said, *I should have done it differently. I should have done it in L.A.*" He looked straight at me, but he didn't seem to see me. His eyes were cold and hard, like green granite.

I felt my throat constricting. "Peter, I didn't kill her. You have to believe that. I don't know what I was talking about, but I didn't kill her."

Why the hell would I say such a thing? *I should have done it in L.A.* Done what? What should I have done in L.A.? I was afraid of the answer.

Andy and I had arranged to meet at Red's Fine Food, a dive coffee shop located a few blocks from the police station but not so close we would be likely to run into any of his fellow officers. Red's was a Black Bay tradition of sorts. It had been tucked away in a corrugated metal shack behind Barnes Auto Body for as long as I could remember, although until today I had never been inside. Now I knew why. From the look of the plates the waiter was bringing out to the handful of mangy lunchtime customers, it didn't seem like particularly "fine food" to me.

I'd gotten there ten minutes early and had taken a seat at the window to watch for Andy's Blazer. Fifteen minutes later he arrived on foot and peeked in the door. He wore mirror-lensed sunglasses and a Gore-Tex jacket with the collar turned up. After assuring himself that the joint was a safe spot for an anonymous rendezvous with a prime murder suspect, he slipped inside and closed the door softly behind him. Without looking in my direction he nodded to me to join him at a table near the back of the restaurant, away from the windows and most of the other diners.

If there was a sure way to attract the attention of Red's slacker clientele, Andy had certainly found it. At the table next to ours a greasy-looking kid in a fluorescent orange knit cap and a Barnes Auto Body windbreaker snickered to himself as he sopped up a puddle of yellow gravy with a slice of white bread.

Our waiter was a stocky fellow about five feet tall with a bandaged left hand and a mouthful of badly capped teeth. He tossed two menus onto the center of the table and pulled an order pad and pencil from the elastic waistband of his nylon sweatpants. I glanced at the plastic sheet and set it aside. When I looked up I caught him eyeing my wedding ring. He asked for our orders with a wink and a nod at Andy.

"Just hot tea with lemon," I told him. I hadn't come here to eat, and nothing I had seen so far had changed my mind.

Andy ordered a liverwurst sub with Swiss cheese, mayonnaise, onions, extra pickles, and a double order of German potato salad. When the waiter shuffled off with our orders, I leaned toward him and rested my elbows on the sticky tabletop. I was anxious to give my report on Deke Brenner without being overheard by the kid in the fluorescent orange cap, who had slid his chair a few feet closer to our table.

"Wait till you hear, Andy. I have new evidence. It changes everything." I spoke with an urgency I didn't feel. My excitement about tracing Brenner to Black Bay on the night of Sid's murder had been eroding steadily since Harlan produced my bloody blazer.

Andy pushed back from the table and folded his arms across his barrel chest. "New evidence? It better be good."

"Come on, Andy. What kind of crack is that?"

"Just that it better be good, is all. If it isn't, there's a fair chance you'll be arrested, possibly as early as Friday."

"Arrested?" I mouthed the words but no sound came out.

He read my lips and nodded. "That's right. We're meeting with Chief Carbone Friday afternoon to make a determination." He said it as calmly as if the *determination* was whether to invite me to serve on the organizing committee for the police officers' Christmas fund-raiser.

"Arrested?"

"Sorry, Fran. It's not my decision. I'm low man on the totem pole. It'll be the chief who makes the final call, and ultimately the D.A.'s decision whether to file charges."

"Based on what you and Harlan tell them."

"Based mostly on what Harlan tells them."

"And he's going to talk Carbone into arresting me." I flashed back to a picture of the police chief chasing after me out on the rocks at Pirate Point the prior week, how he had ruined his snazzy pinstripe suit and how he had been shaking so badly I thought he might be having a seizure. My smart attitude didn't seem so smart anymore.

"You've got to admit the evidence is pretty overwhelming, especially since we found those bloody clothes, after you swore up and down there was no blood on them. That didn't look too good on top of everything else."

"You think I did it too, don't you?"

He stuffed a quarter of his thick sandwich into his mouth. His cheeks were on fire, his eyes glued to his plate.

I clutched my chipped ceramic mug in a death grip. "What now?" I whispered.

He washed down a mouthful of liverwurst with a gulp of Coke and lightly touched my forearm with fingertips that were cold and wet from the condensation on his glass. The instant he made contact he pulled his hand back, like a kid in a shopful of china who's been warned not to touch. "I'll try to help you, if I can."

When I didn't respond, he peered up from his plate and reached for me again, this time brushing my hand with his calloused fingers. It raised goose bumps all the way up to my shoulders, but I didn't flinch.

"Harlan thinks you're planning to plead temporary insanity. He thinks that's why you went to see your shrink on Monday."

"That's absurd." Peter must have told them I was with Dr. Fielding. Why couldn't he have just said I was registering for spring classes at law school?

"Maybe it's not a bad idea, temporary insanity."

"I didn't do it, Andy. I'm not guilty."

"Then why did you see the shrink?"

Jesus, he thought the same thing as Harlan. "Because you guys are driving me crazy, that's why!" My shout sent his skittish eyes scanning the restaurant for eavesdroppers. Fortunately, our friend in the orange cap had left a few minutes earlier and no one else seemed remotely interested in our conversation, but I continued more softly, wary of losing his strange goodwill. "Andy, my mother died of cancer less than a month ago and my twin sister was murdered two weeks later. I think that's reason enough." I could have said more. I could have told him that I had been making incriminating remarks in my sleep, that my own husband thought I was a killer, and that I suspected my sister and I had been abused by our father—and that she'd been blackmailing him over it to pay off her drug-dealing debts. Certainly it all added up to more than enough reason to see a therapist. "Peter shouldn't have told you where I was on Monday."

"Yeah, well, he got nervous and started blabbing. He made a point of reminding us that anything you say to your shrink is privileged and can't be used as evidence against you." He smiled at me through a mouthful of potato salad. "I guess your husband knows where we're heading with this, huh?"

I took a gulp of bitter tea and set my mug down hard. "The appointment with my therapist was only a small part of the reason for my trip. Like I started to tell you, I've uncovered new evidence."

He looked skeptical. "Let's hear it."

I spilled out a detailed account of my excursion to L.A., including how I tracked down Deke Brenner, how he tried to hide that he knew Sid was dead, and how he finally admitted he had been in Black Bay and had argued with her the day she was killed. I told him how Sid had sold off most of her possessions in an attempt to dig her way out of a drug deal gone sideways, about the mysterious new guy she'd been seeing after she broke up with Brenner, and about the potential pot connection between Sid and Brenner and Woody Hanks.

When I finished my story, Andy tossed his wadded napkin onto his plate and motioned to the waiter for another Coke. He waited to be served and took a long thirsty drink before responding. "Interesting," he said finally, bombarding me with onion and pickle breath. Mr. Profound. Why so blasé? Because he was embarrassed that I was a better detective than he and Harlan were?

"It changes everything, doesn't it?"

He shrugged. "Not really. We already knew your sister was into drugs. We sent an officer down there last week."

"Okay, but what about that guy Monty, the one who was threatening her?"

"Know about him too. P. K. Monteil. We found his phone number in Sid's apartment. As it happens, we know just where he was on the night of your sister's murder, and it wasn't in Black Bay."

"Where?"

"L.A. county jail. He's been there for the past six months, on narcotics charges."

"What about his friends? According to Brenner, the guy's loaded. Maybe he hired someone to kill her, knowing he had a perfect alibi."

Andy laughed. "You've seen too many movies, Fran. We talked to Monteil. He said he's never had anything to do with your sister and doesn't know how she got his number."

"That's a goddamn lie." I slumped back in my chair and tried to regroup. "What about Deke Brenner? I can prove Brenner came to Black Bay the night before Sid was murdered and left again the day after. What more do you need?"

"You also told me why Brenner came up here and that he didn't know about the murder until the next morning."

"For Chrissakes, Andy, the guy's a liar. What's wrong with you?"

He slammed his fork down so hard it bounced off his plate, skipped across the table, and landed on the floor. "Nothing's wrong with me, Fran. For your information, Harlan and I are conducting this investigation, not you, and we have some theories of our own, believe it or not. One of them is that the killer has to be someone from around Black Bay."

"Why? Because I'm from here and you think I did it?"

"Whoever killed your sister knew a good place to dump the body. You can't see the cliffs at Pirate Point from the highway, so the killer had to have known in advance what was back there. That means it couldn't have been a stranger. It had to be someone who has personal knowledge of that point, either because they'd been out there themselves or because they'd read in the paper about April Kaminsky." He picked his fork up off the floor and wiped it with his napkin. "I don't suppose you asked Brenner if he subscribes to the *Recorder*, did you?"

"Deke Brenner arrived in Black Bay on Sunday night, twenty-four hours before Sid was killed. He has not accounted for his time the next day, other than to say that he found Sid and they went for a walk. For all we know, they walked out to Pirate Point. It's a good place for a private conversation."

Andy shrugged. "Maybe. I still think it's more likely the killer's a local."

"Okay, then. Woody Hanks. His story about finding Sid's car is bullshit and now it looks like he and Sid may have had some sort of pot deal going on."

"Then why would he kill her? If what you say is true, he loses a customer."

"Andy—"

"Look, Fran. I think you should quit harping on Woody. Woody Hanks may not be one of Black Bay's most upstanding citizens, but he's not a killer."

"But I am? For Chrissakes, Andy, I *am* one of Black Bay's most upstanding citizens. Woody Hanks the pot dealer wouldn't hurt a flea, but Fran Estes killed her sister? I'm sorry, but I don't see your logic."

Once again he reached over to touch me. I wanted to pull away, but didn't. This time he didn't either. He let his palm rest on the table beside mine, our fingers barely touching. His huge hairy paw made my hand seem fragile and smooth, like a porcelain doll's. I forced myself to look at him, and for once he looked back. A bead of sweat ran down the side of his flushed face and dripped onto his collar.

"Like I said, Fran, I'll try to help you best I can."

"You'll follow up? You'll check out Deke Brenner?"

He nodded, but I didn't see it in his eyes.

"What about Woody? Have you gone out to the bluff?"

He shrugged and turned a shade redder than before.

"You haven't, have you?"

He pulled his hand away and reached for his Coke. He took a long drink and crunched a mouthful of ice. "Harlan didn't want me wasting time with that. He said it's just a diversion. He said Woody's not at issue and we shouldn't get all wrapped up in something that isn't relevant."

"But you're going to follow up anyway, aren't you, Andy? Because if I'm charged with killing my sister, I'm sure as hell going to bring up the view from that bluff and you guys are going to look like fools if you refused to check it out."

He didn't respond.

"So whether or not you tell Harlan, you're going out there. Even if you have to do it on your day off. Isn't that right?" I thought I saw signs of surrender in his eyes. "Promise me, Andy." I reached out and squeezed his thick wrist.

"Harlan won't—"

"Screw Harlan. He doesn't have to know unless you find something. And if you do find something, he'll be damn grateful you did."

He didn't look happy, but finally he said, "I'll do it."

19

Sam was on the phone when I got to work Wednesday afternoon, but he broke away long enough to step across the hall to greet me. He caught me slouched in my chair, cursing Harlan Fry and Andy Saybrook.

The creases in his forehead deepened at the sight of me. "I'll wrap up this call shortly so we can talk," he said.

I nodded my agreement without looking up.

"Fran? You okay?" He came into my office and closed the door behind him.

"I'm fine, Sam. Take your time. I've got plenty to keep me busy." I waved a limp hand at the clutter of files and papers spread across my desk and forced a feeble grin.

He backed into the hall, trading places with Millicent Trimble, who elbowed her way past him and ordered him back to his call. "Can I get you anything, Fran? Tea? Cookies?"

At lunch with Andy I had put away what seemed like a gallon of Red's cloudy lukewarm Lipton, and it was still sloshing around in my empty stomach. "Thanks, Mil, but I'm not up for a snack right now."

Her smiling face tightened with motherly concern. "Oh dear. Do you need aspirin? Tums?"

"Nothing, thanks. Just a few minutes of quiet."

She understood my not so subtle hint and beat a hasty retreat, closing the door behind her.

I laid my head down on a stack of green file jackets in the center of my desk and took several deep breaths. According to Andy, if Harlan Fry had his way I would be arrested in two days. Arrested. For murder. It was like something out of one of my childhood nightmares, except this time I had a feeling I would not wake up to find my mother leaning over me, rubbing my forehead. I squeezed my eyes shut and wildly clicked the button at the end of my pen. I didn't think the evidence against me was conclusive, but it certainly added up to a powerful presumption. Overwhelming, as Andy had said. Hell, if I were the police I would arrest me too, in a heartbeat. And if I were on the jury I would be hard-pressed not to find me guilty. Second degree, I'd be thinking, killed her in the heat of a drunken rage.

I jumped at the sound of a soft knock at my door. "Come in," I said, but no sound came out. I cleared my throat and tried again. "Yes? Come in."

It was Millicent. She opened the door a few inches and peered in. "Sam's off his call, if you want to talk to him. I told him to leave you alone until you're ready."

"Thanks, Mil. I'll go see him now."

She disappeared in the direction of the pantry and met me a moment later in Sam's office. She placed a silver tray on his conference table and left without a word. On the tray were two small bottles of sparkling water, a pot of fragrant peppermint tea, a roll of Tums, a bottle of aspirin, a decanter of brandy, a basket of fresh-baked rolls from the Wildflower Cafe, and a plate of cheddar cheese and green grapes.

Sam joined me at the conference table and examined the spread. "She's gone nuts," he said. "Totally nuts."

"She's trying to take care of me, Sam." I picked out a fluffy wheat roll and took a bite, for Millicent.

He nodded and pulled his chair closer to mine. "I think I'll have a touch of brandy. Will you join me?" Without waiting for my response, he poured an inch of amber liquor into two crystal snifters.

Sam wasn't an afternoon drinker, so the brandy was not a good sign. Nor was his shaky hand as he passed me my snifter and raised his own to his pursed lips. I took a quick sip and set the glass aside. I wanted to hear what was on his mind before I hit him with my own bad news.

"I spoke with a representative of the insurance company this morning."

"And?"

"They've put a hold on your payment pending a determination of the cause of Sidney's death."

I managed to swallow the lump of wheat roll lodged in my throat, but even so I couldn't speak.

"Once the investigation is concluded, the full amount will be paid. It's standard procedure."

"They know I'm a suspect?"

He nodded.

Of course they knew. Five hundred thousand dollars was too much money to pay out without asking a few questions.

"Peter thinks I need a lawyer."

"Oh?"

"They questioned me again this morning and read me my rights. They're planning to arrest me Friday." I said the words quickly and watched the last hint of color drain out of his pale cheeks.

Despite my solemn promise to Andy that I would tell no one of our conversation at Red's, I repeated it to Sam practically word for word. He listened in absolute silence as I recounted the evidence against me. When I finished he asked a few questions, his voice calm and clear but devoid of expression, as if he too recognized the hopelessness of my situation.

He rose with me when I got up to leave. "I'm surprised Saybrook would talk to you so openly," he said. "Especially after what happened last time."

"Last time?"

"In the April Kaminsky investigation. He apparently pulled something. He was taken off the case. Remember? It made the front page of the *Recorder*."

"Vaguely." April's murder had been three months old by the time I moved back to Black Bay a year ago last May, so I missed much of the most sensational coverage.

Sam rubbed his forehead and frowned. "As I recall, it was very odd. The *Recorder*'s investigative writer was all over the story. You know the guy—Kevin Grant—the one who's been calling you. He never was able to make much of it, but he sure smelled something rotten."

That explained a lot. "Grant smells something rotten in every story," I said. "He's got a problem with his nose."

"Maybe. I just hope that Saybrook fellow can help you like he says."

I turned away. I wasn't counting on it.

*   *   *

I dialed a number I had gotten from directory assistance and gnawed on my pen while I counted the rings. It took five.

"News desk. Gleason."

"Could I speak with Kevin Grant, ple—"

"Hold on." The phone clattered onto a desktop.

While I waited for the *Recorder*'s star investigative reporter to take my call, I studied the collection of framed photographs on my credenza, particularly one of Sid and me at a party for what looked to be our sixth or seventh birthday. We were sitting at opposite ends of a long table in our backyard, each with our own birthday cake, surrounded by a dozen or so party-hatted children and my mother smiling in the background. I picked up the photo to take a closer look and was surprised that I recognized all but a couple of the kids. April Kaminsky was there, seated next to Sid. So was Andy Saybrook, near my end of the table. We all appeared to be having a grand time. So long ago, I thought sadly.

Before I could get weepy, Gleason came back on the line. "Grant's not in till four. You want somebody else?"

"No, I don't think so. Unless there's someone who worked with him on the April Kaminsky murder story."

After a pause Gleason spoke again, his tone less harried, more interested. "Who is this? You got something?"

"Maybe," I said, not wanting to lose his attention. "I need to talk to someone who covered the Kaminsky case for your paper."

"That'd be Kev, all right. Who is this?"

"My name is Fran Estes. My twin sister, Sid LaSalle, was murdered last week."

Gleason sucked in his breath. "I know Kevin would like to talk to you, Miss Estes." He was excited now. I was talking to another reporter no doubt, and he could smell a story as well as Kevin Grant.

"I need some information from him first."

"What kind of information?"

"I didn't read the stories about April Kaminsky. I need to find out what was in them."

"Shit. That's easy. You need to go to the morgue."

"The morgue?"

He laughed. "Not *the* morgue. Our morgue, here at the paper. You know, where we keep back issues."

"Oh, of course." How the hell would I have known that?

"It's in the basement of our building. We've got a dozen copies of each back issue for the past ten years and before that on microfiche. You can come over anytime and go through all the articles.''

"Like now?"

"Yeah, like now. Kevin should be in around four, and you can come up to the newsroom to talk to him then. I'll tell him to expect you."

"Thanks."

Gleason caught me before I could hang up. "Hold on a minute, miss. You got a phone number where Kevin can reach you? In case you miss him today?"

In case I changed my mind about giving them the scoop, was what he meant.

"I won't miss him," I said, and hung up.

I placed the birthday photo back in its spot on the credenza and gathered up my belongings. There wasn't much to gather. Just my wheat roll and keys and my briefcase, which I hadn't bothered to unpack.

Sam's door was open, so I stopped in to tell him I was leaving. "I'm going over to the *Recorder*, to take a look at those stories about April Kaminsky. Sorry I haven't been much help around here lately."

He dropped the papers he had been reading and hurried toward me from behind his mahogany desk. "For heaven's sake, don't worry about that. When Bob gets back I'll ask him about defense attorneys. Please tell me if there's anything else I can do, Fran, anything at all."

"Thanks, Sam." I bit my lip and turned away, hoping to escape before I started to choke up. I wasn't quick enough.

He put his hand on my shoulder. "You're going to get through this, Fran. You're your mother's daughter. She was a remarkable woman. You are too."

I nodded, grateful for the encouragement, wishing I shared his confidence. I took a step toward the door but stopped and turned back. There was one more thing I had been meaning to ask him. Suddenly it couldn't wait.

"Sam, you knew my folks before they split up."

He looked surprised. I had never before spoken to him of my parents' relationship. "Yes, of course."

"But you represented Mom in the divorce."

"That's correct. Your dad had his own counsel, a divorce specialist from San Francisco." He pulled out a chair at the conference table and motioned to me to have a seat. "What's on your mind?"

I dropped into the chair and gazed at my reflection in the polished tabletop, distracted by the tense face that stared back at me. There was no graceful way to lead into what I was about to say next. "Did Mom ever mention anything about Dad . . ." I fumbled for the right words to express a question I wasn't at all certain I wanted to have answered.

He placed his hand over mine. "Yes?"

"Did she ever say anything about him beating Sid and me?"

His grip tightened on my cold fingers and he briefly closed his eyes. After a moment he shook his head, less decisively than I would have hoped. "She never mentioned him beating you," he said in a small voice. "It bothered her tremendously that he was so stern, and she spoke of that often. Cliff had a bad temper and little patience, as I'm sure you remember well. Not a good combination for raising two small children."

"Nothing about him hitting us, though?"

"No. She told me you were afraid of him because he was so short with you, and your sister acted out whenever he was around. The difficulties with Sidney exacerbated the problem, made him angry and . . . well, resentful." He gave my hand a soft pat. "But Dottie never suggested that he physically abused either of you. She—" His voice faltered, and he looked away.

"She what?"

I wasn't sure he heard me. He removed his hand from mine and laid it lightly across his chest. His face was drawn and colorless.

"What, Sam? Did she say something else?"

"No, it was nothing she said."

"What then?"

"I hate to bring this up. It's just painful old memories."

"I need to know."

He nodded and closed his eyes, as if retrieving memories he had intentionally left behind. "It was around the time your father first filed the divorce papers," he said slowly. "Your mother didn't want him to leave. She depended on him. She didn't know much about business matters, and the thought of being on her own was overwhelming to her. Even maintaining the house seemed like too much to manage along with the two of you girls. It needed a new roof the year he left."

He paused, but it was clear he wasn't finished, so I waited silently for his story to get worse.

"Dottie felt you girls needed a father. She was having trouble controlling Sidney, and you were so independent, always going off by yourself. She worried about you, Fran. She wanted you to be happy, to have friends, to have what she considered a normal life. So no matter how bad her relationship with Cliff had gotten, she wanted to try to make it work.''

"You mean she didn't love him anymore but was afraid to let him go?"

"No, I think she did still love him. At least she thought she did. She told him she wouldn't sign the divorce papers. She wanted to reconcile." His face contorted and his voice faded to a whisper. "Then one night he had too much to drink . . ."

I braced myself. This was going to hurt.

"And he hit her. He shattered her jaw."

I drove in a kind of stupor, shocked and saddened by what Sam had told me, and unspeakably angry—at my father for what he had done, at Sam for knowing what had happened and not doing anything about it, and at a society that would place a woman like my mother in such a helpless, hopeless situation. How many people besides Sam knew my mother's beautiful face wasn't wrecked in a car accident? How many others knew what my father had done to her and kept his ugly secret?

It was nearly three o'clock and drizzling when I pulled up to the headquarters of the *Black Bay Recorder*. I didn't get out of the Jeep at first. I sat there staring through my blurry windshield at the red brick wall in front of me, trying to remember why I came.

After ten minutes my fingers and toes began to go numb, so I dragged myself out of the Jeep and up the stone steps at the front of the building. MORGUE signs led me to a heavy wooden door with chipped black paint. It opened onto a rickety staircase, which I followed down to a large open room with low ceilings, concrete floors, and brick walls. The room was cold and damp, like a meat locker—or a morgue. I pulled my jacket tighter around me and surveyed my surroundings. On one side of the room was a long wooden counter behind which were three desks, each with an ungainly contraption that I took to be a microfiche reader. Everywhere else there were flimsy metal bookshelves stacked to the ceiling with newspapers. The shelves looked ready to topple over at the slightest disturbance, and if one went, the others would go too, like giant dominoes. I'd be in big trouble if the next earthquake hit within the half hour.

Gleason had told me the *Recorder* kept a dozen hard copies of each edition for ten years. At fifty-two issues per year, that meant I was looking at more than six thousand newspapers, most of which hadn't been touched in ages, judging from the heavy smell of dust that hung in the dank air.

There was no attendant on duty, which suited me fine. I headed into the stacks to get the lay of the land, intending to find the paper that came out during the third week of February 1997, and work my way forward until the stories about April Kaminsky's murder came to an end. I located the issues dated February 22, exactly one week to the day after April's body had been found. They were out of reach at the top of the shelf, so I wandered the stacks in search of a footstool. I was dragging it back to my place when I heard the door at the top of the stairs slam shut, followed by a deep voice.

"Hey down there."

I peeked out from behind the stacks and saw a rumpled-looking man in an ill-fitting green suit gazing down at me from the top of the stairs. He was stoop-shouldered and balding, of indeterminate middle age, with rimless spectacles and a pencil behind one ear.

"Hello there," he said in a powerful but not unfriendly baritone, a little like the pope addressing a crowd of tourists from the Vatican balcony. He trotted down the stairs toward me, extending his hand. "Mrs. Estes?" His handshake was firm, his smile warm, perhaps a little too warm. "I'm Kevin Grant. Gil Gleason said you were looking for information."

I returned his greeting and checked my watch. It was barely three-fifteen. If Gleason had his schedule right, Grant was forty-five minutes early to work today.

"I'm sorry about your sister."

I mumbled my thanks but didn't say more.

"Terrible tragedy. Please accept my condolences."

And please give me the scoop, I imagined he was thinking. What he really wanted to say was, *Tell me, did you kill her, like everybody's saying?*

"Gil said you wanted to review the Kaminsky stories."

I struggled to focus, but my frazzled mind kept jumping back to my conversation with Sam an hour earlier. Jesus, my poor dear mother . . . I stared at him mutely and managed a nod.

He shifted his weight from one foot to the other and swept the back of his hand across his brow, as if he were brushing back invisible bangs. "Do you think there's a connection between the Kaminsky murder and your sister's?"

Here we go, I thought. This was why I hadn't returned his phone calls from the week before. "You don't waste any time, do you, Mr. Grant? I'm surprised you haven't pulled out your tape recorder."

He took a step back and held up his hands in mock surrender. "Sorry.

I retract the question. And please call me Kevin. I'd like to help you, if I can.''

Call me Kevin. I'd like to help. No doubt he had heard I was a suspect and was hoping for an exclusive interview with a woman who had killed her twin sister.

He nodded at the door. ''Let's go upstairs and sit down. I have a file with copies of the articles. It'll be easier than going through the stacks.''

I followed him up the steps and into the newsroom, which was quiet and nearly empty, since the next edition of the paper wasn't due out for several days. The room had a dirty feel, as if years of ink and grimy newsprint had worked their way into the very pores of the place. The floors were littered with crumpled papers and cigarette butts. The walls were a dingy taupe wherever they weren't streaked dark brown from a leaky roof. Scattered about were beige computer terminals on gray metal desks. Neutral shades muted to colorlessness by a haze of stagnant cigarette smoke.

At the far end of the newsroom two men were huddled over a desk, deep in a debate about something in a newspaper that lay open in front of them. I recognized the younger of the two from high school. He had been in the class a year behind Sid and me, editor of the *Black Bay High Times*. The other, a gorilla-size man with shaggy salt and pepper hair and a matching beard, was doing most of the talking between puffs on a cigar. He must have weighed three hundred pounds.

Grant followed my eyes and smiled. ''Big guy's Gil Gleason, who you talked to on the phone. He's our senior news editor.''

He led me along an alley of windowless partitioned workstations and into the last cubicle at the end of the row. The space was overrun with junk—newspapers, notepads, pencils, photographs, candy bar wrappers, Styrofoam cups, wadded napkins. The only clear spot was the chair facing the computer. He scooped up an armload of newspapers from the other seat, dumped them on top of a stack of files on the floor, and motioned to me to sit down while he emptied an ashtray into the overflowing wastebasket. Then he dropped onto his own chair with a satisfied grin. ''Coffee?''

I shook my head.

''Okay then. If I'm not being too pushy, maybe you could tell me what it is you'd like to know.''

I started to answer, but he held up his hand. ''First, let me say one thing, Mrs. Estes—''

''Fran.''

"Fran. I'm not looking for a story. If that happens later, it happens. Today we're strictly off-the-record."

Where had I heard that line before? He sounded like a teenage boy not looking for sex. If it happens later, it happens. Right now he just wants to put his hand down your pants. "Look, Mr. Gra—Kevin, I—"

"Wait. Let me finish. A few minutes ago I asked if you think there could be a connection between your sister's murder and April Kaminsky's. Now, I don't have the details about what happened to your sister, but I do know the basics. Enough to know that certain circumstances of her death are a lot like those of the Kaminsky woman. Same killer? Maybe. Copycat? Maybe. Hell, maybe you did it. I won't deny I've heard the rumors. Maybe it was someone else entirely. All I know is the cops fucked up royally in the first case, and it'd be a damn shame if they fuck up again."

I was starting to like this man. "Are you finished?"

"I am."

"First of all, just so you know, I didn't kill my sister. The police think I did, but they're wrong." My hollow voice echoed in my head, as if I were hearing someone else speak, someone without much conviction in her words. Instead of looking at Grant, I watched my restless hands smoothing out imaginary wrinkles in my wool slacks. "Seems to me one obvious suspect in Sid's case should be the guy who killed April, but for some reason the police don't agree."

He nodded but kept his lips sealed in a solemn half smile. His reporter's instincts no doubt warned him not to interrupt a subject on the verge of spilling her guts.

His silent encouragement almost worked. I was dying to unload, to tell him how the cops had been after me since the day after Sid's death, how they had pounced on every bit of evidence against me and virtually ignored everything that might establish my innocence. I controlled myself, but just barely. Despite his earlier assurances that we were off-the-record, I was sufficiently cynical to suspect my comments would somehow wind up on page one if they were juicy enough.

"Unfortunately, by the time they recovered Sid's body it had been so badly mauled by a shark they couldn't tell if she'd been—"

"Raped," Grant said.

"Uh-huh." Let him say it. I couldn't bring myself.

"And if her nipples were sliced off—"

"Jesus, stop it. Please." I buried my face in my hands.

I felt him gently squeezing my arm. His workspace was so cramped he could reach me across the desk without getting out of his seat. "I'm sorry."

I kept my head down and pressed my palms hard against my cheeks. Although I understood generally what had been done to April, I had never heard the details. I still didn't want to know. The same things may have been done to my sister.

"Can I get you something? Water maybe?"

"No. I'll be okay." I shook off his hand and took a deep breath. "You said you have a file with the stories?"

He pulled open the top drawer of his file cabinet and handed me a folder filled with newspaper clippings. "Every story the *Recorder* ran on the case is in that file. I wrote all but a few of them."

He leaned back and lit a Marlboro while I flipped through the clippings. Had he asked my permission to smoke, I would have politely told him no. I didn't like the smell or the burning in my eyes or the reminder of my sister. But he didn't ask, so I kept my mouth shut. This was his office, after all, so he got to make the rules.

There must have been three dozen clippings in the file, each neatly trimmed and taped to a piece of plain white typing paper. They were arranged in chronological order, beginning on February 22, 1997, and continuing through the following August. I scanned the headlines, but didn't read the stories. I didn't need to. I had a pretty fair idea what they said. The first several dealt with the circumstances of April's death and the town's reaction. Later the focus shifted to the Kaminsky family and the progress of the investigation. The last few took a different tack, starting with a front-page article on June 14. Its banner headline caught my eye: "Police Deny Cover-up in Kaminsky Case." This must have been the article Sam Goldman was talking about.

I closed the folder and looked up at Grant. "Can I get copies of these? I'll read them later."

"Absolutely." He looked out over the low wall of his cubicle and waved to a young man in jeans and a wrinkled oxford shirt sitting on top of a desk in the middle of the newsroom, sucking on a cigarette. "Hey, Jeremy. I'll buy you a Coke if you copy this file for me."

The young man dropped his cigarette and loped over. He was probably no more than a sophomore in high school. He wore rimless eyeglasses like Grant's, intellectual yet funky. He grabbed the folder and disappeared.

Grant turned back to me and frowned. "Some of the stuff in that file is pretty graphic. It won't be an easy read."

I gave him a casual shrug that belied my queasiness. I wasn't much for blood and guts, particularly when it hit so close to home. "I have a question."

"Shoot."

"Why'd you say the police screwed up? I saw a headline about a cover-up."

He took a long last drag on his Marlboro and stubbed it out. "Goddamn. I wish I knew what happened. They kept the whole thing under wraps."

"But that's typical, isn't it? I mean, in a murder investigation the cops can't talk about the evidence or they'd never catch the killer."

"It wasn't just evidence they were hiding. There was police misconduct. I'm sure of it. That's what they didn't want to let out."

"Like what?"

"I wasn't able to figure it out. I have a strong suspicion who was at the root of it, though."

"Andy Saybrook."

"Right."

"But you don't know what he did?"

"I never found out. Nobody in the police department would talk about it, other than to admit Saybrook had been pulled off the investigation in midstream. They said it was an internal matter, nothing bearing on the case, but man, they really circled the wagons. When I asked Saybrook about it, he got so freaked out he nearly started bawling, and his partner wouldn't return my calls. After I made it clear I wasn't giving up until I had answers, the police chief gave me a stock statement, probably drafted by his goddamn campaign manager." He reached for another cigarette without missing a beat, but fortunately his pack was empty. "The woman's family knew what was going on, or some version of it, but they wouldn't talk. They were scared, I think. I have an idea the police got to them first, convinced them I was out to cause problems, you know, write something scandalous about their daughter."

"But of course you weren't."

"Hell no. All I wanted was the truth."

It sounded strange to me. The Kaminskys had been friends with my mother. I knew them too well to believe they would be intimidated by a bunch of corrupt cops, especially when it came to finding April's killer.

"I see Andy Saybrook has landed on his feet," I said, hoping to keep him talking. "He and Harlan Fry are assigned to Sid's case now."

"Saybrook took a vacation that summer while the dust settled. He got his old job back, but if I had to guess I'd say he's a short-timer. Dominick Carbone isn't one to tolerate political liabilities, not with an election coming up next year.'' He pulled off his glasses and rubbed his eyes. ''Carbone. Jesus. He jumped all over the Kaminsky investigation at first—he knew the woman, collected her paintings—but when it became clear the case wouldn't be resolved quickly, he distanced himself in a hurry. If Dominick Carbone can't use something to his own advantage, he's just plain not interested. Anyway, he's overstaffed and he knows it. I bet he'll make some cuts before the election, and Saybrook's the logical victim.''

Grant's theory didn't tell me much, but perhaps it explained why Andy was willing to put his butt on the line for me. Apparently he hadn't much butt left to get kicked.

It was dark and windy and starting to sleet when I left the *Recorder*'s smoke-filled headquarters and hurried down the slippery stone steps to my Jeep. The November night had fallen with a vengeance during the ninety minutes I had been inside. I drove north toward home along the coast highway, anxious to be warm and safe and out of reach of the ominous Pacific, churning and thrashing like an angry black bear just beyond the trees bordering the road to my left. A major winter storm was gathering not far offshore. The weather service had issued a small craft advisory earlier that afternoon, and the mountainous inland counties were preparing for the winter's first full-on blizzard. It was good news for the ski areas, most of which were opening the following day, Thanksgiving. For the rest of us it simply meant the beginning of another long cold winter.

Having spent most of my life in Black Bay, I didn't need the weather service to tell me a front was moving in. Living on the North Coast, you learn early to read the warning signs and to respect them. You learn how you can see a storm approaching in the dense purple-gray of the western sky, how you can hear it in the moan of the wind and the rustle of the eucalyptus leaves, how you can feel it in the bite of the damp air suddenly turned cold. Sometimes, like that night, you can even smell it, a kind of musky frenzied scent that lingers in each moist breath.

The highway was already slick from the sleet and well on the way to developing patches of treacherous black ice, so I shifted the Jeep into four-wheel drive and lightened up on the accelerator. When I came to the center of town I turned onto High Street, where the Kaminskys lived in a white clapboard house with the name SEA HAVEN burnt into a varnished cedar plaque on the front door. I coasted past their corner lot and smiled. Parked in the driveway was a black Camero with tinted windows, wide racing tires, and a chrome hood ornament that from a distance looked suspiciously like a Mercedes emblem. The black hot rod meant April's brother Danny had come home to spend Thanksgiving with his folks. In my mind's eye I had a perfect picture of Mr. Kaminsky and Danny in the den, hunched over a game of checkers with a football game blaring in the background, and Mrs. Kaminsky in the kitchen, peeling potatoes or kneading bread dough for the next day's holiday dinner.

We were all just struggling to survive in our own way. For the Kaminskys it would no doubt mean celebrating a traditional Thanksgiving as best they could without April. For Peter and me it would mean spending the day quietly, pretending it was no different from any other. We had received dinner invitations from the Olsons and the Goldmans, but I declined them both. As far as I was concerned, we had nothing to be thankful for this year, and I wasn't interested in pretending otherwise. Peter agreed. Having come from a family of alcoholics, he wasn't big on holidays anyway. Thanksgiving in the Estes family was just one more excuse to get drunk.

The lights were on at our house, a welcome sight as I rounded the final bend in the road. I found Peter in the living room, practicing his guitar in front of a dwindling fire.

I grabbed a quick kiss and stepped over his legs to get to the fireplace. "Keep playing," I said. "I'll crank up the fire. It's going to be a cold one tonight."

"And stormy. I'm glad you're home, Frannie. I was getting worried. I called you at work, but Millicent said you left at three." There was an edge to his voice. I took it to be more than simple curiosity.

I dropped a log onto the fire and shoved it into place with an iron poker.

"Everything all right, Frannie?"

"Yes. Keep playing." I needed a moment's rest before pulling out the folder of articles I had gotten from Kevin Grant. I had decided to hold off telling Peter what I learned from Sam about my mother's shattered jaw. I knew I wouldn't make it to the newspaper articles if I allowed myself to think about that.

He leaned his guitar against the side of the couch, safely out of my reach, and stood up. "The funeral home delivered the ashes this afternoon."

I nodded but said nothing. One more thing to get through.

He disappeared into the kitchen and returned with a burgundy velvet sack, which he placed on the floor beside me. Inside the sack I found a heavy copper box the size of a thick hardcover book and an envelope containing a death certificate, a certificate of cremation, and instructions for opening the box. I looked them over and slid them back into the sack with a heavy-hearted sigh, taking care to smooth its velvet finish and tie its satin drawstring into a perfect bow. A tear rolled off my cheek and made a dark spot on the red fabric.

The struggle was over for Sidney Charlotte LaSalle. So much adversity for such a short life. I wondered if she'd have thought it worth the trouble. Would I, when my time came?

"April Kaminsky's body was found nude, in the backseat of her four-door Subaru station wagon. Her dress and hosiery had been torn off and were found near the body, also in the car. Traces of seminal fluid were detected inside the body, which had been severely mutilated. According to the Sonoma County Coroner's Office, cause of death was a broken neck."

Peter stopped reading long enough to wipe the sweat off his forehead and sneak a peek at me. We had organized ourselves at the kitchen table with my folder of newspaper articles from Kevin Grant and a pitcher of ice water.

He held the paper up close to his face and skimmed the remainder of the report. He was breathing hard, as if the room were running short of oxygen. When he finished he set the page back into the folder facedown so I couldn't see the words if I wanted to, which I didn't.

He looked at me with glassy eyes. "It was a goddamn animal that got her, Frannie. He raped her and cut her up real bad."

I nodded and stared at the stack of papers without seeing them.

Peter picked up the page and scanned it again, as if he couldn't believe what he had read. "Here's something. Listen to this: 'The coroner was not able to identify signs of a struggle, which suggests either that Ms. Kaminsky knew her attacker and consented to his sexual advances or that both the intercourse and the mutilation occurred after she was already dead.' I guess that's encouraging, huh? Sounds like she may have been killed first, before the gross stuff."

Or she may have been too terrified to struggle, I thought, remembering how I had frozen the other day out on the rocks at Pirate Point when I heard something in the trees. I took a sip of water and closed my eyes. We were still on the first article and already I wanted to quit. "I've got the picture," I said. "Let's move on. See what there is about the investigation."

He flipped through a few articles, skimming them for sections that were fit to quote. "Here's an interview with the woman April worked for at the gallery." He laid the page on the table so we could read it together.

As far as the police have been able to determine, Ms. Kaminsky was last seen alive at 5:00 P.M. on Friday, February 14, when she left Jasmine's, the small Main Street art gallery where she worked as a sales associate. According to the gallery's owner, Jasmine Parker, the two women closed the gallery at 5:00 and Ms. Kaminsky left alone in her car.

"April told me she was going out that night, but she didn't say where or with whom," said Ms. Parker. "I assumed she was going over to the Seahorse Pub for a beer, maybe meeting someone there or maybe just planning to hang out with whoever was at the bar. If it were summertime, I'd guess she was going somewhere nicer, like the Sundowner or Cal's, but this time of year there's not much choice. Just the Crazy Frog and the Seahorse, and April never went much to the Frog."

Ms. Kaminsky never made it to the Seahorse Pub, if that was where she intended to go. Bartender Woodrow Hanks, who worked that night from 6:30 P.M. until the pub closed at 1:00 A.M., reported that Ms. Kaminsky did not come into the establishment during his shift. "I knew April real well," said Hanks. "If she'd been there that night, I would have known it. There's only one entrance and I see everyone who comes through. She wasn't there."

Jose Calderon, the day bartender at the Seahorse Pub, concurred with Hanks. Calderon was behind the bar until approximately 6:30 P.M., when Hanks arrived to relieve him. "Woody was 35 minutes late, so I know exactly what time I got off that night," Calderon said. "I know for a fact the Kaminsky girl did not set foot in the joint while I was there."

The next afternoon Ms. Kaminsky's car was spotted from a fishing boat a hundred yards off the coast. The boat's captain radioed the Coast Guard, who identified the vehicle and recovered the body at 5:15 P.M. The coroner later estimated the body had been underwater for 18 to 24 hours.

I ran my finger back and forth through the puddle that had formed at the base of my glass. "I wonder where she was going that night—if Woody was telling the truth about her not showing up at the pub."

Peter shrugged and slipped the page back into the folder. Having never met April, he didn't attempt to speculate. He flipped through a couple more articles and pulled one. "Here's something about the guy following her." He read the story to himself, frowning. "Not much information. The police wouldn't comment on the stalker while the case was open. Neither would the Kaminskys. All it says is the police wanted anyone receiving suspicious telephone calls or noticing any strange behavior to report it to them immediately. *Strange behavior.* Think they could have been any more vague? Jesus. With all the oddballs in this town, how do they expect you to tell the *strange* strange behavior from the normal strange behavior?"

"Let's get to the stuff about the police misconduct." I reached for the file.

He slid it toward me and rubbed his eyes. "Be my guest. I think we're past the gruesome parts."

I found what I was looking for near the bottom of the stack and read it aloud.

Black Bay Chief of Police Dominick Carbone confirmed this week that Officer Andrew Saybrook has been taken off the team investigating the brutal sexual assault and slaying of a 31-year-old Black Bay woman last February 14. The case remains unsolved more than three months after April Kaminsky's naked and mutilated body was found inside her smashed car on the rocks beneath Pirate Point four miles north of town. The police claim to be vigorously pursuing several leads, but sources close to the department have hinted that they are baffled and in fact have little hope of apprehending the murderer, who has become known as "The Valentine's Day Killer."

Saybrook was one of two experienced officers assigned to the case. He reportedly left town over the weekend for an indefinite leave of absence. Police Chief Carbone would not comment on the reason for Saybrook's departure, but he confirmed that Lieutenant Harlan Fry, Saybrook's partner, will remain on the case, working directly with the police chief himself.

"This is an important case," Carbone told the *Recorder* in a brief interview earlier this week. "It warrants having the most experienced team the department can provide. I expect to devote the lion's share of my time in the coming weeks to leading the investigation."

Asked if and when Officer Saybrook will return to active duty, Police Chief Carbone responded, "I don't know, and frankly, it's not uppermost on my mind right now.'' Asked if Saybrook would be reassigned to the Kaminsky case upon his return, he said bluntly, ''No f---ing way.''

''That's our chief of police,'' I said, shaking my head. ''Didn't he know he was talking to a reporter? *No fucking way.* Very eloquent.''

Peter shrugged and pulled the next article out of the folder. It was getting late, and we both were running low on energy. ''Here's a clipping from two weeks later,'' he said, handing me the page. ''Take a look.''

Officer Andrew Saybrook was seen leaving Black Bay Police Head-quarters Monday afternoon, in uniform, having returned to work after a 15-day leave of absence. Saybrook was approached by a reporter and staff photographer for the *Recorder*, but he refused to make a statement. When photographer Roy Chan tried to take his picture, Saybrook knocked Chan's camera to the ground, where it was smashed on the sidewalk. Chan said later he will submit a repair bill to the police department and is considering filing an official complaint.

20

Peter pressed the doorbell and squeezed his arm around my shoulders to shield me from the frigid morning wind. I cuddled up against him and hugged my wool coat tighter around me, tucking my fingers into my armpits. In his left hand Peter held a bottle of Kunde cabernet, our excuse for appearing, uninvited and unannounced, at Rulon and Helene Kaminsky's front door on Thanksgiving Day. Their doormat said WELCOME TO SEA HAVEN, but I wasn't sure the sentiment would apply to us after they found out the reason for our call.

I was stiff and sleepy, propped up by a half pot of coffee that had made me anxious and irritable but no less weary. The previous night had been a long one, made longer by the banging of a loose shutter outside our bedroom window. Twice Peter had gotten out of bed to fasten it down, but his efforts were effective only until the next gust blasted the side of the house. I dozed in twenty-minute catnaps throughout the night, amassing no more than three or four hours total. Technically, it was the storm that kept me awake, but I don't think I would have slept much better if the night had been calm and quiet. My mind was too aroused by a parade of macabre visions of April Kaminsky's raped and mutilated body and by a swelling suspicion that something was horribly wrong with the way the investigation of her murder had been handled.

Kevin Grant had piqued my interest, and my nerves, with his comments about the peculiar conduct of the Black Bay police. The cops had produced no strong suspects in the twenty-one-month investigation of April's murder, and in Sid's case they were doing nothing but trying to pin the rap on me. Meanwhile, a killer was at large, free to look for another target. Or two killers were at large and one or both might be planning to strike again. Who would be the next victim? Another young woman living in Black Bay? The thought had left me cold under our thick winter blankets.

We held off until nearly eleven before calling on the Kaminskys. After reading the newspaper reports about April and hearing of my conversation with Kevin Grant, Peter was as curious as I was to learn more, so I didn't need to sneak over to the Kaminskys' house by myself. He rang the bell a second time and we huddled together, waiting for someone to come. The rain and high winds of the previous night's storm had tapered off, but the morning air was still bitterly cold and damp.

Mrs. Kaminsky was wiping her hands on a white cotton dish towel when she opened the door. "Fran and Peter. What a nice surprise." She stepped back and motioned us into the entryway. "Come in and warm up. Rulon! Danny! Fran and Peter Estes are here." She scooped me into a robust embrace scented with freshly baked bread, holiday spices, and, I suspected, a touch of gin.

"Sorry to barge in unexpectedly," I said. "We wanted to wish you a happy Thanksgiving."

She took the bottle of wine from Peter and stepped back to get a better view. "Look at you, Fran. You've gotten so thin."

By the time she finished wiping the flour fingerprints off our dark coats, her husband had joined us. He squeezed my hand and slapped Peter on the back. "Come in, come in. Good to see you kids."

I felt a surge of fond memories as we slipped off our coats and trooped into the den. It looked much the same as I remembered, just two decades shabbier. Dark oak floors scattered with area rugs, comfortable slipcovered furniture, wood-paneled walls crowded with family portraits. The only new thing was a big-screen Sony TV. It was tuned to a football game, as the Kaminskys' old Zenith would have been.

April's brother rose to greet us, but he kept an eye on the action. "Game's tied with five minutes to go."

Mrs. Kaminsky shot him a football widow's glare but said nothing. Her husband looked as if he sympathized with their son but knew better than to say so.

I waved them off. "Go back to the game, Danny. You too, Mr. K. We'll talk when it's over."

Peter joined the men in front of the TV, leaving Mrs. Kaminsky and me to escape together into the kitchen. The room was big and friendly with a black and white linoleum floor, white tile counters, and a pea green Formica-top table. The sweet smell of gingerbread made me think of my mother.

Mrs. Kaminsky pulled a handful of celery out of the refrigerator. "If you don't mind, I'll work while we visit. If I don't get the turkey stuffed and in the oven soon, we won't eat until after dark."

I ignored the chair she'd pulled out for me at the table. "Can I help? I'm not much of a cook but I'm a great chopper."

We chopped and sliced and reminisced about happier times while I wondered how I would turn the conversation to more recent events. Neither of us mentioned April's murder or Sid's, or even my mother's cancer, and I got the distinct impression Mrs. Kaminsky did not want to discuss painful topics.

After twenty minutes, Mr. Kaminsky came into the kitchen. "Don't mind me," he said, heading for the refrigerator. "I'm just the bartender. What can I get you, Fran?"

"I'd love a diet soda if you've got one, Mr. K."

He poured me a Diet Pepsi over ice and went back for two Budweisers and a liter of tonic water. "Helene, honey? Ready for another?" Without waiting for an answer, he fixed two gin and tonics, heavy on the gin. He set one on the counter beside his wife and disappeared with the other mixed drink and the two beers. Mrs. Kaminsky dropped her knife and went for the glass immediately.

So that's how they're getting through this, I thought, hoping my mother's friend was sober enough to handle a paring knife. The Kaminskys had never been teetotalers, but they were not the type to mix their second gin and tonic before noon. The thought filled my eyes with tears. Would my mother have done the same in Mrs. Kaminsky's shoes?

I blinked hard and wiped my eyes with the back of my hand. "Whew, these onions are strong," I said.

Mrs. Kaminsky nodded and took a swallow of her drink. I noticed her forehead was lined with deep wrinkles and her eyes were droopy. She had aged ten years since her daughter's death.

"That's enough onions, Fran. I'll mix up this stuffing and pop the bird in the oven. Then I can take a break."

When we joined the others in the den ten minutes later, Mr. Kaminsky jumped to refill our drinks. Another football game had started, but he turned down the volume so we could talk. By now he and his wife were clearly feeling no pain. I decided to ask them about April's murder before they were too tipsy to give me straight answers.

"What do you hear from the police?" I directed the question to no one in particular but hoped one of them would respond. "Do they have any leads?"

A silence fell over the room. I glanced at Peter, begging for help.

"We understand Harlan Fry and Nick Carbone are handling the investigation now," he said. "They're looking for similarities between April's death and Sid's. The autopsy didn't tell them much, one way or the other."

Still none of the Kaminskys spoke.

"We haven't been entirely satisfied with the way they've handled Sid's case," Peter continued in a steady but increasingly hollow tone. "We wondered if you felt the same."

It was Danny who finally broke his family's silence. "They've got no leads, Peter. None. Of course we're not happy about it, but there's not a whole hell of a lot we can do, especially after all this time. The killer's long gone by now. We're trying to move on too." His voice had gotten progressively weaker and when he finished he was practically whispering. "Mom and Dad don't like to talk about it."

I stared at a brown stain on the green throw rug in the center of the room. This would be a good time to change the subject, or leave. If Peter and I went away now, perhaps the Kaminskys could salvage what was left of their Thanksgiving.

"I hate to bother you with this," I said slowly. "But I need to ask you some questions. You see, the police think I killed Sid. They're planning to arrest me tomorrow."

Three pairs of dark brown Kaminsky eyes stared back at me in shock.

Peter laid his hand on my leg and gave it a squeeze of support. "If we could understand better what happened to April, we may be able to tie it to what happened to Sid," he said. "If we can do that, maybe Frannie won't be—" His voice cracked. I felt his trembling hand clutching my thigh.

Danny was the first to compose himself enough to respond. "Holy Christ," he said quietly. "Of course we'll help you. Won't we, Mom and Dad?"

Mr. Kaminsky finished his gin and tonic and set his glass down hard on the coffee table. ''What do you need to know?''

I took a deep breath and started the way I had rehearsed in bed the night before. ''The newspaper said April was stalked during the weeks before her death. I assume that's true?''

Mr. Kaminsky nodded. ''Yes, except it wasn't weeks. Just ten or twelve days. April told us about it a few days before her death. She said it had been going on for a week or so. We called the police immediately, of course. They said they'd keep an eye out, but there wasn't much they could do. Blast them. They really were of no help to us at all. Eventually we convinced April to move back home for a while. Her cabin is so secluded out there in the woods. We thought she'd be better off in town with us. She agreed. She was planning to stay with us temporarily, and if the trouble didn't stop we were going to make arrangements for her to spend some time with friends in Sacramento.'' He shook his head and went for his drink. It was empty except for a few ice cubes, but he tried to drain one more sip. ''If only we had done something sooner, she might still be alive.''

''You did what you could, Mr. Kaminsky,'' Peter said. ''You had no way of knowing what would happen.'' He reached for the empty glass. ''I'll get you a refill. Mrs. Kaminsky?''

She nodded and took a long swallow before handing him her glass. ''Yes, please, Peter. You can freshen mine too.'' She looked at me and shrugged. ''It helps dull the pain, you know?''

I smiled my thanks to Peter and turned back to Mr. Kaminsky. ''Can you describe what the stalker did? The newspaper said he was following April and telephoning her, but the stories weren't very specific.''

Mr. Kaminsky swallowed hard and fumbled for his wife's hand. ''Helene, honey, maybe you should get back to your cooking. I can handle this.''

She got up slowly and wobbled out of the room without a word. When she was out of earshot and Peter had returned, he continued. ''It started with the phone calls. Once or twice a night April would get a call. She could hear the bastard breathing, but he never said a thing. At first she figured it was just some kid playing a prank. Then a day or two after the calls began, he started following her, or she thought so, anyway. She didn't mention it to us for a few days because she suspected she might be imagining the whole thing.''

''Did she ever get a look at the guy?'' I asked.

"No. Never saw him. No car, nothing. She just had this feeling she was being followed. One night she was home alone and she heard some-one outside, but Smoky started barking and whoever it was disappeared before the police showed up. That's when she first told us what was going on, and we asked her to consider moving back home. But you know April. She loved being out there in the woods by herself. She had her studio all fixed up. She didn't want to leave it."

"Of course not. She always was one stubborn kid."

Mr. Kaminsky rubbed his forehead and swirled the ice cubes in his drink. "Then the letters started," he said.

"Letters?" This was news that hadn't been in the papers. "What letters, Mr. K?"

"Well, they weren't letters, really. Postcards. Plain white cards like you'd use for a recipe. He slipped them under her door during the night and she found them in the morning. Happened twice. He cut words and letters out of the newspaper and glued them onto the cards. Police said the typeface was common. It matched the *Recorder* and the *San Francisco Chronicle*, along with hundreds of other papers."

"What did the postcards say?"

He closed his eyes and dropped back in his chair, sloshing gin and tonic onto his lap. "I can tell you word for word." He let out a long loud sigh. "The first one said, *Dear Baby, I'm watching you. I want you. Pussy, Pussy. I can taste you already.* The second one said, *Dear Pussy, I can't wait much longer. Going to explode. I'm coming for you soon, Pussy.* She got the second one on the thirteenth of February, the day before—" His voice gave out before he could finish.

I reached over and took his hand. It was wet from wiping his tear-streaked cheeks. Hard as this was for him, I had to ask one more question. "Mr. K?"

He nodded but didn't look up. I wasn't sure he had heard me.

"I need to ask you about the investigation. There were stories in the *Recorder* that hinted at something improper with the way the police handled April's case."

He rocked forward in his chair and rested his head in his hands.

"The paper said Andy Saybrook had been assigned to the case origi-nally, but he was removed. Do you know anything about that?"

He nodded again.

"What happened? What did Andy do wro—"

"Nothing!"

Danny had been sitting silently across from us, but he leapt to his father's side.

"Why did the paper print that article, Mr. K? They made it sound like Andy did something he shouldn't have. Why'd he get taken off the case?"

"You don't understand." His voice was soft again and he wagged his head slowly from side to side. "April was . . ."

"Yes, Mr. K? She was what?"

"Pregnant."

Mrs. Kaminsky picked an untimely moment to slip back into the den. She stood behind us, unnoticed long enough to hear her husband reveal their daughter's secret. The words were barely off his lips when we heard a gasp and a clatter from the doorway. She had fallen back against the door frame and dropped a glazed clay bowl filled with nuts.

I don't know who among us came closest to having a heart attack. Mr. Kaminsky, I guess. His hand shot to his chest and he whirled around in his chair, splattering ice cubes and gin and tonic in a four-foot radius. Mrs. Kaminsky came in a close second. If she hadn't happened to fall into the door frame she might easily have landed flat on her back on the floor, surrounded by a sea of mixed nuts and broken pottery. She glared at her husband, oblivious to the nuts. "Rulon, how could you?" Her voice was low and hoarse. "We had an agreement."

While Peter and I watched in silence, Mr. Kaminsky staggered toward his wife, maneuvering across the nut-covered wood floor as if he were walking on marbles. Danny was right behind.

Mrs. Kaminsky held her husband at bay with a fist shoved into his chest. "No! Get away from me. How could you, Rulon?"

He pushed her hand to the side and grabbed her by the shoulders. "Get ahold of yourself, Helene. For Pete's sake."

Danny slipped in between them to referee. I had a feeling he'd played this role before. "Calm down, both of you. Mom—"

"Your father and I had an agreement, Danny. We were not going to speak of the ba—" She cut herself off with a hand clasped over her mouth.

"I know. But you heard what Fran said. They're planning to arrest her tomorrow. She needs to know—"

"She doesn't need to know *that*."

"For Chrissakes, Mother. We're talking about telling Fran LaSalle, not the goddamn *Recorder*."

He pulled her over to a chair and forced her into it. She let out a wail as she sank into the cushions.

Mr. Kaminsky lowered himself onto the ottoman beside her and put his hand on hers. "I'm sorry, dear, but Danny's right," he said softly.

With her eyes closed she pulled a wad of Kleenex from her pocket and wiped her flushed wet cheeks. After a moment she looked up at her husband and nodded. "Okay. You tell them."

Through the whole scene, Peter and I remained on the couch, not speaking, barely breathing. Peter was the first to find his voice. "Maybe this is none of our business. We don't mean to pry into your private affairs, Mrs. Kaminsky."

Polite Peter. I wanted to slam him in the ribs. Of course we meant to pry. I needed to hear the rest of the story.

It was Mrs. Kaminsky who finally explained. "I noticed something about April that year at Christmastime. I knew before she did, you see. A mother can tell. She would have been three months pregnant the week after she was . . . the week after she died."

I nodded and struggled to keep my mouth shut, to let her tell the story her way, but I couldn't help myself. "And the father? It was Andy?" I hadn't had much contact with April after high school, but still . . . Andy Saybrook? It didn't seem possible.

Mrs. Kaminsky gazed wide-eyed at the nuts and broken glass strewn across the floor, as if noticing them for the first time. She reached down to pick up a few walnuts that had rolled her way. "Maybe. We don't know for sure who the father is—was."

I bobbed my head encouragingly. "I understand." Actually I didn't understand at all, but the words seemed appropriate.

Mr. Kaminsky cleared his throat. "April made a lot of choices her mother and I disagreed with, Fran. We wanted her to go to college, get married, raise a proper family. But April didn't want that. All she cared about was her painting."

I nodded again.

"She knew right off she wanted to keep the baby," Mr. Kaminsky said. "And Andy was going to claim it. They were talking about moving in together—not getting married, just living together. I supposed if it worked out they might eventually get married, but you never knew with April."

Danny pulled his chair into the circle. "Come on, Dad. That plan was history. April had changed her mind. The way she saw it, one baby would be enough. She didn't want to take care of Andy too."

"But you figure Andy was the father?" Peter asked.

"We aren't certain," Mrs. Kaminsky said, her pale cheeks coloring. She went for more nuts, gathering them with one hand and holding them in the other. When she collected too many to hold, she transferred them to a growing mound in her lap. "April dated several men that fall. She was friends with Andy but not particularly close, as far as we could tell. Personally, I think Andy may have just been doing her a favor, you know, so the baby would have a respectable father. Andy didn't date much. It's not like he had anyone else. April would have been a wonderful catch for him." She hesitated, rubbing a filbert between her thumb and index finger as if she were polishing a silver pendant. "Andy wasn't the best, but he wasn't the worst either. There were others. Drifters she'd meet in the bars, local boys who hadn't much going for them, even that awful man who works at the Se—"

"Helene, please." Mr. Kaminsky jerked forward in his chair. "As it happened, before they could tell people about the baby, April was killed. We were the only ones who knew. Afterward, Andy asked us not to tell anyone, and we agreed we wouldn't. That was pretty much the end of it, until the chief of police found out. It was in the official autopsy report, you see. Andy wanted to protect us—and April—so he got the coroner to strike any mention of the pregnancy in the public record. He said he was going to tell Carbone, but I suppose he never found the right moment. Eventually the police chief found out anyway—maybe Andy finally told him—and he was furious. He took Andy off the case and sent him away. Leave of absence, they called it. They conducted an internal investigation—at least that's what they told the papers—and through it all, thankfully, they kept the pregnancy confidential. We understand Andy was cleared of any wrongdoing and allowed to go back to work."

"Not as part of the team on April's case, though," Danny said, lest we think that all was back to normal. "I still think Andy got in big trouble. I've seen him around a few times since. He's not the same guy as he was before. He used to be easygoing and friendly. Now he's all uptight. I mean, I understand him feeling bad about April and the baby, but it's like he got real strange all of a sudden. He never used to be so goddamn strange."

I nodded. That certainly fit the Andy I'd experienced during the past couple of weeks.

Mrs. Kaminsky knelt down on the hardwood floor and began to gather nuts in earnest. "So now you know April's secret," she said, concentrating on the task before her.

Peter and I joined her, picking out chunks of broken pottery so she wouldn't cut herself. Now we knew Andy's secret too.

It was not yet two o'clock when Peter and I arrived home from the Kaminskys', but it felt more like five. A bank of dense black clouds was sweeping inland across the bay and a fierce wind had kicked up. The second wave of the previous night's storm would soon be upon us.

I headed for the fireplace before taking off my jacket. We had turned down the heat when we left that morning, so it wasn't appreciably warmer inside the house than it had been outside.

Peter went straight to the kitchen. When he reappeared moments later he was stuffing his mouth with handfuls of Cap'n Crunch straight from the box. "I thought I'd go bonkers smelling all that home cooking," he said. "I kept hoping they'd offer us something."

"I think that's what the nuts were for."

"I guess. Poor Mrs. Kaminsky. Too much gin."

"Too much heartache."

"Maybe, but drinking won't bring her daughter back. It'll only make things worse. Believe me, I know."

I wadded sheets of newspaper and added them to my pile of twigs and logs. Then I tossed a match onto the kindling and watched its tiny flame take hold.

Peter set his box of cereal on the coffee table and knelt beside me, brushing crumbs from his beard. "What's next, Frannie?"

I had been wondering the same thing. "Ask me again this time tomorrow, if I haven't been hauled off to jail." I looked over at him, but he didn't look back.

"Talking to the Kaminskys wasn't too helpful, was it?"

I crawled onto the couch and sprawled out on my stomach, burying my face in the scratchy wool upholstery. I hated to admit it, but I agreed. Nothing about April's murder or the ensuing investigation seemed to have much bearing on Sid's case, or much chance of diverting suspicion away from me.

Peter climbed onto the couch with me. He straddled my legs and began kneading the knots in my back. He kneaded and I thought. Neither of us accomplished much.

After ten minutes his hands gave out and he returned to his cereal. "You sleeping or thinking?" he asked softly between mouthfuls.

"Neither."

"Any ideas?"

I squirmed out from under him and sat up. "I guess we could confront Andy with what the Kaminskys told us about him and April, but I can't see what good it would do."

"Except make him mad."

"Right."

"You know, Frannie, I'd suggest you reconsider my idea about offering the insurance money to Andy and Harlan, but I guess it's a bit late for that now. . . ."

"Don't start that again, Peter. Bribery is a crime, for Chrissakes. We are not criminals."

"Sorry. Jeez." He finished the Cap'n Crunch in one last sugary mouthful and retreated to the kitchen.

I stayed on the couch and watched our fledgling fire consume little bits of kindling and spit the embers onto the wood floor. When my weary eyes turned the picture into blurry blotches of orange and black, I struggled to my feet and went to find Peter.

He was standing at the kitchen counter with his back to the door. He didn't turn to face me when I came in. I waited for him to say something, but he didn't. He just stood there, staring into the sink. I stayed where I was, two feet into the kitchen, watching the back of his head. At that moment, more than anything, I needed my husband's unconditional trust. I didn't want to have to make a case against Deke Brenner or April Kaminsky's killer or anybody else. I just wanted Peter to believe, because he loved me, that I had not murdered my sister.

When it became painfully clear he was not going to acknowledge my presence, I said, "You having a staredown with the garbage disposal?"

He didn't respond, so I moved a few steps closer. "You know, Peter, Sid and I got in a fight that night, and I have no doubt I gave her a bloody nose, but if I pushed her car over the cliff you'd think I'd have some recollection. If I could remember anything about being out at Pirate Poi—"

He spun around. "What, Frannie? What if you did remember? What would you do?"

I took a deep breath and looked him in the eye. "I'd turn myself in." There. Saying it aloud made it real. "I swear to you, if I determine that I'm the one who killed Sid, I'll turn myself in and face the consequences. That's not something I'm interested in carrying around hidden inside me for the rest of my life." I reached for his hand, but he pretended not to notice. "I didn't kill her, Peter. I'm sure of it."

He said nothing, but his look was definitely not one of unconditional trust.

"Peter, I'm not lying to you."

"Can't we talk about this later?"

"Peter—"

"Frannie, please. Let's just get through tomor—"

The phone rang before he could finish his sentence. He snapped it up on the first ring and grimaced when he heard the voice at the other end. "Happy Thanksgiving to you too," he said with less than total enthusiasm. He looked at me with raised eyebrows and mouthed the words *your father*. "We were out for a few hours, Cliff. Went to visit the Kaminskys." I motioned to him to say I wasn't home, but he didn't see me in time. "Yessir. Here she is."

I took the phone and stared at it in my hand, deciding whether to answer or simply hang up. After my talk with Sam Goldman the day before, I had zero desire to hear my father's voice.

"Hello, Dad."

"Happy Thanksgiving, Frances."

"Same to you. Why are you calling?"

I detected a faint scoff, but he swallowed his retort. "I was calling to wish you a happy Thanksgiving."

"Okay." You've done that now, I thought. So can I hang up? "Where are you?"

"San Francisco. We leave for Texas tomorrow."

"Oh." This was some trip he and Barbie doll were having.

"What are you and Peter doing for Thanksgiving? Cooking a big dinner?"

"No."

"Going out?"

"No. We're skipping it this year."

"Oh, Frances." Once again I had let him down. He made no attempt to hide it. "How does Peter feel about that? It's a holiday for him too, you know."

"He's fine with it, Dad."

"Barb and I are going out to dinner. Why don't you join us? We'll meet you halfway, in Petaluma or Santa Rosa."

"Thanks, but no thanks. We're not up for it."

"*You're* not up for it, you mean. You haven't even checked with Peter."

"I don't need to."

"Because you know it all before consulting him?"

It was all I could do not to start shouting, but I managed to say, "Thanks for calling. I've got to go now."

"Hold on, Frances. Why are you acting this way?"

"I'd rather not get into it. Why don't you just go back to Texas and we can talk again next year?"

I could see his face turn red with anger. It had to be driving him crazy that I was no longer under his thumb. "This is because of the things your sister said, isn't it, Frances? That's why you're acting so childish."

"What *things* did my sister say, Dad? I don't know what you're talking about."

"You know damn well what I'm talking about, young lady."

I clenched my teeth so hard I wondered if my jaw might lock. Peter stood beside me cracking his knuckles.

"Frances?"

"What?"

"For Chrissakes. I never laid a hand on you. If your sister told you otherwise . . . well, I'd just suggest you consider the source."

It was out in the open now. Sid's recovered memories. I felt sick. As far as I knew, what he said was true. Despite Sid's claims, I wasn't sure he had ever hit me, other than the couple of times I got my face slapped for swearing. But it had been a different story for my mother. And maybe for my sister too.

"Never laid a hand on *me*," I said.

"What's that supposed to mean?"

He knew what it meant. Without another word, I laid the receiver back in its cradle. Then I knelt beside the telephone table and pulled the cord out of the wall. Peter circled his arms around me and tried to draw me in, but I pulled away.

"I think I'll go take a hot bath," I said. But first I would unplug the upstairs telephone.

21

I woke Friday morning to the sound of the telephone ringing in the kitchen. Peter had plugged the downstairs phone cord back into the jack before we went to bed, but we had forgotten to reconnect the line in our bedroom. I scrambled over his lifeless body to get to the cord behind the nightstand on his side of the bed. I plugged it in and grabbed the receiver just before the answering machine in the kitchen would have picked up.

"Hello?" I braced myself, prepared to hang up if I heard my father's voice.

"Fran?" The voice was male, but not my father's. I recognized it, but was too groggy to attach a name. "It's Sam Goldman. Did I wake you?"

Sam? Why the hell would Sam call so early? I glanced at the clock on the nightstand. It was eight-thirty, not as early as I would have guessed from the dull gray morning light. A steady rain was beating down on the ledge outside the window. "No, no. I was awake, just about to get up. What is it?"

By now Peter had gained consciousness. He sat upright, watching for a telltale change in my expression.

"I may be jumping the gun by telling you this, but I have some news I thought you'd be interested in." Sam's voice was calm and steady, as always, but my heart started to pound.

"Yes?"

"First of all, I don't have details so I don't want you drawing any conclus—"

"Sam! What news? Good or bad?"

"Bob Green called from the courthouse. The sheriff just brought in Woody Hanks."

"What?"

"Andy Saybrook arrested him. Bob said Woody was cussing up a storm. They had him in handcuffs."

I sank back into the pillows. "Hold on, Sam." Peter was staring at me with a look of panic. "Andy arrested Woody Hanks this morning," I told him.

His mouth dropped open. "Woody Hanks? For killing Sid?"

He grabbed for the phone so he could hear the news firsthand, but I pulled out of reach and put the receiver back to my ear. "Sam, did Bob say why? Are you sure it was for killing Sid?"

"No. That's why I probably shouldn't be saying anything yet. Bob tried to get details, but they wouldn't tell him a thing. We thought if you called Saybrook yourself, you might get a better answer."

"I'll call him right now. I'll let you know what I hear."

I pressed the button on the phone to disconnect and immediately dialed the station house. Not surprisingly, Andy wasn't there.

"Can you get a message to him?" I asked the woman who had answered. She sounded either very bored or very tired, or both. I wondered if I was speaking with Miss Beasley, the onion-headed secretary I had met two days before. "Please. It's urgent."

"Maybe someone else can help you." Her voice had a flat nasal tone. The onion-head.

"No. I need to talk to Officer Saybrook. Can't you please get a message to him?"

"I'll do what I can."

"Does that mean you'll contact him?"

"It means I'll do what I can."

I hung up and turned to Peter, biting my lip, afraid to let myself believe what I was thinking.

He was cracking his knuckles, slowly, one at a time. "Woody Hanks. Wow. I knew the guy was a loser, but why would he kill Sid? I wonder if he killed April too."

I popped out of bed, too nervous to sit still. "Come and get me if Andy calls. I'll be in the shower."

I soaked under the steamy spray for ten minutes before I heard Peter's shout. "Frannie, get out here. It's Andy."

I grabbed a towel and ran dripping for the phone. "Andy?"

"Yeah, Fran, what is it? I got an urgent message to call you. Is everything okay?"

"I heard you arrested Woody Hanks. What's the news?"

"Word sure travels fast around this town. We busted him this morning, thanks to you. I had yesterday off, so I went out to the bluff like you said. You were right about Woody not being able to see back to Pirate Point. The only way to get a decent view is to get deep into those goddamn prickers, so that's what I did. Got poked up like a pincushion, but guess what I found?"

"What?"

"The guy's got a goddamn plantation back there. Covers the whole bluff. He's ripped out all but a narrow strip of brush. Behind it, the whole frigging place is covered with pot plants."

"Pot?"

"That's right. Marijuana."

"What about Sid?"

"What about her?"

"Your meeting with Carbone this afternoon, to decide whether to arrest me. Is it still on?"

"Yeah, it's still on. We're meeting back at the station at three. No news about that yet. But, Fran, I do need to talk to you about Woody."

I dropped onto the bed and let my towel fall into my lap. "What about him?"

"I'd steer clear of him for a while if I was you. Somehow he guessed you were the one who turned us onto him. I don't know how he figured it out. I sure as hell didn't mention your name."

I remembered all too clearly my encounter with Woody and his wolf-dog the week before. I had no desire for another. "What do you mean, *steer clear* of him? Isn't he in jail?"

"Not anymore. He called Howie Jayco. The J-man rushed right down and took care of things. The judge met with Jayco in his chambers, and they got Harlan on the phone. He wound up letting Woody go. Guess Jayco convinced them he'd make sure Woody doesn't run off."

"Howie Jayco? That's reassuring." G. Howard Jayco, the "J-man," had built a thriving law practice defending scumbags like Woody Hanks. He was a Black Bay celebrity of sorts, a longtime crusader for the rights

of the North Coast's bad apples. Drug dealers, perverts, and the occasional wife-batterer or burglar were the J-man's specialty, provided they
could pay his fees, which were rumored to be exorbitant. Pimps, dealers,
and other lucky reprobates with something to barter could pay in kind, I
had heard.

"Damn," was all I could think of to say. Fifteen minutes ago I had a
glimmer of hope. Andy had extinguished the spark.

"Sorry, Fran. If it'd been up to me, we'd still have the guy locked up,
but I guess Harlan and the judge thought different."

The onion-head was at her post behind the counter, typing, when I barged
into the station house that afternoon at five minutes after three. She looked
up but she didn't smile.

"I'm here to see the police chief," I told her.

"Not now, you're not. He's in conference." She nodded at a door
bearing an etched brass plate with the words DOMINICK J. CARBONE, CHIEF
OF POLICE. Through the frosted glass I could make out three blurry figures
inside.

"Please tell them Fran Estes is here. They're expecting me."

She tapped a few more keys and then pushed up to her feet with a
look that said she didn't believe me. She shuffled over to Carbone's
office, rapped softly on the glass, and poked her yellow head inside. A
moment later she retracted her head, closed the door, and said, "The
chief is *not* expecting you. He says you'll have to wait."

"Tell him it's urgent."

She glanced back at the door but didn't open it, apparently wondering
which would be worse, to interrupt Carbone again or to contend with me.
After a moment she stepped away from the door and turned to confront
me, but either Dominick Carbone was a softer boss than I thought or I
looked very determined, because her defiance disintegrated when she saw
my face. She returned to the door and stuck her head inside, providing
me a few crucial seconds to round the counter and sneak up behind her.
Before she could close the door, I jammed my foot in the crack and
pushed it open. "Mr. Carbone, please. I've something important to tell
you."

Carbone was tipped back in an upholstered leather chair with his spit-
polished Guccis propped up on the corner of his desk and his hands
clasped behind his head. Harlan and Andy sat across from him on
straight-back wooden chairs, looking not nearly so relaxed.

When Carbone saw me he jerked upright. "Mrs. Estes. This is a private meeting."

"I understand it concerns me. I'd like five minutes to tell my side of the story."

His lips tightened, but he didn't kick me out. He glanced first at Harlan, then at Andy. "It seems we've been keeping Mrs. Estes apprised of our schedule."

Andy's gaze dropped to the notepad in his lap, but Harlan sprang to his feet. He pivoted to face me and the onion-head, who was hovering beneath me, blocking my path into the office. "Goddamnit, Beasley, get her out of here. Fran Estes, you're fucking nuts if you think—"

"Fry!" Carbone's voice went off like a sonic boom.

Harlan spun around.

"Watch your language, Lieutenant. Sit down."

Harlan lowered himself stiffly onto his chair, but he didn't take his angry eyes off mine.

When Carbone looked back at me, his pursed lips spread into a wide campaign smile. "You have five minutes, Mrs. Estes."

Andy scrambled to pull up another chair, but he was careful not to catch my eye.

My allotted five minutes stretched to twenty-five as I rattled off a shorthand account of my trip to Los Angeles and why I had reason to believe my sister had been killed by any of several people other than myself. "Let me summarize," I said as I wound down. "There's Deke Brenner, who made a secret trip to Black Bay the night before Sid's murder, took off the morning after, and has been hiding out ever since. There's the guy Sid was sneaking around with after she broke up with Brenner, the one she didn't seem to want anyone to know about. There's Woody Hanks, who saw Sid and me leave the bar that night and lied about how he found her car the next morning—"

Harlan pounded his fist on the desk when I accused Woody, but Carbone stopped him before he could challenge me.

"There's P. K. Monteil, a convicted drug dealer, who blamed Sid for cheating him out of seventy-two thousand dollars and who had expressly threatened her. And there's the guy who killed April Kaminsky, who's still at large and for all we know lives right here in Black Bay and is going about his everyday business while he plans his next attack." I took a deep breath and held up my hand to silence Carbone when he started to interrupt. "Just a couple more points, if I may."

"Finish it up, Mrs. Estes. Your five minutes are almost over."

"Yes, sir." I glanced at Harlan. He was clenching and unclenching his fists. "The evidence you have against me is purely circumstantial. You have no one who saw me kill my sister, nor do you have any physical evidence that places me at the scene of the crime. If I'm charged with Sid's murder, the burden will be on the prosecution to prove it beyond a reasonable doubt. That's a tough standard to satisfy under the best of circumstances. It *cannot* be satisfied with the flimsy evidence you have against me and with so many other suspects who have been overlooked. Your case won't even get to the jury. The judge will rule from the bench."

Carbone stood up. His earlier politician's grin was gone. "I know very well who has the burden of proof, Mrs. Estes."

I started talking faster. "Ask Harlan and Andy what they've done to investigate Deke Brenner. *I* was the one who figured out he'd been in Black Bay on the night of the murder and I was the one who found him in L.A. And ask them about Woody Hanks. I was the one who discovered he couldn't have spotted Sid's car like he said he did. It wasn't until yesterday that Andy finally went out there. And what have they done to follow up on Monteil? He *threatened* my sister, for Chrissakes. The guy's a convicted criminal. And—"

"Enough, Mrs. Estes." Carbone leaned toward me across his desk. "I've got the picture. Now I'm going to have a little conversation with my men here. In private." He walked around the desk and opened the door. I felt his huge hand pressing against the center of my back.

As he pushed me out of the office, I said, "Arresting me will be political suicide, Mr. Carbone. I'm innocent and I'll prove it. If you accuse me of killing my sister and I'm found not guilty, you can kiss your future as police chief"—he slammed the door in my face—"good-bye."

22

At five-thirty I went to check the phone in the kitchen, to be sure it was plugged in. I brought it back with me into the living room as far as the cord would stretch and set it on the floor behind the couch, dragging it a few inches closer so when it rang I could reach the receiver from where I was sitting. "Damnit, why don't they call?"

Peter kept his eyes on the business section of the *Chronicle*. "I don't know, but I do know you're liable to pull the cord out of the wall if you stretch it any farther."

"I'm not pulling it that tight. Jesus. I just wish they'd call." I leaned over the back of the couch and stared at the phone.

The telephone didn't ring, but two minutes later the doorbell did.

Peter tossed the paper onto the coffee table and scrambled to his feet. From where he stood he couldn't see who was at the door, but we both had a pretty good idea who was out there. "Here we go," he said in the same voice he might have used if we were about to jump out of an airplane with experimental parachutes.

As I watched him disappear around the corner into the foyer I said a desperate little prayer, complete with a promise to start going to church again if only God would save me this one time. He opened the door and motioned our visitor into the house with a solemn sweep of his arm.

It was Andy Saybrook. He caught his toe on the edge of the doormat and stumbled into the hallway. He had come alone. He fussed with his cap and scowled at Peter, as if he didn't recognize him. "What are you doing here?" he asked.

Peter answered more politely than I would have, but not without a hint of exasperation. "I live here, Andy."

"Yes, of course. I meant, well, I thought you'd be at work."

"I rearranged my schedule so I could be with my wife when she heard from you. Come in, please. We've been waiting." Peter put his hands on Andy's broad shoulders and pressed him forward.

Andy stopped at the French doors. It was cold outside, but his face was glistening with sweat. "We just got out of the meeting."

By now I was sweating too. I pushed aside the afghan I had draped over my shoulders. Andy Saybrook, my former friend, had come to arrest me. If that wasn't it, why hadn't he simply telephoned? Peter stood behind him, cracking his knuckles and trying to smile. Instinctively I raised my arms across my chest and pressed my clammy palms into my cheeks.

Andy moved slowly and awkwardly, his handcuffs jangling with each stiff step. Peter slipped around him and joined me on the couch. He motioned to Andy to have a seat across from us in my mother's rocking chair, Harlan Fry's usual spot. I didn't think it was such a hot idea to have Andy sit there this evening.

Once settled, Andy mopped his forehead and cleared his throat. "Harlan presented the evidence against you to the chief, Fran. You know what most of it is." He paused to inspect the shiny silver snaps that fastened the cuffs of his jacket around his thick wrists. "There's a lot, including some things you may not know."

I nodded. Here we go, I thought. The room began to spin. Beside me, Peter was taking short fast breaths.

"As you noted, much of the evidence is circumstantial." He leaned back and frowned at his cap.

"Tell us what the verdict is," Peter blurted out. "Are you here to arrest my wife?"

Andy sat up straighter. The old rocker creaked under his bulk. "No."

I squeezed my eyes shut and slowly let out the chestful of air I had been holding. Peter dropped back into the couch beside me, groping for my hand.

"Hallelujah," I said softly.

Andy shrugged. "I wouldn't get too excited. I'm not here to arrest you today, but that could easily change if we turn up any more evidence against you."

"You won't."

"We better not. Frankly, I'm surprised the chief went the way he did on this one."

"Why did he?" Peter asked.

Andy paused to fiddle with his cap. "I really can't say. We're going to spend more time on two other suspects. When we rule them out, we'll be back to Fran."

"Can you tell us who they are?"

"One is April's killer, whoever that is, and, candidly, we're still no closer to the answer. The other is Deke Brenner." He looked at me and smiled. "Brenner's more promising, especially with the information you provided."

I stared at his curly red eyebrows and nodded, avoiding Peter's eye. After Andy left I would have some explaining to do about my trip to Los Angeles.

He pulled out a small notepad and a pen. "I'd like to get some more details about Brenner, if I could."

I glanced at Peter's baffled face. It was flushed from the excitement of the past few minutes. "Peter doesn't know about my visit with Brenner yet, Andy."

Peter's eyes flew open to double their usual size. "Visit with Brenner? What are you talking about?"

I spent the next half hour describing how I had tracked down Deke Brenner and confronted him on his front porch. Andy dutifully wrote down everything I said, now and then praising my ingenuity or criticizing my recklessness. Peter kept quiet. I figured he was shocked by what I had managed to accomplish in such a short time and possibly a little disappointed in himself. After Andy left he admitted as much.

"Jeez, Frannie, why didn't you tell me you were running off to L.A.?"

"I tried. You were against it, remember? You told me to leave the detective work to the professionals."

He reached for my hand. "I was worried about you. If I'd known what you were planning I would have gone with you. You shouldn't have gone down there on your own. Christ, if this Brenner guy really is a killer, imagine what could have happened to you. Jesus, Frannie. You could have gotten yourself into really big trouble. Shit."

"Calm down, Peter. Nothing happened, okay?"

"Not yet. The guy knows where we live. If he came up here to get Sid, maybe he'll be back for you, especially when he finds out what you've told the cops."

"I seriously doubt that's going to happen."

He didn't look convinced, but he wrapped his arm around me. His armpit was moist against my shoulder and he smelled of sweat. "I need to take better care of you, Frannie."

"No, you take great care of me, Peter." I slipped out of his grasp and pressed my fingertips against my temples to stop the pounding.

"You feeling okay?"

"Yeah, fine. I'm just a little overwhelmed by it all."

"Hey, perk up, kiddo. Tonight we have something to celebrate."

Oddly, I had no desire to celebrate. I felt nothing, just numb and weary. My mother and sister were dead, and as far as I was concerned my father was too. The fact that I had not been arrested wasn't going to change any of that.

"Don't you need to be at work by ten?" Peter usually tried to squeeze in a nap before he worked the graveyard shift.

"No. I traded shifts with Bobby Olson. Tonight I'm all yours. How about we go out for dinner? We could drive to Healdsburg, have a date."

The only place I wanted to go was to bed, but I tried to summon some enthusiasm. "Let's eat in. You cook something."

"You sure?"

"It's all I'm up for, Peter. I'm beat."

He nodded and jumped to his feet. The news from Andy apparently had given him as much energy as it had drained from me. "Then that's what it'll be. I'm off to Paulsen's Market before it closes."

Five minutes later he was on his way. I waited for the door to click shut behind him before I broke down in sobs of exhausted relief.

After dinner Peter and I relocated to the living room with mint tea and a backgammon board, feeling stuffed and content and more relaxed than we'd been in weeks. Peter was setting up for a third game and I was on my way to refill our mugs when the phone rang.

"I'll get it," I said, guessing it was my father and planning to hang up on him. I had been expecting him to call back after our argument the day before. He typically wasn't one to give up so easily.

I slid across the slick kitchen floor in my stocking feet and snapped up the receiver a half ring before the machine would have clicked on, but there was no response when I said hello. Hoping it was a bad connection, I tried twice more in a louder voice. When no one answered I slammed the receiver down and reeled away from the phone.

Earlier that evening, during dinner, the same thing had happened—twice. The first time Peter answered and the caller hung up immediately. We figured it was a wrong number. The second time I answered and the caller did not hang up. I heard him on the line, breathing into the phone, but he wouldn't speak. I had dismissed it as a prank, probably kids.

This time I couldn't shrug it off. The breathing seemed louder than before, more intentional, more sinister. This was not a harmless prank. Someone was trying to scare us—and he was succeeding.

I started the burner under the teakettle and opened the cupboard where we kept a box of assorted tea bags, but my hands were shaking so badly I wound up spilling tea bags all over the counter. I left them where they landed except for the two I dropped into our mugs. The kettle wasn't whistling yet, but I jerked it off the stove and sloshed warm water into the mugs and across the counter. With a mug in each hand I hurried back into the living room, leaving a trail of tea drops on the floor behind me.

"That was quick," Peter said, reaching for his mug. When he saw my face, his own clouded with concern. "Who called?"

"Nobody. I said hello three times and then hung up."

The look that shot across his face gave me a chill. "Another one."

"Uh-huh."

"Shit." He pushed the backgammon board to the edge of the table, scattering the pieces he had just assembled. "Come sit down. I'm sure it's nothing."

"I hope you're right." I dropped onto the couch beside him.

April Kaminsky's murderer had started with anonymous phone calls. First he telephoned, then he stalked her, then he sent notes on three-by-five cards. I hadn't been able to get the grisly details out of my head since our visit with the Kaminskys the day before.

"You know, Peter, twice since Sid was killed I've had a strange feeling, like someone was watching me or following me."

"Last week, when you thought we had a prowler."

"That was the second time. The first was earlier that same day, out at Pirate Point. I heard something in the trees. That's when I slipped and hit my head."

"You're thinking it may have been the same person who just called?"

"I don't know. I guess I am."

He took a sip of lukewarm tea and made a face. "Me too."

"So what do we do?"

He slammed his mug down in the center of the backgammon board and pulled his hands through his hair. "I'll tell you what we do, Frannie. We get the hell out of this goddamn town, that's what. We go back to San Francisco. There's no reason to stay in Black Bay anymore."

"I can't leave in the middle of the investigation."

"Why not? You heard what Andy said. They think Sid was killed by Deke Brenner or by the guy who killed April Kaminsky. Listen to me, Frannie. If it turns out Sid was murdered by the madman who got April, I don't want you hanging around here waiting to be number three."

I looked at him through eyes blurred with tears. For the first time since the morning my father told us about the insurance policy, Peter was willing to accept that someone else was the killer.

"I'm still a suspect, Peter. It won't look good if I leave town before the case is resolved." It also would hamper my ability to monitor the investigation.

"Bullshit. If they need to talk to you, they can telephone. San Francisco's less than four hours away. You can drive back to meet with them anytime they say."

"What about the house?"

He picked up a pair of dice from the backgammon game and turned them over in his fingers, rubbing them against each other. "I'd like to tell you to keep the house, Frannie. This is your home. It was your mom's home. You've got a lot of good memories associated with this place. But didn't Sam Goldman say the insurance settlement is likely to be held up until the investigation is concluded? I don't know where we'll get the money to pay the mortgage. I sure don't make enough at the MiniMart to cover it." He tossed the dice back onto the board. They came up double ones. "Look, why don't you talk to Sam again? Maybe he can go to court to get part of the insurance proceeds released."

I nodded, but I knew I wouldn't bother. As long as I was a suspect I wouldn't get my hands on that money, and Peter was right, without it we couldn't afford to keep the house. "You know, I have a lot of bad memories associated with this place too, like watching Mom die and now going through all this trouble about Sid. Maybe it's time to leave Black Bay for good."

He stood up and pulled me to my feet. "Come on. Right now it's time to go to bed."

When I climbed in between our icy sheets ten minutes later, Peter was waiting. He slid over to my side of the bed and pulled me in close to his cool naked body. No T-shirt tonight. I reached out for his embrace, but he pushed my hands down from his chest and pressed them hard against his growing erection.

"I need you, Frannie," he said softly, unbuttoning my nightgown and lifting it over my head. "Oh God, I need you." His lips caressed my neck; his tongue traced a wet path to my breasts.

Our lovemaking was intense and quick, less tender than it used to be in San Francisco with the sound of the foghorns moaning out a slow and steady familiar pace, but considerably more passionate. Afterward I slipped out from under his sweaty sleeping body and lay beside him, listening to the wind howling through the pines and telling myself that the worst was over for Peter and me.

I had just drifted off when the phone jolted me back to consciousness. Peter's body stiffened. He rolled over to grab it on the second ring.

There was no one on the other end.

23

We got two more calls the next morning. The first one came at eight, before we were even out of bed, the second an hour later, during breakfast. I stopped chewing when the phone rang and nodded at Peter to get it.

Clutching his fork in one hand, he snatched up the receiver and said, "Who the hell is this? What do you want?" When he got no response he slammed the phone down and called the police.

Andy wasn't at the station so he asked for Harlan Fry and then Dominick Carbone. He ended up reporting the calls to the person who had answered the phone. "That did absolutely nothing," he muttered after he hung up. "I'm not sure the guy was even listening. Sounded like he had a football game on in the background. Theodore Cruise. Know him?"

I shook my head, picturing the two young officers who had been climbing on the boulders when I went out to Pirate Point the day Sid's car was found. Carbone had called them Cruise and Walters. I had no idea which was which.

"He said to call back if it happens again. Probably gets off in ten minutes and wants the next guy to deal with it."

After breakfast we went for a drive, beyond the reach of our anonymous caller. We cruised up the highway as far as Orcas Cove, past the Oceanside Motel where I had first picked up Deke Brenner's trail. On the way back we stopped at a vista point a few miles north of town. It was a sunny day, but cold and windy, so we sat in the Jeep with the radio on and watched the whitecaps samba to the beat of KJZ's Brazilian hour.

After a half hour I'd had enough Brazilian jazz, and enough hiding. "It's almost noon," I said. "Let's drive into town and then go home. I want to get some boxes at Paulsen's Market so I can start packing Sid's things, and Mom's, while you're at work." I still wasn't convinced we should leave Black Bay before the investigation was concluded—and I suspected the police wouldn't like it either—but it didn't hurt to start packing.

Peter started the engine and pulled back onto the highway. "You sure you want me going to work today? I'm not wild about leaving you home alone."

I leaned over and kissed him on the cheek. "I'll be okay."

When we got to the market we found Mrs. Paulsen standing at one of the cash registers near the front of the store, presiding over her small empire like a queen bee in a clover patch. I had known Molly Paulsen nearly all my life. She and her husband had owned Paulsen's Market since before I was born, and she had long been a leader of the Black Bay Ladies' Club, an organization I was proud to say my mother had never joined. Sid and I had been classmates since kindergarten with Sue Ann Paulsen, the oldest of the six Paulsen kids and the only one of them I really didn't like.

I smiled at Mrs. Paulsen as we stepped up to the checkout counter. She was a large woman with a head full of tight silver-blue curls that looked as if they had been sprayed in place with the rollers still in. She was a little too preachy for my taste, but I figured she would be happy to give us her surplus boxes free of charge. I was shocked by her reaction, or lack of reaction, to our request. Without looking up from her register, she waved us toward a door at the back of the store and told us to ask for Joey. Then she slammed the cash drawer, locked it, and stalked away without another word. In her eyes I was still a murder suspect, guilty until proven innocent.

"You want to skip it?" Peter asked as we marched off to find Joey. "I can pick up a few boxes at the MiniMart this afternoon and get some more tomorrow at the U-Haul store in Healdsburg."

I shook my head and kept walking, fists clenched. "No way. She said we could have the boxes. What's it to me if she's a rude old bat?"

Fortunately, Joey Paulsen didn't share his mother's opinion of me. Or if he did, he didn't show it. He helped us fill the Jeep with boxes and offered to save more for us if we wanted. We thanked him and left, his mother's snub dismissed but not forgotten.

It wasn't until we pulled into our dark garage that my apprehension came creeping back. I led the way into the kitchen, to see if we had gotten any calls while we were out. The message indicator was flashing like the red light on a squad car. We had gotten one call, but there was no message.

Peter was late for work again. I watched his Volvo careen out of the driveway at five minutes after two and prayed he would get over to his own side of the highway before another car came at him from around the blind curve just up the road.

The flying gravel had barely settled before the phone rang. I ran to the kitchen to get it but nearly lost my nerve before picking up.

"Hello?" My anxious voice rang out loud and hollow in our quiet house.

There was no response on the other end, although I imagined I heard the soft sound of someone breathing. In and out, in and out. Too rhythmic to be natural.

"Hello? Who is this?"

My question was answered with silence. Total, terrifying silence.

"Fuck you," I screamed. I slammed the receiver in the general direction of the phone. The whole thing bounced off the table and clattered to the floor. For good measure I sent it spinning into the wall with a swift kick and barked another *fuck you* before pulling the cord out of the wall.

I staggered to the kitchen table and buried my face in my hands. I expected a flood of tears, but they didn't come. I was too angry to cry. Was this how April had felt? Angry? Or terrified? Or had she shrugged off the calls as a nuisance because she didn't realize what the caller had planned for her next?

After a few minutes I pushed up from the table and did a quick tour of the house to confirm that all the doors and windows were locked. Then I reconnected the phone in the kitchen and started to dial the MiniMart. Peter had left ten minutes ago, so he should be there by now. Eight-four-seven-six-four-three—I hesitated before pressing the last number. What could Peter do except worry? He might talk me into coming down to the MiniMart as I had the other night when I heard the prowler. I hung up and dialed the police instead.

My call was answered on the first ring. "Police department. Walters," said an efficient male voice. Part two of the Cruise and Walters duo.

"Andy Saybrook, please." I crossed my fingers that Andy would be there. He didn't exactly inspire confidence, but at least he was familiar.

"May I tell Officer Saybrook who's calling?"

Walters made a great receptionist. I wondered if he was any good at police work. I told him my name and braced myself for a snide comment. No doubt he and Theodore Cruise had caught holy hell from Dominick Carbone for letting me climb out on the rocks at Pirate Point a week and a half ago. He told me to hang on and Andy would be with me shortly.

A minute passed. It seemed like ten. Eventually I heard Andy's deep voice.

"Andy, it's Fran. We've been getting anonymous phone calls."

"I heard."

"Well, I just got another one."

"You're at home?"

"Of course I'm at home." What did he think? The anonymous caller was contacting me in a phone booth?

"Alone?"

"Yes. Peter left for work at two."

"What time does he get off?"

"Ten o'clock."

"Have you called him?"

"No. I called you. Theodore Cruise said we should call the police if it happened again."

"Tell you what. I'm just finishing up a report. I'll stop by your place in twenty minutes to check things out. In the meantime, make sure your doors are locked and pull the drapes. If you get another one before I get there, call the station."

I hung up and made another round of the house. I kept back from the windows and lowered the blinds without looking outside, for fear I would find the hungry eyes of a serial killer peering in at me. Afterward I went to wait for Andy in the living room. I added another log to the dwindling fire and turned on the radio. It was tuned to KJZ, the jazz station Peter and I had been listening to in the Jeep, the one my mother liked. A soulful sax instrumental was playing. I didn't know the name of the tune or even the musician, but I recognized it as one of Mom's favorites. The last time I had heard it was the day she died. I dropped onto the couch and leaned my head back into the cushions to listen and remember. Before long a river of tears was flowing down my cheeks.

The doorbell rang at two-forty. Andy was right on time. I wiped my eyes with the sleeve of my cotton turtleneck and ran my fingers quickly through my snarled mass of curls. Fortunately it was only Andy, so I didn't care what I looked like. He heard my footsteps approaching the door and called out to let me know it was him. Thoughtful, as I remembered him from high school.

I opened the door and stepped back so he could come in. "Thanks for coming, Andy."

He took off his cap and gave me a snappy little nod. "Don't mention it."

He sauntered past me into the living room, more confident than I had seen him lately. He tossed his jacket and cap onto the platform rocker and helped himself to a seat on the couch, the spot where Peter and I had sat the previous times he'd been in our house. I moved his jacket and cap to the easy chair near the fireplace and sat across from him in the rocker.

"I'm guessing you put in a good word for me yesterday in your meeting with Carbone," I said. "Thanks."

"Yeah, well, I don't mind telling you, it took some convincing. Harlan's mad as shit."

Did he puff up slightly, or was it my imagination? "Well, I appreciate it."

"Consider it a favor."

A favor? What was that supposed to mean? I considered it his job. "Anyway, about the phone calls . . . like I said, I got another one a half hour ago."

I described the calls and told him I knew they matched the ones April had received. I also told him about my suspicion that someone had been watching me the week before. He stared at me and nodded in the right places, but I sensed he wasn't really listening.

"So what do you think?" I asked. "Could it be April's killer?"

He didn't answer. I wanted to slap him across the face to get his attention.

"Come on, Andy. It could be the same guy, don't you think?"

"Maybe."

"How about Woody Hanks? You think he's harassing me because I sent you guys out to find his pot farm?"

He gave me an absentminded shrug and struggled to his feet. I watched in confused silence as he walked across the room to the chair where I had put his jacket and cap. Maybe it had been a mistake to call him.

He picked up his jacket and reached into the pocket. His back was to me so I couldn't see what he was doing, but warning bells rang in my ears. He turned around slowly.

In his right hand he held a gun.

"This is for you." Andy reached out to me. The silver and black pistol looked like a toy in his huge hand.

I shrank into the carved oak back of the rocking chair, reflexively tucking my hands under my thighs.

"Take it, Fran. It's not loaded."

"You're sure?"

He flipped the pistol open to show me the empty chamber. "Totally harmless without these." He reached into the pocket of his pants and pulled out a handful of shiny silver bullets, which he flashed under my nose and then dropped back into his pocket. With his other hand he set the gun on the coffee table and slid it across to me. "Go ahead. Check it out."

I picked up the pistol gingerly. It was cold to the touch and lighter than I expected. I held it in my open palm, as Andy had, careful not to touch the trigger. Bullets or no, it felt dangerous.

I looked from the gun to Andy and back at the gun. "What's this for?"

"What do you think?"

I let out an uncharacteristic giggle. "I don't know how to use this thing."

"Maybe it's time you learned."

"I don't think so, Andy. I'm really not a gun person."

"You don't need to be a *gun person*. You do need to be able to protect yourself."

"Peter won't like it."

"If Peter cares about your safety he'll adjust."

"Look, I appreciate your concern, but I really don't think this is my kind of thing, not without a permit." I tried to give the pistol back, but now it was his turn to pull away, as if I were passing back a hot potato.

"Don't say no so quickly, Fran. And don't worry about a permit. Give it a chance."

I turned the gun over in my hand, examining it more closely to appease him. It was small and sleek and shiny, just the right size to fit in a woman's handbag. The longer I held it, the more comfortable it felt. Maybe Andy was right. Maybe I should keep it, just for the time being. The idea excited me as much as it scared me.

"I'll teach you to shoot," he said. "There's a gun club south of town. We can go there right now if you want."

"No. Not until I've talked it over with Peter."

"So call him."

I looked back at the pistol. Andy was wearing me down. Next I knew he was standing over me. He reached down, put his hands on my shoulders, and lifted me out of the rocking chair. When I was on my feet he turned me around so my back was to him. He put his thick arms around me and pressed the gun into my right hand. Then he put his hands over mine and pulled my arms up so they were stretched in front of me.

"Aim at the lamp," he said. "Hold your arm straight and concentrate on a spot in the middle of the shade. Steady now. You're shaking."

"I can't help it. I've never shot a gun before."

"You're not shooting one now, either. Remember, it's not loaded. Pretend it's a water pistol and you're going to squirt the lamp shade."

I did as he said, or tried to anyway.

"Relax," he whispered. I felt the words more than I heard them. He smelled of mouthwash and sweat and pine-scented deodorant. "That's it. Nice and easy. Now pull the trigger."

I did. I heard a soft click and Andy's voice in my ear saying, "Pow."

I started to lower the gun, but he kept his arms around me, his hands over mine. I felt a drop of sweat trickle down the side of my face but didn't have a free hand to wipe it away.

He pulled my arm a few inches to the left. "Try again. This time aim at the picture on the mantel, the one in the silver frame. That's your sister, isn't it? Shoot her in the head."

Again I did as I was told, despite his offensive choice of targets. I wished he would let go of me, but he kept a firm hold on my hand. His belly and barrel chest were pressing against my back.

We spent the next few minutes shooting at targets around the living room and we probably would have continued indefinitely had I not run out of patience and squirmed out of his grip. "Let go of me. Let me do it on my own."

He stepped back quickly, his cheeks coloring.

"I think I'm getting it," I told him in a friendlier tone. I hadn't meant to hurt his feelings, but I couldn't stand his arms around me any longer. "It's really pretty simple, isn't it?"

He grunted and walked past me toward the kitchen. "Mind if I get something to drink?"

I placed the gun in the center of the coffee table and followed him. "Help yourself. We have sodas in the fridge."

He opened the refrigerator and came out with a Miller Lite.

"You allowed to have that on duty?" I asked, wishing he had taken a Pepsi.

"I'm not on duty. Got off at two-thirty." He twisted the top off the bottle and took a long swig.

I let him drink standing up. I didn't offer him a seat at the kitchen table or invite him back into the living room. It was a pretty shabby way to treat someone who was trying to help me, but I was anxious to be rid of him. Something about his attitude made me edgy. I was accustomed to him being awkward and shy, not so cocky as he was acting today.

"Look, Andy—"

"You want to go out to the shooting range? We could be back in a couple hours and your husband would never know."

So Peter was *my husband* now. He spoke as if he didn't much like Peter.

"No, I don't want to go to the shooting range. Not this afternoon. I appreciate the offer, but I want to discuss it with Peter first. And, frankly, I'm just too tired today. If you don't mind, I'd like to be alone."

He finished his beer and set the bottle on the counter. "Okay. It's up to you. You know how I feel."

"Yes, I certainly do."

He nodded at the phone. "Tomorrow I'll check into putting a tap on your line. If your caller tries again and you can keep him on long enough, we can trace where he's at. Maybe we'll catch the bastard."

I followed him to the door, remembering what the Kaminskys had told me about April and Andy and the baby. Maybe we would catch the bastard. Or maybe I would end up shooting him through the head with Andy's little pistol. I wondered if that was what he had in mind.

24

Sunday morning over coffee I told Peter about the impromptu shooting lesson I had gotten in our living room the previous afternoon. He reacted precisely as I expected.

"Are you kidding? He wants to give you a gun?"

"*Lend* me a gun."

"You told him no, I hope."

"Not exactly."

"Not exactly? What's that supposed to mean? We don't want a gun around the house, for Chrissakes."

I set my mug down a little too hard, sloshing coffee onto the kitchen table. Yesterday Andy tried to force the damn gun down my throat. Today Peter was insisting I couldn't have it. They both infuriated me.

Peter flipped his bangs out of his eyes and tugged on his beard. He wore a guilty look, but he didn't back off. "It's a dumb idea, Frannie. Andy Saybrook is a gunslinging hillbilly, probably belongs to the NRA."

I felt my blood pressure rising. "Andy's a cop. Carrying a gun is part of his job."

"Fine. You're not a cop, Frannie. Do you have any idea how many people are killed each year with their own guns? It's a big number."

I silently counted to ten before responding. "I know you don't like guns, Peter. I don't either. But I need to protect myself. We don't have to turn this into a political debate.''

''I know that.''

''Then don't say no before you've given the idea a chance.''

''I don't have to give it a chance. I don't want you carrying a gun. Besides, you shouldn't have to protect yourself. We pay our taxes. It's Andy's job to protect you.''

''And if he doesn't? What then, Peter? If you cared about my safety, you'd—''

''Now wait just a minute.'' He grabbed my arm and squeezed it hard. ''Just a goddamn minute—''

''What?''

A second earlier he had been yelling at me. Now he looked ready to burst into tears. ''I do care about your safety.''

I pulled out of his grasp and turned away. ''I'm scared, Peter.''

''I know you are, Frannie. I am too. I hardly slept at all last night, I'm so scared. I just lay there, wide awake, thinking about those phone calls.''

I believed him. He looked as if he had been in a fistfight and came out with two black eyes.

By Sunday afternoon I had managed to talk myself out of the gun. Surprisingly, it took some effort. Bumbler that he was, Andy Saybrook had done a pretty fair sales job. I still agreed with Peter that as a general principle regular folks shouldn't be arming themselves with lethal weapons, but somehow the general principle didn't seem to apply in this case, not with a murdering lunatic on the loose and me looking like a perfect choice as his next victim.

I had promised Peter one thing, however. When the investigation was over—or sooner if he had his way—we would get the hell out of Black Bay. After the heartache and anxiety of the past weeks, I had no qualms about leaving—selling the house and moving away for good. Frankly, I didn't care if I ever set foot in my hometown again. I had few remaining ties to Black Bay and more bad memories than good. All I would be leaving behind were a handful of close friends and a big old house with peeling paint and a pretty view. Peter agreed. Black Bay was nothing to him. Less than nothing.

Timing remained a sticky issue. Peter wanted to pack up and move immediately, regardless of the message our hasty departure might send to the police. I disagreed. Whether he liked it or not, I was a part of the investigation, and from what I had seen of the cops so far I had little confidence they would solve the case on their own. I didn't want my sister to follow in the tracks of her friend, murdered by an anonymous killer, never to be identified, never to be punished.

"I appreciate your concern for my safety," I told him over grilled cheese sandwiches and grapefruit juice. "But you're overreacting." Just as he had ten days before when he concluded I had killed Sid myself.

"Overreacting?" He threw down his sandwich and glared at me.

"See?"

"How can you say that, Frannie? You're getting crank calls, just like April Kaminsky did. You've had someone following you, like she had. Are you going to wait until you start getting filthy little postcards before you believe it?"

"Peter—"

"Frannie, we don't know for sure the same thing didn't happen to Sid. She might have been getting phone calls in the guest room and we wouldn't have had any idea. For all we know, she might have been getting postcards too. Sid wasn't exactly the type to tell us if she'd been having troubles. Have you thought of that?"

I had thought of that, as well as the possibility that Sid had been intending to confide in me the night of her murder, that perhaps she had asked me to meet her at the Seahorse Pub not to ask for money, as I had assumed, but to tell me she was being stalked. That would also explain why she'd had the attendant at the Shell station check out her car for the drive back to Los Angeles. She had been frightened to go home because of her troubles with Deke Brenner and Monty Monteil, but apparently she was even more frightened to stay in Black Bay.

I finished my juice and chewed on an ice cube. "Of course I've thought of that, Peter. But it has also occurred to me that someone might be trying to scare me away. Maybe that's just what our anonymous caller wants, for us to freak out and leave town."

He rolled his eyes and forced a laugh. "No comment."

"Think about it, Peter. Up until now the police have been investigating one suspect. Me. Now, because I've been pushing them, they're widening their net, looking at other possibilities. If I wasn't pushing, the whole investigation might dwindle away to nothing, just like April's."

He shook his head and checked his watch. It was nearly time for him to leave for work. "My little Sherlock. You give yourself a lot of credit."

"I'm not giving up, Peter, not until we find out who killed Sid."

"I see that." He gave me a halfhearted smile and went to rinse our plates.

                              *   *   *

Shortly after Peter left for work Sunday afternoon, I found myself in our bedroom pulling on a pair of black nylon tights, a long-sleeved T-shirt, and my Nike running shoes. With my sore ankle wrapped snugly in an Ace bandage, I headed out the front door and up the driveway to the main road. My usual route started on a path through the grove of pines behind the house, but until our anonymous caller was apprehended I had no desire to be off in the woods by myself.

Before my mother died, I used to go for an hour-long hike or run nearly every day. Barry Stein had gotten me started during our year together in law school. It had soon become a habit, and later while Mom was so sick, an addiction. When she died, I stopped exercising. I didn't feel like running or hiking or doing much of anything that required physical effort.

By the time I reached the end of the driveway I was already short of breath, so I turned north to avoid the steep grade in the other direction. I jogged slowly along the wide gravel shoulder with no particular destination in mind.

After fifteen minutes I passed the turnout at Pirate Point. I had not been back there since the day I dug up the brown button and hit my head on the rocks. A few minutes later I came to the bluff where Woody Hanks had his secret pot farm and, just beyond, a dirt road on the east side of the highway leading to a cluster of ramshackle cabins where Woody and a handful of other ex-hippies lived with a pack of dogs, cats, and chickens in a 1960s-style communal slum.

I was about to turn back when I noticed a black pickup coming toward me down the highway. It slowed as it approached, and I recognized the driver as Woody. For a panicky moment I thought he was going to pull onto the shoulder beside me, but instead he rolled to a stop in the center of his lane and waited while a northbound car drove past. Then he turned onto the road out to his house and disappeared into the trees. If he had seen me, he gave no indication.

As I jogged slowly home I wondered about Woody, whether he was just an everyday slouch who tended bar for a living and sold dope on the side for extra cash, or whether he was something worse. I had never particularly liked the man, but now I thought of him as a potential enemy. He clearly felt the same about me, at least since his arrest two days earlier and maybe even before that. He certainly had led the charge against me by telling the cops about my brawl with Sid at the Seahorse Pub and by making a big deal out of the statements she had made to him earlier that evening about the two of us not getting along. And it hadn't helped that he had reported seeing a red Jeep driving down the highway an hour after Sid and I had left the bar. That part of his story struck me as more fabrication than fact, another shred of evidence that on top of everything else made me look a little bit guiltier but could never be proved one way or the other.

According to Woody's account, he had noticed the red Jeep that night on his way home from work. It was speeding toward him when he arrived at the turnoff to his house, the same place where I had just been running. Because of the oncoming vehicle, he had skidded to a stop on the wet pavement before turning across the highway onto the side road. The Jeep sped by, and he made his turn. He hadn't gotten a look at the driver.

Funny, until seeing him stop today in the identical spot, waiting for an approaching car to pass before he turned for home, I hadn't pictured it correctly. I had envisioned the approaching vehicle coming toward him from the north, driving south. But that wasn't right. If Woody had been on his way home from the Seahorse as he claimed, he would have been traveling south and the other vehicle would have been traveling north, as if it was heading toward the Seahorse Pub and away from Pirate Point— the opposite of where I would have been heading if I had dumped Sid's car over the cliffs and was speeding for home, as Woody and the cops had hypothesized.

I ran a little faster as I neared my house, energized by my discovery of another weak link in Woody's story.

I stepped out of the shower and reached for the white bath towel hanging beside Peter's green one on a pair of hooks on the back of the bathroom door. I dried off quickly and flipped my head forward to wrap my hair in the towel. It was then that I heard someone rattling our back door.

The sound was unmistakable. Someone had opened the screen door and was attempting to open the inside door, which, thank God, was locked.

Without taking time to grab my robe, I bolted across the hall to the phone in the bedroom and dialed 911. The female voice that answered was friendly and calm, asking where I was and what was happening.

"I'm at 58877 Coast Highway. There's someone trying to get in my back door."

"Okay, miss, hold on. Don't hang up—"

I listened for another sound at the back door, but I heard nothing. The silence did not comfort me. "Hurry, please."

"There's an officer in the immediate area. We'll get him right over. Hold on."

It took her thirty long seconds to get back to me. During that time I imagined I heard the screen door slam, but the sound was muffled by my own frantic breathing.

"Hello, miss? You there? An officer is on the way. I want you to stay right where—"

She was cut off by the sound of a siren.

"He's here," I said. "Thank you, thank you." I dropped the phone, grabbed Peter's robe, and ran downstairs. I saw Andy Saybrook through the glass panel in the front door before I flung it open. He wasn't smiling.

"Andy, thank God you got here so quickly. Someone was trying to get in the back door. Did you see him?"

He stepped into the foyer and placed his hands on my shoulders. "Fran, that was me."

"Am I having a nervous breakdown? I'm nuts, aren't I?"

"Maybe you should ask your shrink."

Andy stared at me from the other side of our booth in the Wildflower Cafe. His expression was cold and unyielding. For someone who typically had trouble making eye contact, he was doing remarkably well today.

"Thanks for the vote of confidence, Officer Saybrook."

"That's not what I'm here for. They're paying me to figure out who killed your sister, not to provide psychiatry services." He examined his double-decker meatloaf sandwich and squeezed a thick corner into his mouth.

"Okay, Andy. Let's cut the crap. You were the one who came to see me. Why?"

We had ended up at the Wildflower Cafe because Andy insisted he needed to talk to me. A half hour earlier, while I was showering after my run, he had arrived at my front door. When no one responded to the doorbell he checked the window in the garage and saw my Jeep was there, so he went around to the back. He said he wanted to make sure everything was okay, because he knew Peter was at work and I was home alone, but I couldn't help but wonder if he was motivated less by concern for my safety than by an urge to peep in my windows.

After he had scared me half to death I wasn't in the mood to invite him inside, so I proposed instead that I put on something more presentable than Peter's robe and we go out for a cup of coffee and a bite to eat, my treat. Conveniently for me, he hadn't eaten since breakfast, so twenty minutes later we slid into a booth at the Wildflower.

Andy was in a foul mood. I had expected when his food arrived he would brighten up, but halfway through his monster sandwich he was still crabby. I didn't care to know why, although it was obvious his ill temper was directed at me. Maybe Harlan was torturing him for defending me to Carbone Friday afternoon and he felt obliged to pass on a little of the misery.

"So, tell me, Andy. What's up?" My voice was unnaturally chirpy and sure to irritate the hell out of him, but I was determined not to reward his bitchiness by showing the least bit of discomfort. "Is there news in the investigation?"

He picked at a piece of gristle stuck between his two front teeth and took a long slurp of his chocolate shake. "No, but I do have a couple of matters to discuss with you."

"Such as?"

"For starters, I think you should install a burglar alarm. That way we can avoid a repeat of what just happened back at your house."

"We can avoid a repeat if you don't try to let yourself in my back door again."

"Fran, you live in a secluded house surrounded by trees and you have a husband who works nights. You need an alarm. I know someone who can get you set up for pretty cheap. I'll have him call you. After he installs the system, I'll come over and show you how to set the codes."

"How cheap is 'pretty cheap'?"

He thought for a moment. "Your place is a good size with a lot of windows. I'd say you could get the whole job done, including the garage and guest room, for less than a grand."

Less than a grand, but no doubt more than the seven hundred Peter and I had in our checking account. "Don't bother, Andy. As soon as this business with Sid is cleared up, Peter and I are leaving town. I don't want to invest hundreds of dollars in a house we're planning to get rid of in a month or two."

He pulled the last bite of his sandwich out of his ready jaws. "Leaving town?"

"We're moving back to San Francisco and selling the house. We can't afford to keep it. I'm going back to law school. Peter's going to get a real job."

"What do you mean, you can't afford to keep it? What about the insurance? When do you get your hands on the five hundred grand?"

I poked my fork around in my salad, pushing the olives off to the side. The insurance was none of his business. "There's no longer any reason for us to live here, now that my mother has passed away." I stabbed at a cherry tomato, skewering it on the second try. It squirted pink juice and tiny gold-green seeds across the table. The liquid missile hit Andy smack in the middle of his tan polyester shirt, but he didn't notice.

"Black Bay is your home, Fran."

"No it's not. Not anymore. San Francisco is my home. That's where my friends are."

He cringed openly at my last comment, whether out of resentment, disappointment, or surprise I couldn't tell. What planet was this guy from? Certainly he didn't claim some personal stake in my choice of a place to live?

"I see. You're off to Frisco. Just like that. Peter didn't say—" He stopped in midsentence and looked away.

"Peter didn't say *what*, Andy?"

He coated a french fry with ketchup and stuffed it into his mouth.

"Andy, when were you talking to Peter?"

"It's nothing, Fran, forget it."

I dropped my fork and stared across the table at his hunched frame, trying to make sense of our latest exchange. Why was he acting this way? And what the hell had he been talking to Peter about? A red heat crept up my neck into my face. I took a sip of Diet Coke and pressed the icy glass against my burning cheeks.

"Fran? What's wrong?" He reached across the table for my hand, but I pulled away.

"Nothing." I leaned back in the booth and closed my eyes. When I opened them again, he was gazing at the remains of his sandwich with a strange half smile.

"Andy, I need to ask you something."

He shrugged, a little defensively, I thought. "So ask."

I took another swallow of Diet Coke and watched a bead of condensation run down the outside of the glass. "Did Peter offer you money to keep me from getting arrested?"

His mouth fell open but no sound came out.

"He did, didn't he?"

He cleared his throat and licked his lips. His pink cheeks had gone white. "Why do you say that?"

"Never mind. I get the picture." I let out a chestful of air. "Shit."

Finally he said, "I don't think you do get the picture, Fran. Yes, Peter offered me a financial incentive to come up with something to help you, but I told him no. I don't do that sort of thing. What I did in the meeting two days ago, I did on my own."

I saw him staring at my hands, which were balled up in fists on the edge of the table. I pulled them into my lap before he could reach for one. "Do Harlan and Carbone know?"

He shook his head.

"And you're not going to tell them?"

"I don't plan to, but I'm not making promises."

I nodded. "It was Peter's idea to do that, Andy, not mine. He suggested it to me, but I told him no. Did he mention that?"

He looked down at his napkin and began meticulously folding it back into its original shape. "I'd rather not have this conversation."

"I'd rather not have it too, but you need to know I do not condone what my husband did."

"Okay. You've made your point."

"Peter was trying to help me, Andy, but it was a stupid thing to do. I don't need to bribe anybody. I'm innocent."

"I got it, Fran."

I wasn't so sure he did get it, but so long as he kept his mouth shut I should be okay. We sat in silence until I said, "So why are we here? Why did you come by my house this afternoon?"

"Oh. I wanted to talk to you about Deke Brenner. He's missing."

"Missing?" I pictured Brenner on his front porch, his straight-faced denial that he had been in Black Bay on the night of Sid's death, and later, his look of distress when Reginald showed up.

"Bill Walters went down to Los Angeles to talk to the guy. Couldn't locate him. Neighbors haven't seen him for days."

"That seems to be Brenner's pattern. When I found him last week, he said he'd been staying at a friend's."

"Well, he's gone again. You got an address for the friend?"

"No. Not even a name."

"Any other ideas? Any buddies who'd know where he's at? Anyone he'd be in touch with?"

"Sid's neighbor knows him. Sunshine Scott. I'm not sure she'd know where he is, or if she did know whether she'd be keen on telling, but it's worth asking. And you should ask about her friend Reginald. He knows Brenner too."

Andy shook his head. "We already tried Ms. Scott."

"She wasn't helpful?"

"She's moved. Cleared clean out and didn't leave a forwarding address."

I didn't get it. Why wouldn't Sunshine have told me she was planning to move? "Walters went to her apartment?"

"No. He called. Got the building manager. She was there cleaning the place for the next tenant. She told him Miss Scott left the week before and didn't say where she was going to."

He dug into his black-bottom pie and motioned to the waitress for coffee. I watched him stuff himself in silence, wondering what the hell had become of Sunshine and whether she was in trouble—or off somewhere with Brenner. I tried to remember if she had told me Reginald's last name. Maybe he'd know where she was.

As soon as Andy finished his pie, I paid the bill and got up to go. He followed me out to the Jeep and asked whether I had spoken with Peter about the gun. He still wanted me to have it, he said, especially if I wouldn't install a burglar alarm.

I climbed into the Jeep and started the engine. The afternoon overcast had turned the air cold, and I had no desire to stand on the curb for the next half hour arguing about his damn gun. "The answer is the same as I told you last night, Andy. Thanks, but no thanks. We don't want a gun in the house. I'm comfortable I can survive without one."

He turned and walked away without thanking me for lunch or saying good-bye. "I'm glad you're so goddamn sure of yourself," he muttered.

When I got home from the Wildflower Cafe, I tried Sunshine Scott's old number but got no answer. I considered calling Peter next, to chew him out for trying to bribe Andy, but I was too angry to risk speaking to him. I decided instead to occupy myself by tackling the daunting task of packing up my sister's belongings.

I pulled on a sweatshirt and went out to the room above the garage. I unlocked the door and pushed it open an inch or two, just enough to peek inside. As usual when I came out here, I felt ill at ease, as if I were sneaking into a place I wasn't meant to be. I had never spent much time in this room, never had any desire to. To me it would always be my father's office, his secret hideout where the rest of us were not welcome.

I stepped inside and deposited my supplies at the foot of the bed. I had brought with me an extra large Charmin toilet paper box from Paulsen's Market, a stack of old newspapers, a roll of strapping tape, and a package of Hefty garbage bags. There wasn't much in the guest room to be packed, not more than a few pictures and knickknacks, towels and bedding, and Sid's clothes, which were still scattered about, untouched since Harlan and Andy had rifled through them nearly two weeks ago.

I took a deep breath and flipped on the ceiling light. It was cold in the poorly insulated room, but I walked around the bed and pushed the window open. Even at fifty-five degrees, fresh air was preferable to the smell of stale cigarettes, the scent of my dead sister.

I started with Sid's clothes, which I intended to stash in the basement until after the investigation was concluded. I shoved her jeans into a garbage bag, then tossed in a T-shirt and a pair of thick-soled black shoes, but that was as far as I got. This stuff, however meaningless, was my last remaining connection to my twin sister. I emptied the bag onto the bed and went to get her canvas duffel from the closet. Item by item, I smoothed out the clothes and folded them—no doubt more carefully than Sid had ever done herself—and placed them neatly into the duffel.

Her shoes were the last things to be packed. Impulsively, I kicked off my Nikes and tried them on. They fit perfectly but they felt strange on my feet. They were so Sid. And so not me. Next I knew, I'd pulled a baggy black sweater out of the bag and put that on too, and I undid my ponytail, letting my curls spill freely over my shoulders. When I looked in the full-length mirror behind the door I was shocked by the woman looking back. I could have been Sid. I'd lost weight the past few weeks, so I was thin like her, and hollow-cheeked, with dark circles under my eyes. I made faces at myself, Sid's faces, and attempted a few of her stupid jokes, laughing before the punch lines, as she always had.

A half hour later, cold and weary and out of Sid impressions, I took off her funky shoes and sweater and pulled my hair back into its conservative ponytail. Sid's spirit had left the room, and I wanted to be out of there too.

The phone in the house rang as I was knotting the drawstring on the fully packed duffel bag. It was not a welcome sound these days, not since Friday night, when our anonymous caller had started his campaign of terror, but I was perversely determined to keep answering. I abandoned the duffel on the bed and ran for the house, pulling my keys from my pocket as I bolted two at a time up the steps of the front porch. By the time I reached the phone in the kitchen, the machine had answered and I heard the tail end of Peter's recorded greeting telling our caller to leave a name and number at the beep. My hand froze on the receiver.

He surprised me this time. I had expected to hear a quick click, but he left a message of sorts. Instead of hanging up, he stayed on the line, breathing. I pulled my shaking hand away from the receiver and stood there, staring at the phone. The breathing continued, heavy and rhythmic. I made myself listen, straining for some sound that might be a clue. There wasn't much. I heard no background noise, no street sounds signaling he might be in a phone booth, nothing unusual.

Then I did hear something. The faint sound of a dog barking in the distance. An instant later the line went dead.

I saved the message and replayed it twice. Both times I heard the same muffled barking.

I popped the tape out of the machine, went back outside to close up the guest room, then drove into town. I found Andy in the parking lot at the station house, walking toward his Blazer. I pulled up beside him and rolled down my window. He looked surprised to see me, but not displeased.

I told him about the latest call and about the barking dog in the background. He took the tape and promised to listen to it, but he wasn't as excited as I thought he should be.

"Fran, everybody's got a dog around here. Every cop on the force has one. Matter of fact, I can't think of a person in this whole damn town who doesn't either own a dog themselves or have a neighbor with a dog. Even you and Peter. Don't the Olsons still have Brownie?" His remark was punctuated by the barking of the black labrador retriever who lived in a chain-link pen across the street from the station. "See what I mean?"

"Point taken, Andy, but I still think you should listen to the tape."

I started to roll up my window, but he stuck his hand out to stop me. "Where are you going?"

"Home."

"Alone?"

I nodded.

"Listen to me, Fran. You need to consider your safety. It's going to take a few days before we can get a tap on your line. Until then, you shouldn't be home by yourself, not without some protection."

By *protection* he no doubt meant the pistol he had tried to foist upon me the night before.

I hated to give in to him, but I was not anxious to go home alone, and Peter didn't get off work for more than four hours. I tipped my head at the passenger seat. "Get in."

It was past five-thirty when Andy and I drove south out of Black Bay, heading for the shooting range. By now the sky was pitch black and the wind was whipping off the ocean. The highway was less densely sheltered by trees at this end of town, and in places it hugged the very edge of the steep bluffs. I had to fight to keep the Jeep from being blown into the oncoming lane or over the rocky ledge.

Andy had turned the radio on loud, so rock and roll oldies blasted from the dashboard. The sound quality ranged from fair to poor, depending on the level of static, which rose and fell with the vicissitudes of the hilly terrain, but neither of us made any move to find a clearer station. He fidgeted beside me and stared out at the darkness, gnawing at his finger-nails and periodically mopping his brow. Soon I had to open my window a crack to cut the smell of his sweat.

Three miles south of town we passed Heavenly Acres, the cemetery where my mother was buried. A quick succession of headstones flashed in the Jeep's headlights like an eerie slide show set to a screeching Aero-smith guitar solo. The final headstone was a four-foot granite cross lean-ing precipitously to one side, as if it was too old and tired to stand up straight anymore. Part of its crossbar had cracked off and was lying in the grass. I caught only a glimpse as we sped by, but the image burned in my mind like a reflection of the broken crosses in Sid's apartment. With a shaky hand I turned the knob on the radio to stifle the acid rock.

After ten minutes of painful silence, Andy pointed to a dilapidated metal building that looked more like an abandoned warehouse than a shooting range. "That's it. Turn in at the first driveway."

The gravel parking lot was empty, unlit and uninviting. It was an ob-stacle course of potholes, most of which I managed to hit en route to an entrance at the far end of the building. A peeling faded sign over the door said TURNER GUN CLUB AND SHOOTING RANGE. It looked as if it had weathered more than a half-century of North Coast winters.

We jerked to a halt when the Jeep's left front tire dropped into one last pothole at the front of the building. Andy jumped out as soon as we stopped, but I took my time, suddenly reluctant. I watched in the rearview mirror as he marched around the back of the Jeep to get me. He had his own gun in his holster and the smaller pistol in his pocket. His broad square jaw was pulled down in determination.

In the space of two seconds I went from feeling comforted by Andy's presence to being terrified of him. Here we were, alone together at an abandoned building in the middle of nowhere. As far as I was aware, nobody knew we were together, much less where we had gone. I was struck by an urge to get as far away from him as I could, as quickly as possible.

The car key was still in my hand, but before my trembling fingers could stick it back into the ignition, Andy opened the door and took a firm hold of my arm, ostensibly to help me out of the Jeep. Fighting him would have been pointless. So would yelling for help. No one would hear me out here, and he could shut me up with a single blow.

He was saying something as he escorted me to the building, but his words were drowned out by the sirens screaming inside my head. When he let go of my arm to open the door, I took a step backward, contemplating a dash to the highway, but he stepped back with me, blocking my escape route. He pressed his hand between my shoulder blades and told me to go ahead. I leaned into the opening, prepared to see a dark vacant void.

There was a light on inside. It was dim, but adequate for me to see that the building indeed contained a shooting range. My knees buckled in relief as I stepped over the threshold.

Andy grabbed my arm to keep me from tumbling onto the concrete floor. ''Jesus, Fran. You really are nervous about guns, aren't you?''

''I'm nervous about a lot of things these days, Andy.''

He dragged me along by the elbow. ''You should be. That's why we're here.''

For the next hour we wore heavy plastic earmuffs and shot at two-dimensional men printed in black on big white sheets of paper. Amazingly, I was a natural. My first few shots missed the target entirely because my hands were shaking and my eyes were closed, but my aim proved true when I settled down.

''This is easy,'' I told Andy after blowing four holes in the paper man's chest. ''Maybe I was meant to be a cop.''

He didn't look impressed. ''It isn't so easy with live ones,'' he said. ''Especially if they're shooting back.''

25

Peter slipped out of bed early Monday morning. I heard him in the shower at eight o'clock, but I rolled over and pulled a pillow over my head, hoping for another hour of sleep. I had spent much of the previous night awake, wondering if our anonymous caller was the same person who had killed Sid, and if he was, whether I would someday find myself shooting at him with the pistol I had hidden in my underwear drawer.

Shortly before nine, Peter tiptoed into the room and set a breakfast tray on the floor beside me. He was careful not to disturb me, so I kept my eyes closed until I heard his Volvo pull out of the driveway. Then I rolled over and hoisted the tray onto my lap. On it were a thermos of coffee, a blueberry muffin, the *San Francisco Chronicle,* and a note informing me that he was going to Automotive Discounters in Healdsburg and wasn't likely to be back until after I left for my appointment that afternoon with Dr. Fielding in San Francisco.

I savored the coffee and read the paper all the way through before I got out of bed. At ten-thirty, showered and dressed, I took the pistol from the dresser drawer and moved it to my shoulder bag. I expected I would be uncomfortable walking around with a concealed weapon, but not so uncomfortable as I'd be if I left it at home for Peter to find. I pushed the gun to the bottom of the bag, tucking it under my address book. Then, on a whim, I pulled out the book, turned to the *S*s, and dialed Sunshine Scott's number in L.A.

To my surprise, someone picked up after four rings. The voice was foggy with sleep but unmistakably Sunshine's.

"Sunny, it's Fran Estes."

"Hey, girl, why you calling me so early?"

"It's ten-thirty, not so early."

"It's early to me. I had a late night." She let out a loud yawn to emphasize her point.

"I heard you moved."

"Moved? Are you nuts?"

"When the police called you looking for Deke Brenner, the building manager told them you didn't live there anymore."

"Yeah, well, I didn't need them bugging me about D.B. I did my good deed when you came down here last week. I'm through."

"They say he's missing."

"They're right."

"How do you know?"

"Reginald stopped by his place yesterday. D.B.'s truck was there, parked in front of a fire plug. It had three days' worth of tickets. Reginald didn't like the looks of things, so he let himself in. There was a plate of spaghetti and a glass of milk on the table, but no D.B. Reg said the milk smelled like it'd been there for a while."

"Sounds like Deke left unexpectedly." Assuming Reginald was telling the truth.

"Without his truck?"

"Someone must have picked him up, a friend maybe."

"I'll tell you who I think picked him up, hon."

"Who?"

"That guy Monty, the asshole who was after Sid and him for the money they lost in that drug deal."

I nodded to myself, even as I realized it could not have been Monteil. "The police have already checked into that guy, Sunny. P. K. Monteil. He's in prison, has been since before Sid was killed."

She laughed. "Guys like him have associates to do their dirty work while they're out of circulation, girl. They don't stop operating just because they're in jail."

I thought the same thing. Unfortunately, the police had not agreed. I made Sunny promise to call if she heard any news of Brenner and let her go back to bed.

* * *

"It began with my father, years ago when Sid and I were kids. Right from the start we were rivals for his affec—attention. There wasn't enough for one, let alone twins. Sid tried to get him to notice her by misbehaving. I took the opposite approach. Neither of us succeeded, although I'd have to say she failed more miserably than I did. Basically, she drove him off. If it wasn't for her, my folks might have stayed together."

Elizabeth Fielding waited for me to go on. When I didn't, she said, "And you resent her for that?"

"I guess so. I mean, I'm not saying my parents had a great relationship. Maybe it's an exaggeration to say they would have stayed together, or should have, but there's no question Sid made the situation worse."

I took a sip of ice water and leaned back against the brocade upholstery of the high-backed antique easy chair. Exaggeration? Who did I think I was fooling? The beige rice paper on the wall across from me became a blank screen upon which I projected a replay of my father, in a drunken rage, slamming his fist into my mother's jaw. The incident Sam Goldman had described a few days earlier was as horrifyingly distinct as if I had witnessed it in person—so graphic I half wondered if maybe I had. I shook my head to dislodge the image. The focus of this conversation was supposed to be my sister, not my father.

"Tell me more about your childhood, Fran." Dr. Fielding faced me across the rosewood coffee table, straight and still in her black suit and crisp white blouse. Much of today's conversation was old news to her, but she had suggested we go back over my history with Sid as if we had never discussed it before, to get the benefit of a fresh perspective.

"Not long after Dad left, the competition turned to boys. Sid made a point of stealing any boy remotely interested in me. She didn't necessarily want to date them herself, sometimes I think she didn't even like them, but she didn't want me to have them either."

Dr. Fielding nodded, but said nothing.

"You see, Sid always had a special quality guys really went for. She was exciting, and dangerous. Whenever it seemed like I had a chance at some guy, she'd appear out of nowhere and sweep him off his feet, and then of course she'd dump him."

It was true. As a teenager, Sid had been rude, arrogant, and wild. It earned her a lot of criticism and, curiously, a lot of admirers. I learned quickly to keep my prospective boyfriends as far away from her as possible.

"Funny, the only guy I dated who never showed any interest in Sid was Andy Saybrook. He's a cop now, assigned to investigate her murder."

"Andy took you to the homecoming dance. You and he had several dates."

"That's right. Junior year." I was impressed with Doc Fielding's memory, but not overly so. There weren't many other boyfriends for her to have confused with Andy. "Anyway, either Sid never went after Andy or he turned her down. It's not surprising, I suppose. Andy wasn't Sid's type. She'd have chewed him up and spit him out before he knew what hit him, like she did with the others, only faster."

"You never spoke to Sid about this?"

"No. We didn't talk about things like that. Then I went away to college and she didn't, so the rivalry kind of faded."

"But it never disappeared entirely."

"No, not entirely, and because of it we were never again what I'd call friends."

By the time our fifty-minute hour was up, I was losing my voice. We had talked for nearly the full session about Sid and resolved nothing. Then we spent a few minutes on my father. Eventually I got up the nerve to tell her what I had learned from Sam Goldman about my mother's broken jaw.

After a long contemplative pause, she pulled off her glasses and said, "This may not be the best time to delve into this, Fran, but when you're ready I'd like to refer you to a colleague of mine who specializes in repressed memory syndrome."

I shrank back in my chair and shook my head. "I don't think so."

"It's not something I would ordinarily encourage, but under the circumstances I think it's called for. We have two strong indicators—your sister's accusations of childhood abuse and now this discovery about your mother. I think it would be useful to probe some of your own memories on the subject."

"I don't know." A week ago, when I first mentioned the topic of repressed memories, I was curious to explore Sid's claims about our father and maybe even recover some clue about what had happened the night she was killed, but now I wasn't sure I wanted to remember, not if it involved my mother.

"Think about it. We can start whenever you're ready. There's no need to push yourself. You've got a full plate right now as it is."

I debated whether to ask her if a propensity for violence could be inherited, but in the end I decided not to run the risk of an affirmative answer. I was halfway to the door when she inquired about Peter. It was the wrong question if she wanted to end our session.

I briefly described an argument I'd had with Peter the night before. He had come home from work in a particularly cranky mood and had immediately started complaining about one trivial thing after another, hinting in each case that I was to blame. After numerous attempts to fend off his jabs with humor, I snapped. I accused him straight out of suspecting I had killed Sid, which he of course denied, launching me into a tirade about how he had betrayed our relationship by mistrusting me. I did not mention that I knew he tried to bribe Andy. I was afraid if we got into that I might blurt out things that couldn't be patched over later. We argued for a good half hour and went to sleep angry. That was the real reason he had left for Healdsburg that morning before I was up and why I didn't open my eyes until after he was gone.

Dr. Fielding motioned for me to sit back down. "Tell me more about it. We have time before my next appointment."

"Last Wednesday Andy Saybrook told me they were planning to arrest me for murdering Sid, but two days later they decided not to, at least not yet. I found out yesterday that Peter tried to bribe Andy to get me off. He had suggested the idea to me a few days before, but I told him absolutely no."

"Why do you think he did that, after you told him not to?"

"I know why he did it. He thinks I'm guilty, or he thought so until we started getting anonymous phone calls. When Peter found out about the insurance policy on Sid's life, he was as quick as the cops to conclude that I must have killed her myself. How should I feel about that? My own husband thought I was a murderer."

"Why don't you talk to him about it? In a calmer moment maybe you both can understand a bit better how the other is feeling. When Peter called me before our session last week, he was extremely distressed about what had happened to Sid and about the course the police were taking with the investigation. He was frightened for you, Fran, very frightened. It's my experience that people often behave in an uncharacteristic manner when they're frightened. They do things they later regret. They grasp at straws, so to speak."

Grasping at straws. The thought did nothing to comfort me. I promised Dr. Fielding I would discuss it with Peter, but I expected it would be easier to bury my anger and move on.

* * *

It was nearly four-thirty when I left Dr. Fielding, so I had to race across town to get to the law school before the registrar's office closed. To the dismay of the registrar's assistant, I made it with a mere five minutes to spare. Martha Betchmor, commonly referred to by the student body as Martha Bitchmore, was a large gray-haired woman in her midfifties, non-descript in every aspect, except her sour disposition.

"This office closes at five o'clock sharp and I can't stay late to ac-commodate your tardiness," was her response to my cheerful "hello" when I rushed into the room. "Why don't you come back another time?"

I ignored her suggestion and made my way to the course catalog and registration forms spread out at the end of the counter. While she stood beside her desk clucking like an old hen, I pulled a blank form from the pile, scrawled my name and student number at the top, and checked off the first five entries. I was finished in fifteen seconds. Along with the majority of my classmates, I would rearrange my schedule during the first week of classes.

"You haven't done that properly," Bitchmore told me when I shoved the form toward her across the counter. She made no move to take it.

I flashed her a smile and turned to leave. "I like surprises. Now you can close up early."

I sprinted up the stone stairs to the law library. Barry Stein was just where I expected, in his carrel, head down, nose stuck in a thick casebook. I crept up behind him and put my hands over his eyes.

He took my fingers in his and pulled them up a couple inches so my wrists were at his nose. "Hmmm . . . I smell something good . . . good memories." He stood up, turned to face me, and drew me into his strong warm embrace. "Good to see you, Frankie. What a fantastic surprise."

I hugged him back and buried my head against his shoulder, squeezing my eyes shut to keep the tears from spilling out. They came quickly these days, regardless of the emotion. I gave him a light kiss on the chest, too light to be noticeable, and pushed away, blushing and laughing. "You look like you could use a break. Let's get coffee."

He snapped his book shut and flipped out the light above his desk. "I have a better idea. It's five o'clock and I'm starving. How about I skip my workout tonight and we grab an early dinner, to celebrate?"

"Celebrate?" For an odd, uncomfortable instant I wondered if Sheila had come back to him.

He grinned at me. "I got a job at the San Francisco public defender's office. They had one slot and more than a hundred applicants. I start next July after the bar exam.''

"Oh Bear, that's wonderful." I was back in his arms.

A half hour later we were facing each other in a secluded booth in a tiny French bistro, immersed in soft candlelight and the scent of garlic and butter. It felt like a date, too much so. The minute we sat down, I realized it had been a mistake to run to Barry so soon after venting my frustrations about Peter to Dr. Fielding.

But if it was a mistake to be alone in a romantic restaurant with Barry Stein, at least it was a pleasant one. As the evening wore on, Barry got tipsy on wine and, if only in my imagination, distinctly amorous. Periodically he took my hand in his. Once, in the middle of a story, he drew my fingertips to his lips and kissed them. It was an unconscious gesture on his part, I suppose, brought on by three glasses of zinfandel, but I wasn't drinking. I was sober and nervous and intensely aware of his touch—and increasingly consumed by a vivid fantasy of the two of us back at his apartment making love in the big brass bed he used to share with Sheila. Had I encouraged this? How else to explain the flowing black knit skirt and gray cashmere sweater I had worn that day instead of my usual blue jeans or wool trousers? How else to explain the Chanel No. 5 I had dotted on my wrists and behind my ears?

I excused myself and hurried off to the rest room, where I took several deep breaths and warned myself not to get carried away. When I came back to the table, Barry slid over and patted the cushion beside him. "Sit here," he said. "They only had one serving of crème caramel left, but it's big enough to share." A single dessert plate and two forks were waiting on the table.

I didn't want dessert, but I slipped in beside him and took a bite. The booth was small and our arms touched when either of us moved. I wondered if he could tell how hard my heart was pounding; certainly he couldn't miss my trembling hands. I set down my fork and took a sip of water. He did the same.

Then he kissed me. On the lips. It was innocent enough at first, like a wayward peck on the cheek, but when I didn't pull away he followed with one that meant more. He leaned in closer and I felt the pressure of his chest against my breasts. My hand slid up his arm and came to rest on the back of his neck.

When I heard myself whisper his name, I panicked. Suddenly I saw myself on the edge of a cliff, standing at the very brink, about to cheat on my husband. I was ready to do it. I wanted to do it, even though I knew there would be no going back, not completely. The guilt terrified me. Certainly I owed Peter better than to jump into bed with my best friend. I slipped out of the booth and stumbled back to my seat on the other side of the table. What was I doing? In a public restaurant, for God's sake? I scanned the room for our waiter and waved him over. I canceled our cappuccinos and told him to bring the check immediately.

Barry was quiet during the drive back to his apartment. Stunned, I guess. He said nothing when I explained that I needed to be home by ten o'clock or Peter would worry. When I pulled to a stop in front of his apartment building, he suggested I come inside and call Peter to tell him I was running late, but he didn't look surprised when I declined.

"I'm sorry, Frankie." He opened his door but didn't get out of the Jeep. Instead he reached over and squeezed my hand. "That was the wrong thing to do. I'm so sorry."

I shook my head and managed to tell him that I needed to be on my way.

He nodded and climbed out. He stood on the curb watching as I drove off. It took all my willpower not to go back to him.

26

I saw the back of the truck as I rounded the last curve before home, a big dark-colored pickup on the shoulder of the highway just past our driveway. I couldn't tell if it was moving at first, but from the speed with which I approached I suspected it must have been stopped or nearly so. In any event, by the time I was within fifty yards it was back on the pavement, heading north.

I held my breath until I got beyond the double row of pines that separated our property from the Olsons'. Once past the trees I could see that the lights were on in our living room and Peter's Volvo was parked in its usual spot in front of the garage. Of course he would be home by now. It was nearly eleven and he got off work at ten, but I was relieved nevertheless. I flipped on my blinker, fully intending to turn into the driveway, but at the last minute curiosity drew me on.

The pickup was nearly out of sight by the time I decided to follow, so I pressed the accelerator to keep from losing it on the winding road. Fortunately the night was dark and moonless with no trace of fog. The truck's taillights were distinct red specks in the distance. Everything else was black. Without taking my eyes off the road, I reached to the passenger seat for my shoulder bag, pulled it onto my lap, and slipped my hand inside. My fingers went straight to Andy's pistol. It felt smooth and hard and comforting to the touch. I gripped the butt of the gun in my right hand, drew it out of the bag, and carefully placed it nose down between my thighs. I wanted it close at hand, although I most certainly did not expect to use it. I planned to get just near enough to see who was at the wheel of the pickup and then go home.

At sixty miles per hour I gained ground quickly, but before I could make out the driver, the truck's turn signal came on. I slammed on my brakes and dropped back, watching as it slowed to a crawl and turned into the short steep driveway leading down to the Seahorse Pub. Hoping to get a better view, I swerved onto the shoulder and rolled to a stop at the edge of the driveway. Seconds later, a tall drooping stalk of a man slipped out and hurried across the shadowy parking lot to the pub's entrance. As he opened the door, he glanced over his shoulder and scanned the lot and the driveway. His eyes locked on mine for an instant before he disappeared inside. It was Woody Hanks.

Without pausing to think, I skidded down the rutted hill and parked under a flashing neon Budweiser sign. I stuffed Andy's pistol back into my bag and trotted across the lot, not allowing myself the masochistic luxury of remembering the last time I was here, exactly two weeks ago. When I stepped into the stuffy gray haze of the smoke-filled pub, I caught a glimpse of Woody's brown mackinaw as he slipped through a door behind the bar. I barged into the room with as good a swagger as I could muster.

If I'd felt out of place meeting Sid here two weeks ago, I felt doubly so tonight, on my own. A scratchy country-western tune blared from the jukebox, vying with the raucous clamor of the pinball machine, more racket than justified by the meager crowd. A geriatric cowboy was shooting pool by himself in the far corner of the room. Across from the bar a lone teenager in low-slung green trousers banged away at a furious game of pinball. That was it, except for the bartender, a busty blonde with shiny red lips and powder blue eyelids. She was leaning back against the cash register with her arms folded across her rib cage, as if to prop up the fleshy pink breasts swelling out of her low-cut sweater. Her hair was platinum, a metallic buttery shade that comes only in a bottle. It hung nearly to the top of her tight jeans in two thick braids, Heidi-style, each with a beaded leather string knotted at the end. In the merciless glow of the fluorescent light above the bar, she looked old enough to be Heidi's grandmother and made up enough to be a circus clown. I motioned to her, but she didn't let on that she had seen me.

"Hello there. Yoo-hoo." Even my voice seemed out of place in this environment.

Heidi didn't budge from her position at the cash register, but she tilted her chin up slightly and appraised me in silent disdain, jawing a wad of gum. In my expensive gray sweater and black knit skirt I must not have looked like someone who had come to drink.

"Excuse me," I said with feigned confidence. "I'm looking for Woody Hanks. Please tell him Fran Estes would like to talk to him."

She kept chomping. "Woody ain't working tonight."

"Maybe not, but I saw him go behind the bar. Please tell him I'd like to speak with him." My voice was louder than necessary and probably a bit too smooth to win much sympathy, but it was the best I could do under the circumstances.

Her face disappeared behind a huge pink bubble, which she expertly sucked back into her mouth with a loud pop. Had I attempted the same maneuver I would be picking Bazooka off my chops for the next half hour.

"Just tell Woody I need to talk to him." My voice cracked. "Please. It's about my sister."

I had found the magic words. Her expression softened and she stopped chewing. Like everyone else in town she knew about Sid's death and, presumably, that I was a suspect. She may not have recognized my name, but I looked too much like Sid for her to mistake me for anyone else. She dropped her arms, letting her big bosoms sag as she stepped away from the cash register. "Wait here. I'll see if he's around."

"I saw him go back there," I reminded her. "Tell him I won't take much of his time."

She was gone nearly a full minute. When she reappeared, Woody was with her. He strode toward me around the end of the bar, walking the walk, as if he was headed for a showdown. Instinctively my hand went for my bag.

"What do you want, bitch?" He stopped three feet from me, just out of arm's reach.

I climbed onto a bar stool and nodded at him to do the same. He didn't.

"I want to ask you some questions."

"And why should I answer them? If I remember right, last time I talked to you I wound up with the cops on my ass. It'll be a fucking miracle if I don't wind up with my balls in the slammer, thanks to you."

"I didn't know what you were doing out on that bluff, Woody. How was I supposed to know you had a pot field back there?" If I had known, I still would have ratted on him, but that was more information than he needed at the moment.

"What the fuck do you want with me?"

"A few minutes ago I saw your pickup on the side of the road in front of my house. I want to know what you were doing there."

He scowled and shook his head. His eyes narrowed to black slits. He was doing a passable job of looking offended, but I suspected he was just buying time.

"Tell me, Woody, why were you there? Don't think about it. Just tell me."

"Fuck you, smart-ass. I was passing by on my way here. I saw someone in the woods behind the house, so I slowed down to have a look."

Yeah right. "And?"

"Whoever it was disappeared." He patted the pockets of his leather vest, as if he was looking for cigarettes, or a joint, but he came up empty.

"I don't believe you."

"I don't give a fuck what you believe."

"I'm sure you don't."

I decided to try my luck with a new topic. "Tell me, Woody. When I came in here Monday night two weeks ago, you and Sid were chatting it up. And she'd spent lots of time here during the previous week. What did you talk about?"

"None of your goddamn beeswax."

Beeswax? Who said that anymore? "Pardon me, but it is my beeswax, Woody. My sister was murdered. I'm trying to find out who did it."

He examined his dirty hands and began picking at a hangnail.

"Did you and Sid ever talk about April Kaminsky's murder?"

He put his finger up to his teeth to get a better grip on the hangnail. "Maybe."

"Does that mean yes?"

"Sure, we talked about it. Everybody talked about it. It was the biggest thing that happened around here since the last time Sid was home. Naturally, we talked about it."

"You told her April had been stalked before she was murdered?"

"I suppose so."

"And she was interested in that?"

"Everybody was interested in that."

"But did Sid seem especially interested? Like she had a personal interest?"

He gave up on his hangnail and looked at me. "What the hell are you getting at?"

"Did she seem nervous?"

"Sid LaSalle always seemed nervous. She was a nervous kid. Now look, sister—"

"But did she seem extra nervous? Like maybe she was being stalked too? Like April?"

The color drained from his hollow cheeks. His hands went first to his beard and then to the silver studs on his leather vest. Eventually he buried them in his pockets and glanced over his shoulder at Heidi's grandmother. "Hey, Val. Bring me a beer."

"What do you think, Woody? Did she seem nervous like that?"

He waited for his beer and leered at Val's beefy back end as she sashayed back to the cash register. Then he grabbed the bottle off the bar, took a long guzzle, and wiped the slobber off his beard with his shirtsleeve. "Sid was interested in what happened to April, including the stalker, but not particularly interested, not like she had a *personal* interest. I told her what the newspaper said, that some loony-tune was calling April and following her around before he killed her."

"Was she afraid?"

He chugged the rest of his beer and waved for another. "Why the hell are you asking *me* all this shit? I had nothing to do with Sid LaSalle. Nothing."

Val slid his second beer across the bar and looked at me. "You want one too?"

I shook my head.

"It's on the house. You look like you could use it."

I could practically still taste the beer and rum I'd had here two weeks ago. I pushed back from the bar and smiled. "No thanks. I've got to be going."

I started to say good-bye, but Woody wasn't finished yet. The beer had loosened him up.

"If you told me someone'd been bothering Sid, I might venture a guess who it was."

"Who?"

"Guy named Fenner—something like that. He followed her up here from Los Angeles. Big guy with white hair and a girlie voice."

"Deke Brenner?"

"That's him. Asshole tried to tell me he was her boyfriend, but she never mentioned no boyfriend to me."

"He told you that himself? In person?" Brenner specifically told me he had intended to contact Woody about buying pot but he never got to meet with him, never even spoke to him on the phone.

Woody's dirty fingers wandered back to his beard. "Uh, maybe I'm not remembering quite right . . ."

"You're remembering right, Woody. I know all about Deke Brenner. He came up north to find Sid. And to buy pot, from you."

He went back to work on his hangnail. "He's gonna be fucking pissed when he finds out what happened to his stuff."

"Did you do a deal?"

He nodded. "Fenner—Brenner—whoever he is, he'll be back anytime now to pick it up, but I ain't got nothing for him. The cops wiped me out, thanks to you."

"He's coming back to Black Bay?"

"That's the plan. He wanted to inspect the stuff before taking delivery. Real suspicious sonofabitch. Paranoid. Didn't want to carry it home on the plane, so he's driving all the way from fucking L.A." He took another swig of beer and slammed the bottle down on the bar. I leaned back to avoid the bullets of spit. "Asshole took off without leaving me any way to get in touch with him. Shit. These days even thirteen-year-olds got pagers, but that jerk can't leave a goddamn phone number."

"When is he supposed to be back?"

He shrugged. "I'm surprised he ain't here yet."

I leaned into the pub's heavy wooden door, giving it substantially more shoulder than turned out to be necessary. It swung open easily and I pitched forward, diving chest-first into an unsuspecting Harlan Fry, who had pulled the door open from the outside just as I threw my weight at it. It was like hurling myself at a brick wall. "Jesus! Harlan, you scared me."

"Whoa, freight train coming through." He stepped around me into the bar and looked back with a mean grin, begging me with his body language to come after him.

I let him go without a word. I'd like to think I was too smart to be goaded into an argument that could wind up getting me arrested, but more likely I was simply too tired to bother. Instead I hustled the ten feet to my Jeep and walked a circle around it, peering in the windows, wishing I had a flashlight and wondering if there might be someone waiting for me in the backseat, fixing to dispose of me at the bottom of the cliffs where April and Sid had ended up. Finding no stowaways, I climbed in and shifted into low gear to power up the steep gravel driveway.

It was midnight by the time I got home. Peter met me at the door.

"For God's sake, Frannie, where have you been? Why didn't you call?"

I turned away to hang my jacket on a hook in the hallway. I was still furious with him for trying to bribe Andy and my anger no doubt showed. "I stayed in San Francisco for dinner and then stopped at the Seahorse Pub on the way home."

"The Seahorse Pub? Why the hell—"

I waved my hand to shut him up. "Hold on. Let me explain before you go nuts. I would have been home an hour ago, but when I got to the Olsons' I saw a truck stopped by our driveway. When I got closer it took off, so I followed."

"Jesus Christ. What if whoever it was caught you following him and came after you? Why didn't you come inside and call the police? This business of playing detective is going to get you in trouble, Frannie."

Somehow I didn't think it would help my cause to tell him I had the comfort of Andy's pistol between my legs. "By the time the police got here, the truck would have been long gone. I just wanted to catch up close enough to see who it was."

"And?"

"It was Woody Hanks. He stopped at the Seahorse, so I went in after him."

"Oh, that was a bright idea. Woody Hanks is a drug dealer, Frannie. Why would you follow him into that joint?"

"For Chrissakes, Peter. First of all, Woody is hardly a *drug dealer*. Small-time pot farmer, yes. Drug dealer, no. Besides, the Seahorse Pub is a public place. It's not like I was following him into some abandoned warehouse." As I nearly had with Andy the night before. "You won't believe what he told me."

"I'm sure I won't. Let's have some tea and talk about it. I have something to tell you too."

"Make mine herbal," I said as I headed upstairs. "I'm going to change." And put my gun somewhere where he wouldn't be likely to stumble across it.

I dropped my bag on top of the dresser and stuffed the pistol into the far corner of my underwear drawer. Eyeing our bed longingly, I pulled off my sweater and skirt and started toward the bathroom to get my robe. It was then that I noticed the white bar wedged diagonally across our bedroom window. Startled, I went over to take a look. It was a sturdy wooden post, one of several stored in our basement that had years ago been part of our back porch. I gave it a tug, but it was lodged in tight and didn't budge.

I pulled on my robe and trudged downstairs to find out what was going on.

"It's a security bar," Peter said. "So someone can't slide the window open from the outside. I've already done all the windows upstairs and I'm going to hit the downstairs in the morning. Good idea, huh?"

"Yeah, great." The bar gave me the creeps. "Do you really think it's necessary?"

"You don't? Do you know how easy it would be for somebody to climb onto the roof of the porch and get in through a window? The locks on those things aren't worth shit."

"I guess you're right." He was absolutely right, of course. Any burglar worth his stocking mask wouldn't need more than a few seconds to break into one of our windows, locked or unlocked. "It just seems like a pain in the butt, is all."

His face grew serious. "Pain in the butt? Come with me. I want to show you something."

I followed him into the hall. When he opened the door to the den we were met with a blast of cold air. He flipped on the light and stepped aside.

I stifled a scream. The room's big picture window was shattered. Amidst a sea of broken glass lay a jagged black rock the size of a cantaloupe.

Peter kicked a piece of broken glass across the hardwood floor. "It happened while I was at work. I got home to find a smashed window and a blank message on the answering machine."

I said nothing. Suddenly the security bars didn't seem like such a waste of time.

"The good news is nobody got in. Look—" He tiptoed a careful path to the window through a minefield of glass shards, as if I couldn't identify the damage well enough without him pointing it out to me. The rock had taken out nearly a quarter of the windowpane, leaving a gaping hole in the lower right-hand corner. A series of cracks radiated from it like bicycle spokes. "The window's shot, but the hole isn't all that big. Nobody could have fit through it."

I nodded and did the math. The window had been broken sometime before ten o'clock, when Peter got off work. It had been almost eleven by the time I saw Woody Hanks's pickup near our driveway, stopped there because he had seen someone in the trees behind the house, or so he said.

Peter stared at the window. His frown made angry furrows across his forehead.

"What time did you get home?" I asked.

He jumped at the sound. "Huh? Oh. Ten o'clock. You know that."

"Exactly ten o'clock?"

"A few minutes after, I guess. Maybe ten-fifteen. Bobby showed up a little late. Why?"

"Woody said he saw someone run into the trees behind the house, but that wasn't until nearly eleven. We've got forty-five minutes to account for, at a minimum. You didn't hear anything when you came home?"

"Nothing."

"Did you see anything strange, like a car or truck by the side of the road?"

He thought about it and shook his head. "No. Nothing out of the ordinary. Right after I got home I went upstairs to change clothes and pee. Then I came back downstairs to fix something to eat. When I walked past the den I noticed the window was smashed, so I made sure no one had gotten into the house and just closed the door. I figured you'd want to see it before I touched anything. Then I went into the kitchen and got some food. I was in there until after eleven, listening for your Jeep. If somebody had been sneaking around outside, I should have heard something."

"I wonder if Woody was lying about seeing someone back there."

"Wouldn't surprise me."

"But why?" I shivered and stepped out of the draft.

Peter picked his way back to my side, crushing bits of glass with each step. "Let's talk in the kitchen. I'll sweep up this mess and board up the window after you're in bed." He put his arm around my shoulders and firmly turned me away from the damage.

As if on cue, when we entered the kitchen the telephone rang.

Peter stiffened and pulled his arm away. "I'll get it," he said, but he didn't move toward the phone. Neither did I.

He grabbed it on the third ring. "Hello? Who is this?" His voice was loud and remarkably steady, considering how badly his hand was shaking.

I clenched my fists and braced myself for him to hang up or demand again who was calling, but his jaw relaxed and his face fell into a tired smile. "Oh, hello. Yes, she's home, safe and sound. . . . Right . . . Okay then. I'll tell her." He hung up and let out a loud sigh. "That was Barry Stein, checking to be sure you made it home okay."

Barry. I nodded and bit my lip.

"He called earlier too, said you'd left the city in time to be home by ten-thirty. They've got a new number by the way. Must have moved."

Apparently Barry hadn't told Peter that Sheila had left him. I didn't either. I watched in guilty silence as he dialed the phone.

"I called the police about the broken window and again when you weren't home by eleven," he said. "I better let them know you're—yes, may I speak to Theodore Cruise, please?"

I turned on the burner under the teakettle and dropped into a chair at the kitchen table. After Peter hung up, he filled our mugs and joined me. "So, tell me about your day." His tone was light and cheery. It begged for a like reply.

I bobbed a peppermint teabag in my steaming mug and searched for a safe subject. I considered confronting him about his attempt to bribe Andy but decided to leave that argument for a time when I had more energy. "Same old stuff with Dr. Fielding. She says I'm crazy." I didn't feel like talking about it, and I suspected Peter didn't either. He wouldn't want to risk reminding me of his desperate call to my therapist the week before.

"Crazy, huh? I don't need Dr. Fielding to tell me that. What else? How are the Steins?"

"Fine." I concentrated on my tea bag and remembered the feel of Barry's lips on mine. "I registered for spring classes."

"Great. What are you taking?"

"Let's see . . ." I shook my head to cast out thoughts of Barry. "Constitutional law, copyright, criminal procedure, and evidence." It sounded better than confessing I really didn't have the faintest idea.

He looked at me with an odd expression, as if he could tell I was hiding something. "You'll be glad to get back to law school, huh?"

"I guess so." I would be happy to get back to a normal existence. I wasn't so sure about law school. Without Barry, it wouldn't be much fun. But with him it would be torture.

Peter dumped a tablespoon of sugar into his tea and watched it dissolve. "Okay, so why don't you tell me about it?"

I took a sip to wet my cotton mouth. "What do you mean?"

"You know. Your latest adventure. What happened at the Seahorse Pub?"

"Oh that."

"Yeah, that. What happened?"

I told him about Woody's dealings with Deke Brenner and watched his eyes widen, especially at the part about Brenner coming back to Black Bay.

"You need to report that to the police."

"I guess."

"You guess? Frannie, three days ago Andy told us Brenner was their top suspect. You've got to warn them to be on the lookout."

I cringed at the thought of my collision with Harlan an hour ago outside the Seahorse Pub. "You're right, as usual. I'll call Andy first thing to-morrow."

"Why not tonight?"

"Because I'm too damn tired to do anything more tonight, Peter." I stomped over to the counter and dumped my tea down the drain. I left the soggy tea bag in the sink and stalked out of the kitchen without saying good night. Halfway up the stairs I called out a guilty apology and waited until he yelled back not to worry about it.

We usually left the blinds open in our bedroom, since there was no view from the highway into our window, but that night I closed them to hide the security bar. I dropped my robe at the foot of the bed, climbed in, and pulled my knees up close to my chest so I was huddled in a little ball. I could hear Peter downstairs, rummaging around in the broom closet, beginning the task of cleaning the den and boarding up the broken window.

I sandwiched my head between two pillows and squeezed my eyes shut, determined not to think about Barry or allow myself to second-guess my actions earlier that evening. I was utterly exhausted, but wired, as if I had just polished off a double espresso instead of a few swallows of herbal tea. I tried to conjure up innocuous thoughts that wouldn't work me into another sleepless night, but soon enough I slipped into a rehearsal of the report I would give Andy when I called the next morning to warn him that Deke Brenner might be on his way back to town. The thought left me shivering. Where the hell had Brenner disappeared to? Was he hiding out in his friend's carriage house in Los Angeles? Or spending the night at the Oceanside Motel twenty minutes up the highway? At two-thirty I got up and moved Andy's gun from my dresser to the top drawer of my nightstand.

27

So our boy's coming back to town, is he?'' Andy sounded positively gleeful when I called him late Tuesday morning to report what I had learned from Sunshine and Woody about Deke Brenner's disappearance and his intended return to Black Bay. ''We'll be ready for him this time. As soon as we hang up, I'll issue an APB. We'll nail that sonofabitch as soon as he sets foot in Sonoma County.''

I didn't share his enthusiasm. ''That's great, Andy, but if Brenner really was on his way back to Black Bay, why would he leave his truck illegally parked and his dinner on the table?''

That brought him down a notch. ''Good question.''

''Besides, he specifically told Woody he was going to *drive* up from L.A. so he wouldn't risk getting caught carrying pot on the plane.''

''Maybe he rented a car.''

''Yeah, maybe.''

''I think I'll hold off on that APB.''

Peter came into the kitchen as I hung up. It was almost eleven-thirty, but his hair was a tousled mess and his eyes were red and puffy with sleep. He had been up past three the night before boarding up the broken window in the den and had slept fitfully when he finally came to bed. ''Who was that?''

''Andy.''

He yawned and shuffled toward the coffeepot.

"Your *friend* Andy," I said.

He didn't catch my meaning. "He's not *my* friend. You're the one who dated him. Guy's not much of a cop, if you ask me."

"Why not? Because he won't take a bribe?"

He set the coffeepot down and turned slowly to face me. "What are you talking about?"

I fought to keep the emotion out of my voice. Over the course of another long night I had resolved to broach the topic, but this was not quite how I had planned to do it. I started over. "Andy's been acting real strange lately, Peter, like he thinks I owe him something."

He leaned against the counter, looking confused, his coffee forgotten. "That's crazy. Why would you owe him anything?"

"I can't imagine, unless you offered him some of our insurance money, like you suggested last week."

"I didn't do that. You said not to." He looked me straight in the eye without blinking. Only the desperate staccato clicking of his fingernails betrayed his anxiety.

"Peter—"

He went back to the coffeepot and filled his mug.

"Don't lie to me. I asked Andy. He admitted it."

He spun around, his face pinched with anger. "Goddamnit, Frannie, we had to do something. You were too proud to do it yourself."

"Proud? We're not talking about *pride*, Peter. This has nothing to do with pride." My voice grew more shrill with each word. "We're talking about murder and bribery, but we are most certainly *not* talking about pride."

He took a deep breath and let it out slowly, refusing to raise his voice. "We're talking about doing what it takes to keep you out of jail."

"There's no need to keep me out of jail. I didn't kill Sid."

He took a swallow of coffee and struggled visibly to get it down.

"You know you only made me look worse by doing that."

"No I didn't. I didn't push it that hard. I suggested it to Andy, off-the-record, but he said no, so I dropped it. It went no further than that."

"*Off-the-record?* Who the hell did you think you were talking to, Peter? A newspaper reporter? The police do not go off the goddamn record."

I stormed out of the room and slammed the door behind me. Two minutes later I was in my Jeep, speeding toward town, still swearing.

*   *   *

Millicent was out to lunch when I got to the office, so I had to use my key to get in. I was sorry to have missed her. I needed someone to cheer me up—and calm me down.

Sam Goldman was in his office on the telephone, and Bob Green was out, as usual. I went through the motions of turning on my computer and pulling out a few files, but I knew I wouldn't be able to work. To pass the time until Sam was available and to keep my mind off Peter, I made some calls of my own. I dialed Barry Stein's number first. I expected to get his answering machine and did.

"Hello. This is Barry. I'm not here right now, but leave your number and I'll call you back."

Basic message, but the sound of his voice made me smile. "Hi, Bear. It's Fran calling to say thanks for dinner last night and to apologize for running out like I did. Please don't be sorry about what happened. I'm not. Anyway, thanks for dinner, and congrats again on the job. No need to call back. Bye."

I hung up quickly and closed my eyes. Damn. Why did I tell him not to call back? I did want him to call, but now of course he wouldn't.

I tried Sunshine next. She kept a wild schedule, so I figured she might be home, probably just waking up.

"Helllooo."

"Sunny, it's Fran."

"Hey girl, what's the news?"

"No news. I thought maybe you'd heard from Deke."

"No sign of the guy. Reginald thinks he's hiding."

"Hiding? From the police?"

"From the police, from all the people he owes money—including Reginald, who's madder than shit at the guy—from that Monty character, from you. Who knows? D.B.'s got lots of folks he'd rather not deal with these days. His truck disappeared. I'm betting it's been towed."

We chatted for a few minutes, but Sunny had no more information. I reminded her to call if she heard anything new and then went to talk to Sam.

He was still on the phone, but he hung up when he saw me. "Fran, how are you?"

"I'm okay."

"Just okay?"

I told him about the police's decision not to arrest me—yet—and about

my anonymous caller and how Deke Brenner was missing. I had not
intended to mention Peter's attempt to bribe Andy, but in the end I told
him about that too.

His face was pale and drawn, but he tried to smile. "It's quite something that Peter went ahead and offered the bribe after you told him
not to."

" 'Quite something' is right. You know why he did it, don't you?
Because he thought I was guilty." I picked up a plastic paper clip and
started to twist it. "In his heart of hearts he *still* thinks that, even now
that the police are investigating other suspects. I can tell. He gets all
twitchy and short-tempered, and he looks at me strangely sometimes, like
he mistrusts me." The paper clip snapped in half, and I tossed the pieces
in the general direction of the wastebasket.

"Come now, Fran. I can't believe anyone who knows you as well as
Peter does would think you killed your sister. He might be convinced the
police think you did it, but I can't believe he thinks that himself."

We sat in silence while I searched for a better explanation for Peter's
behavior. All I came up with was one that was worse. I sucked in a deep
breath and held it. "Sam?"

"Yes?"

"What if Peter killed her?"

His eyes flew open. "Peter? What makes you say that?"

"I don't know. Damn. The way he's been acting, I guess. It's different,
ever since the morning we found out about the insurance. He's been
desperate to get me off the hook, Sam, desperate. Even to the point of
risking a bribe." I felt sick to my stomach and light-headed.

"Clearly Peter is upset by what's happened. I imagine—"

"Jesus, Sam. What if he did it?"

"Okay, Fran. Hold on a minute." He reached across the desk and took
my hand. "Let's say Peter did do it. Why? Why would he kill Sidney?
He doesn't strike me as a violent man."

"Peter never liked Sid. And he really didn't like the way she was acting
after Mom's funeral." I squeezed his hand to stop my own from shaking.

"So he killed her? That doesn't make sense. He could have gotten rid
of her easily enough by sending her back to L.A. Why would he go to
the trouble of pushing her off a cliff? He's got no mo—" He cut himself
off with a frown. "There is the insurance, I suppose. He certainly will
stand to benefit when you collect the money."

"He will, except fortunately he didn't know about the policy until after

Sid was already dead. The first he heard of it was when Dad called the day after Sid's car was found."

"Any other motive? Any particular trouble between them?"

I thought for a minute but couldn't come up with anything. "Nothing specific, except Peter didn't like Sid, and he knew she and I didn't get along. Maybe he thought he was doing me a favor by getting her off my neck. After Mom's death I wasn't coping with her very well. I made some comments. Shit. Maybe he took them a little too literally."

"I understand there was tension, Fran, but unless we come up with something more concrete, I think we're off track. People like your husband don't kill without a compelling reason."

I reached for another paper clip and started twisting, too worked up to abandon my suspicions so quickly.

Sam sensed my determination and pulled out a scratch pad and pen. "I don't have much experience with criminal law, but I do know the police look for three elements: motive, opportunity, and means. All three must be present before someone can be classified as a viable suspect." He jotted the three words on his pad and put a dash under *motive*. "How about opportunity? Where was Peter the night Sid was killed?"

"At work. He had the graveyard shift from ten that night until six the next morning."

"Could he have left during that period, taken a break to kill her and then gone back?"

I grinned—a little sheepishly—and tossed the paper clip onto the desk. "No, I guess not. Not according to the police. They say they checked the MiniMart's security videotape and Peter was on camera all night."

Sam put a dash under *opportunity* and smiled. "So, not much motive and apparently no opportunity. The final element is means. Can we eliminate that too?"

"He would have had the means, I suppose. He's stronger than Sid, and if he had approached her that night she would have trusted him. She'd probably have gotten in his car or met him somewhere if he asked her to, although I have a hard time picturing his Volvo pushing her VW over the cliff and making it back to the highway without getting stuck in the mud. It's like quicksand out there, and Peter's not much of an off-road driver."

Sam put a question mark under *means*. "As I count it, we're scoring about one-half out of three. I'm not convinced."

"Me either."

He tore the page off his scratch pad, wadded it into a ball, and tossed it into the wastebasket. For a few minutes at least, I had gotten Peter back for mistrusting me.

Sam had less than a half hour before his next conference call, so we walked to Fritzel's Deli for sandwiches to eat at our desks. We were next up in line when I heard a familiar voice behind me. I glanced over my shoulder and saw Harlan Fry standing four feet away.

He caught my eye and nodded. "Hello, Mrs. Estes."

I had been deciding between a BLT and a turkey club, but now I didn't feel like either. I told him hello and turned back to the counter. Sam ignored him and ordered a ham and Swiss on rye. I asked for the same thing, figuring it would be the fastest way to get us out of there. I did not let myself look back at Harlan until we had our lunch bags and were ready to go. As I feared, he had not gotten into line to order a sandwich.

We walked past him and out the door without a word, but we made it no more than a few steps down the sidewalk before he caught up to us. "I wonder if I might have a word with you, Mrs. Estes."

"Yes. What is it?" I made myself look him in the eye.

"I understand you interrogated Woody Hanks last night at the Seahorse Pub."

"I was in San Francisco yesterday, Lieutenant. When I got home at eleven o'clock last night, I found Woody's truck stopped in front of my house. I followed him to the Seahorse to ask what he was doing there. I learned later that someone threw a rock through one of our windows. I suspect it may have been him."

Harlan, of course, did not inquire about the broken window. Since it did not support his theory of the case, he apparently wasn't interested. "Let me remind you of one thing, Mrs. Estes. You are still a suspect. Your meddling might backfire on you. Don't think that just because we haven't arrested you yet, we won't."

Sam placed his hand on my arm. "What's your point, Lieutenant?"

"My point, Mr. Goldman, is simply that your client will be in big trouble if she interferes in any way with the investigation of this case."

"Are you telling me my client is not permitted to ask Woody Hanks why he was parked outside her house at eleven o'clock at night?"

"No, I didn't say that."

"Good. Let's be sure we understand each other, Lieutenant. My client's sister has been murdered and my client is trying to determine who's responsible. To that end, she has a right to ask whatever she pleases of whomever she chooses.''

Harlan glared at me. ''Your client has already been caught attempting to destroy evidence and lying to the police, Mr. Goldman. I'm warning you both, she won't get away with it again.''

He wheeled around and marched across the street to his Blazer, leaving us standing there, lunch bags in hand, watching him drive away.

After a speechless moment, Sam put his arm around my shoulders and steered me toward the office. ''Don't let the tough-guy act get to you, Fran. Fry's a fool for going after you, but now he's too far into it to give up gracefully. Let him humiliate himself if he insists on it.''

Millicent was back at her desk by the time Sam and I returned from the deli. She sprang to her feet at the sound of our voices outside the door.

''Hello, you two. Fran, dear, how are you?'' The phone rang as she rounded the corner of the reception desk, but she continued toward me with outstretched arms. ''Sam, could you get that, please?''

With an amused ''Yes, boss,'' he went for the phone.

Millicent swept me into a much-needed embrace. ''If I'd known you were coming in, I would have brought a pecan pie for you to take home.'' Her thin fingers pushed my hair out of my eyes. ''You look tired, dear. Are you okay?''

''I'm fine, Mil. I didn't get much sleep last night, that's all.''

By now Sam was standing over us. ''Sorry to interrupt, ladies, but I just transferred Jerry Hazelton into my office. I need you to pull his file, Milly. I've got no idea where you've hidden it.''

Millicent gave my arm a firm pat and whispered ''job security'' as she scooted off to the file room.

I retreated to my office and settled in with a yellow legal pad and a sharp pencil. I planned to compile a list of people who might have killed my sister and review each of the suspects using Sam's motive-opportunity-means test.

Millicent looked in before I had written any names. ''Can I get you anything, dear?''

''No thanks, Mil. I'm just going to sort through my thoughts and make a few phone calls. I'll come out later and we can visit.''

She pointed at my unopened Fritzel's bag. ''You will eat your lunch, I hope.''

''Yes, ma'am.'' I dutifully pulled out my sandwich and took a bite.

"By the way, a man called for you this morning. He wouldn't leave his name, said he'd try you at home."

I nodded and did my best not to show my excitement. Maybe there would be a message from Barry Stein waiting for me at the house. For the first time in days, I would be eager to check the answering machine.

As soon as Millicent disappeared I wolfed down my sandwich and picked up my legal pad. I sketched out a chart with four columns, which I labeled *Suspect, Motive, Opportunity,* and *Means.* Under the *Suspect* heading I listed Deke Brenner, Woody Hanks, P. K. "Monty" Monteil, and two nameless candidates who I identified as "Anonymous Caller" and "April's Killer." At the bottom of the page I made a final entry called "Others/Sid's New Boyfriend?" Then I went back to the top of the list and inserted Peter's name. He would make a good warm-up.

Under the *Motive* heading for Peter, I wrote: "Killed her for me? Didn't know about the insurance." Under *Opportunity,* I wrote: "At work. Security video." Under *Means,* I wrote: "Yes, except for the mud."

I looked at my chart and smiled. The exercise might be pointless, but it made me feel as if I was at least trying to do something.

I went on to Deke Brenner. In the *Motive* column, I wrote: "Lover scorned. Drugs." Under *Opportunity:* "Followed Sid to Black Bay. Has no alibi for that night." Under *Means:* "She would have trusted him, but how did he know to dump her at Pirate Point? Did she take him there herself?"

For Woody, I wrote under *Motive:* "Creepy behavior. Drugs." Under *Opportunity:* "Last known person other than me to see her alive. Found her car the next morning. Under *Means:* "She would have trusted him. He knows Pirate Point would be a good place to dispose of the body."

The phone rang before I started on Monteil. Hoping it would be Barry, I grabbed the call before Millicent could beat me to it.

"Fran?"

Not Barry. "Yes? Who is this?"

"Kevin Grant from the *Recorder.* We met last week."

I groaned inwardly. "Yes? What do you want?"

"I was hoping to talk to you about the investigation of your sister's death. The police won't discuss it with me, but my sense is they might be, well, floundering."

"Your *sense?*"

"I do have a few sources, but unfortunately they've not given me much to go on."

"And you think I will?"

"I thought we could trade information."

"I don't think so. If the police don't feel it's appropriate to make a statement, I'm sure I shouldn't either. So, I'm afraid I have nothing to say—" I stopped just short of hanging up and added in a more cordial tone, "I'd be happy to hear your information, however."

He laughed. "That's not much of a trade." I could see him in his cluttered cubicle at the newspaper, grinning as he spoke. "I understand you've become the Sam Spade of Black Bay and the cops don't appreciate it."

"Off-the-record?"

"Sure."

"The cops don't appreciate my efforts because I've turned up more leads and better evidence than they have."

"Their attitude doesn't strike you as suspicious?"

"It strikes me as egocentric."

"It strikes me as suspicious. If I were in their shoes, I'd sit on my goddamn ego and remember that a woman has been murdered. If I really wanted to solve the case, I'd take the help anywhere I could get it."

"Are you insinuating that the cops don't want to solve the case?"

He lowered his voice to a conspiratorial whisper. "Between you and me, that's exactly what I'm insinuating. I might be wrong. I hope I am. But two women have been murdered. The circumstances are similar. The first case was never solved and probably never will be. The second case is headed in the same direction. The cops hushed something up in the first case and now they're turning away perfectly good assistance from someone who wants to help them solve the second one."

"You're omitting the part about that someone being their prime suspect. That's why they don't want me meddling."

"That's what they say."

I thought through his theory. His criticism of the police was well-founded, but not for the reasons he thought. The information they had *hushed up* in the first case was the fact that April was pregnant and Andy was going to claim the baby. That fact was embarrassing, but not necessarily relevant to her murder. As for his second point—about the police not accepting my assistance—it certainly applied to Harlan Fry, but not so much to Andy or Dominick Carbone. They hadn't been exactly receptive or tactful, but they had listened.

"Fran? Any comment?"

"No. Sorry."

"You think about it." He sounded frustrated. "If you decide you want to brainstorm, you have my number. My home phone's in the book. Call anytime."

"Okay."

"I mean it. We're on the same side here, Fran. I want nothing more than for your sister's killer, and for April Kaminsky's killer, to be caught, prosecuted, and punished. I'm not sure the police feel the same."

I considered what he said after we hung up. His judgment might be clouded by his desire for a front-page story, but I nevertheless added Andy Saybrook, Harlan Fry, and Dominick Carbone to my list of suspects.

After my conversation with Kevin Grant, I took a half-hour cookie break with Millicent and then resumed work on my suspect chart, which had grown to two legal-length pages. I filled in the blank boxes as best I could for Monteil and for the newly added Black Bay police officers, but there weren't many details I could include for my anonymous caller or for April's killer, except to question whether Sid had been sexually assaulted before she was killed.

With the skeleton chart completed, I went back to the beginning to flesh out my notes and perhaps eliminate some of the names. Peter was my top suspect, in placement on the chart if not in probability of guilt. I was still furious at him for trying to bribe Andy, so I decided to make a couple of calls before crossing him off the list. Maybe later I would tell him what I had done, so he could experience what it felt like to be a murder suspect.

I had to check my Rolodex for my father's phone number in Dallas. He'd had the same number for years, but we didn't talk often enough for me to have it memorized. The recorded greeting on his answering machine said he was out of town, on holiday, but would be checking messages and returning calls. I reminded him to record a new greeting and asked him to call me as soon as possible.

I called the station house next. I did have that number memorized, unfortunately. My friend the onion-head answered and put me on hold.

After two minutes Andy picked up. "What now, Fran?"

"Hello to you too, Andy."

"Hello. I have another call holding. What do you want?" He covered the phone and said something to someone else while he waited for my response.

"You know that gun you gave me?"

"Uh-huh." He went back to his other conversation, clearly uninterested in what I had to say.

"I shot Peter."

"Jesus Christ! You what?" That got his attention.

"Not really."

"Fran—"

"Look, Andy, I need your help."

"My help?" His tone had gone from distracted to panicky to skeptical in the space of a few seconds.

"I want to check out the MiniMart security video for the night Sid was killed. You guys still have it?"

"Yeah, we still have it, but the answer's no. I'm not handing out that video to anybody, especially you."

"Why not? I thought you said it doesn't show anything except Peter sitting there all night."

"That's right, but it could turn out to be evidence. The case is still open. That tape is not leaving the station, Fran. Forget it."

It occurred to me that I should have done this in person. I seemed to have better luck with Andy face-to-face. "Can I come in and watch it there?"

"Absolutely not."

"Why not?"

"Why do you want to see it?"

"I'd rather not say." If he had half a brain, it would be obvious.

"Then that's why you're not seeing it. You are a suspect in this investigation, Fran, in case you've forgotten."

"Believe me, I haven't forgotten, Andy. If you won't let me see the video, could you check something for me?"

He let out a loud *I'm-being-imposed-upon* sigh. "What?"

"Two things. I'd like to know what Peter was wearing that night and whether the tape runs for a full eight hours."

"I remember what he was wearing. A plaid work shirt and jeans. I can't tell you what color the shirt was because the film's in black and white. As for the tape running for eight hours, I already told you it covered Peter's entire shift. I assume that's eight hours, give or take. There's no date and time marker, so I can't say exactly. Now, if that's it—"

"Wait, Andy. That doesn't answer my question."

It did answer one of them. I was happy to hear Peter had been wearing a plaid work shirt and jeans. It was what I had expected, since he wore pretty much the same uniform all the time, and what I thought I remembered he'd had on that night. But Andy's cavalier response about the length of the tape didn't suffice. Sam had asked whether it was possible Peter had taken a break to kill Sid sometime during his shift. I had told him no, but in truth I didn't know that for sure. I was familiar enough with the MiniMart's security camera to know that it was positioned to capture a single stationary shot of the store's front entrance, checkout counter, and cash register. It was operated from a switch on the back of the camera, enabling it to be deactivated by someone who was offscreen. Unless there was some activity within the camera's view at the time it was turned off or when it was turned back on, the film wouldn't necessarily show any break. But if Peter had switched off the camera and gone out to kill Sid and dump her over the cliff at Pirate Point, the time he spent on camera that night would have been considerably less than eight hours. The scenario was a bit far-fetched, perhaps, but possible.

"What's your question, Fran? I've got to take this other call."

"I need you to time the video to see how long Peter's shift lasted that night. And I'd love it if you'd watch it straight through to see if there are any obvious breaks in the film."

"Jesus, Fran—" From the tone of his voice I gathered he had finally figured out what I was getting at.

"Please, Andy."

"What the hell is going on?"

"Nothing. This is nothing, really."

"It's not nothing if you're telling me your husband wasn't at work for a full shift that night."

"Look, just check the video. If you find something troubling, we'll talk about it. Promise me you'll talk to me first and not—"

I was cut off by a rap at my door. Millicent stuck her head in and whispered that my father was holding for me. I told her to find out where he was and tell him I'd call him right back, but she said she had already tried that and Dad had refused to say where he could be reached.

I went back to Andy. "My father's on the other line, long-distance. I have to take his call. Will you check out the video and discuss it with me before you talk to anyone else?"

"I'll talk to you first, but if I find something I have to report it."

"That's fine." I was happy to cross that bridge if we came to it. I didn't expect we would.

I forced my brain to shift gears and nodded to Millicent to transfer my father's call. "Thanks for calling back, Dad. Where are you, anyway?"

"What does it matter where I am?" He sounded rushed and grouchy, as Andy had. "I'm at home, of course. Why are you calling? Is there news about your sister?"

"No news, unfortunately. I have one quick question and then I'll let you go." We no longer bothered with a pretense of affection.

"What's that?"

"When you were here for Mom's funeral, did you and Peter discuss insurance?"

"Insurance? Does he want to get into the business?"

"No. I mean the policies on our family, you know, Sid and me. Did you happen to mention them?"

"No, of course not." He hesitated. When he continued his tone was warmer. "When will you have the money?"

"Not for a while. They've held up the payment until the investigation is over." As an insurance agent, he should have known that.

"Frances?"

"Yes?"

"I have something to ask you. You see, I've gotten myself involved in . . . well, an investment opportunity. It's temporarily drained my cash. I thought . . ."

I squeezed my eyes shut, awaiting the blow.

"Maybe I could borrow some of the money once you get it. In view of the fact that I'm the one who paid the premiums for all these years, I think it's only fair."

First my sister and now my father. Apparently my family thought I was better suited for banking than for law. "What kind of investment opportunity, Dad?"

"That's confidential, Frances." His voice cooled a good ten degrees. "It's really none of your concern."

"Excuse me, but if it's my money it is my concern."

"Well, I'm not prepared to discuss it with you."

"Fine. Then I'm not prepared to make a loan."

We sat for an interminable fifteen seconds before he started snarling out loud. "You seem to have forgotten something, young lady. Your sister did too—"

"We forgot what, Dad?"

"Goddamnit, I'm still your father."

"Yes, you are. But you're not still the boss."

"Frances—"

"Sorry, Dad."

"You owe me that money, Frances."

"I owe you nothing."

With that, I quietly hung up the phone and buried my head in my hands.

It was after seven when I left the office. I stopped at Paulsen's Market on my way home to pick up a chicken breast and a box of rice pilaf, but I wound up leaving the store with a sourdough baguette, a wedge of brie, a six-pack of diet root beer, and two red licorice ropes. Peter was having dinner in San Rafael with his former supervisor from Intersoft and wouldn't be home until late, so I was on my own for the evening. If brie and red licorice couldn't make me feel better, nothing could.

I drove slowly, stretching out the drive so I could catch all three Van Morrison songs playing on the local FM station's dream set. I had hummed along through "Moondance" and was belting out the chorus of "Brown-Eyed Girl" when I noticed that the same pair of headlights had been behind me the whole time.

I stopped singing and snapped off the radio. "Okay, Fran," I said aloud. "Chances are that car isn't really following you, it just happens to be going in the same direction." And it just happened to be content to poke along doing forty in a fifty-five-mile-per-hour zone.

I sped up to fifty-five, but the headlights did not drop back. Nor did they at sixty. Or sixty-five. If anything, they seemed to be coming closer. Reluctant to pull over for fear the other driver would too, I continued to accelerate, now cruising considerably faster than was prudent on the narrow winding highway.

The lights disappeared when I squealed around the last major curve before home but seconds later they returned in full force, much closer now, blinding me with their high beams and dashing any hope I might have had of distinguishing the type or color of the vehicle. When I got to our driveway I drove on by, heading for refuge at the nearest all-night gas station ten miles up the road in Milton.

I squeezed the steering wheel in a sweaty death grip as I sped past the turnout at Pirate Point and approached the Seahorse Pub, where a station wagon was pulling onto the highway and into my path. Praying no one would suddenly appear over the crest of the next hill, I laid on my horn and swerved into the oncoming lane, forcing the surprised driver onto the shoulder as I careened past. In my rearview mirror I watched my pursuer do the same and could only hope the driver of the wagon had been sufficiently terrorized to return to the pub and call the police.

North of the Seahorse the highway veered sharply closer to the cliffs, clinging to the very edge of the coastline as it wound its way along what in daylight was some of the North Coast's most spectacular terrain. I drove with one foot on the accelerator and the other on the brake so I could maintain as much speed as possible through the sharp curves. Without taking my eyes off the blur of gray pavement disappearing beneath me, I peeled my right hand off the wheel, wiped it on my jeans, and reached to the passenger seat for my handbag. If necessary I would make a quick detour into the ditch and pull Andy's gun.

The first blow struck while I was driving one-handed, fumbling for the pistol. It sent the Jeep lurching forward and onto the right-hand shoulder. I jerked my hand free, sending the bag and its contents spewing onto the floor and out of reach. I managed to get the Jeep back onto firm pavement just in time to take the next hit. This one sent me fishtailing across the oncoming lane, straight for the cliff.

On the far side of the highway there was no gravel shoulder. Only air, and fifty feet below, rock and water. In slow motion I wrenched the wheel hard to the right, acutely aware of my gaze skimming the jet black Pacific and my tires grappling for purchase on the ragged edge of the pavement. They grabbed, but with no more than a few inches to spare.

Gulping for air and leaning so far forward my chin knocked against the steering wheel, I felt the Jeep respond to my panicky pressure on the accelerator. Any faster and I would catapult off the road even without help from my pursuer, but I was incapable of easing up. My frenzied gasps were punctuated by the squeal of rubber on cement as I surged into the next curve. My heart threatened to explode in my chest. With each desperate jerk of the wheel, the seat belt cut more deeply into my collarbone.

I braced myself for a third jolt, but it didn't come. After several excruciating seconds, I diverted my eyes from the road to my rearview mirror just long enough to see that the other driver had fallen two car-lengths behind. I kept up my speed and didn't risk checking again until the first lights of Milton beckoned in the distance, by which point he had dropped back considerably.

By the time I blasted into town he had abandoned the chase, but I was still choking with fear when I pulled into a twenty-four-hour Chevron station and staggered out of the Jeep. My legs were too shaky to offer much support, and I stumbled to my hands and knees, half sobbing as I scrambled across the lot to the cashier's booth.

* * *

Ten minutes later a black and white Blazer squealed up behind my Jeep. A lanky blond kid in uniform spilled out and jogged into the station where I was waiting with the cashier.

"Hello, Mrs. Estes," he said. "I'm Theodore Cruise. We met a couple weeks ago at Pirate Point."

He offered his hand and I took it gratefully, although my own was still clammy and trembling. "Yes, of course. Thanks for coming."

"The dispatcher said you were being followed."

I nodded. "To put it mildly."

I thanked the cashier for letting me use the phone and led Cruise outside to show him the fresh dents in my bumper. I described to him what had happened and how I had not been able to get a good enough look at the vehicle to provide even a minimal description.

He listened to my account with far less skepticism than I likely would have received from Andy or Harlan. "You did the right thing by coming here, Mrs. Estes. I'll check back at the Seahorse; maybe they can identify the driver of that station wagon. Then I'll take a ride up and down the coast, see if I find any unsavory characters."

I nodded my thanks and kicked a pebble into the street. I wasn't particularly reassured by his plan, but what else could he do? "I know you've talked to my husband about the anonymous phone calls we've been getting the past few days," I said. "I'm wondering if this could be the same guy." I also wondered if it was the same guy who had stalked April Kaminsky before he killed her.

He nodded. "Or the one who gave your sister problems a few weeks back."

I assumed he was referring to Sid's murderer, but his comment was oddly put, and Sid had been killed only two weeks ago. "*Problems*? You mean the guy who killed her?"

"No, before that, the one who tried to run her off the ro—" He saw the look on my face and stopped. "You didn't know about that?"

"Somebody tried to run her off the road?"

"Yeah. I'm surprised she didn't tell you herself. Andy Saybrook took a call from her one night about a week or so before she was killed. Some asshole tried to run her off the highway. Unfortunately it happened on a dark stretch and it was pouring down rain, so she didn't get a look at the vehicle. There wasn't much that could be done about it at the time. As far as we know, it didn't happen again."

"How come I wasn't informed of this?"

He shrugged. "Nobody was. Andy didn't mention the call to anyone until a few days ago. Last Friday afternoon he and Harlan Fry met with Chief Carbone to brief him on the investigation. That's when Andy brought it up for the first time. I wasn't in the meeting myself, but I heard the ruckus and asked Andy about it later. Seems he'd been too busy to enter the incident in the official log when it first happened and then he just plain forgot about it. He still had his notes of what your sister said, but because the call had been mishandled Harlan insisted the whole thing should be ignored, like it never happened. Apparently Harlan really threw a fit over it, but in the end the chief decided it could be relevant to your sister's death, like maybe that's what happened to the Kaminsky woman, some guy ran her off the road and then went after her."

"Is that why I'm not sitting in jail right now?" Cruise tactfully had not pointed out that the primary purpose of the briefing last Friday had been for Carbone to determine whether there was enough evidence to justify my arrest. Sid's call would have muddied the case against me.

His rosy cheeks turned rosier. "Part of it, I guess. The chief figured the incident would come out in court if you were brought to trial. If nothing else, it'd be a way for your attorney to create a reasonable doubt."

"I understand," I said, but I didn't really. The Sid I knew would not have called the police to report somebody trying to run her off the road. It wasn't in her nature to call the police about anything, certainly not without later complaining about it to me and Peter. I had a sick feeling that Andy's memory of Sid's call might have been prompted by his conversation with Peter about the insurance money.

"Look, Officer Cruise, I'd like to go home and have dinner. I wonder if you'd come with me to make sure it's safe."

He followed me home and walked with me through the house, but his jittery fingers twitched toward his holster at every sound, grating on my already raw nerves. Nobody was there and we found no sign that anyone had been, so he left, promising to drive by periodically until he went off duty at ten-thirty. I locked the door behind him and carried my groceries into the kitchen, where I sat for a moment massaging the welt on my collarbone. The light on the answering machine was blinking, so I pressed the play button, hoping for a message from Barry Stein. All I got was silence.

I ate my baguette and brie at the kitchen table, but they didn't provide much comfort. I skipped the root beer and red licorice. At nine o'clock I took my gun upstairs and went to bed, where I lay listening to the wind and straining for the familiar crunch of the Volvo's tires pulling into our gravel driveway. It wasn't until Peter crawled in beside me at midnight and I snuggled up against his cool back that I finally felt my anger and fear fading into sleep.

28

I was in the kitchen nursing a glass of diet root beer and picking red licorice out of my teeth when the phone rang Wednesday morning. I dove to get it before Peter picked up in the bedroom, still stubbornly hopeful Barry might return my call.

When my anxious hello was met with silence I slammed down the phone, but seconds later it rang again. I snapped up the receiver, prepared to scream a string of my best obscenities, but before I got it to my ear I heard Peter sleepily saying hello.

"Fran Estes?" There could be no mistaking the high-pitched male voice.

"I've got it, Peter," I said, waiting to hear the click of the upstairs line before I continued. "Deke Brenner?"

"Yeah."

"Where are you? Why are you calling?"

He took so long to respond I thought maybe he had changed his mind, but finally he said, "I need to talk to you . . . about Sid. I have some information I think you should know . . . about somebody who might have killed her." He spoke in a slow, lilting drawl, as if he was high.

"What is it?"

"I can't tell you over the phone. I need to see you."

See me? I sucked in my breath. Was Brenner back in Black Bay? Had he been at the wheel of the vehicle that nearly knocked me off the road the night before? Could he be the one who threw a rock through our window the previous night? "Where are you?"

"I'm at . . . fuck, I don't know . . . about fifteen minutes from your house."

"Are you coming here?"

"No. Where can I meet you—alone?"

I laughed at the absurdity of his suggestion. "There is nowhere you can meet me alone, Deke. How about meeting me at the Black Bay police station? If you have information about Sid, they should hear it too."

"Fuck you."

"Look, Deke, as far as I'm concerned, until proven otherwise, you're the sonofabitch who killed my sister. There is not a chance in hell I'm meeting you alone."

"I didn't kill Sid and I can prove it, smart-ass. Can you do the same?"

I took a swallow of root beer. "I do want to hear what you have to say, but I'm not going to do something stupid. How about you tell me over the phone?"

"No. I need to . . . show you something." His jerky cadence did nothing for his credibility. I suspected the something he needed to show me might be the weapon he planned to kill me with.

I tried to think of a good compromise, someplace where we could be alone but not entirely. I couldn't come up with much. "How about the Chevron station in Milton? Nobody knows either of us there. We could meet outside in the lot."

"No way. If the cops find out I'm up here they'll be on me like flies on shit."

"Why? If you haven't done anything wrong, there's no reason to be concerned."

"I didn't say I haven't done anything wrong. All I said is I didn't fucking kill Sid."

"Did you come back up north to buy pot from Woody Hanks? He's been expecting you."

He didn't answer.

"Have you talked to Woody yet? The cops shut down his operation."

"I told you I have information about your sister, smart-ass. You want it or not? Cause if you do, you better come up with a place for us to meet, alone, in private—and you better come up with it soon or you'll lose the chance."

Now it was my turn not to answer.

"You hear me?"

"I heard you. I'm thinking."

"What's it going to be?"

"Come to my house. We can meet in the garage. My husband's still in bed. He'll never know."

"No way. We meet somewhere totally private or not at all."

"This is crazy, Deke. Why should I trust you? How do I know you have anything of interest to me?"

"Fuck . . ."

I waited for him to continue, but he didn't.

"Deke? You still there?"

"Does the name Pete mean anything to you?"

Pete? As in Peter? I gripped the edge of the table. "What did you say?"

"You heard me." He knew he had me now. His voice was louder and stronger than before. "You want the information or not? It don't matter to me one way or the other."

Clearly it did matter to him or he wouldn't have gone to such lengths to convince me to meet him. That alone should have been a big red flag, but in the pressure of the moment I caved. I heard myself saying, "Okay. I have a place. There's a vacant cabin off the coast highway just north of town."

It was a foolhardy plan and I knew it, but it was the only thing I could come up with short of telling Brenner I didn't care to hear his information, which was impossible now that he had mentioned Peter, as he no doubt had known it would be. But he didn't know I would be carrying Andy's gun, and if I got into trouble I would be prepared—and I hoped able— to use it.

"How do I get there?"

"It's five miles north of Black Bay, just south of a bar called the Seahorse Pub. There's a paved road that heads into the woods on the east side of the highway. The sign's hard to see because of the trees, but it says Alpine Vista. The cabin is on the right side of the road, a half mile in. I'll meet you out in front, in the driveway. It's the only place back there. The road heads on into the hills for a few miles and then just dead-ends. Nobody ever goes back there. The cabin's vacant. The woman who owns it is gone."

The woman who owned it was dead. I had just given him directions to April Kaminsky's old place.

He told me to meet him there at noon and hung up.

* * *

The phone rang again seconds after my conversation with Brenner, but not before I had begun to panic at the thought of what I had just agreed to do. My hand was shaking as I picked up the receiver and said hello.

"Frank?"

It was Barry. Finally. I stumbled over to the kitchen table and dropped into a chair. "Hi, Bear."

"Is this a bad time? You sound out of breath."

"No, I'm glad you called. I need some advice." I told him about Brenner's call and our date at April's cabin. I did not tell him that Brenner had enticed me to meet him by mentioning Peter.

Barry confirmed what I was thinking myself. "You're nuts, Frankie. You just got done telling me how this guy is a top suspect in your sister's murder, and now you say you're going to meet him at some secluded cabin out in the woods? Promise me you won't go out there on your own. If you won't call the police, at least tell Peter. Bring somebody with you. Promise me that, at least."

I didn't promise. I changed the subject instead. I thanked him again for dinner and apologized for the way it had ended.

He stopped me before I got very far. "Oh no you don't. Don't steal my line."

"You have nothing to be sorry for. Really, Bear."

"I made you uncomfortable."

I started to disagree, but he wouldn't listen.

"Don't make this harder than it already is. I have a speech prepared. Let me give it, okay?"

I swallowed hard and softly said, "Okay."

"I had no business being so forward the other night. I got carried away." His voice was low and shaky. "I'm sure you know how I feel about you, Frankie. I've always thought that if it weren't for Sheila and Peter, we'd have made a great pair. So now, with Sheila gone, I got, well, carried away. The product of a light class load, I guess. Too much time for daydreaming." He attempted a laugh, but it fell flat. "It won't happen again. I owe you and Peter an apology."

I struggled for a response but didn't end up saying anything. In fairness to Peter, Barry and I both owed him an apology, but I was still too angry at him to admit it. *We'd have made a great pair.* Barry thought so too. I was elated and miserable at the same time.

He continued his speech, but my mind had darted off in its own direction—until I heard him talking about coming to Black Bay for the weekend. "How about it, Frankie? I'd love to get out of the city, and I haven't seen Peter in ages."

I wasn't sure I wanted Barry and Peter in the same room. Lately my husband would suffer by comparison. "You really want to drive all the way up here? It's liable to rain all weekend. And Peter will probably have to work most of the time anyway."

"That's just it. I'd feel better if you didn't spend so much time alone, not with everything that's been going on. I'll keep you company. I don't have classes on Friday, so I can drive up in the morning and get there in the early afternoon. I'll leave Sunday evening. How about it?"

I knew I'd probably regret it later, but I couldn't turn him down. "Only if you bring mu shu pork and kung pao chicken."

"You're on."

"And a double order of potstickers."

"You drive a hard bargain, Frankfurter, but I'll even throw in steamed rice and fortune cookies."

"Okay, you're invited."

I called Sunshine Scott next, and woke her up, as I knew I would. It wasn't yet ten o'clock, after all.

"Damnit, girl, can't you understand I keep different hours than you?" Her morning voice was raspy and gruff. "You call back at a civilized time, say two o'clock."

"Sunny, wait. Don't hang up. I have one quick question. It's important."

"What?"

"Has Deke Brenner ever mentioned the name Peter to you?"

"Not that I remember. Why?" Her words were muffled by a yawn.

"He—"

"Wait a minute. There's Pete Van Gilder, who lives down the hall, one of Reginald's buddies. He was friendly with Sid. Too friendly. She didn't like him much, thought he might be a narc. D.B. hates the guy. They're always getting into it over one thing or another. That who you're looking for?"

"I don't know. Deke didn't give a last name." I told her about my conversation with Brenner and pointed out that I had automatically assumed he was referring to my husband.

She laughed. "The only thing I'd *assume* about D.B. is that if you talk to him for more than ten minutes, he's bound to tell you a half-dozen lies. The guy's living in a fantasyland. He belongs in one of two places—

jail or a mental ward.'' She was fully awake now and back on her anti-Deke bandwagon.

"Thanks for the advice, Sunny. I think I know what motivated Deke's comment. I'll take what he tells me with a grain of salt.''

"No, you take it with an ocean of salt, girl. Now I'm going back to bed. When I get up I'll mosey on down the hall and have a chat with Van Gilder. You call me this afternoon after you've talked with D.B. and we'll sort out the shit from the shinola.''

I held off until after eleven o'clock before I crept upstairs to get my gun. I thought if I waited long enough, Peter might come downstairs or at least take a shower. No such luck. He was still half asleep when I tiptoed into the room.

He smiled up at me and yawned. "Morning. Who was that on the phone earlier?''

"Nobody. I mean, just a client. Of Sam's. I'm going in to the office for a few hours. You're working two to ten today, right?''

"No. Graveyard. Bobby Olson's coming over later to work on the Volvo.''

I proceeded to the dresser, watching in the mirror to see if his eyes followed me. For the moment he was gazing at the ceiling, but he would have a perfect view if he bothered to look down. My bag was sitting on top of the dresser and my gun was in the second drawer down, tucked amidst my underwear. I pulled open the drawer, slid the bag into it, and reached back to the far corner of the drawer. Praying Peter wasn't paying attention but afraid to check again, I grabbed hold of the gun and slipped it into the open bag. It came with a pair of panties attached, but I didn't bother to disentangle them.

"Frannie?''

I pulled the bag closed and wheeled around, no doubt looking guilty as hell. "Yes?''

"Who was the second call from? Our anonymous friend?''

I took a breath. "No, it was Barry Stein. He's coming up Friday, for the weekend.''

"Really? You just saw those guys the other night. Why do they want to schlepp all the way up here?'' Peter didn't sound excited about the prospect of houseguests. He also didn't know yet that Barry and Sheila were separated.

"Sheila left Barry, Peter. He's coming by himself.''

"She left him? Like they broke up?''

"Yes. I think Barry's lonely. That's why he wants to get together."

"Wow. Why didn't you tell me before? Barry and Sheila. The perfect couple." He flopped back down in bed. "I guess you never know, huh?"

"I guess not." I pulled a wool jacket out of the closet and headed for the door. "I'll see you this afternoon."

"Yeah. Have a good one."

I was five steps down the hall before I went back to give him a kiss and a hug.

He had gotten out of bed and was standing at the door. "Hang in there, Frannie. We'll get through this."

I prayed he was right and hurried off.

At the risk of running late for my rendezvous with Deke Brenner, I drove into town, intending to take Barry's advice about bringing a chaperon. I stopped by the office first, but Sam was out visiting a homebound client and couldn't be reached. I didn't want to upset Millicent with the truth, so I assured her it wasn't important, chatted a few minutes and promised to drop by later. From there I started toward the police station, but at the last minute I decided against stopping, my intuition telling me I would be better off on my own.

I spent the ten-minute drive to April Kaminsky's cabin fighting off thoughts that it was somehow sacrilegious for me to be meeting Brenner there. The cabin had once been a special place for Sid and me. We had discovered it together on a hiking expedition when we were kids, a dilapidated shack in the woods with no running water or electricity. We adopted it as our secret hideaway and spent countless summer afternoons there, hanging out with two or three other girlfriends, including April. As a high school graduation present, the Kaminskys bought the cabin and the surrounding half acre of land and helped April convert it into a rustic art studio, complete with indoor plumbing, an efficiency kitchen, and electric heat. She and her cocker spaniel, Smoky, had been living there year-round when she was murdered.

When I got to within a hundred yards of Alpine Vista, I pulled onto the shoulder and coasted to a stop. I was already five minutes late for my appointment with Brenner. Another minute wouldn't matter. I wiped my sticky palms on my jeans and moved the gun from my bag to the right-hand pocket of my jacket. With my finger on the trigger, I closed my eyes and visualized being with Andy at the shooting range. If I ran into trouble with Brenner, I would pull out the gun. Hopefully the intimidation factor alone would be enough for me to get control of the situation. If not, I would shoot him in the shoulder or the leg. In the unlikely event that he produced a weapon, I would aim for his chest. As I eased back onto the highway, I remembered what Andy told me when I bragged about being a good shot. *It's not so easy when they're shooting back.*

I rolled down the window to let the breeze cool my burning cheeks and turned onto the narrow asphalt road cut through the pines. After a few seconds the cabin came into view. A beat-up blue pickup was parked in the driveway. I couldn't see Brenner from the road, so I gave a quick honk to let him know I was coming. When he didn't appear, a knot took hold in the pit of my stomach. I pulled into the driveway and inched up beside his truck, steering with my left hand and squeezing the pistol with my right. It was not until I was parallel with the pickup that I saw him.

He lay on his back near the front wheels. A puddle of blood encircled his head like a crimson halo. On the far side of his body, a dark red river flowed along a crack in the blacktop and spilled over the edge of the pavement.

29

I made myself get out of the Jeep and go to Brenner, to be sure he was really dead. His eyes and mouth were shut and he didn't appear to be breathing. The sweet sickly smell of blood mixed with a fainter odor of urine nearly made me gag, but I dropped to my knees and forced myself to lean my head down close to his, listening for a breath, a gurgle, anything. I heard nothing. With one hand covering my nose and mouth, I reached for his neck to check for a pulse. His body was warm, but I found no hint of life.

When I pulled my hand back my fingertips were wet with Brenner's blood. The sight of it sent me bolting for the edge of the driveway, where I retched in the bushes. Then I staggered to a faucet near the back of the cabin, praying it was connected. The water came out cold and strong. I washed the blood from my hand and splashed my face, rinsing the sour taste from my mouth and taking a long drink straight from the tap.

Steadier now, I pushed to my feet and braced myself for an unavoidable second look at Brenner's dead body, but as I turned toward the front of the house, something—intuition perhaps, or a noise—caused me to look up. My breath caught in my throat.

Directly above me was a small wood-frame window divided into four square panes. In it I saw, or thought I saw, the silhouette of a person looking down at me, but in the time it took me to register that I had observed anything at all, the figure had vanished.

Terror shot through my body like an electric shock, leaving me dizzy and nauseated, with a painful tingling in my limbs. If I had in fact seen someone at the window, there could be only one explanation. Brenner's killer was still here, inside the cabin, and he had seen me looking at him.

My mind screamed at me to bolt for the Jeep, but my body refused to cooperate. My knees weakened and my bowels threatened to give way. Trying to believe my imagination had finally run amok, I managed one stiff step and fought to take another.

What I heard next definitely was not my imagination. It was the sound of the screen door at the front of the cabin swinging shut. The sound confirmed my fear. It also jarred loose the chink in my brain that had caused me to freeze.

I took off into the thick cover of trees and brush on the south side of the cabin, charging ahead with my hands outstretched to part the thorny branches that whipped my face and clawed at my wool jacket. I did not look back to see if I was being followed. I didn't have to. I could hear the thrashing in the underbrush behind me. The soil was soft and soggy from the recent rains, and I ran like a drunkard, stumbling and staggering and tripping on tree roots, blasting through the weaker vegetation and bumping like a pinball off the sturdier trunks.

Before long my lungs and my legs began to tire and then to burn. Knowing one or the other would soon give out, I glanced over my shoulder to gauge my chances of escape. My pursuer was a dozen yards back, but still coming. From my quick glimpse I could make out little about him, except that his face and head were hidden in some sort of dark mask.

Then he fired at me.

The shot missed badly and ricocheted off a distant redwood, but it nevertheless knocked me onto all fours, as if I had stepped on a land mine. I scrambled to my feet, sobbing now, but determined to keep running until the bastard shot my legs out from under me. I veered sharply to my right, hoping to get out of his gunsights and onto a course that led more directly toward the highway.

There was no second shot. Although I assumed he was still on my tail, in truth I didn't know for sure. I was too frightened to look and gasping too loudly to hear.

After I had been running for what seemed like miles but probably was no more than a few hundred yards, I caught sight of a clearing and a car cruising past on the highway. I tried to call out but produced little more than a groan, and the car continued on its way. Moments later I staggered into the center of the road, where I was able to make better time despite my exhaustion. I fled south toward civilization and, I prayed, safety.

Hope came in the form of a big rig that bore down on me from around a wide curve. The driver blasted me with his horn, but he had no choice but to slam on the brakes and skid onto the gravel shoulder when I didn't get out of the way. He ground to a halt some fifty yards down the road.

By the time I reached the back of the truck, the driver was out of the cab and marching toward me. He did not look happy but he stopped swearing as he drew near. "What the hell . . ."

He was a giant of a man, only average height but built like the rig he was driving. He was stout enough to be obese, although on closer inspection I saw that his bulk was rock hard. He wore jeans and a dirty black T-shirt stretched tight across his barrel chest. His hair was long and snarled.

"Please, you've got to help me," I stammered. "There's a man back there who's been shot and now the killer is after me. Please—"

He took one look over my shoulder and whisked me to the front of the truck without wasting time on questions. He shoved me into the cab through the driver's door and climbed in behind, grunting as he threw the rig into gear. Neither of us spoke until we had rolled to a stop a mile down the highway, at which point he demanded to know what was going on.

I attempted to summarize my experience back at the cabin and in the woods, but what came out was a breathless, incoherent babble. After a few unsuccessful tries to calm me down, the trucker—Babe, he called himself—held up a hand to silence me. He radioed the police, then produced a tall green thermos from behind his seat.

"Here. Shut up and drink this."

I took the thermos but eyed it skeptically.

"Go ahead. It's only coffee, I promise. You could use something stronger, but coffee's all I got. It's black and it's hot. It'll have to do."

I took a grateful sip. It was only coffee, thick and acidic, but it tasted fabulous. I sank back in the seat and drank some more. By the time the black and white Blazer pulled up and Harlan Fry jumped out, I was down to the last few swallows.

We sped back to April's cabin with sirens screaming and lights flashing. It occurred to me that if Brenner's killer was still in the area he would be instantly warned to get the hell out of our way, but I kept my mouth shut.

I told Harlan where to turn onto Alpine Vista, although he seemed to know well enough where he was going. We screeched to a halt a few feet from the body and he jumped out, barking at me to stay in the vehicle. I was glad to comply. I had no desire to get anywhere near the cabin or, for that matter, to see or smell any more of Deke Brenner.

Harlan gave the body a cursory examination, enough to determine there was nothing left to be done for poor dead Deke. Then, with his gun drawn, he approached the cabin. He peered in a window and tried the front door. It opened and he disappeared inside. Moments later he returned to the Blazer, his gun back in its holster. Without a word to me, he radioed the station and instructed the dispatcher to organize a search of the vicinity and to summon Theodore Cruise to the scene. He also told her to contact Dominick Carbone and the coroner's office. Interestingly, he did not mention Andy Saybrook.

When he finally turned his attention to me, his vehemence came as no surprise. "You want to tell me what the fuck you were doing out here with Deke Brenner?"

I cleared my throat. "I wasn't doing anything with him. He was dead when I arrived."

"That's a fresh body, Mrs. Estes. How long ago did you find him?"

I glanced at my watch. "It's quarter to one now. I got here at twelve-ten or so. I was scheduled to meet him at noon, but like I said, he was already dead when I arrived. Whoever did it was still in the cabin. He saw me from the window and chased me into the woods, shooting at me."

"Shooting at you." Harlan did not sound predisposed to believe me.

"Yes. Shooting at me." As I shifted position I noticed a hard lump pressing against my hip. Andy's gun. Ironically, when I had finally found myself in a situation where I might have needed it, I had totally forgotten it was there.

"You had an appointment with Brenner," Harlan said. "Out here."

I explained how Deke had called me that morning, insisting that we meet somewhere private. "He said he had information about someone he thought might be Sid's killer. He also said he wanted to show me something. Check his pockets. Maybe there's a note or something."

Harlan ignored the suggestion. "Did you go inside the cabin?"

"No. I drove up, found the body, and got chased through the woods." I saw no reason to mention the part about throwing up in the bushes. "Obviously, the person who chased me is the one who killed Brenner."

He raised his thick black eyebrows. "Is that what you think, Detective?"

I stared at the scar above his eye where he'd had stitches a couple weeks ago, but before I could compose a suitable retort another vehicle pulled into the driveway. Theodore Cruise jumped out of his Blazer and jogged toward us. He took one look at Brenner's body and went pale.

Harlan rolled down his window and Cruise hurried over. "Dead?" he asked in a small voice.

Harlan chuckled. "No, Teddy, he's taking a nap. Why don't you wake him?"

Cruise bit his lip but didn't respond.

Harlan opened his door and looked back at me. "Get out of the vehicle, Mrs. Estes."

I did as he said and walked around the back of the Blazer to meet him, staying as far away from Brenner as possible.

He pointed to Cruise's Blazer. "Get in." To Cruise he said, "Take her back to the station. Do a GSR."

As I was climbing into the Blazer I heard Harlan add, "Better read her her rights first. I think our friend here may have gone on a little killing spree."

Back at the station, Theodore Cruise and I sat facing each other in the closet-size room where I had been questioned by Harlan and Andy a week earlier. We had spoken little on the drive from April's cabin, although he did admit, apologetically, that he had not been able to track down the driver of the station wagon I had sped past on my wild ride to Milton the night before.

He placed a cardboard box in the center of the table, but its top was shut, so I couldn't see what was inside. I didn't ask. I expected I would find out soon enough. As instructed by Harlan he read me my rights, though from his tentative tone I gathered he was embarrassed by the formality. After he confirmed that I was prepared—stubbornly and stupidly—to go forward without legal counsel, he extracted a plastic place mat from the mystery box, laid it before me, and directed me to place my hands on the plastic, palms up.

It was then that he noticed my jacket sleeves, which were still damp from the soaking they had gotten under the faucet back at the cabin. The sight made him cringe. "You haven't recently washed your hands, have you?"

I looked down at my palms and nodded. ''When I checked Brenner's pulse, I got blood on them. I rinsed it off.''

He slumped back in his chair and pulled his fingers through his short blond hair. ''Shit. This test is worthless in that case.'' He squeezed his eyes shut. ''Goddamnit.''

''What test?'' I asked meekly.

''Gunshot residue. If you fired a gun within the past couple hours, there'd be residue on your shooting hand. The test won't work if you've washed your hands.''

''Sorry.'' I silently cursed myself for touching Deke's bloody neck. I had known very well by looking at him he was dead, but still I checked for vital signs—for no good reason except I had watched too much TV in my lifetime, so it seemed like the right thing to do.

Cruise sat brooding in his chair, at a loss for what to do or say next.

''Can't you do the test anyway?'' I asked. ''I didn't use soap.''

He gave me a look that said he could not believe I had said something so dumb. ''And have a negative result for you to use as evidence you didn't shoot the guy? Fry would crucify me.''

I shrugged and watched him stew. He had lost my sympathy with his last comment. Theodore Cruise wasn't the only one Harlan was likely to crucify. Only in my case, the term applied more literally.

After a few painful moments, he packed up the cardboard box and pushed back from the table. ''One of us will be in to take your statement, Mrs. Estes. Wait here.''

I managed a weak laugh. ''I wasn't planning on going anywhere.''

I sat alone in the interrogation room for almost an hour. Cruise did not return after he left with his gunshot test kit, probably because he was afraid he would only make things worse if he dared to question me. I spent my solitary confinement reliving my close call back at April's cabin, and in my more lucid moments, developing theories against Woody Hanks and P. K. Monteil.

Finally Harlan came in. As I was expecting, he was in a foul mood. He subjected me to a barrage of questions regarding my previous contact with Brenner and my activities that morning, taking every opportunity to intimidate me with hints of my pending arrest. When I reminded him how Sid and Deke had both been threatened by Monteil, he grudgingly acknowledged that Monteil had been released from prison a week after Sid's death, and his current whereabouts were unknown. Although he wouldn't admit it, I suspected the Black Bay police might consider Monteil a bit more seriously than they had before.

I brought up Woody Hanks next, not expecting Harlan to be receptive.

He leaned back in his chair, folded his arms across his chest, and said coldly, "I'm all ears, Mrs. Estes. Enlighten me."

I took a deep breath. Harlan might let me talk, but it would be up to me to make him listen. I told him about Deke and Woody's pot deal and how Deke had been planning to make a second trip to Black Bay to pick up the shipment in person. "He called me this morning at nine-thirty, totally out of the blue, to say he wanted to meet in private to give me information about someone who might have killed Sid. He said he was fifteen minutes away, but—this is important—he scheduled our meeting for *noon*, a full two and a half hours later. At the time it didn't strike me as odd, but now I'm wondering what he had planned for all that time between nine-thirty and twelve. Maybe he called Woody and arranged to meet him at April's cabin before his appointment with me. Maybe Woody went out there and told Brenner he had no pot for him and Brenner got mad. Maybe they got into an argument and Woody shot him."

Harlan stood up and opened the door. "Or maybe you killed Brenner because he had evidence against *you*. Either you have a hyperactive imagination, Mrs. Estes, or you're trying desperately to attract attention to anyone but yourself."

I followed him into the corridor. "Are you going to question Woody?" I asked the back of his head.

When we reached the door to the public waiting area, he pushed it open and said, "You're dismissed, Mrs. Estes. Go on home and stay there. Don't even think about leaving your house until you hear from me that it's okay. You set foot off your property before I say so and your ass is in jail."

30

It was three o'clock when I finally got home, utterly exhausted from the day's trauma. I was happy to see Peter and Bobby Olson in the driveway, working on the Volvo. Bobby's presence meant I could steal a few minutes of private time before I had to tell Peter what had happened.

He emerged from under the hood of the car and tucked a strand of long brown hair behind his pierced ear. "Hey, Fran, how's it going?" He wiped his hands on a greasy terry cloth rag and came over to kiss my cheek as I climbed out of the Jeep.

I returned the kiss and for appearances gave Peter one too, although after my conversation with Brenner that morning I wasn't feeling particularly affectionate.

"Say, was that your dad I saw downtown a couple days ago?" Bobby asked.

I shrugged. "Last week, maybe." I didn't want to talk about my father, especially with Bobby, who was too young to remember what an asshole he had been. I nodded at the Volvo. "You guys keeping this clunker alive another few hundred miles?"

"Absolutely." He let the hood down softly and gave it a pat. "She's a classic. You take care of her right, she'll run forever." He pulled on a battered leather jacket and began gathering his tools.

"Don't let me chase you away."

"Nah. We're all finished." He glanced at his watch and snapped up his toolbox. "I've been here nearly two hours already, and I'm supposed to meet a buddy downtown in a half hour. I'll have to visit some other time."

After Bobby disappeared through the row of pines separating our property from his parents' lot next door, I reluctantly followed Peter into the house. He washed up in the downstairs bathroom and joined me in the kitchen, where I sat clutching a cold Miller Lite. A second bottle waited on the counter. He twisted off the top and took a swallow.

I kept my eyes on the table. "Deke Brenner is dead."

When Peter stopped choking, he said, "Jesus, what happened?"

"He came back to Black Bay. Somebody shot him in the head."

"Wow. How do you like that? Brenner did come back, just like Woody Hanks said he would."

"Not entirely. Brenner had information about Sid's murder. He came up to . . ." I let my voice trail off, waiting for a reaction.

Peter's unblinking eyes widened. "To what?"

"To report the information."

"What information?"

I had to hand it to Peter. He was doing a remarkable job of looking genuinely confused and curious. I was not so smooth. My mouthful of beer turned sour, and I had to struggle to get it down.

"Frannie, what's going on? Are you okay?"

"Brenner called this morning. He wanted to tell me what he'd found out about Sid."

His jaw tightened, but still he kept his composure. "And?"

"When I left here this morning, I didn't go into work. I went to meet him at April Kaminsky's cabin out on Alpine Vista."

I finally hit a nerve. Peter slammed his bottle down on the table. "You went to meet him at April Kaminsky's cabin? Are you crazy? You went to meet that guy in the fucking wilderness?"

"He claimed to have information about who killed Sid."

"Yeah, right. Who'd he say?"

I stared him in the eye, attempting to muster the courage to answer him honestly.

"Who, Frannie?"

You! I wanted to scream it. *You killed her, Peter. Deke confirmed what I already suspected.* Instead I shrugged and said to the tabletop, "He was dead before I got there."

Over a second beer I told Peter how I had come to find Brenner's body in April's driveway, how I had been chased through the woods by the likely killer, and how Harlan Fry had accused me of making it all up.

He reacted pretty much as I expected he would. His frown deepened into a full-fledged scowl, betraying horror and frustration but little sympathy. "Jesus Christ, Frannie. How many times did you hear from me or Andy or Fry that you shouldn't mess with the cops' investigation?"

"So that's it? I could have been killed, Peter, and I may be arrested for murder—two murders—and all you have to say is *I told you so*?" My voice cracked with exhaustion and stress, and most of all, with disappointment. I had hoped for—and thought I deserved—better than this.

He shook his head. "No, that's not all I have to say."

"Peter, I didn't kill Sid and I *certainly* didn't kill Deke Brenner. I think I can safely say you and I both know that."

"I think we can safely say what you and I know doesn't make any damn difference."

I got up and marched into the living room, slamming the kitchen door behind me. Peter's guitar lay on the couch and his sheet music was spread across the coffee table. I swept them not too gently into a pile on the floor, turned the stereo on loud, and flopped down on the couch with my feet on the table. After fifteen minutes he passed me on his way upstairs. Neither of us said a word.

The living room was cold and growing dark, but I didn't bother to start a fire or switch on a lamp. I stared at a mound of ashes in the fireplace, trying to sort things out, all but oblivious to the incongruously upbeat big band beat blaring at me from the bookcase. At some point the phone rang, but I let Peter get it.

Could it be that I had all the pieces of the puzzle but I was too blind to see how they fit together? I felt as if I'd been spun in circles so many times I was too dizzy to stand up straight. My suspicion of Peter, however unfounded, had been aggravated by Brenner's cryptic comment that morning. *Does the name Pete mean anything to you?* Of course it did, and Brenner knew it. Was that the only reason he said that? To tempt me? Because he knew by mentioning Peter he would get me to agree to meet with him? Sunshine Scott said Deke Brenner was a liar, and she knew the guy a lot better than I did, so why should I believe Brenner when he pointed the finger at my husband?

I pictured the chart of suspects I had made the day before. Peter was on the list for reasons born more of emotion than of logic. I wanted to lash out at him for suspecting me. I wanted him to be on the hot seat for a while, to see how it felt to be mistrusted. But if Peter had killed Sid—

despite the obvious weaknesses of motive, opportunity, and means—I was left with a disturbing tangle of loose ends that couldn't be tied into a neat little bow. Peter did not kill April Kaminsky; he'd never even met the woman. He didn't kill Deke Brenner either, having had no way of knowing Brenner was in Black Bay, let alone out at April's cabin. And he wasn't the asshole who was harassing me with anonymous phone calls. I knew the incidents might not all be related, but surely there must be some connections.

Woody Hanks was a more promising link. Woody had known April well. She had bartended at the Seahorse Pub and was a regular there. He knew Sid too. She used to hang out at the Seahorse before she moved to L.A., and she went back there whenever she was in town. Woody didn't know Deke Brenner very well, but he had unsuccessfully attempted to do a drug deal with the guy. And Woody was just the type of sleazeball who would take pleasure in harassing someone with anonymous phone calls, in throwing a rock through her window, and in running her car off the road—particularly someone who had gotten him into hot water with the police.

I didn't see Peter at first when I opened my eyes. It was nearly completely dark in the living room and I had fallen asleep, so I wasn't aware he had come back downstairs. The stereo was still on, but at a considerably lower volume than before, and my mother's red and green afghan had been wrapped around my legs and pulled up to my chin. He sat facing me in the easy chair next to the fireplace.

"Hi, Frannie." The expression on his face was lost in the shadows, but his tone was friendly if somewhat tentative.

I answered him with a yawn. As I regained consciousness, I reluctantly acknowledged that what had happened earlier that day was not just a bad dream.

"Go back to sleep if you want." Presumably he would continue to sit there in the dark watching me. The prospect was hardly conducive to slumber.

"What time is it?"

"Five o'clock."

I hadn't been out for more than a half hour or so, but it felt like longer. It also felt like longer than seven hours since I had breakfasted on red licorice and root beer. "I need food," I said, pulling myself to my feet.

He followed me into the kitchen. "Want me to fix you something?" He had apparently done some thinking about his unsympathetic attitude earlier that afternoon, and although he didn't want to come right out and say so, he was sorry.

I squinted indecisively in the blinding two-hundred-watt light, inclined to go for the immediate gratification of Triscuits and brie. "Like what?"

Before he could answer, the phone rang.

It was Harlan Fry, summoning me to the station house for further questioning.

Andy ushered me back to the interrogation room, where Harlan and Carbone were waiting. The tiny windowless space was crowded enough with two people; with four of us it was oppressive. Harlan directed me to a solitary metal chair on the far side of the table, and Andy took the remaining seat across from me, to the right of Carbone, who had appropriated the middle chair like a warlord flanked by his serfs.

Carbone took over after Harlan read me my rights, seemingly oblivious to his lieutenant's sulky glare. "Okay, Mrs. Estes. As you were advised by Lieutenant Fry, we have a few more questions. We spoke to Woody Hanks this afternoon. He made some interesting remarks, a few of which require explanation."

Shit. What had Woody told them now? "Such as . . . ?"

"Such as, where were you Monday morning between, say, nine-thirty and ten-thirty?"

I thought for a moment. I had gone to San Francisco Monday for a three o'clock appointment with Dr. Fielding, but I hadn't left the house until eleven. "I was at home."

"Alone?"

"Yes. Peter was in Healdsburg buying parts for his car."

Carbone nodded slowly and pulled on his chin. He didn't take his eyes off mine and he didn't blink. "That's interesting. So nobody can vouch for your whereabouts?"

I felt faint for a few seconds until I remembered my telephone conversation that morning with Sunshine Scott. "I made a phone call to Los Angeles around ten-thirty. Check with the phone company."

"We'll do that. You're sure you weren't in Guerneville that morning?"

"Guerneville?" I didn't try to hide my surprise. Guerneville is an eclectic resort community on the Russian River a half hour east of Black Bay. It was not on my way to San Francisco. "I'm positive, Mr. Carbone. I was not in Guerneville Monday morning."

"Ever hear of The Sportsman?"

"Sure. It's a sporting goods store. In Guerneville."

"Ever been there?"

I shrugged. "Once or twice, years ago. I don't fish or hunt."

"Ever been downstairs?"

"No. I didn't know they had a downstairs."

He nodded again but cocked his head slightly, as if to say he was surprised by my answer—or didn't believe it. "So you're totally unaware that there's an illegal gun shop operating in the basement of The Sportsman?"

"Totally unaware." But not totally surprised. The Sportsman was in a tough neighborhood, adjacent to Guerneville's sleaziest bar. The store catered to rednecks and drunks as well as legitimate hunters and fishermen.

"You have no idea why Woody would say he saw you there Monday morning at ten o'clock? Or why he'd say you bolted up the stairs and out of sight before he could get near you?"

I shook my head in disgust and disbelief. "I have a very good idea why Woody would say those things, Mr. Carbone. To make it look like I killed Deke Brenner."

"Now why would he want to do that?"

"Maybe because he killed Brenner himself. Did you bother to ask Woody what the hell *he* was doing in an illegal gun shop?" I started to explain again how I suspected Brenner had met up with Woody at April's cabin before I was scheduled to arrive at noon, but Carbone cut me off.

"Okay. We understand your theory on that, Mrs. Estes. New topic. The night your sister was killed."

"Yes?"

"You and she were drinking at the Seahorse Pub and you got into an argument."

"Yes."

"Do you recall saying, in the course of that argument, 'I'll dump you where you'll never be found'?"

"No. Of course not."

"But you were so drunk you really don't remember what you said or didn't say. Isn't that correct?"

I shook my head, although what he said was true. "I wouldn't have said that. If Woody told you that, he's lying."

"And is he lying as well about seeing a red Cherokee on the highway that night an hour after you left the bar?"

"Probably. Can't you see what's going on here? Woody's trying to pin Sid's murder on me, and now Brenner's, because he must have killed them himself. He probably killed April Kaminsky too. The guy's a psychopath.''

Harlan glared at me and grunted, but he didn't say a word. Apparently Carbone had instructed him to keep his mouth shut. He looked ready to burst.

Carbone paused to review his notes. Before he resumed his questioning I remembered something. "Wait a second. Woody mentioned seeing a red Jeep before, but from his description the Jeep had to have been driving *northbound* from Pirate Point toward the Seahorse Pub. If I had killed Sid and dumped her over the cliffs I'd have no reason to be driving back in the direction of the pub afterward. It doesn't make sense. He's either making the whole thing up or he saw some other damn Jeep.'' I looked over at Andy, who was cowering in the corner. "Tell them, Andy. We've discussed this before.''

Without so much as a glance at Andy, Carbone said, "I'm afraid you've got the details wrong, Mrs. Estes. Woody said the Jeep was traveling southbound when he saw it, the same way you would have been going to get from Pirate Point to your house.''

"That's not what he said before. He's been talking to Howard Jayco, hasn't he? His story is swinging back and forth like a goddamn pendulum.'' I turned to Harlan. "Have you offered Woody some kind of deal if he provides evidence against me? Is that it? Woody tells you what you want to hear, and he gets off the hook for that pot farm of his? Ninety percent of your evidence against me comes from that liar.''

Harlan could restrain himself no longer. He slapped his palms down on the table and sprang to his feet. "Woody Hanks wasn't the one whose husband offered us five hundred grand to let his wife off the hook.'' He pointed a finger at my face. "You're going to jail, Mrs. Estes—''

Carbone jumped up and grabbed Harlan by the shoulders. "Damnit, Fry, shut your trap.''

Harlan allowed himself to be pushed back into his chair, but he was still pointing at me. "Woody Hanks is doing his civic duty by seeing that you pay for what you've done. We'll get you, Mrs. Estes, and we'll get your husband too, for attempted bribery.''

Carbone looked ready to slam a fist into Harlan's mouth. "That's enough, Lieutenant.'' He swung open the door and jerked his thumb in the direction of the corridor. When Harlan didn't move, he seized him by the collar and pulled him to his feet. "Out. I'll finish this alone.''

Andy remained in his seat in the corner, silently observing Harlan's ejection. Carbone turned back to me without acknowledging his presence. "Do you have anything to say for yourself, Mrs. Estes?"

"Yes. I didn't kill my sister or Deke Brenner. This is crazy."

He folded his arms across his broad chest. "You're going to have to do better than that, I'm afraid. Today is Wednesday. I'm going to the D.A. Friday afternoon to get a warrant for your arrest unless someone changes my mind in the meantime."

"Jesus Christ. Woody Hanks is lying through his teeth. Check out what he's said and you'll see. Call the phone company. At ten-thirty Monday morning I was at home talking to Sid's neighbor in Los Angeles, Sunshine Scott. Here, I'll give you her number." I reached into my handbag, which I had dropped on the floor beside my chair. My fingers found Andy's pistol first and I pushed it to the bottom of the bag. I pulled out the address book, flipped it open to Sunshine's number, and read it aloud.

"I'll check with the phone company, Mrs. Estes, although I don't see what it proves. I've seen you racing around in that Jeep of yours. If you left Guerneville at ten o'clock, I have no doubt you could have been in your house and on the phone by ten-thirty."

"The story about Woody seeing my Jeep that night is a crock of shit too." I looked over at Andy, but he wouldn't meet my eye. "Andy, come on. You know Woody changed his story for no good reason except to incriminate me. First he said he saw a red Jeep heading up the highway toward him. He had to wait for it to go by before he could turn onto the road out to his house. Now he says it was heading south, the same direction he was supposedly going."

Without looking up, Andy said softly, "We asked Woody to think carefully and tell us exactly what he saw that night, Fran. This is how he remembers it."

"Well it's not how he remembered it before. And now, according to Mr. Carbone, he remembers hearing me threaten Sid the night she died. He didn't remember that two weeks ago either."

"Correct."

"How long ago did you bust Woody's pot business, Andy? Friday? It seems to me his memory's gotten a hell of a lot sharper in the past five days."

Andy didn't respond. Carbone watched me and pulled on his chin.

I leaned forward and stared into Carbone's dark eyes. "Friday was the day Woody Hanks hired Howard Jayco to defend him. It also was the day Jayco and Harlan Fry convinced the judge to let Woody out of jail.

And it just happens to be the same day Peter and I started getting anonymous phone calls. You tell all that to the D.A. when you ask for an arrest warrant, Mr. Carbone.''

Andy stayed with me in the interrogation room after Carbone dismissed me and stalked out. He closed the door so we could talk in private, and surprisingly, neither Harlan nor Carbone insisted on monitoring our conversation. Either Andy was too insignificant to be noticed or, more likely, they trusted him not to blow their case. I reminded myself once again that Andy was a cop first and my friend second.

"You shouldn't talk to the chief like that," he said.

"Like what?"

"You're not very respectful. You keep calling him Mr. Carbone. He likes to be addressed as Police Chief Carbone."

I forced myself to laugh. "Tell me you're kidding, Andy."

"He doesn't like you much, Fran. He thinks you're cocky and manipulative—and that's a direct quote. He is planning to go to the district attorney on Friday and he will get that warrant. He's never once gone in for an arrest warrant and been turned down. He didn't arrest you last week because he wasn't confident the D.A. would agree, but now that Brenner's been killed and it looks like you might be involved with that too, he's feeling the pressure to get you off the street."

"Off the street? Are you telling me Carbone thinks I'm a danger to society?" I tipped my head back and stared at the light bulb dangling from the ceiling. "This is surreal."

"People have been talking, Fran. A lot of folks think you killed your sister. The town's going to go nuts when they find out Sid's boyfriend was killed and you were the one who found the body. The chief's got to do something. He's an elected official."

"Aha. That's it, isn't it? Dominick Carbone's more interested in getting reelected than in finding the truth. And Harlan's the same; he just wants another damn notch in his belt."

Andy rolled his eyes and shook his head, but he wouldn't look at me.

I took a breath and lowered my voice. "I need your help, Andy."

He gazed mutely at a coffee stain in the middle of the table.

I reached across and waved my hand in front of his eyes. When he looked up I touched his forearm and smiled. His ruddy cheeks turned crimson.

"I guess you felt you had to tell Harlan and Carbone about Peter offering you that money."

"No. Your stupid husband went to Harlan too. He was the one who reported it to the chief. I still haven't told them Peter tried to bribe me too."

I bit my lip and sank back in my chair. "Oh shit."

"Yeah. *Oh shit.* It doesn't help your case, Fran. You and your husband seem to have very little respect for the police."

"It's not that, Andy. I don't know what Peter had in his head when he did that. It was wrong. I know that, and so does he."

"Yeah, well, it's a little late to be figuring that out now, isn't it?"

I straightened in my chair and tried to focus on something less hopeless. "Were you and Harlan the ones who talked to Woody this afternoon?"

"Harlan handled it. I came in late."

"Howard Jayco was there too?"

"Yeah."

"Did Harlan make a deal to go easy on Woody in exchange for dirt on me?"

He shrugged. "Maybe. It wouldn't be inappropriate to trade away a marijuana charge to get evidence in a murder investigation."

"But it would be inappropriate for a Black Bay police lieutenant to encourage a lowlife like Woody Hanks to make up a pack of lies to frame an innocent person, wouldn't it?"

"Jesus, Fran. There you go again." He made a move to stand up. "I don't know what you and Harlan have against each other, but—"

"Okay. Forget what I said about Harlan. I still think Woody's lying. How certain was he that it was me he saw at The Sportsman? Could he be making that up?"

"Hard to tell. He was a little hazy on the details, I'll grant you, and the guy running the operation was busy with another customer and doesn't remember seeing you or anybody else come downstairs."

"But you and Harlan believe him?"

"Harlan does. I'm reserving judgment."

"Tell me, what was Woody wearing when you talked to him?"

"What was he wearing? What's that got to do with anything?"

"Nothing, probably, but humor me on this one, Andy. What was he wearing?"

He thought about it and said, "Sweatshirt and jeans."

"And his brown mackinaw?"

"Yeah, he had that with him too."

"I don't suppose you noticed what kind of buttons the jacket had?"

He laughed. "No. I don't suppose I did."

"Do me a favor, Andy. Check back with Woody and take a look at his mackinaw. Check the buttons. See if they're all there."

"You going to tell me what this is about?"

"Absolutely. *After* you check his jacket."

He looked irritated, but I suspected he would do what I asked.

"New topic, Andy. What kind of gun shot Brenner? Was it like the one you gave me?"

"We don't know yet. We'll get that information from the coroner later tonight." He shook his head. "We're both up shit creek if it's a match."

"Harlan and Carbone don't know you gave me the gun, do they?"

"No one knows."

"How about Brenner's body and his pickup? He told me this morning he wanted to show me something relating to Sid's murder. Did you find anything?"

"Nothing. Only interesting thing that turned up was a stash of cocaine in the glove box."

"No letters or photographs or anything like that?"

"No. He had a grocery bag on the seat of his pickup with a T-shirt, a pair of boxers, and a shaving kit with a razor and toothbrush, but that's it. He had nothing in his pockets other than his wallet and some change."

"Nothing in the wallet?"

"It was empty except for eighty bucks, his driver's license, a couple credit cards, a blank check from his own account, and an old receipt with your phone number on the back."

Neither of us said anything for a minute or two. Finally Andy pushed back from the table. "Look, I should get going. You can call me or Harlan if you think of anything else."

I nodded and stood up slowly. I had another question but I was reluctant to ask it.

He moved to the door, but I put my hand out to stop him. "Wait, Andy. One more thing."

"What is it?" He gave me a wary look.

"Did you check out the videotape from the MiniMart, like I asked you?"

"Oh, that." He sounded relieved. I wondered what it was that had made him nervous, what question I wasn't asking. "As a matter of fact Bill Walters watched it last night, start to finish. Peter was there for exactly eight hours, four and a half minutes. There were no breaks in the film."

I fell back against the wall and closed my eyes. "Thank you, Andy," I said softly. *Thank you, Peter,* I repeated to myself.

Peter heard me pull into the garage and met me in the hallway. His pale face looked healthier than it had in days, thanks to a good night's sleep and a sunny afternoon spent in the driveway tinkering with his car. "How'd it go?" He smiled hopefully but kept his distance.

I shrugged and smiled back, finding it considerably easier to smile now that Andy had confirmed Peter was at the MiniMart from ten o'clock on the night of Sid's murder until six the next morning with no unexplained breaks. "It went okay. Woody Hanks made some wild accusations. I had to set them straight."

We loaded up a tray with brie, green grapes, Triscuits, and a bottle of chilled chardonnay, and Peter carried it into the living room. I told him about my interrogation more or less faithfully, although my account took on an increasingly optimistic spin as I went along. By the time I finished my second glass of wine, I heard myself saying in a confident, almost triumphant tone that Woody Hanks was now a top suspect. It was wishful thinking, perhaps, but Peter and I both needed something to cling to.

"So there you have it," I said as I popped the last grape into my mouth. "My guess is they'll have a case prepared against Woody within the next few days—for killing Deke and Sid, and hopefully April too. We'll rest easier and so will the Kaminskys. So will the whole damn town."

He smiled and closed his eyes. When he opened them again he poured himself the last of the wine and swirled it in his glass. "And you'll be vindicated."

I nodded.

He took a swallow and said softly, "I was an ass to have ever believed they could successfully pin this on you, Frannie . . ."

His eyes searched mine, pleading for me to tell him that it was okay, that all was forgotten. I couldn't. After two glasses of wine on a nearly empty stomach, I couldn't fake it. I managed a halfhearted smile and said, "No, Peter, you were an ass for believing I was guilty."

He stared into his glass and chewed his lower lip. "I'm so sorry. I can't tell you how sorry I am." He looked close to tears.

I scooted forward on the couch and prepared to take the tray back to the kitchen. "I'm sure I'll get over it, Peter. It's not like I've never been an ass myself. I just hope we've learned something from all this, something about trust."

He polished off his wine and set the empty glass on the tray. "Right. Maybe in the end we'll take something positive away from this whole terrible tragedy."

I tried to nod, but I knew he was wrong. "I don't think I'd go that far, Peter. Just surviving will be an accomplishment." I headed for the kitchen without waiting for his response.

We were on our way to bed when the phone rang. I ran upstairs to grab it in our room. "Hello?"

I heard the caller breathing, but he said nothing.

"Who is this? Woody Hanks? Woody, if it's you, you're going to jail, you sonofabitch."

I slammed down the receiver and turned to Peter. He was staring at me and cracking his knuckles. "How do you know that was Woody?"

"It's got to be him. It sure as hell wasn't Deke Brenner. Woody's harassing me because I'm responsible for the cops finding his pot farm. The guy's a lunatic."

Peter looked nervous. "Do you think it's a good idea to confront him like that?"

"I'm sick of those calls, Peter. If it is Woody and he knows we know it, he'll think twice before he calls again."

Either the caller wasn't Woody or I was wrong about him thinking twice. We got another call fifteen minutes later, just after we had crawled into bed, and again every hour on the hour until three o'clock in the morning, when Peter pulled the phone cord out of the wall.

31

We stuck close to home Thursday morning. Peter didn't have to be at work until ten o'clock that night, but I didn't dare disobey Harlan's order not to venture off our property without his permission. Our anonymous caller left us in peace until almost eleven. I was cleaning the refrigerator and Peter was mopping the kitchen floor when the phone rang. I answered without saying hello and hung up as soon as I heard the breathing.

Peter kept his eyes on the floor, mopping ever more furiously. "Call the police, Frannie. They need to do something about this."

Theodore Cruise took my call. He promised to pass my message on to Andy and Harlan, but had nothing else to offer. He sounded anxious to be rid of me.

"What about the tap for my phone, Officer Cruise? Andy told me last Sunday he'd have one within a couple days. Do you know if anything's being done on that?"

"No, Mrs. Estes, I really don't. I'll make sure Andy calls you. He and Lieutenant Fry are due in at eleven. They should be here any minute."

"Tell Andy I'm unplugging my phone. If he wants to reach me he'll have to drive out to the house."

I dialed Sunshine Scott next, but she didn't pick up. I left a message on her machine about Deke Brenner's death and told her I would call back later with details. Given Sunny's strained relationship with Brenner, I expected she wouldn't be too broken up by the news.

Afterward, at Peter's suggestion, I went out to the guest room above the garage to finish packing Sid's things, leaving him behind in the house to wait for the contractor who was coming to replace the boarded-up window in the den. I trudged up the steps to the guest room with leaden feet. I hadn't been out there since Sunday afternoon, when my packing had been interrupted by the anonymous message with the dog barking in the background. I made a mental note to ask Andy if he had listened to the tape.

Sid's duffel bag, stuffed full of her neatly folded clothes, was lying where I had left it on the unmade bed. I moved it to the floor and dragged an empty toilet paper box to the center of the room. I crammed a pillow into the bottom of the box to serve as padding, then pulled the pictures off the walls, wrapped them in newspaper, and piled them on top of the pillow. Next I turned to the bed. I gathered up the patchwork quilt and stuffed it unceremoniously into the box. I did the same with the nubbly old wool blanket and went back for the sheets. They should have been washed before they were packed, but I had neither the energy nor the inclination.

When I pulled the fitted sheet off the mattress, a flash of white caught my eye. A small bit of paper had popped out from between the mattress and the box spring, an envelope maybe, or a postcard. I stooped to pick it up and saw a three-by-five card on the scuffed wood floor between my blue and silver running shoes. I reached for it tentatively. The underside of the card felt rough to the touch. I was barely breathing when I flipped it over and saw the words and letters crudely pasted there. *Dear Pussy: Watching you. Waiting for you. Can't hardly wait.*

With trembling hands, I shook out the sheets and slid the mattress off the box spring, but there was nothing else. Just the one postcard. Why the hell hadn't Sid told me about it? Why hide it under her mattress instead of reporting it to the police? I sank onto the edge of the box spring and stared at the blur of white and gray quivering in my sweaty fingers. Had there been other warning signs? Had she gotten anonymous phone calls like April Kaminsky? Had she been followed? How could she have failed to see that this note meant serious trouble?

I tried to reread the postcard, but the sight of it made my stomach turn, so I stuffed it in my pocket. Subconsciously my hands drifted upward and my arms folded across my chest. My fingers dug into my sides. April's attacker had sliced off her nipples. Had he done the same thing to Sid? If she had only confided in me. I would have known to get her out of here, back to Los Angeles or to San Francisco, anywhere but Black Bay. Ironically, she had been afraid to go home because she was having trouble with Deke. Big dumb Deke Brenner, barefoot junkie and wannabe drug dealer. He was a sweetheart compared to the author of this little note.

I thought back to Sid's behavior in the days before her murder. She had been sullen and distant, but that was nothing new. Or was it? My own twin sister, and I didn't know her well enough to tell. Had she been afraid? She'd been smoking nonstop and drinking a lot, but more than usual? I didn't know. The attendant at the Shell station told Andy he had serviced Sid's car the afternoon before her murder so it would be ready for the drive home to Los Angeles. Her plan to leave town made perfect sense to me now.

My legs gave out when I tried to stand up. I slid to the floor and slumped against the bedframe. The last time I'd seen my sister had been more than two weeks ago at the Seahorse Pub, where Woody Hanks had willingly served us enough alcohol to pickle an elephant. I recalled feeling ill at ease, especially at first, before the beer and rum had broken down my inhibitions. And I had been curious. Sid had asked me to meet her at the Seahorse because she wanted to ask me something. Or was it that she wanted to tell me something? I couldn't remember. I had foolishly assumed she was after money, so I brushed her off. Now it seemed that if I hadn't been so defensive of my pocketbook, she might have told me about the postcard. We would have gone straight to the police and she would be alive today. Instead, I picked a fight before she could say what was on her mind.

Twenty minutes after finding the *Dear Pussy* note I careened up to the police station and skidded to a stop in the passenger zone, leaving a thin layer of tire tread on the side of the curb. Before scrambling out of the Jeep I reached into my pocket, again, to be sure the three-by-five postcard had not somehow slipped out.

Harlan and Andy were both on duty, manning dingy metal desks near the front of the bull pen. Theodore Cruise sat in the far corner of the room with his back to the other two.

I pulled the postcard from my pocket and tossed it onto Andy's desk. It landed faceup.

He cocked his head to read the upside-down message without touching the card. ''Holy shit,'' he said in a hoarse whisper.

Harlan leaned over to take a peek. He said nothing, but his eyes widened with interest.

"I found it under the mattress in the bedroom above the garage," I said. "The room where Sid was staying."

Andy did a doubletake. "Under the mattress in Sid's room? You mean *she* put it there?"

"I assume so. Certainly the guy who left it for her would have put it somewhere a little more visible, don't you think?"

He shot me an annoyed look. "I was trying to establish that the note was directed at Sid, not you. Naturally I assumed with you barging in here . . ."

My cheeks grew warm. "Oh no. We're still getting anonymous calls, but no notes."

Harlan popped a peppermint candy into his mouth and bit down with a crunch that sounded as if it broke a few teeth along with the candy. "When did you find this?"

"Just now. I went up to the guest room to pack Sid's things. It fell out when I pulled the sheets off the bed."

Without explanation, Harlan headed for a door at the far end of the bull pen, nearly colliding with Theodore Cruise, who had come over to see what all the excitement was about. Cruise told me hello and glanced down at the postcard, which was still lying where I had tossed it on Andy's desk. He sucked in his breath at the sight of it, but none of us said anything more until Harlan returned. He was holding a sheet of white typing paper and a small clear plastic bag. While the rest of us looked on, he lifted the note off Andy's desk by sliding the paper under it, then dropped it into the plastic bag.

"I assume you've fingered this thing so completely there's no chance we'll get any prints." He said it as if I should have known better. Maybe I should have.

"Sorry. I wasn't thinking too clearly."

Cruise reached for the bag. "Can I see?"

Harlan grudgingly handed it over, and Cruise proceeded to examine the card through the plastic, nodding to himself.

"It's the same as the notes April Kaminsky got, isn't it?" I asked.

Andy's hulking shoulders tensed visibly at the mention of April. "How did you know about those?" he asked.

"Her folks told me."

"I see." He sounded stunned. Was he wondering whether the Kaminskys had told me about the pregnancy too?

"So, it is, isn't it?" I asked.

"Is what?"

"The same as the notes April got."

His eyes were focused over my head, on something across the room. I looked behind me, expecting to see that someone else had come into the bull pen, but no one was there.

"Yes," Harlan said for him. "It looks like the same fucked-up son-ofabitch."

"Same s.o.b. or a pretty good copycat," Cruise said. "Seems like he got himself some stickier glue for this one, though. Made a bit more of a mess."

"Copycat?" I looked from Cruise to Andy to Harlan.

Harlan shook his head. "Not likely. Unless the Kaminskys have made a habit of talking about those notes, nobody knew about them except the family and the police, and now you. Goddamn newspaper reporter sniffed around long enough, but never found out. If he had, the whole fucking world would know and every psycho in the state would be doing the same damn thing." He snatched the evidence bag from Cruise and turned to go.

"So now what?" I asked before he could escape. "What will you do with that?"

"Now we check for fingerprints. Won't be any though, other than yours and your sister's. Weren't any on the Kaminsky notes and won't be any on this one either."

"Then what? If this is a serial killing, shouldn't you guys be getting assistance? Like from the FBI or at least the county sheriff?"

His only response was the clunk of the peppermint candy he spit into Andy's metal wastebasket. He walked to the door quickly and without comment, but before he left he turned to me. "My order still applies, Mrs. Estes. You get home and stay there. Leave your house again and you're under arrest. There'll be no more exceptions."

Before leaving the station I asked Andy if I could use his phone. He relinquished his chair and moved to a desk several feet away where he picked up a document and perused it, pretending not to eavesdrop.

I called Barry Stein. By the sixth ring I began to fear he had switched off his answering machine, but finally it picked up.

I turned my back to Andy and said in a low voice, "Hi, Bear. It's Fran. I need your help. I'm calling from the police station. The guy I told you about yesterday morning was dead when I showed up to meet him, and I'm still getting threatening phone calls, and now I've found a letter in Sid's room that suggests she was stalked by the same lunatic who raped and murdered that other woman a year and a half ago. I wonder if you could come up to Black Bay today instead of tomorrow. Peter has to work tonight and I'm really afraid to be at home by myself—'' My voice started to crack, so I talked faster. "If you can, just come. We've got our phone unplugged so you won't be able to call. If you get to the house and I'm not around, there's a key to the front door taped to the bottom of the flowerpot on the second step from the top. Let yourself in and call the police. Tell them to get a message to Dominick Carbone.''

I hung up quickly and looked back at Andy, who obviously had heard every word. I made a mental note to find a different hiding spot for our key after tonight.

The contractor was still working on our broken window when I got home. By now he had enlisted Peter's help and the project did not appear to be going smoothly. I volunteered to lend a hand, but Peter told me through gritted teeth that he would appreciate it if I left the room. I was happy to oblige.

I went into the living room and sat in my mother's rocker, staring out the window at the distant cypress trees on the rocky ledge above the ocean. The day was sunny and warm for early December, but I had no desire to go outside. I prayed Barry would get my message and head for Black Bay that evening. If he departed San Francisco by six o'clock he would arrive before Peter left for work at ten, but if he didn't go home after classes he might not get my message until it was too late to drive up that night, and I would be alone until morning. I briefly considered asking Peter to stay home from work or requesting police protection. Oddly, neither alternative appealed to me. I wanted to be with Barry, only in part because I was frightened.

At one o'clock I fixed tuna salad sandwiches for Peter and the contractor. I let them eat alone and told Peter I would be upstairs, beginning the task of packing up some of my mother's things and Sid's stuff in her old bedroom.

By five o'clock, we were exhausted and operating on autopilot. It had been a long and stressful day on top of a long night of anonymous calls. Peter had joined me in Mom's room at two-thirty when the window repair was finally finished, and together we boxed up her belongings with little conversation to cut the tension.

Our first casualty occurred at five-fifteen. I had emptied Mom's dresser and was closing the top drawer when it happened. The drawer, warped by years of damp North Coast weather, jammed. After three unsuccessful attempts at sliding it shut, I shoved hard. It still didn't budge, but I rocked the dresser so sharply the whole thing tilted to the side and an antique vase full of pink silk roses toppled to the floor and shattered. The vase had belonged to my maternal grandmother, a wedding present from her mother back in the 1930s.

I stared in shock at the broken vase and scattered roses, desperate to have the prior seconds back to do over. Peter heard the crash and hurried in from the hallway where he had been taping and marking boxes. He stood behind me without speaking, letting me mourn the vase in peace. He knew its significance. He had admired it the first time he was in my mother's room, and she had told him it was her most precious possession.

"How about we take a time-out?" he suggested after a long silence. "I'll fix us some dinner and then we can get back to it."

"I'm not hungry," I said, although in truth I was weak and light-headed. I had eaten nothing all day except a few bites of tuna salad while I was making lunch.

"You need to eat, Frannie. I'll make spaghetti, okay?"

I shrugged. "If you make it, I'll have some."

"Fine. You want to keep going up here or join me in the kitchen?"

"I'll keep going."

"First let me clean up that broken vase." He knelt down and scooped the fragments onto a sheet of newspaper. "I'd offer to try to glue it back together, but I think it's beyond repair. Unless you want to save the pieces, I'll throw it away."

I nodded and dove onto the bed, burying my head in the pillow. When he tried to comfort me I sent him away. "Go make dinner. I'll take a nap and be down in a half hour." At the speed Peter functioned in the kitchen, there was no way he would have a meal on the table in less than thirty minutes.

He left reluctantly but without argument, switching off the light on his way out. While he was still on the stairs the phone rang. He sprinted for the kitchen and grabbed it on the second ring. I couldn't hear what he said to our caller, if there even was anyone on the line, but I knew I wouldn't sleep until I found out who had called. I slid out of bed and pulled on my sheepskin slippers.

Peter hung up before I got to the kitchen. "Another one?" I asked.

"No, actually. Wrong number."

I suspected he was lying to spare my nerves, but I didn't question him.

He nodded at the table. "Have a seat. I'm trying to scare up some food around here. Our larder is pretty bare these days."

"How about some of that frozen lasagna from Mrs. Olson?"

"All gone."

"I thought we had a lifetime supply."

"Sorry, sweetie. I finished the last of it a couple days ago."

"What else is there?"

"Not much." He pulled open the refrigerator and stared into the emptiness. There was a small hunk of moldy cheddar cheese, a tangerine, a carton of milk, and an assortment of condiments. Nothing substantial enough to make a meal, unless we wanted more tuna. He slammed the door. "We've got nothing decent to eat in this whole damn house. Not even a jar of spaghetti sauce."

"Well, like I said, I'm not very hungry."

"Frannie, don't be that way. You've got to eat."

I shrugged and resisted the urge to tell him he wasn't my mother. He probably was starving, which would account for his crankiness. The same went for me.

"I'll make a run to Paulsen's," he said. "You can take that nap if you want, or better yet, come with me. I know you're tired, but I think it would be best if you came along."

A small voice inside my head—inside my gut, really—told me to go with him. Another slightly louder voice reminded me I still had Andy's pistol should anything happen while he was gone.

"You go ahead. I'm sure I'll be okay for twenty minutes." More likely it would be at least forty minutes, but I figured I could last that long too.

He looked ready to argue, but he swallowed his objection. "Okay. I'll hurry. Spaghetti with tomato sauce, right?"

"Whatever."

I followed him when he went upstairs to get his car keys and wallet. He pulled down the covers of our bed. "Climb in. A catnap will do you good."

I did as I was told, determined this time to get some rest. He leaned forward for a quick kiss on the cheek, but I grabbed him and pulled him closer. Maybe I was being foolhardy by letting him leave me alone. "I love you, Peter."

"I love you too, kiddo. I'll be back soon."

Then he turned out the light and was gone.

* * *

I pulled the covers up to my chin, more for security than for warmth, and squeezed my eyes shut tight, even though I knew I wouldn't sleep. Huddled alone in our bed, I waited for the phone to ring or another rock to crash through one of our windows. I should have gone with Peter to Paulsen's Market. Five minutes after he left I began listening for the Volvo, but all I heard was the wind in the trees and an occasional car speeding past on the highway. After ten minutes I gave up. I climbed out of bed, switched on the light, and pulled on my slippers. Then I dragged an empty box into Sid's bedroom and began filling it with her collection of red and black candles.

I wrapped the candles in newspaper and placed them carefully into the box. First a red one, then a black, then red again, and so on. Soon I realized it would take me hours to complete the job at the rate I was going. And for what? I never wanted to see the damn candles again, nor did I expect they would be of value to Goodwill. They belonged at the garbage dump. With that concluded, I began tossing them unwrapped into the box, breaking as many as not.

I would get rid of the candles in Sid's Los Angeles apartment too, or as Sunny recommended, I would hire someone to do it for me. I didn't quite know what to do about the broken crosses. Was it a sin to throw away a cross? If so, was it a sin if you paid someone else to do it for you? It was something I would rather not get into if I didn't have to. Maybe I could find somebody who would want them, like a church, although I wasn't sure how I would explain why all the little Jesuses were missing their arms.

Before long I heard the front door click shut, signaling Peter's return. I had been so deep in my thoughts of Sid and her candles and crosses, I hadn't heard his car pull into the driveway. He had been quick, true to his word. He'd been gone less than a half hour.

I hurriedly dumped a handful of candles into the box and started to pull the punk rock posters off the walls. I wanted to be done with Sid's room before Peter left for work so he could carry the boxes out to the garage to wait for next Tuesday, when they would be hauled away with the rest of the garbage.

I was nearly finished before it dawned on me that something was wrong. Two things, really. First of all, Peter hadn't yelled up to let me know he was home. It was odd of him not to call to me, although perhaps explained by the fact that he assumed I was napping and didn't want to wake me. The other thing was more troublesome. I couldn't hear him downstairs banging away in the kitchen, no sound of the refrigerator opening and closing, no clatter of pots and pans being pulled out of cupboards.

I stopped and listened, praying for a familiar sound. I heard nothing but the wind.

32

I stood where I was for nearly a full minute, listening for some small noise to confirm Peter was downstairs. Maybe he had bought a newspaper and was sitting at the kitchen table, reading. I strained for the distant sound of a page turning. All I heard was a small pop, the sound of the candle I was holding as it snapped under the pressure of my panicky grip.

It did not occur to me I might be imagining the whole thing. The click of the front door had been unmistakable. I knew this old house too well. Suddenly it struck me what a huge mistake I had made by not going downstairs after Peter left to lock the dead bolt and put the chain on.

When the candle in my hand snapped again, I forced myself to set it on the bed. Despite my efforts to be silent, I was sucking in short sharp breaths, loud gasps really, so if someone was sneaking around downstairs I would have trouble hearing him over the noise I was making just to keep from suffocating on my own fear. Take deep breaths, I told myself. Deep, quiet breaths. I must have wasted thirty seconds trying to calm myself. A goddamn serial killer might be lurking one floor beneath me and all I could do was deep breathing exercises.

The next thing I heard was a creak on the steps, the sound of someone creeping up the stairs. It was barely noticeable, but undeniable. Our steps did not creak on their own. Someone was coming upstairs. I listened closely and heard the soft padding of footsteps. They were moving slowly, barely moving. They were not the sound of Peter coming to check if I was sleeping. They were the sound of a stranger sneaking up on me.

My feet were glued to the floor and my heart threatened to explode. Only a few minutes had passed since I first heard the front door close, but it seemed like hours. Peter must have been gone more than thirty minutes by now. He would be home anytime, if I could just hold on. *Damnit, Peter, hurry. Please hurry.*

I scanned the room in desperation. The window. From Sid's room, I could climb out the window onto the roof of the porch and jump down the twelve feet to the ground. If I didn't break a leg in the fall, I could run to the highway and hail a passing car.

I stepped closer to the window, close enough so I could see the driveway and confirm that Peter's Volvo was not there. I took hold of the security bar he had installed a few nights before. Some good it did us when our intruder walked in through the front door. I pulled on the bar. It didn't budge. I gave a harder pull, but to no avail. In a panic, I tugged again and again, but the bar was jammed into the window frame so tight it might have been cemented. One more jerk with all my strength did nothing but strain a muscle in my shoulder.

I stopped struggling with the security bar long enough to listen again for the intruder. I heard nothing at first. Then another footstep. He was on the carpeted stairs, inching toward me one slow step at a time. Apparently he hadn't realized I was aware of his presence.

Andy's gun. It was still in the nightstand beside my bed, where I had hidden it the night before. God, why hadn't I thought to keep it with me? To get to the gun I'd have to go into my bedroom, the middle room, which meant walking several feet down the hall toward the top of the stairs. I didn't want to get any closer to the intruder than absolutely necessary, but I had no choice. There was no other way out of Sid's room and no doubt he would work his way through the rooms until he found me at the end of the hall.

I wiped the sweat off my forehead and moved toward the door. I inched along quietly in my suede-soled slippers, praying the intruder would continue to move slowly enough for me to get to the gun before he reached the top of the stairs.

I wasn't breathing when I stepped into the hall. My lungs had seized. My eyes bore into the hardwood floor in the hallway, watching the distance diminish between me and my bedroom door.

Three feet from my room, I heard another tiny noise from the steps. His breathing maybe. I forced myself to look in the direction of the stairs, prepared to be face-to-face with a monster. What I saw sent a tremor through my body. On the pale gray wall was a distorted black spot, the shadow of the intruder. He stood against the wall, midway up the steps, just out of view.

I had no choice but to keep going. I moved faster now, still trying to be quiet but incapable of controlling my desire to bolt for the gun.

I made it to my room, but the instant I was inside I heard the footsteps coming at me. They were moving faster now too. My intruder knew I was on to him. There was no longer any need to sneak.

Hurry, Peter.

My nightstand was on the far side of the room, by the window. Rather than take time to circle the bed, I dove onto it, intending to scramble across it to the nightstand.

Several things happened at once as I threw myself onto the bed. I heard a loud crash, the sound of someone slamming through the bedroom door. And I felt a strong grip on my ankle. Horrified, I stopped scrambling and turned to face my attacker.

He was disguised in baggy overalls and a heavy canvas jacket. He wore leather gloves, and his face was covered by a black ski mask, his eyes hidden behind dark glasses. He was not big, probably no more than an inch or two taller then me. I couldn't tell how heavy he was under the loose-fitting clothing, but I could see he wasn't Woody Hanks. He was not nearly tall enough.

"Who are you?" I croaked the words out of my dry throat, surprised by my ability to say anything at all.

He didn't respond. Instead he reached into his pocket and pulled out a knife, keeping a firm grip on my ankle with his other hand.

I was too frightened to move. I stared at the black ski mask in terror, whimpering and gasping for air.

He pulled on my ankle and jerked his head toward the door, motioning for me to get up off the bed and walk out of the room. I didn't budge. I couldn't. I was frozen with fear, a cowering lump in the center of the bed, curled in a fetal position. I tried to scream, but no sound came out.

When I didn't move, he tossed his head again, this time more insistently. Why the hell didn't he just tell me what he wanted me to do? Because I would know him if he spoke?

I began to sob and finally recovered my voice. "Who are you?" I screamed. "Who are you?" When he didn't answer, I yelled out for Peter, wailing his name at the top of my lungs.

The intruder tugged again on my leg, and I tried to twist out of his grasp. Seconds later I felt the blade of his knife slice down my calf and I saw that my jeans were slit open and rapidly soaking up blood from a deep cut in my leg. I screamed again and began to thrash about the bed, desperate to kick my way free.

He responded by pulling harder on my ankle and dragging me toward him. The cut in my leg burned as if it were touching a hot coal. Still struggling, I flashed to an image of April Kaminsky's mutilated body. The same thing was about to happen to me, unless I could somehow get across the bed to my gun.

Another jab of the knife blade sent pain shooting through my leg, into my back and out to my fingertips. I yelled out but allowed myself to slip toward the edge of the bed.

"All right," I sputtered. "I give up."

As I slid closer to the edge, I felt his grip on my ankle loosen. He didn't let go, but he relaxed his hold slightly, apparently believing I had capitulated. This might be the only chance I would have.

With a sudden frantic kick, I broke free of his grasp. I shot across the bed, spun over the other side, and landed on the floor in front of the nightstand. He headed after me around the foot of the bed and dove at me as I ripped open the drawer and groped for the gun.

The next several seconds were obscured in a panicky tangle. I heard what sounded like our front door slamming followed by the sound of footsteps. Peter, thank God. But my relief lasted only a second. If it was Peter, how could I have missed the sound of his Volvo in the driveway? By now the footsteps were on the stairs.

I felt the nose of the pistol and pulled it out of the drawer at the same instant as the intruder grabbed my shoulder and jerked me back. I spun around, gun in hand but not in position to shoot, just in time to see Peter charge through the bedroom door, a look of horror and determination on his face as he bolted across the room.

"Jesus, Frannie—"

I fumbled to get the gun into the palm of my right hand so I could aim and pull the trigger, but my hands were sweaty and my fingers were stiff and clumsy with fear. I felt the knife tear into my shoulder. I shoved my weight into my attacker and screamed for Peter as we stumbled to the floor.

He lunged toward us, pulling us apart and giving me the split second I needed to get the gun ready to shoot. He yelled at me to stop, but I was past turning back. I pulled the trigger.

The intruder dropped to the floor and Peter fell on top of him. "Frannie! What have you done?"

In a single motion, he seized my pistol and ripped the ski mask and dark glasses off the intruder, who lay motionless on the floor. I saw a nightmare come true. Sid's face, so like my own, emerged from under the mask, her lifeless eyes wide open, staring off into space. When I looked up, I saw Peter pointing the pistol back at me, his own eyes wide and crazy.

"You killed her," he said. "Damn you. You killed her." He raised the gun so its nose was just a few inches from my face.

I fell back in confused surrender. I was stuck between the bed and the nightstand and the wall. Peter blocked the only path out. I was bleeding profusely and by now was too weak to put up a fight. "Peter, what—"

"Shut up."

"Sid was alive. And you knew it." I felt numb and disoriented. I stared down at Sid. Her wild curls were spread in a semicircle like an Indian headdress. Her eyes were as blue in death as they had been in life. I understood now. I was supposed to be the one sprawled on the floor and she in my place, alive, with Peter. I looked back at him. "You and Sid? You did this?"

Tears were streaming down his cheeks. He brushed them away with a shaky hand and took aim at my head. "You. You killed her."

"Put the gun down, Peter, please. Put it down." I tried to roll out of the way but managed only to fall back against the nightstand. Peter didn't lower the pistol. His expression was ugly with hatred and anger.

I closed my eyes and prepared for the inevitable jolt. I was woozy from the loss of blood and oddly calm, resigned to my fate.

Before he could pull the trigger there was a commotion downstairs, the sound of our front door slamming again. My feeble cry was silenced by his fist in my face, but I found new life in the diversion. I retaliated with a solid swat at his shooting hand.

The next thing I heard was a loud crack followed by a searing pain in my chest. I cried out in agony and fell back, clutching my side, but I managed to launch a series of frenzied kicks. Mostly I hit nothing but air, but finally my right foot connected. It was enough to dislodge the pistol from Peter's grip before he could shoot me again.

We scrambled across the floor for the gun and came up with it together. I kneed him in the groin. He grunted and doubled over, still clutching the gun. With my last bit of energy, I kneed him again, this time harder, and while he gasped for air I wrestled the gun free.

Without hesitating, I turned the gun on my husband and fired. I hadn't taken time to aim, but it's hard to miss at point-blank range. He moaned and fell forward into my lap.

Seconds later I saw Barry Stein charge into the room. He crashed across the bed toward me, his arms outstretched. His lips were mouthing my name, but I couldn't hear the words. As he pulled me out from under Peter's limp body, he dissolved into a bright white light.

EPILOGUE

I waited for nearly an hour before they brought him in. Sixty minutes of thinking it through one more time, one last time. I came here for clarity and, as Dr. Fielding put it, for closure.

My husband and twin sister had betrayed me. Big time. They set me up to take a fall on a murder charge, and when that didn't work they tried to kill me and make it look like a serial killing. All for a lousy five hundred thousand dollars. Ironically, after all my efforts to prove that I did not kill my sister, in the end that's exactly what I did.

A stocky pock-faced guard led my soon-to-be-ex-husband into the visitation room. He was wearing prison blue and his hands hung low in his lap, chained together. It was all I could do not to look away in revulsion.

"Hello, Frannie," he said in a dull, unfamiliar voice. He kept his head down, his eyes focused on his feet. He slumped into the chair across from me.

We were just three feet apart, separated by a wire screen. It was the first time I had seen him since the trial ended six weeks before. His sandy hair was cut short; his goatee was gone. He looked pale and thin and unhappy. It occurred to me that I should act as if my heart went out to him in some small way, but I didn't bother. The paler, the thinner, the unhappier, the better, as far as I was concerned.

"Hello, Peter. You don't look well."

He shrugged and said nothing.

I stared at him, gathering my thoughts. Dr. Fielding was right. This was indeed cathartic. All of the sadness and confusion I had felt over the past several months were gone. The anger was still there, as strong as ever, and so was the disgust, but none of the sadness.

"Why did you come, Frannie?"

"I have some questions." My voice was strong and clear and steady.

"Ask away." He sat hunched over in his straight-back metal chair. He gazed at the concrete floor, unable to meet my eyes. I noticed a small bald patch forming on the top of his head.

"So?" he said. "Let's get this over with."

"You in a hurry, Peter? Got someplace to go this afternoon?"

He offered no response to that.

"Actually, you're absolutely right. I should get to the point. I am in a hurry. I have lots of things planned for this afternoon, and for tonight and next week and the next fifteen to twenty years." Why I chose to be cruel, I don't know. I hadn't planned it that way. I swallowed hard before I continued, to check my rising temper. "I want to know why, Peter. Why did you do it? And don't tell me it was the money. Why the hell did you get involved with Sid in the first place?" *And how could you live with me, in my mother's home, for eight long months, knowing it was all a sham?*

"I dunno. It was just so . . . easy. In a way, it was your fault."

"My fault? Have you lost your mind?"

"You were the one who wanted me to get together with her when I was down in L.A. She came on to me. She had a way about her, you know? It's like she cast a spell on me."

"Cast a spell? Give me a break." The witchcraft excuse hadn't worked with the jury, and it wasn't about to work with me either.

"She offered some excitement in my life at a time I didn't have much. I was working like a fucking dog, Frannie. And you were more interested in your mother than in being my wife."

"You weren't getting enough attention from me, so you went after my sister? My twin sister, for Chrissakes? What the hell was in your head?"

"I didn't plan it that way, Frannie. It just happened. Being with Sid was like a drug. I was on this wild trip whenever I was with her. I wanted more and more, and before long I was so hooked I couldn't think of anything else but being with her."

"So you decided to screw me so you could have her. Did the concept of divorce ever occur to you? If you wanted to be rid of me there was an easier way.''

"Yeah, I know, but Sid got this idea about going after the insurance money. If either of you died, the other would be rich, but . . . well, we didn't want to, you know . . .''

"You didn't want to kill me? How thoughtful. You just wanted to have me convicted of murder and locked away for the rest of my life, so you could step up as next in line under the insurance policy.''

He said nothing. There was nothing to say.

"It really put you in a bind that I didn't go down easily, didn't it, Peter? Too bad for you that I beat the cops to the button from my blazer you planted out by the rocks at Pirate Point. And the talking in my sleep, the incriminating things you told me I said? Did you think you'd convince me I really did kill her, so I'd confess?''

"Something like that.''

"It nearly worked too. I played right into your hands by getting so ripped that night at the Seahorse—with the help of whatever it was Sid slipped into my drink—that I didn't know what the hell happened and couldn't explain how her blood got on my clothes and in the Jeep. And then you really got lucky. You couldn't have planned for that other woman's body to be found so soon after Sid disappeared, or for the fact that it was totally unidentifiable except for her earring, which you so cleverly switched on your way home from the morgue with one that Sid had been wearing that night at the pub.''

I paused and looked at him, but he wouldn't meet my eye. "You must have been flying high at that point.''

We sat in silence for a full minute. The only sounds were his knuckles cracking and the soft clinking of the chains around his wrists.

"But your luck ran out when Andy made up that bit about Sid reporting someone trying to run her off the road. That's what tipped the balance in my favor, even after you practically admitted my guilt when you offered to bribe Andy and Harlan. So then you had no choice but to kill me. I mean, shit, if they weren't going to arrest me, what else could you do? I suppose it didn't hurt that the insurance would be double if Sid and I were both dead. A nice little five-hundred-thousand-dollar bonus for switching to Plan B as it were. Whose idea was it—to kill me and make it look like the third in a series? Did you think of that, Peter?''

"No. It was Sid. I never wanted—''

"No, of course not. It was all Sid. I forgot. Sid made you do it. The anonymous phone calls, the *Dear Pussy* note under her mattress . . . How handy for you that the Kaminskys described in such detail the postcards April got.''

I closed my eyes and tried not to think of April. Her murder remained a mystery. Her killer was still out there somewhere.

"And Deke Brenner?" My voice was shaking now. "Just an innocent victim, in the wrong place at the wrong time.''

"Thanks to you.''

I nodded. Unfortunately, Peter was right about that. Brenner had been shot—by Sid, according to Peter's defense attorney—after I unwittingly sent him to her hideout in April's cabin. Peter had been listening on the upstairs phone when I set up the meeting with Brenner, and he had rushed out to the cabin ahead of me, warning Sid we were coming and later chasing me through the woods. The bullet in Brenner's head matched those in a gun tucked inside Sid's overalls the night she sneaked into our house intending to stab me to death and dump my body over the cliffs at Pirate Point. It was the same gun that had been sold to a young woman matching her description in the basement of The Sportsman a couple days before. We would never really know for sure which of them pulled the trigger.

"Poor dumb Deke Brenner. He was just trying to help." Brenner's evidence against Peter had been legit, if somewhat sketchy. He had asked around in Los Angeles about Sid's mysterious new boyfriend, the one she had been reluctant to introduce to Sunshine. The manager of the restaurant where Sid waited tables told him Sid frequently got calls at work from a guy up north named Pete and she occasionally called him back. The manager checked an old phone bill and jotted down the number on the back of a receipt the police later found in Brenner's wallet.

The metal feet of my chair screeched like fingernails on a chalkboard as I slid back and rose to leave.

Peter's head twitched, but he didn't look up. "Wait, Frannie. Let me—''

I turned to go, keeping my back to him as I walked away so he wouldn't see the pain in my face, physical pain, mostly. It was sheer agony to walk without a limp. A sliced tendon takes a long time to heal. Longer than a glancing gunshot wound to the rib cage, I had discovered.

"Frannie—''

"I've got to be on my way, Peter. I have too many things to do, too much going on. See ya around. Oops, no, I guess I won't.''

I let the door slam behind me and reached for my crutches, which I had left against the wall just outside the visitation room. I signed out with the prison administrator and crutched my way quickly and efficiently toward the main exit. At the top of the concrete steps I stopped and looked down at the parking lot, searching for my Jeep. It was already scooting toward me.

By the time I reached the curb, Barry was waiting with the passenger door open. He helped me in and tossed the crutches onto the backseat. Then he climbed in behind the wheel. The engine was still running, but he didn't pull away at first. He studied my expression and touched me lightly on the arm. He didn't ask how it went with Peter. He knew I would tell him when I was ready.

As we drove out of the prison lot, I reached for his hand. He gave it to me but kept his eyes on the road. I drew his fingers to my cheek and watched through misty eyes as his lips turned upward in a tentative smile. I smiled back.